WITHD✓ P9-BYJ-813
from the
Norfolk Library

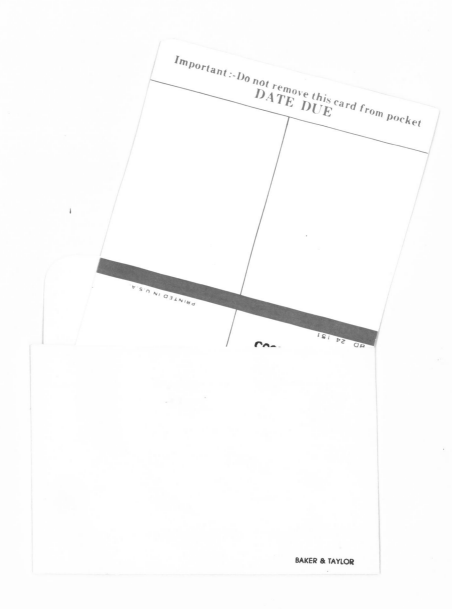

Important :- Do not remove this card from pocket

DATE DUE

PRINTED IN U.S.A.

HD 24 131

BAKER & TAYLOR

Also by Amy Herrick

At the Sign of the Naked Waiter

The Happiness Code

Amy Herrick

VIKING

NORFOLK LIBRARY
P.O. BOX 605
NORFOLK, CT 06058

VIKING
Published by the Penguin Group
Penguin Putnam Inc., 375 Hudson Street, New York, New York 10014, U.S.A.
Penguin Books Ltd, 80 Strand, London WC2R 0RL, England
Penguin Books Australia Ltd, 250 Camberwell Road, Camberwell, Victoria 3124,
Australia
Penguin Books Canada Ltd, 10 Alcorn Avenue, Toronto, Ontario, Canada M4V 3B2
Penguin Books India (P) Ltd, 11 Community Centre, Panchsheel Park, New Delhi —
110 017, India
Penguin Books (N.Z.) Ltd, Cnr Rosedale and Airborne Roads, Albany, Auckland,
New Zealand
Penguin Books (South Africa) (Pty) Ltd, 24 Sturdee Avenue, Rosebank, Johannesburg
2196, South Africa

Penguin Books Ltd, Registered Offices: Harmondsworth, Middlesex, England

First published in 2003 by Viking Penguin, a member of Penguin Putnam Inc.

10 9 8 7 6 5 4 3 2 1

Copyright © Amy Herrick, 2003
All rights reserved

PUBLISHER'S NOTE: This is a work of fiction. Names, characters, places, and incidents either
are the product of the author's imagination or are used fictitiously, and any resemblance
to actual persons, living or dead, business establishments, events, or locales is entirely
coincidental.

LIBRARY OF CONGRESS CATALOGING IN PUBLICATION DATA
Herrick, Amy.
   The happiness code / Amy Herrick.
      p.   cm.
   ISBN 0-670-03197-6
   1. Brooklyn (New York, N.Y.)—Fiction. I. Title.
PS3558.E746 H3 2003
813'.54—dc21   2002029625

This book is printed on acid-free paper. ♾

Printed in the United States of America
Set in Goudy
Designed by Nancy Resnick

Without limiting the rights under copyright reserved above, no part of this publication may
be reproduced, stored in or introduced into a retrieval system, or transmitted, in any form
or by any means (electronic, mechanical, photocopying, recording or otherwise), without the prior written permission of both the copyright owner and the above publisher of
this book.

To my girlfriends,
Alice, Eileen, Erica, Dina, Kate, Leah, Shelley, Theresa,
for all the laughter and comfort and stories

And in memory of Paul Walker

I would like to express my gratitude to my agent, Edite Kroll, for all her support and noodging, and to my wonderful and exacting editors, Janet Goldstein and Susan Hans O'Connor. Boundless thanks, as well, to my mother, Audrey Herrick, whom I can always count on to be an appreciative audience, and to my husband, Sam, for all the happiness he brings me.

The Happiness Code

This story takes place a few days or years into the future (depending on when you begin reading) and, as such, if you keep off to the side of your mind the endless catastrophes and marvels that will always vex and hound us and, with luck, drive us along in the direction we need to travel, everything here is exactly the same as it always has been and always will be.

Part One

1. The Jelly Jar

*P*inky wanted another baby.

Not that she hadn't thoroughly enjoyed herself the first time around, but it had been like having her ship stormed and looted and set on fire in the night. Now that she knew what to expect, she wanted the chance to really drink it all in. She wanted to smell the smells slowly—the milky and the foul and the freshly shampooed. She wanted to lean over the cradle and savor the entire concert—the howls and the squawks and the neighs, the caroling vowels and the precise stuttering moment when the consonants made their entrance. She wanted to kiss, again, the buttery plump little belly. She wanted to watch with exacting adoration as the baby unfolded like one of those flowers in a speeded-up film, opening week by week from a helpless nobody in particular to someone upright and astonishing and unlike anyone else in the nearby universe.

Just like Teddy had.

Now, no one should imagine that she wasn't still mad for her firstborn, that she wasn't still dazzled by the curve of his sleeping cheek, the feel of his warm sticky hand in hers, or by the questions he asked her:

"How long would it take you to die if you got locked in a refrigerator?" "If I stuck my finger under Niagara Falls, would it get ripped off?" "What do you think would happen if the fire on the sun went out for just two minutes and then came back on?"

No, she loved his questions and everything else about him. She loved the things she found in his pockets, the pebbles and feathers, the unclaimed keys he collected for his key collection, the little carcasses of dead insects, the wine corks and the washers and the ball bearings, the discarded vitamin bottles he found in the trash and filled with his own perfumes and other potions, the lint-covered Chiclets and the adjustable rings with bright-colored stones. Once, the eyeball of a trout, given to him, as he explained, by the man in the fish store.

She loved the way he undertook each new project or game with an expression of utmost seriousness, as if he were preparing to do heart surgery, or the way he sat at their eighteenth-floor window, scanning the skies with narrowed gaze, watching for fighter planes or hurricanes.

She trembled with tenderness for him. He was as dear to her as air and light.

But he was the second reason she wanted a second child. For, if there was anybody who needed a sidekick, it was surely Teddy. It had become clear to her in the last year or so that there was something too singular and sober about him. He needed somebody who would give him a different angle to see from, a youthful companion, ready to instruct and be instructed, who could lighten things up a little. Somebody on friendly terms with the absurd, who would blow spit bubbles and would think it was hilarious if you hid your face behind your hands and then showed up again. Somebody who would knock his towers down.

Obviously, this wouldn't do Arthur any harm, either.

The problem, of course, was Arthur himself.

Arthur hadn't wanted children in the first place. In his opinion, earth was no longer a good place for bringing new people on board and probably never would be again. But popular sentiment, most especially Pinky's, had been against him. He had let his guard down and he had lost the first round. This did not mean, however, that he intended to agree to a second child. He had not only *opinions* on this score, but convictions. He took the responsibility of becoming a father for the grave matter that it was, and to his surprise he realized that, given the opportunity to undo the original mistake that had led him here, he wouldn't choose to undo it. But any idiot could see that if there was any hope to be salvaged for this planet at all, what was needed was fewer human beings, not more of them. For a couple to produce a single child was one thing; two children were unconscionable.

For a year or more, Arthur had held out quite successfully against Pinky's campaign. Then Marina, a colleague at work, came to him with a most unusual request and he found himself on the horns of a dilemma.

She and Arthur had been working together for two years in the bio-engineering department, where Marina was the lab assistant on Ken Fishhammer's HDR Deficiency Project and Arthur was a database administrator. She was not particularly talkative, but she had imparted at least the facts of her history to him, how she had escaped a certain highly destabilized Eastern European country after she had been forced to watch her family home burned to the ground with her parents barred inside. Her parents had been dissidents and intellectuals, and she had been a medical student at the time when this had happened. It had been through her father's academic connections at the university and to Ken Fishhammer in particular that she had gotten this position. She had brought her younger sister Katya with her and Katya was now a student at the university.

Arthur was pretty sure from the flatness in her delivery of these facts that there was more here than she was telling. And she may have owed Ken Fishhammer a debt, but he didn't think she liked him much. Not any more than Arthur did. Arthur admired Marina's reticence and her self-containment, was deeply respectful of all that she had endured, and had no wish to know more of her hidden thoughts. As far as he was concerned, she was the perfect work partner for him and they had formed an efficient alliance, keeping Ken's demands in check and easily completing their tasks on schedule.

It had come to Arthur as a great surprise when she made her request.

But being Arthur, he did not pry. He did not ask her, *Why now? Or, Why me? Or, How would you manage?*

It wasn't merely because of his lack of interest in the personal (something Pinky always complained about), but was more because there was something both pleading and forbidding in the way that Marina stood there.

So he said he'd think it over and he went home and he did. He thought again about what Marina had done and what she had lost and about what had happened to her face.

In the end, he decided to give her what she sought because, although on one hand it compromised one of his most sacred principles, on the other hand he saw it as an opportunity to make his own small repayment to the common human debt.

The next morning he went downstairs to the lab, where he knew he would find her tending to the test subjects. If she had chosen at that moment to explain to him how much she loved these mice and about the inspiration they had given her and about what she planned to do with Arthur's gift, he almost certainly would have changed his mind. But she said nothing, so he handed her the small jar. The label had been left on and one could see that it had once held strawberry jelly. But it had been carefully washed and rinsed out, and there, on the bottom, was a couple of tablespoons of what she needed.

She held it in her hand wonderingly. What was inside added no more perceptible weight than a thimbleful of snow, a mouse's heart, a single fallen leaf.

Partly because he had one of his headaches, which gave him the peculiar and unsettling sensation of pulling up to an intersection and hearing a fire engine approach from a direction he could not determine, and partly because he saw her blush, Arthur nodded and backed out of the room.

Marina's father had always said, to your destiny there is only one bus. You must arrive at the corner on time. So she stayed at the lab that evening until everyone had gone home and then slipped into the refrigerator room, where she turned off the switch on the light sensor. She crossed the room softly in the dark and opened the refrigerator door. The neatly arranged trays of culture dishes glistened up at her from the cold interior. A container of yogurt, an unopened can of Coke, and a small green plum perched uneasily on the top shelf as if trying not to rub shoulders with any of the silently gleaming army of little dishes placed beside them.

She reached into the back, where she knew that Ken Fishhammer stored the second set of chromosome vectors, his secret ones, and she searched blindly with her hand for a good pick, for a lucky choice, for the tiny arrow that would fly straight. It wasn't for herself, really, that she searched, but for the others, her parents and her sister and the rest, wishing to grab for them a little happiness in compensation for all their suffering. At that moment she heard footsteps coming down the hallway. Her hand closed upon one of the little dishes. She slipped it into her bag and stepped behind the door where she hoped she would not be seen.

In a moment, through the little window in the door, she saw Ken Fishhammer go by and the light flick on automatically as he entered the room across the hall where the mouse cages were kept. He looked distracted and determined, as if he were searching for something he had lost, and was muttering angrily to himself.

Just then, one of the Vector Two mice began to "sing" and Marina was filled with a terrible foreboding. She knew Ken did not like it when they did this.

They "sang" every day after the sun had set. For most of the afternoon these mice would leap and tumble and jump over each other with great delight. Then suddenly they would throw themselves down around the floor of their cages and look at each other and their small world with oddly alert and joyful expressions and one of them would begin chittering and cheeping away, a complicated tuneless aria. It wasn't always the same mouse who sang, but the song, she was sure, was always joyful.

And Ken, she knew, was for some reason much irritated by this singing. A great mystery. Wasn't this one of the behaviors he had worked for so secretly and so hard?

She only hoped that he would quickly find whatever it was he was looking for and leave.

The little mouse continued to squeak rapturously.

"Oh, for God's sakes, shut up," she heard Ken say, and then there was the sound of the latch being released and the door creaking open. The mouse's song stopped abruptly. He must have been frightened by Fishhammer, she thought.

The cage door clicked shut.

She heard Fishhammer cross the room and stop and then move some things around.

"Where the hell are they?" he muttered. He paused and then headed toward the door.

She could hear a great rush inside her own ears, and for a second she thought it was the guilt of her conscience come to drown her like the ocean inside a seashell, but then she realized it was only the adrenaline signaling her heart to pump faster in case he should find her and she should need to move quickly.

She calmed herself and her pulse grew quieter. In a moment she heard him give a little grunt of triumph and then she heard the jingling of keys as he hurried back out the door and down the hallway.

After waiting a few moments to be safe, she crossed quietly over to the mouse room and checked the cages.

In most of them the mice were settling down for the night, burrowing into their wood shavings, but in one cage she noticed that all the mice seemed to be huddled busily around something. When she looked more closely, she saw that they were eating, with great gusto and pleasure, one of their companions, who lay at an odd angle in their midst as if its neck had been broken. The noise they made as they ate was not mouselike, nor human, nor funerallike, either, but made her think of the hum of telephone wires or the sound of light traveling through the dark spaces between the stars.

She stared at this scene with horror for a moment and thought of taking the poor mouse from them, but did not. Loaded as she was with so many black and bloody memories that could never be laid down, she swung her canvas bag over her shoulder and headed out into the night. The snow had stopped and the sky had cleared. The stars looked down upon her, bright, she thought, with approval.

Arthur decided that he could not tell Pinky what he had given Marina, because she would have interpreted his act in a highly personal and overcomplicated light, because she would have been jealous, and because telling her might have caused her to interfere in the matter, which, he was certain, would not have been Marina's wish.

Arthur was normally a man who had no trouble holding his own counsel, but, inexplicably, he was nagged by a desire to tell someone what he had done. Running with Maury on Saturday morning, Arthur found himself briefly relating the events of the last few days. He had no wish to break trust with Marina in any way, but given the nature of Maury and the fact that their relationship was mostly limited to this weekly run inside the boundaries of Riverside Park, he decided that his secret would be safe enough.

Furthermore, although he anticipated that Maury's thoughts on the matter would be novel and interesting, since they would be based on Maury's unfathomable theory of life, which involved universal harmonies, predestination, and diet, Arthur did not imagine it would give him much serious pause.

After he told Maury the story, Maury did not say anything for a minute, but just went on running. Maury always held himself like a waiter carrying a tray of champagne glasses. Whether he was running, standing, or sitting, he seemed to make his way through life with an inscrutable glide, his face still and serene. Today, however, when Arthur glanced over at him, he saw his shoulders quivering and his eyes alight. He appeared to be amused. After a little thought Maury said, "Well, I've got a joke for you."

"Okay."

"Why does it take two million sperm to get through to one egg?"

Arthur shrugged. "Why?"

"They're all afraid to ask for directions."

For a while they jogged along in silence while Arthur contemplated this.

"One of your problems," said Maury, "is that you don't really know what it is you wish for. When you don't know what you wish for, it's hard to see where you're going."

Arthur didn't understand what this had to do with Marina and the jelly jar, but he jogged along, attempting to give Maury's accusation fair consideration. And it was true, he supposed. He didn't spend a lot of time thinking about desires that were unlikely to be fulfilled, which is what he thought a wish was. "You mean, if some person with the power to give me whatever I chose offered it to me, what would I choose?"

"Well, something like that."

Arthur thought about it some more. "I would wish for human progress," he said after a little while.

Maury laughed. "Yes, I think you would."

"Well, what would you wish for?"

"Oh, I always wish for the same thing. But I'm much more self-indulgent than you. I wish for my eyes to open wide enough to see what's invisible."

Arthur decided that whatever it was that he had been hoping for from Maury, this wasn't it. He resolved again to speak no further about the matter.

Early in March, the DNA Research Advisory Committee came bursting into Ken Fishhammer's offices, asking questions and pointing fingers. The university community was scandalized and outraged. Apparently, Fishhammer's project was not what it seemed. It was immediately closed down.

Arthur was relieved. He had guessed some months ago that Fishhammer, in trying to cure the HDR deficiency, had made an inadvertent discovery, a discovery of a powerful side effect that came along as a companion. And apparently he had the presumption to think that not only could he harness it, he could avoid the illegalities involved in messing with such a thing. Arthur did not believe that Fishhammer could succeed or that, if he did succeed, he would bring anything but one more variety of human-made catastrophe into the world. Even so, he never would have willingly involved the authorities himself.

He was curious, though, about who *had*. He made some inquiries here and there, but could find out nothing.

Ken Fishhammer was asked to resign his chair. Arthur and Marina, who, it was decided, were innocent bystanders, were sent their separate ways to work on other projects within the department.

Several months after the project had been shut down, he met her coming out of the cafeteria and saw that she was pregnant.

"Hello," he said.

"Hello."

She had a fine line of perspiration over her upper lip and he remembered how it had been for Pinky being pregnant in the heat, how she was always wearing a dripping wet washcloth over her small red frizzy head and waddled through the apartment moaning and muttering terrible threats to some invisible opponent. He looked into Marina's eyes a little apologetically, but she gazed back at him with a distant, dreamy gaze.

"I heard you were working on the soybean project. How's that going?" he asked.

To his alarm, she laughed. "Soybeans? You want to talk with me about the soybeans?"

"Well . . . how are you feeling?" he asked awkwardly.

Unexpectedly she leaned forward and gave him a small, sisterly kiss. "Artur, you must take care where you are going. You have many eyes like the potato who is walking in the dark."

He stared at her.

She looked at him tenderly. "Do you miss, sometimes, our mice?" she asked him.

"Well . . . no," he answered truthfully.

She sighed and rested her hand gently on her protruding stomach. "I do. I wish to know that they are well."

The mice were gone. Nobody had been able to find them. Arthur had his suspicions about what had happened to them because he knew that innocence was not, at least in this particular district of the galaxy, worth two dimes and a nickel in the way of protection. He thought she ought to know this herself, but he said nothing to her.

She waited, but when he said nothing, she told him, "Today the chili is with no meat. I know you like this. Perhaps someday we will meet for lunch."

Since he could not tell if she was making him an invitation or trying to end the conversation, he smiled and wished her well and continued on into the cafeteria to get some lunch.

Early in October, the baby was born. He was delivered easily. When the time came, Marina gave one long ripping and grunting push, and there he was in the doctor's hands, looking fresh and dewy and perfect as a pearl. His large dark brown eyes were sprinkled with sharp gold flecks that sometimes caught the light and sometimes didn't. His gaze was unusually focused right from the beginning and he started smiling when he was only three days old—not that grimacing gas smile that infants make, but the smile of someone genuinely thrilled to see you. At two weeks old he slept through the night like an angel and woke up refreshed and prepared for excitement. Within a very short time he was busy-fingered and insatiably curious, grabbing for anything he could get hold of. By four months old, when it was normal for a baby to become hysterical if anyone but those he knew well tried to come near him, this fearless baby chortled invitingly to every passing stranger and batted his long dark lashes, opening his arms and begging to be lifted up. He loved being bounced and thrown into the air.

He was as good as gold, as sweet as honeysuckle. Even her sister Katya, who did not like babies and said he was a demon, pretended to eat the little pieces of squashed banana that he tried to feed her, and let him stick his fingers in her ears. Marina knew, without a doubt, that he was one of those meant to change the direction of things to come. She also knew that, despite the stories to the contrary, we are all tied to our destiny by a thread no stronger than a spider's silk. So she watched over him as all babies are meant to be watched over, as if he were the last one on earth.

Pinky missed the birth announcement. She missed it because it arrived on the very same day as the notice from the landlord informing them that he was not renewing their lease because he needed the apartment for his mother.

Pinky had been working on Arthur to move out of Manhattan for the last two years. They would need more room if she ever succeeded in convincing him to have a second child. They needed more room anyway. But he had been fixed in his argument that sane people did not give up a rent-stabilized apartment. There were only about three hundred rent-stabilized apartments left in the city and he considered renting one of them a great social honor and responsibility. Now, however, there would be nothing he could do. Perhaps they could find a little house with a backyard somewhere.

In her excitement, she did not notice that other small square envelope.

But Arthur found it. The photo was not a very good one. The baby's face was out of focus, or no, it was the background that was un-intelligible. Was that the ocean behind the infant? Or a dark and over-pillowed blue sofa? The baby's face, caught in just that singular moment when the stroke from the lighthouse shines out across the water, shone out from the uncertain interior of the smudged photo and beamed itself into the room. Arthur gazed at it solemnly for sev-eral minutes, then dropped it into the paper recycling slot in the wall and waited until he heard the automatic shredder turn itself on and then off.

2. Mitchell's Fruit Trees

*K*en Fishhammer went home on the day that the project was shut down and locked himself in his study. His wife kept the children away from the door.

It enraged him, of course, the foolish timidity of the regulators. They were willing to support him for researching a cure for a disease almost no one had heard of, but for this accidental discovery that promised so much more, which would almost certainly create a monumental shift in our ability to promote general human well-being, for this they stampeded in, confiscated all they could find of his files, shut the program down, and publicly reprimanded him.

Luckily, he had gotten wind of what was coming just in time to kill off the Vector Two mice and dispose of them, and then to copy and erase what needed to be copied and erased from the data records in his compubank.

The hardest part was to have gotten so close to knowing for sure and then to be cut off in this way. If he had had just a little more time, probably nothing could have stopped him, not the Advisory Committee, nor whatever forces had brought them to this critical moment.

He took his meals in his room for three days and he thought about abandoning his research and going back to practice medicine, or perhaps taking up teaching.

He wasn't good at those things and he knew it. He knew, too, that he was never going to be able to rest until he found out where that missing chromosome vector had gone.

On the third day he called Mitchell Newman at Venturetech. He had been loath to sell himself to the private sector and had held out for many years, but he knew that evolution is not so much a matter of the slow accretion of little mutations and small changes, but a history of sudden jolts and leaps forward. And that for those in the right place at the right time, willing to jump through when the gate swings briefly open, the rewards can be great. Mitchell Newman, he had reason to believe, was one of those willing to take the risks needed. Ken had never met him, but Mitchell had called him several times in the past, trying, Ken assumed, to lure him over to Venturetech. He recognized the strange, hoarse voice instantly.

"So I gather your situation has changed somewhat," Newman said. He might have been amused.

"I've left the university."

"And now, at last, you are ready to talk to me."

"Yes."

"Of course, your legal situation has become a little dicey."

"It would surprise me if you took that much into consideration."

"I take everything into consideration."

"If you're not interested in my project, I'm sure I can find someone else who will be."

"You know, Thomas Hardy said that happiness cannot really be more than 'the occasional episode in the general drama of pain.' You really believe you have found a way to outfox that destiny?"

"Well, that's the point, isn't it?" Fishhammer replied stiffly.

"All those pharmaceutical disasters, the Prozacs and mood elevators. It took a long time for the final effects of these to show up."

"This is different. The pharmaceuticals masked symptoms. This is genetics. This is human programming. We're talking about changing things at their source, shaping the human disposition. This is, perhaps, where evolution has meant to lead us all along. Your company can be the vehicle to make this possible. Or not."

There was a long silence. Then Mitchell Newman said, "Are you aware that someone borrowed one of your chromosomal vectors?"

Ken stood up and went and gazed out his window. There were his two daughters, building a castle or a house or something in the sandbox he had made for them. The little one leaned over and accidentally tumbled the fragile building over. The older one, seeing what had happened, raised her shovel furiously and whacked her little sister hard on the shoulder. The little one began to cry.

"Do you know where it is?"

"Come in to my place in the morning. I will tell you what I know. Perhaps it will make you happy. If it does, we'll find you a corner to work in."

Mitchell had started out in cosmetics, but gradually he began to stake some claims in bioengineering, where he had great good fortune. Most of his triumphs, initially, were in the agricultural area (where it had remained largely impossible for the governmental agencies to place effective restraints), but as his company began to grow, he took on more and more animal and human research. He was a notorious eccentric, reclusive and unpredictable, a brilliant inventor and no friend of the DNA Research Advisory Committee. He drove around in a 1972 Volkswagen Beetle held together with coat hangers and gave away hundred-dollar bills to strangers on the street and it was said that sometimes his company vice presidents could not find him for weeks at a time.

Ken was not particularly surprised by the fact that Newman made no effort to meet him in person. Nor did he particularly care.

The little corner he was given was in an extremely well secured basement level of the building that did not appear on any of the public floor plans, and it had as well-appointed a laboratory as any you might find anywhere. Not only did it have its very own capillary sequencer, its staff was largely robotic, distracted by nothing and able to work twenty-four hours a day.

Each morning he drove off before the sun rose and entered the facility just as everyone else was waking up. He used his biometric identi-key to let himself into the elevator and down he went. The dim and winding hallways in his corner of the building were softened by a live green grasslike carpet that seemed to mow itself. The laboratory areas and his own office space were clean, bright, and indifferently furnished.

Then, down at the end of the hallway was the area that he had requested for his tests and observations. These were two interconnected rooms, one equipped to care for and please a young child, the other all tile, easy to sterilize and wash down, with an examining table, cabinets holding all of the necessary instruments and measuring devices, and a small restraint chair with nonconductive straps.

The observation area was completely satisfactory. The living area, however, had been arranged in a more fanciful way than Ken would have liked. It was carpeted with the same strange grasslike material that covered the hallway. Full-spectrum lights, devised undoubtedly through some expensive technology, gave this room a sunny, summery feeling, although it was several stories belowground. But what bothered Ken most were the fruit trees—three of them—growing robustly out of huge wooden planters. Two of them were of the old-fashioned variety—an apple tree, bearing small green fruits, and a peach tree, also with its branches beginning to hang heavy. The third, which stood beside a small table piled high with various toys appropriate for a baby, was a tree most certainly never seen before on this earth. It was about as tall as a man, with leaves that were silvery on one side and dark green on the other, and the fruit it bore was walnut-sized, but flat and disklike, and red as fire engines.

The fruit trees—he had heard it rumored—were Newman's passion, but that they should be imposed upon *his* experiment Ken found somewhat irritating. It was not, however, a matter he felt it worth quibbling about.

During the first weeks of Ken's arrival there, Newman continued to show no interest in meeting up with Ken in person, but they spoke to each other a few times on the voicelinker. After that Ken found himself working in uninterrupted solitude. Within the next eight months he managed to reproduce about half of the work he had done at the university. He did not speak directly to Newman again until the day he received the birth announcement from Marina. On that day, Ken called Newman and asked him what he intended to do.

"What do I intend to do?" Newman asked. His voice sounded rusty and hoarse, and slightly surprised. "Why, not a thing."

"I want that baby," Ken said.

"Well, naturally. Of course you do. Who wouldn't? He's a baby from another world. He's everything you've dreamed of."

"You've seen him?"

"He's too young for us right now. He needs his mother."

"We can provide for him anything his mother can provide."

"I'm surprised at you, Ken. All the millions of years of evolution through which you've sifted so patiently. You're going to blow it all away because you couldn't wait until the right moment?" Newman coughed, trying to clear his voice. "Events will conspire. They always do. That baby's got to ripen up a little bit. And I'm a big believer in breast milk. However, I'm keeping a careful eye on him, so you have nothing to fear. I want you to hold your impatience in check for a little while longer and allow time to take its course."

3. Moving Day

*A*rthur managed to stall their landlord for several months. But by spring, he saw there was nothing further to be done and he gave in to Pinky and agreed to buy a little house in Brooklyn. Pinky found a part-time teaching job at a senior center in what would be their new neighborhood. It wouldn't start until the fall, so she would have several months off to deal with the upheaval. Moving day arrived in mid-June in spite of all of Arthur's resistance.

Pinky awoke that morning and jumped up out of bed and rushed in to see that nothing had changed in her painting during the night. When she was satisfied that everything was as it had been, she hurried over to their eighteenth-floor window and looked up at the sky and then down at Broadway. The sky over the buildings appeared clear and light and cloudless, while down below it was still shadowed and gray-lit, and everybody hustled along in the usual hustle. She was looking for an omen, some sign of what was to come. Now that the fates had finally gotten it together to move her out of this nasty little apartment, she was looking for some encouraging signal that the other project she had been working on for the last few months—the most important one—might soon arrive at a happy conclusion.

However, if there was an omen out there, she couldn't see it. It was one of the gravest disappointments of her life that she could not foretell the future. Countless times her mother had picked up the phone just before it rang, or said, "God bless you," to someone, just before they sneezed. Her grandmother could go much further than this. For instance, she could always tell when two people she knew were going to fall in love and get married, often long before they met. She generally knew when someone of her acquaintance had died in the night and she was very proficient at foretelling floods and tornadoes and other weather-related disasters. Furthermore, she had several other dubious talents, including—it was said—the ability to lift small kitchen objects into the air without touching them. Pinky thought she had a recollection of a small green plum hovering in the air over the kitchen table. She had tried this herself, but had never been able to lift so much as a cornflake, let alone shift the fixed stubbornness of Arthur's mind on anything he had fixed it on.

But at least he had agreed to move out of Manhattan.

The cat, who had been watching her sleepily from inside a half-packed carton of books, now came out, padded over to her, and jumped up on the windowsill. In his periods of repose, which took up most of his day, he had a heavy, shape-shifting quality, like a sack of flour, but when the situation called for it, he was amazingly light on his feet. He landed in front of her with a soundless grace and she cried out in surprise. As she did, all at once there was a blaze of light.

Pinky looked down and saw that the street below had become real and of consequence in a way that it had not been a moment before. Each peach and apple and snapdragon in the fruit and vegetable market on the corner appeared to burst into flame. A woman struggling to untangle her six terriers who had gotten tangled up on their leashes stopped what she was doing and straightened up and peered at the sky. The mob of bloodthirsty pigeons who had been jostling and shoving and pecking at some hunks of stale Italian bread lifted themselves into the air as if they were a single bird. The two guys in front of the Chinese restaurant dropped the large slippery gray fish they had just unloaded from the back of their van and the fish flipped over on its stomach, slapping its tail against the sidewalk.

Then, when she looked up, there it was, the sun rising slowly and majestically as the hump of a camel over the chimneys and antennae of the roof opposite.

Surely this was a sign, although being tone deaf, as it were, to such matters, she didn't know whether to read it as a good or bad one, but being also composed of some fundamentally optimistic and cheerful fiber, she let the question go for the moment and turned her mind hopefully to the day ahead.

When Arthur came into the living room brandishing two table lamps, she wanted to tell him how happy she was, about how well her painting was coming along, and furthermore, about the possibility of the omen, but she looked at him and held her tongue.

Arthur, she often sensed, was ill at ease in the face of exhibitions of cheerfulness, and furthermore, he was very opposed to omens.

However, since moving days are much like wedding days in that they have a momentum of their own that can only be ignored at great peril to the participants involved, she blew him a kiss and turned her back on him and went on throwing things into boxes, and before she knew it, all the rugs had been rolled up and all the little odds and ends had almost been taken care of and Arthur was yelling at her because she hadn't labeled things properly and Teddy was demanding to know where his remote control Infernal Pod Racer was. (This most recent gift from her mother had come in the mail a couple of weeks ago. She loved sending Teddy the most garishly high-tech toys she could find, partly in the hopes of pleasing Teddy and partly, Pinky suspected, to get a rise out of Arthur.) Pinky assured Ted that they would find it as soon as they got to the new house, though she knew, almost certainly, that it would not turn up before next spring.

At the last minute she tried to call her friend, Fran, to tell her everything, that this was it, they were leaving. But when she went to pick up the voicelink receiver she found that the lines were down. This was just like Fran, who enjoyed making herself unavailable during emergencies.

Then, just as it was time to pack herself and Teddy and the cat and her easel into the car and drive on ahead as they had planned, the cat could not be found.

She did not panic at first, but went carefully through all the upside down furniture, and went out into the hallway and called and called and called. Teddy was beside himself, egging himself on to ever greater visions of catastrophe. The cat could have fallen out the window, splattered on the ground eighteen stories below, or suffocated at the bottom of a carton of books, or been eaten by the dog at the end of the hallway. They checked all the closets and the cabinets and under the sink, and a rising tide of dread began to grow in her.

They were just beginning to open boxes when Arthur caught them.

Arthur claimed that he didn't like cats. But Pinky knew that that wasn't the point. The point was that he was jealous of Oedipus. It was one of the things Arthur couldn't see but Pinky knew was there. She knew it with certainty the way she knew with certainty where the edge of the dresser was when she got up in the dark to pee. She also knew that, although he believed he didn't love her and, even worse, believed that she didn't love him, that love was just one of those foolish constructs people employed to make themselves look good—here, too, he was missing the point.

"I'm not leaving without Ed!" Teddy wailed.

Arthur ignored him. "You cannot be serious," he said to Pinky. "You're not actually going to start unpacking boxes to look for that flea mat? We're paying this moving company two hundred and fifty dollars an hour and you're going to start unpacking? *I* will find the cat. Don't worry, he's under something somewhere, vomiting up hairballs. Leave me the carrier. He'll show up and I'll bring him along."

This, of course, was unthinkable—to leave without the cat. He had been her family long before she met Arthur and Teddy.

But, again, she was faced with it, that there was some mysterious force that, for reasons of its own, regularly set forth unthinkable things for people to do. There was no getting around it.

She told Teddy not to worry. Daddy would find the cat. They had to get going now.

Teddy wept as silently as a lover does when he hears his beloved has drowned at sea.

Pinky took her easel and her painting and the heavy little rug she always stood on when she was working, into the elevator and down to the lobby and out into the car. Then she went back and got Teddy. She led him downstairs and helped him into the car, too. Then she went around to the other side and got in.

She leaned out the window, into the lovely morning, and told Arthur, who was supervising the loading of all the improperly labeled boxes into the van, to leave the doorman the cat carrier and a couple of dollars for a tin of smoked oysters in case he needed some bait to lure the cat out, although chicken skin would be better since chicken skin was his favorite, but it might be hard to find.

Arthur nodded impatiently. "Go ahead," he said. "Don't worry. I gotta go supervise these guys. I'll meet you at the house."

She pulled her head into the car reluctantly. She turned to look at Teddy. "Don't look back," she advised him, "or you'll turn into a pillow of salt." For just a brief moment Teddy stopped to look at her with interest, but then he resumed his lamentations and they drove off down Broadway.

At around the time Pinky was discovering that the cat was gone, Marina asked Katya to watch the baby. They needed a couple of things from the store. Katya sighed. She owed her older sister much, since it was Marina who had kept her wits about her and managed to get the two of them out of their country after their parents had been incinerated, and it was Marina who had gotten herself a research assistantship and Katya entrance into the university, as well. So she came out of her room where she had been studying and lifted the baby onto her lap.

"I must walk to freshen myself in the air and then I will stop at the corner," Marina explained. "We need some coffee and some bread and the baby needs a banana for supper."

Katya sighed and held her tongue. Their parents, with some foresight, had insisted they learn English against just such a day as this, and now Marina insisted that they always speak English together, but she always spoke it in just the way she liked, with her lisp and her fanciful embroideries, and did not allow Katya to correct her. The baby, who had a seductive air about him like a little red berry peeping out from beneath a green leaf waiting for somebody to come along and eat him, tried to imitate her sigh, but to his surprise and delight, his breath instead came out with a little *pputt pputt* sound. He giggled and leaned forward to suck on her chin as a way of showing how pleased he was with himself.

"Now, remember, most importantly, where is the voicelink number for the department for fire and ambulance." And she pointed to the little card posted over the computer box.

Katya looked at her sharply. "What is it? You think we will burn the house down?" Katya asked as she disengaged the baby from her chin.

Marina shot her sister a look of disapproval and then leaned forward and gave the baby a little kiss. Just as he always did, he batted it away lightly as if it were a mosquito. Another sign of strength, she thought with satisfaction, and stood up.

There was almost no traffic and Pinky didn't get lost even once. They turned onto their new block and there was the house down at the end, with its bay window and yellow flower boxes, looking like it was pleased to see them. The street was quietly busy—a boy whizzed silently by on a skateboard without glancing at them and a woman bumped an auto-pram up her front steps. Down the block a man was standing on his roof waving a pole at a flock of pigeons circling around and around overhead. Everything was exactly the way she had imagined it, except, perhaps, for the disheveled fellow sitting on the stoop next door (he had greasy blond hair that stuck up uncombed around his head and he drank from a paper bag and stared at them incuriously) and except for the fact that she had lost her cat, who knew her better than anyone else in the world and whose loss would leave an open, gaping wound in the side of her life.

She unlocked the front door and took Teddy inside. He was quieter now, but still shuddering and leaking tears. They stood silently, for a moment, in the small bare hallway. Then they walked through the echoing and freshly painted rooms. When they reached the back door, she opened it. Teddy looked at her for moment and then stepped out into the garden. The screen door swung shut behind him.

Leaning against the kitchen sink, she watched him through the window. He looked around at the trees and up at the sky, worried as a little swallow who has gotten picked up by a hurricane and blown a thousand miles off course.

~~~

Around this time in the late morning, Marina stepped under the green and yellow awning of the fruit and vegetable store and carefully selected several bananas. She had never had a banana before she came to the United States. Such fruits had simply not been available where she came from. Now she could never get enough of them and the baby loved them, too. As she was pulling one carefully away from the bunch, a green van leaped the curb and barreled across the sidewalk and rammed straight into her. It was an old van that had been repainted at least once. Even if it had had the new high-density rubber bumpers it probably wouldn't have made any difference. As she went flying through the air, it cannot be said that the whole of her life flashed before her eyes, but she did find herself standing in the river that ran by the summerhouse they went to when she was a little girl, trying to catch, with her hands, the little silver fish that darted around her ankles. This time, for once, when she lifted her hands up, they did not come up empty, for there, in the small clear cupful of water, swam a single silver minnow who looked straight up at her and winked, and as he winked the sun rose and set a hundred times, and then it was dark.

Teddy, of course, unaware of the car that leaped the curb and sent Marina flying into the perfectly arranged pyramids of peaches and cantaloupes, did not feel the moment of impact, but a few seconds later he had a strange sensation, as if a hand laid itself lightly upon his chest and then passed through him. He felt disoriented. He looked about the garden expectantly. Perhaps it was the cat giving him some warning that he was about to appear.

But the cat, who was his blood brother, was nowhere to be seen.

A bird, however, who might have been sitting in the tree over Teddy's head, began to sing. It whistled and chortled and trilled. Its song went up and then down, and then it got ahead of itself and burst into a great gabble of overexcited notes. The notes cascaded down out of the air, and tumbled, light as little scraps of paper, onto the lawn.

When Teddy looked up to find the bird, it was easy to spot because it was sitting, not in the tree after all, but on the top of a very curious, very tall and narrow metal ladder in the far corner of the yard. It was almost as tall as the house itself, and when Teddy went to look at it more closely to see how it could stand so straight up like that, he saw that it grew right out of the ground like the ivy. When he tried to shake it, it didn't move at all, as if it had somehow rooted into the earth. The bird sat on the top rung and made its announcement per- haps to the entire morning at large, perhaps to some specific visitor it was expecting to descend the ladder. Then the bird lifted its wings and, with a flash of white, flew into the tree.

The tree was a wonderful tree. He'd never seen anything like it be- fore and he wondered if, possibly, it was the only one of its kind in the world, for it was hung all over, just out of his reach, with furry green golf balls.

The cat would have loved the tree and the bird.

Tears came to Teddy's eyes as the possibility occurred to him that just when you got to a place you really wanted to be, something else would always be lost.

He sat down in the grass to think this over, but was distracted by a smell that he was sure he had smelled before. What was it? He couldn't remember at first, though it was a powerful and sublime smell and he associated it clearly with the boredom of sitting on an itchy sofa. Then it came to him. It was the perfume of a hundred old ladies gathered to play cards at his grandmother's house. What if they were all here now, gathered in his new backyard? He opened his eyes in alarm, and at first he found nothing—just the grass and the tree and the bird—but then he saw her, over in the next yard, a small woman in shiny black capri pants with silver zippers on the legs and a straw hat. She was holding the largest pair of scissors he'd ever seen and she was clipping at a thorny bush all covered with yellow flowers. It was from her, appar- ently, that the smell was coming. Abruptly, she turned and stared at him. Not wishing to meet her eye, he gazed about her yard and noted that the whole place was filled with the thorny flowers. These, though lovely, filled him with a sort of dread and he looked back at her. If he had been asked to place her in time, he would have put her between his mother and his grandmother, but as it was, he didn't consider her age, only how behind the tightness of her gaze there was a fallen look, like a cake after all the candles have been blown out.

"You don't have any cats, do you?" she asked.

Teddy looked at her in confusion. How could she have known about the cat?

"Because I don't want any cats coming in here and peeing on my roses. And please stop staring at me like that." She turned away from him with a loud sniff and disappeared around the other side of her house.

He took a deep, shuddering breath. Although he had imagined many awful consequences to leaving their apartment behind, he had not imagined this woman next door. It was hard to completely prepare yourself for the worst. He tried to see around the corner where she had gone, but there was nothing but shadows. Her words, however, seemed to hang about in the air like little black bugs, although when he looked more closely he saw that what he was staring at was an actual swarm of gnats or flies. His heart beat quickly with joy and excitement, and he forgot all about the misfortunes of the morning.

When the policemen came to the door later that afternoon, Katya knew right away what it was they were going to say. She felt the news they were carrying press against her blouse and into her ribs with cold little prongs, like a sharp metal fork.

She did not invite them in. Her family had never invited policemen in. She stood very straight. She did not move a muscle.

The policemen felt as if they were delivering their news to a lovely carving of granite and wondered if perhaps she were deaf or an idiot.

But as soon as they had finished delivering the message, they were both relieved and disconcerted to see her fall to the floor on her knees and begin to rip at her clothes and scream. One of them tried to comfort her, but she swatted and whacked at him, until Mrs. Morales from upstairs heard the commotion and came running down and gathered her in her arms and held her.

In a while they all went into the apartment and Mrs. Morales brought Katya over to the sofa and the policemen sat on the hard chairs. They told Katya the events of the accident as they had reconstructed them. While the policemen spoke, they wondered at the loud clanging and crashing that came from the kitchen.

"So although your sister has met this terrible accident, we want you to know that she died instantly, with no idea of what hit her."

Clang! Boom!

"You believe this is good?" Katya threw at them. "That she does not know what hits her? My sister, who keeps her eyes open even in her dreams to protect us from every tragedy?" Katya wept loudly.

Kabang!

The policemen looked at Mrs. Morales questioningly. "Do you know what's going on in there?" one of them asked her.

Mrs. Morales got up and went into the kitchen and returned a moment later with the baby in her arms. He had the preoccupied air of one who has been interrupted in the middle of taking every single pot and pan out of the cupboard. When he saw the strange policemen, however, he perked right up. He held out his arms to the one nearest him and the policeman gingerly lifted him up in his big hands. The baby looked up into the policeman's face and held his breath as if he fully expected to be hit with the news that he'd just won the lottery.

"How's it going?" the policeman asked the baby softly.

"Dweebo." The young orphan laughed and pulled off the policeman's hat.

Hearing her nephew's musical voice, Katya stopped sobbing for a moment and looked up at him. And at the moment that she wondered in despair what she was going to do, how she could possibly manage to take care of the two of them, she saw her sister standing in the doorway of the kitchen beckoning to her.

Now, Katya did not believe in ghosts, but she did believe in the boundless ingenuity of the survival instinct. She had no doubt that the phantom she saw before her was a product of her own imagination, and she also had no doubt that she would do well to pay attention to it. She excused herself to Mrs. Morales and the policemen and got up and followed the figure into the kitchen, where it led her over to the emergency numbers posted on the wall. Now she scanned them, frowning: police, fire, ambulance, poison control, the pediatrician. At the bottom was a name that she could have sworn had not been there the last time she had looked. It said: *A. Sorenson—Data Base Administrator (for using only in grave emergency)*. This was followed by a local exchange and number.

Katya stared at it, frightened. Was this the answer to the mystery she had not dared to question her sister about? She took the list down from the wall and folded it carefully and put it in her pocket and looked around for her sister but did not see her.

She went back out into the living room. Her face was pale, but her eyes were dry. The policemen were relieved to see that she had pulled herself together.

"I must come to the police station? There are papers?"

"Yes, but tomorrow is soon enough for that," the officer said. "Perhaps this kind lady will keep you company tonight?"

Mrs. Morales nodded.

The baby's small face beamed out at everyone from inside the policeman's hat.

"This is a happy baby," the policeman said.

Katya stared at him grimly. "Since it is too late for herself, this is what my sister wishes for. To make sure that into this world she brings a happy child." She reached for the baby and, reluctantly, the policeman passed him over to her. Katya handed the officer his hat and said, "Myself, I think it is a dangerous affliction."

That night, at bedtime, Pinky told Teddy the story—one of his favorites—about how he wouldn't be here today if it weren't for the flu epidemic of 1918. But only half of her was with the telling. The other part of her was listening to the low busy hum that only she herself could hear. She could feel the dull ache in her side as this month's applicant stepped up its efforts and tried to wiggle itself free of its moorings.

"And so," she said, "the first wife of my great-grandfather and the first husband of my great-grandmother died from the flu and both your great-great-grandparents, who hadn't had time to have any children, were lonely and sad."

They were lying in Teddy's new room on a mattress on the floor, since they hadn't put the bed together yet. She had switched off the lamp and the room was awash in the tremulous pinprick lights of the two dozen fireflies Teddy had imprisoned in a jar. The fireflies, had there not been so many tragedies—the move, the loss of the cat, the terrible woman next door—would have made his day. He held the jar up in front of him as she told the story.

"Then one windy Easter Sunday, your great-great-grandfather was bicycling down Crown Avenue when he saw a large black bird with a single streak of green in its wing come swooping up the hill towards him. This was an unusual-looking bird, one he had never seen in this part of Pennsylvania before, so he screeched to a halt to get a better look and the bird got closer and he saw that it was not actually a bird, but a small black hat with a green feather tucked in the front. He reached up and grabbed it out of the air."

The hum became a little louder and then she felt it. The translucent, shimmering egg, that half a possibility of a person, gave a little pop as it worked its way free at last, and, right away, foolish with hope, it started down her left fallopian tube toward the dark meeting place. It hummed its little hum as it went. Naturally, she wasn't going to mention this event to her own child, so she proceeded with the story.

"Your great-great-grandfather hung the hat carefully on the front of his handlebars and proceeded slowly down the hill. When he had nearly reached the bottom, he saw what he was looking for. Standing on the corner in the evening dusk was a lovely young woman, trying to pat her hair into place as she looked frantically about her.

" 'Is this yours, by any chance, miss?' he asked her, as he held out the little hat.

"It was, of course, her hat, and she was extremely grateful and happy. She took it and put it on her head and he was sorry to notice that she wore a wedding ring. He would have liked to ask her out for an ice-cream soda or something, but of course he couldn't do that if she was married. He had no way of knowing that her husband was dead, just like his own wife was dead. Also, it was getting dark very quickly. In those days it used to get dark much quicker than it does today and in those days ladies did not talk to strange gentlemen after dark. So he just bowed to her and got on his bicycle and rode away. And that would have been that, of course, if, my great-grandmother had not happened to take the Phoebe Snow train down to New York the following weekend."

"But she did, didn't she?" Teddy asked anxiously.

At this moment the voicelink began to ring. "I'll be right back,"

Pinky said. "Don't worry." She pushed his hair back from his furrowed brow and smiled at him reassuringly, but he merely sat there frowning at his fireflies.

She zigzagged her way around the boxes and ran down the hall to the closest receiver. It was her first voicelink call in the new house. Perhaps it was the doorman calling to say he had found Oedipus.

It was not, however, the doorman, but Fran.

"So? You're in?"

"Well, we're in. Yes, we're in. But something awful has happened."

"Like what?"

"I should have known that something was going to go wrong. There were omens. There was this lady with six dogs and then the sun came up."

There was a pause while Fran digested this. "You think a lady with six dogs is an omen?"

"And then, just as we were getting ready to leave, the cat disappeared. He disappeared into thin air. There were the moving men and he had just vanished. Arthur wouldn't let me unpack the boxes to look for him. Arthur's pleased, I think. He says the cat will turn up, but he doesn't believe it. And Teddy's heart is totally broken. He says it's the worst day of his life."

"Teddy always says it's the worst day of his life."

"And he won't let me unpack his toys or clothes or anything until we find him."

"First of all, Pinky, don't worry about that cat. You know that cat knows how to take care of himself. He's probably sitting in some old lady's apartment right now eating oysters off a Wedgwood plate. He'll turn up.

"As for Teddy, send him over to *me* for a couple of weeks. You know how I love him, and nothing would make me happier than to give him a little attitude adjustment."

"Oh, Arthur would never part with him for that long. He needs to keep a very tight eye on Teddy's influences. He'd be afraid you'd say 'fuck' in front of him, or let him watch a vidvert with naked breasts or violence in it. No, what we need to do is to find Arthur a major distraction. That will take some of the heat off of Teddy. That's why my project is the only answer."

"Which project is that?"

"You know what I mean. *My Project.*"

"Oh, that project. Yeah, well, you're right. That's probably a good idea."

"But I don't want to talk about it. It might jinx it. Something might be happening really soon. How are you?"

Fran laughed. "How am I? Well, I had a terrible day.

"We got this new guy today over from Rikers. He tried to commit suicide by swallowing a battery. He ended up over here with us and now he's discovered that we're a no-smoking unit and he's trying to get himself transferred back. I told him I couldn't let him go back until, A, he shat out the battery and, B, he convinced us he was not going to do anything suicidal again, which would take some time. When I told him this, he put his hands down flat in front of him and stared at me like Anthony Hopkins in *Silence of the Lambs*, but then he just started to cry."

"Well, I hope you gave him a cigarette. Did you give him a cigarette?"

"Of course I didn't. It would have been all over. He would never have done any work with me if I'd given him a cigarette. Plus then I'd have to give everybody a cigarette."

"I would have given him the cigarette."

"Of course you would have given him the cigarette. You're a kind, empathic person. But my job isn't to make people feel good. I work in a psychiatric forensic unit. My job is to give these guys some shovels and pickaxes so they can dig themselves some tunnels out of here. Oh, oh, my mother's calling in on the second line. She's undoubtedly checking in to see if I ate all my peas or met any nice men yet."

"Why don't you just ignore it?"

"I can't. You know I can't. If I ignore it, she'll get in a taxi and come over and tell the super she thinks she smells gas coming out of my apartment and he'll call the police and then there'll be cops all over the place and they'll probably knock the door down like they did last time."

"Maybe you'll meet a nice policeman."

"My mother will never be happy with anything less than a doctor."

"Well, send her my regards."

~~~

When she got back to Teddy she found him asleep, the jar of fireflies clutched in his hand. She took it carefully from his grasp and carried it over to the window, which was wide open and had no screen in it yet. She opened the jar and softly instructed the fireflies to make a break for it. It was a long time before the whole lot of them figured out they were free to go. There was no excited passing of the word. Each one had to figure it out for itself. It struck her as funny that here these guys had been given this gift of being able to find each other across miles of darkness using their little lanterns, but when they were all packed in a jar, shoulder to shoulder, they couldn't pass each other a simple message like, *Hey, the lid's off. Make a run for it.*

She thought about her great-grandfather coming down the aisle of the Phoebe Snow, punching tickets, and how in just a moment he would ask her great-grandmother for her ticket, and how this time he would notice not only her black hat with the single green feather, but also that the rest of her clothes were black, and how this time they would get into a conversation and he would ask her respectfully who she was in mourning for, and when she told him she was mourning her husband, his heart would leap up in excitement, and once again, if the story didn't change, which Teddy was always anxious it somehow might, the path that led to all of them, to herself and to Teddy and the worlds that went with them, would, once again, spring into being.

When she went back downstairs, Arthur was arranging the spices in the spice rack. He was humming and chewing Bazooka gum. She could smell the scent of the gum in the air.

"Please tell me you're not putting those in alphabetical order."

"What's wrong with alphabetical order?"

"What good does it do you, Arthur? You put things in alphabetical order and then you can never find them anyway."

He ignored her and went on humming the tune to Ravel's *Bolero*, one of his favorites. This was a good sign. She would rearrange the spices tomorrow when he was out of the house. She came up quietly behind him and slid one hand expertly up his T-shirt and then, before he could turn around, she slid her other hand down into the back of his jeans. "Don't move. It's a stickup," she whispered in his ear.

"Jesus, Pinky, when are you going to get a little sense of modesty?" He turned around and grabbed her hands and pulled her body up close to his.

"Soon," she promised.

"You're after something."

"Nothing. If you turn that light switch off over there, nobody will be able to see what we're doing."

He turned off the light switch. "What are we doing?"

"Nothing."

"Right now?"

"Yes. We gotta break in the new kitchen."

She could feel that he was forgetting all about arranging the spices. If he forgot about the spice jars, there was a good chance he might forget about other matters. She felt victory within her grasp and slipped off her green T-shirt with the alligator tie-dyed on the front. She wore nothing underneath and took a step back while she raised her arms to take out her barrette so that he could see her bare freckled skin shine with its own light in the darkness of the kitchen. Her red, ill-mannered hair flew out about her head and shoulders.

A little unauthorized sound escaped him and she smiled in the dark.

The door was open to the backyard and she could feel all the green things and the fireflies practically knocking each other down trying to get a look at what was going on.

She leaned up against the dishwasher and waited. She gave him plenty of room. She acted like she hadn't a care in the world. After a few minutes of proving to himself that he was in complete control of the situation, he came forward again and put his hands around her waist, his thumbs on her rib cage. He kissed her with that urgency that always took her by surprise and that seemed to her to disprove everything he wanted to believe about himself, given how he avoided such demonstrations during the general course of his day.

Then he leaned back, but he kept one hand on her as he used the other to pull off his T-shirt.

When their skins came back together there was, at first, a brief shock of coolness like you get when you turn the pillow over, but almost immediately the coolness evaporated.

Her breath came faster, which excited him, and he put his hands down into the back of her shorts and pulled her up against himself. Then he put his mouth on her ear and said, "Do you have your buzzer on?"

It wasn't a good idea to lie to Arthur, but she kept her voice light against the unevenness of her breathing. "I'll go get it if you want me to, but it'll take me a few minutes to find it. I think it's in the bottom of the dresser where I put my underwear."

He groaned. "Did you unpack the way you usually unpack? If it's like your old Ringling Brothers Barnum and Bailey Three Rings Tights and Panties drawers, you won't find that thing in years."

She laughed and slipped her hand up inside his baggy shorts on the furry tender inside of his thigh and applied a slightly rough upward pressure. She hated the idea of the damn thing anyway. It was a flat adhesive-faced disk that became activated as soon as it touched your skin, and as soon as it was activated it set up an imperceptible high-frequency vibration that, for some reason, confused and disoriented the eager sperm so that they were not able to find their way to their appointed destination.

She waited, treading water lightly.

Arthur sighed into her ear with some exasperation. "How can you be so disorganized, Pinky?"

"I'm sure we have nothing to worry about."

He pulled back and looked at her. "Sure, nothing except a squalling, peeing, shitting, unformed human being who will require constant supervision and unrelenting attention to shaping its character in the face of a world gone nuts with greed and violence and terrorism." Arthur unzipped her shorts and pulled them down.

She could hardly believe her luck. He was going to go ahead with it anyway. How could this be? The thought came to her that the cat had been the barter price for this gift. She was filled with equal parts of remorse and gratitude.

"Well, luckily for both of us, I came across some of these handy little things when I was arranging the cereal boxes. I found them in the oatmeal. I don't know what the hell they were doing in there. It must have been another one of your peculiar packing arrangements."

She watched with a sinking feeling as he leaned away from her and fumbled in the pocket of his shorts. She remembered with regret

how she had thrown the things into the Quaker Oats container because she hadn't been able to find the toiletries box. She'd figured
they'd eventually resurface.

And so they had.

He handed the thing to her to hold, while he started to take his
shorts off.

"Oh, Arthur, I'm sure we don't need this."

Arthur laughed. "One is all they get out of us," and he took the
foil packet out of her hand and deftly tore it open.

Afterward, they leaned up against the new dishwasher and she for-
gave him. This was not only, she knew, because of the way sex made
you oversimplify matters. But it was also because, as they stood there,
he held on to her for several minutes more than was completely necessary, just the way people do when they find themselves in strange
countries or lost in the woods. She knew how easily he got lost.

She followed Arthur upstairs to bed, but, too restless to sleep, went
to check on Teddy (who was sleeping with his fist under his chin,
frowning slightly), and then she drifted down the hall to the room that
was to be her studio. The heavy little rolled-up rug rested in the center
of the newly polished floor and her paintboxes and canvasses and easel
leaned up against the wall.

As she stood there in the doorway, she thought about how if there
was any one thing that might help to save Teddy from the seriousness
of himself, it would be to get himself an assistant, somebody he could
split the responsibility of being Arthur's child with. But she simply
didn't know from where was going to come the inspiration that would
persuade Arthur again.

She stepped into her little studio and began to set things right,
opening the easel and setting her paints out on the table. She went
over and picked up her painting and put it gently on the easel. This
painting was a mostly shifting violet and blue abstract, except for
down in the bottom in the center, where there sat a storefront window
frame and then, inside this window frame, disappearing deeply and
busily into the depths of the canvas, was the dinner hour in the
Golden Yen Chinese Restaurant. The painting she knew was almost
finished, but she wondered uneasily if, now that she no longer lived

across from the Golden Yen Chinese Restaurant, she was going to have a problem.

Pushing this worry aside, she grabbed hold of the fringed end of the rug and gave it a hard *thwack*. The rug unrolled halfway, slowly and balkily, and then stopped. She gave it a kick and it rolled unwillingly a couple more times and then, suddenly, with a final bump, laid itself out flat. In the center, to her surprise, was someone's fur hat. She did not know what to make of this. No one in their household wore fur hats. As she stepped closer to get a better look, something odd happened. The hat stretched and stood up.

"Oedipus!" she screamed, kneeling to pick him up.

He didn't apologize or even look at her. He wriggled impatiently out of her grasp and jumped down to the floor, where he began licking at a slight disarrangement of his fur with an ostentatious show of annoyance.

"Teddy was out of his mind! How could you have been so inconsiderate?"

Methodically, he finished the task at hand; then, in that half-sitting, half-standing posture from which a cat reviews his position, Oedipus gazed alertly around the room, missing nothing. When he was done with his inventory, he padded over to the windowsill, jumped up, looked out, and then froze in what appeared to be absolute shock.

She went over and looked out with him and tried to see what it was he was seeing, and then she realized he had never looked out of a window before and not seen cars and traffic lights and people going in and out of D'Agostino's.

Was it like landing on Mars? she wondered. Was it like a blind man being able to see for the first time? Would he be able to bear the extraordinariness of it—the rustling of the tree, the scent of the roses, the fireflies blinking in and out of the darkness?

He gazed out. His body was perfectly still, yet he stared with a ferocious intensity at the darkness before him. His concentration was extraordinary, as if he were not only looking out there, but looking inward for some piece of information left him by his father or his father before him, a key that would let him make sense of the inexplicable scene that lay outside this window.

Of course, there is no dawn of recognition that goes across a cat's face, but suddenly she could have sworn she saw a bloody gleam of intent in his eyes that she had never seen before, and then just the white tip of his orange tail twitched, and she leaned forward and slammed the window shut with a bang.

4. The Watergun

*W*hen he heard the news about Marina, Ken was furious and he called Newman immediately.

He assumed that the man was somewhere nearby in the building, but the connection was thin and seemed to drift in and out, as if Newman were traveling through clouds, high up and far away.

"And you think I had something to do with this poor woman's death?"

Ken couldn't tell if he was amused or angry. "Did you?" he asked.

"I'm not offended at the question, in case you're wondering, but I certainly think you misunderstand me."

"Did you or didn't you?"

"She had some very serious enemies. Political enemies, I suppose you'd call them. You're aware of what happened to her parents?"

"Yes."

"They were burned alive in their own house."

"I know that. I knew her father."

"Speak up. I'm having trouble hearing you," Newman said.

"I know what happened to her parents."

"She was perfectly innocent, you know," Newman's voice seemed to whisper hoarsely.

"It's time for us to bring the baby in here. I want you to leave this to me. This is an extremely important matter. This is not one of your hybrid corns or anti-wrinkle creams we're working on, here. This is probably the biggest thing you're ever going to get your hands on," Ken said loudly across the static. "I'll let you know if I need anything. Please don't interfere."

"Absolutely. It's your turn now. Anything you require. I'm most eager to see what kind of results you get and I can't wait to meet the little fellow."

The next morning, Pinky was standing at the counter rearranging the spices when Teddy came down the stairs carrying Oedipus in his arms. He was dressed in a wrinkled pair of blue shorts and a white T-shirt. He came and stood in front of her and looked at her anxiously.

"I was dreaming that Phil, the doorman, had called to say he found Oedipus, and then I woke up and there he was, sleeping on my stomach."

"Yes! Isn't it wonderful? I thought you'd be happy. I thought you'd be overjoyed. Why are you wearing that face?"

"Because what if this is one of those dreams inside a dream? What if I'm not really holding the cat? What if I'm still sleeping in my bed?"

She looked at him with interest. "You mean maybe I was just dreaming when I found him last night rolled up inside my rug?"

"No! No. Of course not. *You* aren't dreaming. *I'm* dreaming. You're inside my dream."

"Oh, I see."

At this moment, the cat, who had been wiggling and squirming, trying to get free of Teddy, leaped out of his arms, giving him a small scratch on his wrist as he went. Teddy let out a yelp of pain and then watched with fascinated interest as the blood welled up.

"Taste the blood," Pinky suggested. "If it tastes salty, then it means you're awake."

Teddy looked at her suspiciously, but brought his wrist up to his mouth and took a lick.

"Well?"

"It's salty," he said, "but couldn't something taste salty in a dream?"

Oedipus, eager to get out and unused to the properties of screen doors, jumped up and tried to climb it and got his claws stuck. He hung there, waiting for someone to help him. Pinky unhooked him and set him on the floor. The cat looked up at Teddy.

Teddy frowned. A small breeze, from out of nowhere, shouldered its way up to the screen, peered in at them, and then pushed its way ef-

fortlessly through the thousand tiny holes and released a smell, difficult to name, which seemed to drive the cat frantic with desire and
made Pinky suddenly oddly aware of the dishwasher where she and
Arthur had leaned last night.

"Could I have a bagel to take with me?" Teddy asked grimly, as if
he were preparing to set forth on a journey to one of the cold rims of
the world.

"Sure, but if this is a dream, it will only be an air bagel and you'll
wake up in your bed hungry. And remember, this cat has never been
outside in his life, except to go to the vet. I don't know what he'll do.
Maybe he'll go crazy. Keep an eye on him."

She gave him the bagel and opened the back door. The cat did not
hesitate for a moment, but dashed out into the grass like he'd been
shot from a cannon.

When he reached the center of the yard, he stopped suddenly in
his tracks and looked toward the sky going up and up without a ceiling
in sight, and the hair on the back of his spine and his tail stood
straight out. Then he slunk down so his belly fur brushed the ground
and slid, as inconspicuously as he could, into the bushes.

Teddy followed along beside him while the cat stealthily paced the
boundaries of the backyard, slinking in and out of the undergrowth.
Teddy watched him for a while, but then, unable to help himself, he
began to look for bugs. It was the kind of morning the world has been
leading up to for years. There were luminous blue morning glory trum-
pets that trembled on the fence. There was a honeysuckle hedge that
filled the air with its perfume. Blood-red roses hung sweetly from their
thorny stems and the fuzzball tree was hung all over with fuzzballs.
Everywhere the place crawled and buzzed and hummed with bees
and ladybugs, crickets and flies, beetles and ants. The place was a paradise of insects, creatures it had been almost impossible to find in Manhattan, where the microchipped robot ant and roach terminators had
all but eliminated them. Teddy was fascinated with bugs simply for
themselves, of course, but he also needed them desperately for his
experiment.

His attention being elsewhere, Teddy did not notice when Oedipus stopped at the chain-link fence that separated their yard from the
giant scissor lady's yard. Oedipus lifted his nose and sniffed the air, too.

There was something that seemed to seize hold of him, for he stiffened and then peered through the chain links intently. After a moment he began poking along where the dirt and dead leaves collected at the bottom of the fence, until he found a small depression in the ground. He widened this a little by scraping at it with his paw and stuck his head through, and then, a moment later (and it was impossible, if you were watching closely, to see how this was done), he shrank his pudgy, pillow-shaped self into something no bigger than a wet and thieving rat and slid into the hole he had made.

Teddy came awake just in time to notice the tail end of the cat vanishing under the fence.

"Ed!" Teddy cried in alarm.

A moment later, Teddy spotted him sauntering through the giant scissor lady's garden. He paused here and there, sniffing, looking for something. Teddy peered around anxiously, but saw no sign of the lady.

"Ed! You've got to come back. You shouldn't be there."

But the cat ignored him, acted as if he had never seen Teddy before in his life and didn't wish to be introduced to him now. Teddy was wounded, but Oedipus paid no attention. He sniffed at a small red rose, but apparently this wasn't what he was looking for. He lifted his nose, searching for something else, and then headed toward a white wooden trellis against which a tall climbing rosebush had been trained. The bush, when you looked at it closely, was loaded with buds in tight green-pointed casings. They weren't ready to open yet, but in some you could see slivers of creamy pink pushing against their constraints. Oedipus sniffed carefully around the thorny base of the bush and then sniffed again. When he recognized, at last, what he was looking for, he opened his eyes wide and stared fearlessly up at the ascending sky. Then he made a 180-degree turn, so that his rear end was almost up against the rosebush. His tail lifted and quivered slightly. He released a bright, straight-as-an-arrow stream of pee into the foliage.

The cat, having relieved himself, sat there fearlessly as if this new world were his own personal oyster.

In the shadows of the alleyway next door, something moved. A moment later the giant scissor lady appeared. She was wearing her black capri pants with silver zippers and a straw hat. She was also carrying the nozzle end of a garden hose, which unwound behind her as she approached.

"Ed!" Teddy hissed.

Perhaps the cat heard him. Or maybe not. But, in any case, the scissor lady pointed the gunlike nozzle at the cat and depressed the trigger. The cat was astounded. He was horrified. He leaped his big sack-shaped self to the top of the fence with a terrific screech. When he landed on Teddy's side of the fence, he turned briefly to see to whom it was he owed this insult. Then he turned and disappeared haughtily, dripping, stepping on wet disdainful tiptoes down the alleyway.

That morning Arthur had read the newspaper carefully and saw that, as usual, things were shrouded in darkness. Along with a report on another ten percent decline in ice at the Arctic cap, there had been a train wreck in Moscow claimed by two unrelated terrorist groups, and an outbreak of a never-before-seen virulent influenza in Japan, claimed by no one, but suspicious-looking. Arthur checked on his antibiotic supply in the upstairs medicine cabinet and then wrote a brief letter to the *Times* expressing his continued disgust with the New York Olympics plans, which would not only increase the prospects of calamity here tenfold, but had already caused the eviction of several hundred low-rent families with no other place to go.

Once he had sent the letter, he set off for the university. Halfway there, he was hit with one of his headaches. This one was like several bell towers going off at once. He considered turning around and going home, but knew it would be of no use. Whatever was going to happen, would happen.

He had no sooner walked into the front office than the department secretary told him the news of Marina's death. This, of course, he had not expected. He stared at her, dumbfounded, his head throbbing.

The secretary, noting his pallor, wondered if he had been in love with Marina. Stranger things had happened. She waited for him to ask for more details of the accident, but he said nothing and, after a moment, simply walked out and went down the hall to his own office.

He was stricken with remorse. What had he done?

He, who always strove to keep his life simple and fair and uncluttered, how was it that these things happened to him?

Although he tried to keep his mind upon the data in front of him (an experiment having to do with cow eggs implanted with human cholesterol genes), he found it hard to do so.

He kept taking the little jar out and turning it around in his mind.

Would Marina have expected or wished for him to interfere? Hadn't Marina merely approached him as a means to an end? As far as he could tell, she had had no personal interest in him, and if she had wished for his involvement in any further way, wouldn't she have let him know? Was it not, after all, the sister whom Marina would wish to inherit what was left behind?

And what of Pinky? Did this unforeseen occurrence change his responsibility to her? He knew that to tell her what he had done and what had happened would probably be much the same as inviting hell and all its minions to camp out in and around his house. And what the consequences might be for all the other interested parties was impossible to foresee.

All day he kept coming back to these questions, but by evening he had gotten no further in settling what he should or should not do. He determined, as he rode the subway home, to put the matter out of his mind for the time being. He walked out into the cooling green evening and turned the corner to his block. As he passed the house next door to his own, a man watering a stone urn full of geraniums hailed him.

"You're Teddy Sorenson?"

Arthur looked at him with a start. "No, I'm Arthur. Teddy is my son."

"Well, welcome to the neighborhood. I'm Billy Edelman. I have a package here from UPS for your son. Everyone must have been out when it came this morning. I've got it right here in the front hall. Let me get it for you."

He emerged a moment later with a long rectangular package. He handed it to Arthur, and Arthur turned it around slowly and looked at the return address.

"From my wife's mother," he said and felt a twinge of apprehension. He gave the box a little shake and it rattled slightly. "Well, thanks. My son will be excited. You been in the neighborhood long?"

"Almost twenty-five years," the man said with a laugh.

"You knew the previous owners of our house well?"

"We were great friends for the first fifteen years or so. Then there was a disagreement between the women. A horticultural friction. Something about the gardens. I believe the other woman used some of the new bioengineered seeds in your garden over there and my wife was horrified and worried about what effect it would have on her roses. My wife is a rose breeder. It was a pretty vicious business. Susan can get a little carried away. She's very sensitive. But the worst thing was that the women didn't want the men to talk to each other, either. Howie and I had been playing chess together every week for all those years. We were pretty evenly matched. I was maybe a little better than he was."

"So you stopped playing?"

Billy gave a little glance behind him, then looked back at Arthur cunningly. "Is that what you would have done?"

"I doubt it."

Billy looked at him searchingly, then sighed. "Whaddaya gonna do? Howie's gone." He turned away and looked up at some point along the roof line of the brownstones across the street. When Arthur followed his gaze, he noted a row of four or five small gargoyles jutting out from the eaves of the house opposite. It was impossible to make out their features from this distance. When he looked back at Billy's face, he saw that although it was, for an older man, an alert and supple face, it had the kind of gray cast to it that goes along with a bad heart.

Arthur was surprised to hear himself say, "I play a bit. Perhaps we could have a game one night."

Billy's gray face lit up. He cracked his knuckles. Arthur sincerely hoped that this was not something he did while playing chess. "This is a wonderful piece of news, a wonderful invitation. Maybe we could meet for a game, say, Thursday night."

"Thursday? Well, that's possible, but I'll have to see how the unpacking is going."

"We could meet down at the park? Down by the lake? If the weather's good. There's some chess tables. That's where Howie and I went after the garden wars began."

Arthur looked at Billy more sharply.

Billy laughed. "People are made funny, don't you think? The way they always want to be rubbing up against each other, living next door to each other, throwing parties, getting married, and then it turns out they're not really made right to be doing that. Better to meet somewhere on neutral territory now and then, and then go back home."

"Yes, I agree with you," Arthur said, although he felt upset and unsettled, and he associated the outdoor playing of chess with a certain wantonness. "Well, I'll stop over later in the week and let you know."

Susan Edelman came over that very evening in the middle of the argument about the watergun. His mother wanted him to have it and his father did not.

The watergun was solar-powered and would emit, depending how you set its controls, a jet stream accompanied by a zapping sound, a silent smokelike mist, or a loud belch and a sudden explosion of bubbles—all designed to confuse and confound one's enemy. It was about a foot long and had a poisonously lime-green detachable tank, shaped like a bomb. When the box was opened, Teddy stared in disbelief. He had never owned a gun, let alone a gun such as this.

Before Teddy could reach out and touch it, Arthur let forth a hard, impatient sigh and lifted the box out of Teddy's reach.

"She's either going mad or it's a carefully planned campaign," his father said. "She knows perfectly well what my feelings are about toy guns." One of Arthur's eyes was slightly higher than the other. Under normal conditions, you hardly noticed this, but for some reason, when he became angry or upset, this asymmetry became much more marked.

"Isn't that the most grotesque thing you ever saw?" he said to Teddy. He put the gun, still in its box, up on top of the refrigerator.

Teddy went into the small sunroom, which they had told him he could use for his projects. It would have been nice to have the gun in here with him now, if only just to look at, but he turned his mind to his work. He had been experimenting with this particular project on and off for some time now, and he had a great feeling this place was going to bring him success. Certainly the work would go more quickly, since he would have all the bugs he needed to do his test trials on.

There were still boxes all over the place, but there was a long low table under the window. As he neatly laid out his notes, his chemistry set, and an odd assortment of other materials, he could hear his parents beginning the argument. His parents argued all the time. They might argue about how long it takes to hard-boil an egg or if beauty meant anything or what was the mathematical probability that the earth would be hit by an asteroid in the next ten years or whether or not it was extravagant to buy raspberries.

Her side of the argument would go flashing through the apartment like a ball of fire, clumsy and hot, knocking over tables and lamps, while his father stood there as critical and considering and unassailable as the air in a doorway.

Teddy hated it when they did this.

He concentrated on his work. He took out a clean petri dish and put in a teaspoon of sulfur, a teaspoon of charcoal, and then added a dash of salt. He stared at this thoughtfully, then went into the kitchen and borrowed his mother's extra bottle of green dishwashing liquid from under the sink and came back and squirted some into the mixture. He was stirring this up when the doorbell rang.

His parents stopped just like angels fighting in midair with swords and looked at each other accusingly. While they each waited for the other to give some explanation for this interruption, Teddy got up from the floor and answered the door.

The woman was no longer carrying her scissors and she had taken off her straw hat.

Teddy's parents gazed at her uncomprehendingly as they came in slowly from that distant dimension of complete obliviousness to which people travel when a small marital disagreement turns out, as usual, to hold within it the very seeds of life and death.

"It's the lady from next door," Teddy explained.

"Ah," Arthur said. "This must be our neighbor Billy's wife. Susan, isn't it? Won't you come in?"

Susan gazed impassively around the still-disordered living room and said, "No, thanks. I just wanted to suggest to you that you put your name and house number on your laser bins. I don't want to point any fingers, but there have been a lot of missing bins lately."

Pinky smiled again, happily. "Oh, really? That's wonderful. In Manhattan, where we come from, people who have their own garbage bins get special electric shock devices to put on them. Of course, we lived in an apartment building, so everything just went down the chute and got laser-crisped in the incinerator in the basement."

"I never go into Manhattan."

"Oh, I don't blame you. I'll probably never go back there again except for emergencies. And I promise to put our names on our bins."

"Secondly, I wanted to mention to you that there was an orange cat urinating on my roses early this morning. I watered him quite thoroughly with my hose and I think he is unlikely to come back, but if he does, I will not be so lenient with him next time. If, by some chance, he happens to be your pet, I suggest you train him to stay on your side of the fence. One of my roses in particular is quite valuable. It should start blooming any day now and under the right conditions will bloom all the way into early winter. I bred it myself and I expect it to take first prize in its category."

Teddy looked over at his mother. She had told him that when she was a little girl her whole face had been covered with freckles. Now, however, there were just a few left, sprinkled around her nose and cheeks. Whenever she was taken by surprise—which was quite frequently—her face would grow even paler than usual and her freckles would stand out, as they were doing now, like a throw of birdseed against the snow.

He looked up at his father. It wasn't always easy to tell with his father, but Teddy gathered that he was amused.

After a moment of silence, Pinky said, "I'm sure it must have been some other orange cat. Our Oedipus is litter-trained and very polite."

Teddy's father snorted.

Pinky glared at him and then looked back at Susan. "In any case, I know I read somewhere that cat pee is full of vitamins. It's probably very good for roses."

"If my roses are going to receive any vitamins, naturally I will prefer to dispense them myself."

"Well, of course. But you realize that cats are not great believers in fences," Pinky said.

"Oh, don't worry, I will make a believer out of this cat."

Teddy looked at the two women's faces. Teddy noted how, up close, Susan's face was finely etched all over with tiny cross-hatches like reptile skin. Her shadow, he knew already, was going to be treacherously sharp and unpredictable and he would have to be on the lookout for it wherever he went, like the way you had to be on the lookout for broken glass when you ran about barefoot. But in his mother's face there were complications, a tug-of-war between feelings, which was, of course, perfectly commonplace with his mother, and a phenomenon he watched with some interest, but also contempt. She was furious, he could see, but she also felt some inexplicable need to be polite, or maybe even kind.

"Well, I hope your getting settled in has gone smoothly. Let us know if there's anything we can do for you."

"Yes, we will."

Here Susan withdrew, and the door slowly swung shut.

There was another long silence. His father jingled some coins in his pocket.

"The nerve," Pinky said at last. "Don't you think? The toad-faced nerve. I'm gonna go over and pee on her roses myself if she touches my cat."

Teddy said nothing. He had things he could have added, but he knew when it was best to keep quiet.

"That cat is a gangster, Pinky. A lowlife. He deserved a good hosing down."

"Arthur! How can you say that? He was only marking his territory! He's waited nine years for a little territory of his own, and now that he's got it, he's doing exactly what his natural, healthy instinct told him to do."

"Well, if his instinct tells him that the Edelmans' backyard is his, his instinct is leading him into serious legal error."

"He's not a lawyer, Arthur. He's a cat. He doesn't know anything about *legal*."

"Well, if you can't teach him that this is our backyard and that's theirs, then you better keep him in the house, because she can pretty much do whatever she wants to him if she catches him over there."

Teddy decided he'd better go outside and check on Oedipus.

The summer dusk was descending softly through the branches of the fuzzball tree. He looked around and spotted Ed, half hidden in the ivy behind the ladder that leaned on nothing. The cat sat upright, his tail folded neatly about his rear legs, which were tucked beneath him. He was either watching something attentively or asleep. It was hard to tell which.

Teddy went over and knelt beside him. The cat's fur, which was still slightly damp, felt unusually soft. "You're going to have to watch out, Ed. I'm not joking."

The cat did not reply. His attention flicked to something rustling in the corner under the birch tree. He crouched low and slipped softly through the grass toward the small disturbance. He went slower and slower, stopped, and then somehow flattened himself so that he was almost as close to the ground as a pancake. He slid forward a few steps at a time, then took a sudden leap and landed in among the trailing branches of the tree with a small, precise thump.

On the western side of the sky there was still a large swath of pale orange light. Teddy lay down on his back in the grass and stared up at this light. He felt as if he were inside a cantaloupe. Inside the house he heard his mother yell that fences were for perverts.

This puzzle of how different they were, and who, then, Teddy was supposed to be, was a worry. His father had once explained to Teddy the process of meiosis, of eggs and seeds and cell division and what a clever way it was for nature to make sure that each baby was a completely new and different person, and yet carried with himself or herself pieces of all the parents and grandparents who had come before. Not entirely sure he understood what his father was talking about, he had once tried his mother on the subject, but she had answered cryptically that he should pay no attention to his father, that she had won him in a bet.

The cantaloupe, he saw, was going from the sky. There was only silence now from the house. Oedipus, in the gathering dark, was a gray silent shadow. He slid up to Teddy and dropped something small at his feet. Teddy lifted it up and his first thought was that it was a tea bag, for it was wet and limp and warm. Looking closer, however, he realized that it was a dead mouse.

"Ed, you murderer," he said, but carried the mouse carefully over to the light at the back porch, where he examined it with curiosity, having not so far had many encounters with death and knowing it to be one of the great scientific puzzles of the universe.

Katya, who had located Arthur's street on a city map and discovered it to be a short bus ride from her own, now appeared at the end of the block and came strolling slowly down the street pushing a stroller (Mrs. Morales had passed this on to them, since her grandchildren had all outgrown it. They could not afford one of the new motorized ones.) She came along the sidewalk, appearing to gaze at the house numbers with casual interest, but as she neared Arthur's house she slowed down even further and began to limp as if a small stone had gotten caught in her sandal. In front of the house she stopped and leaned up against the railing, removed the sandal, and glanced up at Arthur's front window. Her timing was as good as she could have wished. The bay windows were all open to the rose-scented evening and a lamp had just been switched on in the living room. Standing there, feeling around between her toes for a nonexistent pebble, she was allowed to see the following scene.

Pinky stood in the archway between the dining and living area with a small loaf of bread in her hand, and said in a loud, angry voice that she hoped that now that they owned a house Arthur was not going to turn into one of those small-minded tyrannical petty Beaujolais types who put up fences so they can get horny peeping through them.

Katya could see that Arthur was neatly placing books onto a bookshelf. He bent down and picked up some more, perhaps from a carton on the floor, and then straightened up again and looked at Pinky with amusement. "What? Petty Beaujolais? What do you mean? You mean petty bourgeois? Is that what you mean?"

"Wipe that superior smirk off your face, Arthur Sorenson. You know what I'm trying to say. I'm talking about how you, who always scorned the idea of private property, have now joined your enemy and all of a sudden you're into fences like that dried-up shoe-leather face next door who's worried that the sky will fall in if a little cat pee gets on her roses."

"The issue here is not my thoughts concerning private property, but the fact that the cat has a criminal mind. He steals food, he claws the furniture, and he pees on other people's roses." Arthur turned his back on her and leaned down to get a couple more books from the carton.

As he did so, Pinky lifted the loaf of semolina bread and threw it at him, hitting him on the shoulder. He stood up and gazed at her indignantly. Katya could see him quite clearly as he stood near the bookcase next to the front window. She examined his face carefully and critically. It was, she thought, a scholarly face, a little too pale and little too unused to the light of day, but striking, as if it had appeared here by one of those strange leaps of heredity, straight from some ancient lost race.

"Do you imagine you will convince me of something by lobbing loaves of bread at me?"

"I wasn't trying to convince you of anything, I was just trying to soothe my nerves."

Because Pinky stood farther back in the room, Katya could not see anything but her small furious silhouette. The outline of her head seemed disproportionately large and alive because of the numerous small tendrils of hair that had managed to escape from their rubber band as they always did when Pinky became excited. When Pinky now took a step toward Arthur and moved into the light, Katya noted the bright carrot color of this hair.

This color was so different from Marina's rich chestnut that she was filled with sudden sorrow and she began to weep again.

But only for a minute this time. She was fairly sure that what she had seen here was what her sister would have wished her to see, that the effort was both familiar and part of the forward struggle of humankind. So she wiped her eyes, slipped her shoe back on, then took up once again the handles of the stroller and moved off down the block.

Later, when Pinky went upstairs to mess around with her paints and soothe her soul, Arthur sat there at the kitchen table without turning the lights on and watched his young son working intently at some mysterious task out in the backyard. After a while he put his head down between his hands.

Arthur did not believe in love—that is, the kind of love where one party sees the other party as the long-lost missing half of the lover's soul, or the password that will move the rock that covers the opening to the cave that holds the treasure that we have all been sent to search for—any more than he believed in God or the human soul or that trees speak with the moon at night. He considered it a delusion, a self-deception of the most reprehensible order. All schoolchildren from the earliest moments onward should be educated with historical and psychological examples as to the ignorant superstitiousness of expecting romantic love to be a solution to anything.

Nor did Arthur think much of marriage. Clearly people living or working together in close quarters for any length of time almost always created between them the most absurd problems and suffering. As for the producing of children, since he was realistically pessimistic about the future of the human race, he had from the outset told Pinky many times that he had no intention of contributing any fruit from his loins to the sinking ship.

But, of course, things had not gone the way he had planned.

Teddy had been conceived, in spite of Arthur's honorable intentions. Once Pinky was pregnant, he had been badgered mercilessly by his own parents, who wished for him to marry, and then by hers, and then, when one evening he had brought it up for discussion with her, she laughed.

"Ignore them," she said. "You admit you do not love me, that you do not think you will ever love anyone. The day will come when we will tire of each other and we will want to move into greener backyards. I know you to be an extremely fair guy and I'm sure that you will always do your share for our child without needing any legal contract to make you do it. So why bother? Let's just enjoy the moment."

He was so outraged by this naive and unrealistic statement that he proposed to her on the spot. "We'll do it at home. We'll get that goofy Ethical Culture guy to do the ceremony and we'll make it potluck. No presents, though. I don't want to let ourselves get weighed down with a whole lot of trashy unnecessary junk right from the beginning. I despise it when people get married so that other people feel obligated to give them a whole lot of wasteful clutter."

She said it was okay with her, if that's what he really wanted.

They had an all-night, drunken, and potluck wedding. The Ethical Culture minister, who saw that he was binding together two truly just and righteous and kindhearted people, outdid himself in goofiness, and people brought presents anyway—mostly good useful items: a new broom, a window bird feeder and birdseed, mixing bowls and wooden spoons. Arthur let her keep the presents, but he took half the money they were given and gave it away to causes he considered deserving.

That all of this had come to pass, was baffling, but he had accepted it with a rational humility and he had even learned to accept the state of terror that being a father put him into, how it drew attention to and illuminated all manner of things he had never thought of before that might go wrong. But he had learned to calm many of these fears and had even, in some respects, found himself enjoying the great opportunity of raising a child.

So now it seemed terribly unfair that, having come so far and having worked so hard to master these difficult, unasked-for things, this new dilemma should be thrown at him. Not, of course, that he expected fairness.

He lifted his head and saw Teddy playing at his mysterious game out there in the dark.

"Teddy!" Arthur called out into the darkness, and Teddy, standing under the back porch light examining something, looked up, startled, and dropped whatever was in his hand. The thieving cat darted forward and picked it up and carried it off into the night.

Arthur opened the screen door and stepped outside. He was startled for a moment by the perfumed air, by an actual night sky hanging with stars over his head. He had never been a man much drawn by the temptation of owning things. Yet here, for just a moment, he felt the pleasure of ownership, as if, having bought a house, he had also bought himself the bit of sky that leaned over it. He worried for a moment that Pinky had been just in her accusation that he was betraying his own principles, that he might, without even noticing it, by small increments find himself joining the madding crowd of petty Beaujolais drinking, Welbutrin popping, vidvert scanners. But then, again, knowing himself for exactly what he was, he knew this was preposterous. He stepped forward and put his arm about his son's shoulders.

Teddy looked up at him expectantly and Arthur wasn't sure what it was he wanted to say. Then he remembered that he had wanted to talk to him about the watergun. "You didn't really want that gun, did you?" he asked.

Teddy didn't answer right away, either. "Well," he said at last, "I haven't really got much time for it right now. I'm working on a big project." He paused. "But I guess Grandma really wanted me to have it. So maybe, when I'm done, I should play with it a little?"

Arthur put his fingers through his son's fine hair. "You know how I feel about guns."

Teddy sighed.

"But your mom seems to think I did wrong in not consulting you. She seems pretty upset."

"What is it with Mom?" the boy said stiffly.

Arthur, moved by an impulse not easy to name, bent and kissed the child's forehead.

Immediately Teddy reached up and wiped the warm, invisible mark away with his hand.

"Your mother tends to get farblondjet rather easily," Arthur said.

"What's that mean?"

"Farblondjet? It's a Yiddish word, I guess. It means she gets herself all turned inside out about stuff."

"Why? Why does she get like that?"

"Well . . . in this case I think it's because she's after your happiness."

"What do you mean? She wants my happiness?"

Arthur laughed. "No, no. She wants you to be happy because it would give her happiness. She thinks you're too serious."

"Do you think I'm too serious?"

Arthur sighed. "I don't know if I'm qualified to be the judge of that. It may be that I'm too serious myself."

"Do *you* want me to be happy?"

"Of course, but I'm not sure, in any case, that people are designed to be generally happy. I think happiness is just something that comes along now and then when you're busy working at something else. But whatever the truth of the matter, I don't think toy guns are a good place to start looking for that particular pot of gold. Why don't you tell me about your big project?"

Teddy looked up at his father, then glanced around suspiciously as if he suspected that there were spies hiding up in the rustling leaves of the fuzzball tree.

"I can't talk about it here," he said in a low voice.

Arthur lowered his voice. "Is it something new, an important invention?"

"Yes, sort of."

"Well, just tell me this," Arthur whispered. "Is it a project that will help to push the darkness of human ignorance back a little further or are you only in it for the money?"

It was hard to tell, but Arthur thought he saw Teddy blush. After a moment, Teddy said, "Don't worry. If it makes us rich, I'll give most of the money away."

"I couldn't have asked for a better son," Arthur said.

The cat, who had perhaps had enough of the abundant and mysterious night for the time being, came out of the bushes and sauntered up to the back door. He looked at the two of them, rather pityingly, Arthur thought, then began casually washing his bloodstained paws while he waited for someone to let him in.

5. Pepper Tree

*W*hen Ken Fishhammer had begun the project four years ago, he was working on the problem of *delivery*, how to get the *good* genes into the cells so that they replace the *bad* genes. This was the big issue occupying much of the human bioengineering field and had been for the last decade, and he knew that there were many others like himself who were right on the verge of breaking through to a solution.

But he doubted that there was anyone else who had met the same improbable stroke of good luck that he had met, the stroke of good luck that would lift his work, if he succeeded, into the realm of legend.

He understood the irony of it, that a cold-eyed, single-minded, exacting fellow like himself should have stumbled up to these particular gates, but so it was.

When he started, he had been using the HDR deficiency as the platform for his experiments with chromosome vectors. HDR was a rare genetic disorder, which caused the overproduction of a certain enzyme, which then caused the buildup of something like small seltzer bubbles in the blood and, in turn, weakened the valves of the heart and eventually caused its early and fatal short-circuit. He had chosen this disorder because no one else was working on it and because it was the type of disorder that is a perfect target for gene therapy, since the cells that needed a new gene were in the bone marrow and easy to get at.

But he had been working with the disorder for only a year or so when he came to a most unforeseen realization.

He had known from the beginning, of course, that people with HDR deficiency rarely made it past their twenty-fifth year, but as he was working with these people he also came to see that they were a most unusually cheerful bunch. For a while he thought this merely some odd sort of psychological quirk, a response to the certainty of death, a kind of adrenalined inflation of the spirit such as soldiers sometimes experience as they go into battle.

But then, when he had managed, at last, to locate the offending gene and, further, had managed to introduce this gene into mice, the mice, too, became preposterously good-natured.

Fishhammer could poke them with needles, give them electric shocks, keep them close to starvation, but they remained determinedly friendly and pleased with whatever hand he dealt them. He tried over-crowding the cages, introducing strange males to nesting females, even housing one of the cages next to a startled-looking owl he had bor-rowed from some strange project they were doing upstairs on sleep cy-cles. But the mice cheerfully took it all in stride, moving over and making room, developing new cooperative behaviors of building and grooming that he'd never seen before, and sometimes cheeping in a comradely manner to the owl next door.

It came to Fishhammer that he had within his grasp the possibility of locating a gene—a single simple gene—that could confer a lifelong talent for happiness.

The only problem was finding a way to separate the desired dispo-sitional effect from the enzyme deficiency with which it was linked. And then, of course, to find a reliable way to deliver the new gene. He had worked carefully and very quietly, of course, since all personality improvement engineering research had been outlawed several years previously, in the wake of the great Clone Debates, and he made cer-tain to continue his original efforts to find a cure for the HDR defi-ciency. HDR was a rare disorder and no one had paid much attention to him, and he had been able to make swift and unhampered progress.

Then, at the moment of his breakthough, just as he was almost certain that he had safely separated the two linked genes, the clowns, the DNA Research Advisory Committee, that ridiculous pack of sniveling, self-righteous fools, had come in and shut him down.

So it was that a good year after the lab was shut down, Ken arrived at Katya's door and stood there for a moment listening curiously. He recognized the overture to *Der Rosenkavalier* coming perhaps from a radio and then there was a loud crash, followed by a woman's voice, it-self musical, but also desperate, followed by a loud stream of scold-ing words, half English, half some other Eastern-European-sounding language.

He knocked loudly and the voice stopped and then the music.

When she opened the door, she was holding the baby in her arms. He was scantily clad in a diaper and a not very clean white T-shirt. He had one hand on his aunt's cheek as if he wished to comfort or reassure her, but now he turned and gazed with luminous anticipation at the stranger standing in the doorway.

"Katya? I'm Ken Fishhammer."

"Come in," she said nervously. "Come in. The apartment . . . you will excuse our mess."

The small apartment, though sparsely furnished, was crowded with books and toys. If Katya had made an effort to tidy up the living room for her visitor, it was to little avail, since the baby had almost certainly followed behind her, pulling out whatever she attempted to put away and, apparently, just in that minute before Fishhammer knocked he had climbed up on the dining room table and pulled down a small wicker shelf filled with framed photographs.

Katya bent down now and swept up an armful of these and put them on the table. One, whose glass front had cracked down the mid-dle, she laid carefully aside.

"My parents," she explained bitterly. "Who think if only to edu-cate everyone then we can clear away darkness in people's minds, but now they are ashes sleeping in the pit."

She went over and sat down on the sofa. The baby crawled out of her lap and stood holding on to her knee with one hand, looking with great interest at Fishhammer.

"You don't believe we can clear away this darkness?"

She looked at him angrily. "No. It is a darkness we each arrive into the world with. Each one can become a monster filled with cruelty and hunger."

"Flapoosh!" the baby said.

They both turned to him. He was wonderful-looking, a little comi-cal, with his loosely curling, almost black hair that stuck up on the top like a rooster's comb. The little flecks of gold in his eyes sparkled.

"I think you are right. Our troubles are wired inside of us, but perhaps someday we will find a way to fix these troubles."

Katya did not say anything, but stared at him with the face of a stone water nymph in a dry fountain in winter. The baby, however, had made up his mind, and began to make his way over to Ken by lunging recklessly from one piece of furniture to the next. When he reached Fishhammer's knee, he held on tightly and peered up into his face with interest.

Fishhammer smiled stiffly at the baby, then looked again at Katya. "It must have been terrible for you, losing your parents like that, and now to lose your sister. The baby, I suppose, must be very disturbed by the loss of his mother?" Now he reached out and patted the baby on the head.

The baby smiled back at him, then leaned forward unexpectedly and grabbed the expensive mechanical silver pencil that Fishhammer kept in his shirt pocket. Fishhammer tried to snatch it back, but quick as lightning the baby dropped to his knees and crawled away out of reach, then stopped. He stared at the pencil briefly, then put it in his mouth and continued crawling across the carpet.

Katya, he saw, had not noticed this. She was watching something in the doorway.

He kept an eye on the pencil and said, "I grew very fond of your sister, you know, as if she were one of my own daughters. And she, I would like to think, was very fond of me. I was, naturally, very concerned when I learned that she was pregnant. She had quite enough difficulties to contend with, without having to also care for an infant. Did she ever speak about the child's father to you?"

"My sister was very private on this matter."

"She was a proud woman. Perhaps she was ashamed of her mistake, a mistake which, after all, can happen so naturally."

"My sister was ashamed of nothing."

Fishhammer looked at her uneasily. She still seemed very distracted by whatever it was she was gazing at. "Did she ever speak to you about the research we were doing?"

"No."

"You're sure? I believe she understood the importance of the work I was doing. She was one of the best researchers I ever had."

"What is it you want?" Katya asked abruptly.

He was silent for a moment. "Did your sister leave no will or instructions?"

"No."

"What are your plans? How will you manage?"

She smiled for the first time. "My plans are same. I will go to school to learn the market and the financing. I will get a job in multinational company, one which has interests everywhere, but especially in the country of my birth. I will raise myself to a position of great power."

He stared at her quizzically, unsure whether or not she was kidding. It was the middle of the afternoon and very hot. The fact that she offered him nothing to drink was probably not a good sign. Then again, perhaps such niceties were inconsequential or foreign to her.

He checked again on the progress of his pencil and saw that the baby was now crawling toward the window. When he reached it, he got up on his knees and, with the silver pencil still in his mouth, grabbed for the low windowsill. As soon as he was standing, he gave a loud grunt of triumph, took the pencil out of his mouth, and slid it forward across the ledge. Ken realized that although there was a window guard, there was no screen, but before he could leap across the room, grab the baby by the hair, and yank the pencil from his hand, it was too late. The baby pushed the pencil all the way forward until it dropped out into space and disappeared.

Ken, who had started toward the baby in fury, now forced himself to sit back. He took out his handkerchief and wiped his face. He was very thirsty.

The baby watched the place where the pencil had last been, completely captivated, as if he knew that he had somehow managed a great magic trick, but hadn't a clue how he'd done it.

Katya seemed now, at last, to notice the baby. "Andre!" she said sharply. "Do not put anything out window!" She looked at Fishhammer. "He is always throwing things from window. You would not believe how many things he throws out onto street."

"Why don't you get a screen?"

"My sister did not like such things. She said she did not want anything between herself and the air. Even in the winter, she would keep the window wide open. But I myself put in these little gates to make sure the baby would not fall out."

On the windowsill next to the baby was a small green plant with numerous shiny red and yellow peppers. The baby now turned his attention to this plant.

"Is it poisonous?" Fishhammer asked quickly.

She smiled again. "No, it is not poisonous."

The baby pulled, obviously with some expertise, on one of the small red peppers and plucked it from its stem. He took a little nibble. He wrinkled up his nose. He took another little nibble.

"They're sweet?" Fishhammer inquired.

She shrugged.

"Well, Katya, your plan sounds like a good one, but I think it will be very difficult to manage with a small child. Have you thought about this?"

"I am thinking about this problem constantly, with great attention," she said simply.

Fishhammer took a breath. "I am going to make you a bold offer. Perhaps you will accept it as a kindness to your sister. Perhaps you will accept it as a kindness to me."

She looked at him calmly and with full attention.

"My wife and I are doing pretty well. My wife is a wonderful mother. We have two children, girls, but we always talked about wanting a third. I'd like to offer to adopt your nephew. It would make us extremely happy. We could give him most of the things Marina would have wanted for her son, I think—a loving family, decent schools, college eventually. I believe this is what your sister would have wished."

He waited for her to say something, to make some response, but she was watching him.

"Naturally, we see that, although your life would become far more manageable without the care of a child, to give him up would still represent a grave loss for you. We would like to offer, by way of compensation—and also as a gift in memory of your sister—some assistance with your *own* education."

Now Katya's beautiful eyebrows, like two small seabirds, lifted as if upon a slight breeze.

The baby turned and raked the two of them with an amused glance and then began to work his way back to Fishhammer. He zigzagged across the room by lunging from one piece of furniture to the next. He moved with supreme and alert confidence, like a mountain climber traversing the edge of a high and narrow cliff. When he reached Fishhammer's chair, he gazed up into his eyes and then smiled his broad smile.

"He is a terror," Katya said.

The baby offered him a pepper. "Daboo."

Fishhammer took it in his hand and smiled ingratiatingly.

Katya stood up. "My sister wished great things for her child. Your offer is most generous. Most kind. I know that Marina would like for me to give it every possible consideration. I must make some arrangements. You will leave me your phone number and I will call you in a few days."

Fishhammer rose and shook her hand and, gazing into her cool and determined eyes, felt certain of his own triumph.

Once he'd taken his leave, he hurried down the stairs and out onto the sidewalk and cast about, looking for his silver pencil. There it was on the sidewalk, not far from a copy of *The Idiot* and a box of raisins that had opened and scattered all over the ground.

The pencil was still intact and working. He put it back in his pocket with a smile of satisfaction and realized that he was still holding the tiny red pepper. His mind on other matters, he popped it in his mouth and bit down.

He let out a scream of agony and spit the thing onto the sidewalk, but the juice of the pepper burned and tore at the inside of his mouth. He salivated and spit, and salivated and spit, and the tears poured down his cheeks. When he was able finally to see again and draw a breath of air, he stumbled off down the street in search of a place where he might find some water.

6. The Nine Lives of Cats

$\mathcal{T}$he gift from Teddy's grandmother continued to be debated from many angles. Late one afternoon, he heard the following scrap of the conversation as he passed by the sunroom, where his mother was talking on the voicelink:

"Why? You might as well ask me why Niagara Falls falls down instead of up. Or why the Tin Man doesn't have a heart. These things are just laws of nature. And it's just a law of nature that Arthur has to pick all the seeds out of his watermelon before he eats it. Whaddaya mean, what do I mean? You know exactly what I mean. You're a shrink. Arthur is afraid if he doesn't get all the seeds out of his watermelon, one day he'll swallow one and a little watermelon will start growing in his insides and then he'll go crazy and start doing bad things. And that's what's happening with Teddy and this watergun thing. He's afraid that if he lets Teddy have the gun, it will be like a watermelon seed growing in his insides and one thing will lead to another and before you know it Teddy will be out there drawing swastikas on people's front doors and then he will save up his allowance and get a real gun and he'll sneak it through the metal detector at school and at recess he'll shoot everybody in the schoolyard, and then he'll finish off his day by hijacking a plane and flying it into the Verrazano Bridge.

"Don't laugh like that. You know I'm right."

Teddy imagined his beautiful, dark-haired godmother throwing her head back and snickering her little horse snicker. This was what she often did when his mother made one of her explanations. For him, the explanation would often seem to be at first a trail he could follow, but when he followed it, it would suddenly thin out and vanish into the woods, leaving him completely lost among the whispering trees.

He decided he had heard enough. He opened the back screen door. The cat, who had been waiting there, slipped out between his legs. Teddy carefully carried out his petri dish containing an array of items carefully crushed and mixed by hand. Each day this mixture was a little different. One at a time, scientifically and methodically, he had tried all the chemicals in his chemistry set, and when these didn't get him anywhere he had started adding every commonplace material that he could think of. He had tried sugar and flour, soap powder and dust balls, tea leaves and spit. He had tried orange pips and crushed Cheerios, honey, marshmallow fluff, and sand from the corner of his eye. Today he had added some coffee grounds and a dab of super-stiff hair gel. Something was still missing.

From the sunroom, Pinky noted the bang of the door.

Fran said to Pinky, "You're right. Some of this is just what Arthur carries around inside. But some of this is his way of dealing with the environmental anxieties. It's not an easy time. You know that. These are coping mechanisms—all this control stuff and these exaggerated catastrophe fantasies. He's nuts, but, so what else is new? You should hear what I hear down at the prison hospital."

"I know," Pinky sighed. "I know. But what I'm really worrying about is that I think he's painting himself into one of those dark spider-webby corners again."

"You mean another depression? You think he's going into one of those?"

"Yeah."

"Bad?"

"Well, you know, he gets those headaches, but now they just keep hanging on. And he just fuzzes out on me. He hardly talks. He's worrying about something, but he says he's not."

Fran was silent for a moment. "If you catch him right now with one of those nice endorphin patches—they only work for a week or two, anyway—and get him in with a sharp cognitive person, I bet that would do the trick. Before he gets down there too far."

Pinky sighed. "Not till hell freezes over and the angels come down with their ice skates. He'll never agree. He says what he has is just the human condition and last time he told me that if he ever got low like that again, I should just get him shock treatments like they used to do."

Fran sighed. "It's such a shame. There's some really good mood modification work being done these days. I wish we could get him to talk to somebody. What's he thinking about? Do you know?"

"How do I know? He has a very large catalog of things he obsesses about. He could be thinking about whatever horrors are on the front page of today's paper, or maybe he's thinking about what happened to his grandfather in the Holocaust or how his father spent his whole life looking for that little baby uncle of his who got lost in the war."

"Yeah, well, he's got a very nice inheritance of shit there. And trauma experiences like that get passed along from generation to generation, but it's truly awe-inspiring to see how each succeeding beneficiary always manages to grab some au courant anxiety out of the air to give it a fresh new shape. Why, look at old Teddy."

Pinky moved worriedly into the kitchen and peered through the screen door at Teddy, who seemed to be dipping something into his petri dish. He looked completely and radiantly absorbed in whatever he was doing. "I don't think Arthur talks much to Teddy about what happened with his grandfather."

"So? You think that matters? This stuff gets absorbed right through the pores of the skin. You don't need to talk about it."

Pinky had no doubt that was true. "Speaking of which, how's your mom?"

"Did I mention to you that she showed up at that party I went to last weekend?"

"You're kidding!"

"No, I'm not. There I am, talking to the only single and reasonably noncomatose-looking male in the room (who obviously had been invited for the sole purpose of having somebody to introduce me to), and I'm engaging him in some introductory repartee to see if, by any chance, he might meet some of my basic qualifications, when what do I hear but my mother jangling her charm bracelets in my ear."

"But how did she get there? Who invited her?"

"What are you talking about? You think my mother needs an invitation for this kind of thing? Sabotaging my life is her specialty. She barges her way into this party and within five minutes she tells this guy the story of How My Great-Grandmother Came Over on the Boat with Ten Children and the Littlest One Died in Her Arms, How She Met My Father, the Bum, When He Leaped Onto the Subway Tracks to Save Her Alligator Shoe, and How She Almost Gave Birth to Me in the Produce Section of Key Food. She embarrassed me. She mortified me."

"You see, Fran, this is what I don't understand. I always think of you driving around your life like you were at Coney Island in a little bumper car, mowing people down. But whenever your mother shows up, you just seem to freeze in your tracks."

"That's how you think of me, Pinky? Driving around in a bumper car mowing people down? That's very beautiful."

"I mean it. How come whenever your mother shows up in *her* little car, you let her just ram you straight into the wall?"

Fran gave her little neighing laugh. "You'd have to fritter away the past eight years of your life, as I have, studying psychoanalytic and family systems theory, before you had the faintest inkling how a relationship like mine and my mother's turns into the pathological entity it's turned into. But this is just more of what I'm talking about, how we can't escape these little bequests they pass on to us."

"But Fran, why don't you just tell her to shove off? Tell her you're having a private conversation."

"I can't do that."

"Why not?"

"Because then she'd go out into the rain weeping and gnashing her teeth and what would I say to her the next time she called?"

"Say, 'I hope you had a nice walk.' "

"Look, the point is, I'm absolutely sick of having people try to fix me up. If I could have one wish, that's what it would be, that people would stop trying to matchmake me."

"No, it wouldn't."

"Sure it would. If people would just quit it, I wouldn't have to go through these monotonously depressing and uninstructive ritual disappointments. And also my mother wouldn't get so much fuel for her fire. I want you to swear that you will never again try to set me up with anyone."

"I don't have any single men left that you haven't already had stuffed and mounted on your wall."

"Swear."

Pinky was pretty sure that if Fran could have one wish, that was not what it would be, so she crossed her fingers and said, "Okay. I swear."

"So?"

"So, what?"

"What are you gonna do about the watergun? Why don't you just go ahead and give it to Teddy?"

"You know, I'd love to do that, but Arthur would be furious. He says he's gonna mail it back to my mother, but it's just sitting there on top of the refrigerator."

"If he's leaving the thing out like that, on top of the refrigerator, it means he isn't entirely sure what he's doing. Want me to come and mess around with his mind a little? And while I'm at it, maybe I can get him to open up a little about whatever slavering beast it is that has him by the throat this time."

"Would you? Oh, Fran, that would be great. That would be lovely. Come for dinner on Sunday. We'll have a barbecue."

Not long afterward, Arthur arrived home from work. He sat on the little patio, watching Teddy search for bugs in the underbrush. After a while Arthur was able to get himself to get up and go inside and change into his shorts.

He told Pinky he was going to go out for a run and then he had an appointment. He would find himself something to eat when he got home later in the evening.

"An appointment? What kind of appointment could you have in those little shorts and that stinky tank top?"

"I'm going to play a game of chess in the park."

She looked at him in pleased astonishment. "In the park? With who?"

"A guy."

"A guy? What guy? Have you made a friend?"

Arthur sighed heavily and put his right foot up on the kitchen windowsill and began to stretch. "Did I say anything about a friend? Why are you always trying to complicate things? I simply made a date to play a game of chess."

"The point of friends isn't to complicate things, sweetheart. The point is to expand your web. To help you see that you're not standing out in space all alone."

He was leaning down over his right foot and pulling, but he stopped for a moment and considered this slowly. "Were I a spider or an astronaut, what you say might just conceivably make sense, but just being a regular sort of schmo, I'm perfectly content with the friends I've already got, thanks."

"But who do you count as your friends, Arthur?"

Arthur now cocked his head sideways and looked at her irritably. "You know who my friends are."

"Well, who? Who do you think of as your friends?"

Arthur straightened up slowly and switched legs. He pulled himself down over his left one and said, "First of all, there's Stuart at work."

"Stuart at work is a guy you work with," she explained patiently. "He's not a friend. A friend is somebody you exchange all your innermost secrets with. A friend is someone who defends you to the death from your enemies or donates a kidney if you need one because your body won't tolerate any of those new synthetic ones."

"A, my kidneys are fine. B, who would want to be my enemy?"

"It's just as important to have enemies as to have friends. Name another."

"Maury. I feel very close to Maury."

"Maury! Maury is a guy you ran with. You ran with him because he happened to be out there. A friend is someone you stop and look in the face every once in a while. You stop and look at him and say to yourself, *Who is this lovely person I'm looking at?* Did you ever do that with Maury?"

Arthur smiled. "I've looked at Maury many times, Pinky, and *loveliness* was not a word that flashed into my mind when I did."

Pinky smiled back at him. She hadn't been able to engage him in an argument all week. "He was a convenience, that's all."

Arthur stood up. "And it's got to be a real pain in the ass, right? If it's not a real pain in the ass, and if you're not all the time compliment-ing each other's hairdos and such, then it's not genuine friendship, right?"

"Oh, come on. You're always poking fun at him, at his enlighten-ment thing. If you didn't run with him, you probably wouldn't have tolerated him for a second. Now that we've moved, you'll never see him again. Do you even know his last name?"

"Runners don't have last names. It's part of the creed."

"Well, I bet it's different with the crowd who plays chess in the park. Maybe you'll find somebody you can really talk to. That would be good."

"I doubt that these people who play chess in the park are going to be big talkers."

"You might be surprised."

"What would you know about the crowd who plays chess in the park?"

She smiled at him.

There was a curious pause as there appeared between them the slightly-higher-than-eye-level wall of fog that holds within it every-thing that has not been said between two people who are living to-gether, side by side.

"Never mind," she said. "I'm glad you're going. Have fun. But keep your eyes peeled for lightning. They were predicting a storm for later."

Arthur ran slowly. On the block right before the entrance to the park, the sidewalk, for some reason, was still made of its original slate, and the rectangles of gray stone heaved up here and there, pushed out of their places by the roots of old trees. He was surprised to find himself so pleasantly affected by the softness of the evening.

By the time he had reached the top of the hill, he had broken out into a light sweat. Across the street he saw three crows, whom he thought seemed familiar, sitting on the iron fence watching him. He ran once around the park, then slowed down as he approached the chess tables. Billy Edelman sat at the last table, contemplating a chess position that was laid out on the stone board. Over his head was a tree full of hairy green seedpods. As Arthur drew closer, he saw that several of these hairy green seedpods had landed on Billy's head and shoulders. In front of the table lay the lake, still as glass and filled with reflections and counterreflections of the sun going down and the great trees that stood around its perimeter.

"Hey," Arthur said. "I made it."

Billy looked up and smiled at him.

Arthur found that he felt a little better. The running always helped. It was, he supposed, the endorphins. He stretched and then lowered himself onto the stone bench across from his new neighbor. He took out a couple of sticks of Juicy Fruit and offered one to Billy. When Billy refused, he unwrapped both of them and stuck them in his mouth. He was relieved to see that Billy looked better, also, than when he had last seen him. His face had a little more color in it and his skin looked less clammy.

They both turned and contemplated the interior roadway, which was, on this long July evening, filled with a stream of joggers, bikers, roller bladers, race walkers, and an occasional pogo sticker bouncing by, pogo sticks having temporarily returned to fashion. A stroller, with a baby deeply asleep inside of it, rolled by apparently on its own, although it was followed fairly closely behind by a jogger holding out a remote control device.

"Of what significance is it, do you think, all these people going around and around in a circle?"

Arthur grunted. "Good for the cardiovascular system."

Billy studied the stream of people. "Well, you know what this always reminds me of? It was an old, old story. Remember? They took it off the bookshelves—*Little Black Sambo*."

Arthur looked at him blankly.

"The little kid who tricked the tigers into going around and around in a circle until they turned into butter."

"Ah."

"Shall we play?"

"Sure."

They began to set up the board. Arthur gestured at the lake. "It's a beautiful spot. You find it inspires your playing?"

"I hate this spot. If I had any other choice, I'd never come back again."

Arthur looked at him in surprise and then out at the water. It was impossible to tell how deep or clear it was, it lay so still and full of or-ange light. At the edge stood a single old man with a bucket and a fish-ing rod, waiting patiently.

There was a burst of laughter from the table down at the end of the row. Arthur glanced over uneasily and then back at Billy. "You come for the company, then? Some good competition down here?"

Billy followed Arthur's gaze and smiled. "They come to get away from their wives."

"Is that what you do?"

Billy gestured with his hand for Arthur to begin, so Arthur moved Pawn to King Four and Billy replied in kind. Arthur played Knight to King's Bishop Three and Billy played Knight to Queen's Bishop Three. Bishop to Bishop Four and Bishop to Bishop Four. Arthur played Pawn to Queen's Knight Four. Arthur was surprised at Billy's response, which was one of eccentricity, and seriously weakened his own position in the center. After several more moves of this sort, Arthur decided that Billy played inventively but amateurishly. He should be easy to beat.

However, about two-thirds of the way into the game, Billy rather abruptly said, "No, I come because my son drowned in this lake."

Arthur's head snapped up sharply, as if he had been grabbed by the hair. He stared at Billy and noticed how several more seedpods had dropped onto his shoulders and shirt. This somehow did not seem to him a good sign.

"I'm sorry," Arthur said. "I'm terribly sorry. I'm sure this is some-thing you don't like to talk about," and he looked away.

"He was fourteen. He had gone out skating at night with a friend, which wasn't allowed, of course. But to do what is not allowed is a driving imperative when you are fourteen. Up until that night he was no stupider or unluckier than any other boy his age."

Arthur moved his head very carefully in case he was about to get a headache and then he took out and considered this same problem that he had considered many times before. How a parent's sphere of influ-ence could not be everywhere at once. How when they stayed close to you, you could manage the odds somewhat, but as they moved away from you, they fell into the arms of chance over which you had no power.

Arthur forced himself to look at Billy, but Billy was looking out at the lake, where a large white bird was sailing toward them. It drew behind itself a long thin delicate line over the glassy water.

"Quite a number of people have fallen through the ice in that lake over the years. The water is very deep in places. You'd be surprised. People usually are. I'm sure my son was surprised."

"When did this happen?" Arthur asked. The words felt as if they were coming through wads of wet cotton as he said this, so full of dread was he.

"Twelve years ago." Billy took Arthur's pawn with his king. "Check."

Arthur, distracted, moved Bishop to King Two.

"Time, of course, is not such a linear thing as its public relations department would lead us to believe. There are certain moments that always seem much closer in time to the present than others." Billy moved Knight to Bishop six. "Checkmate."

Arthur sat up, startled. How could this have happened? For a wild and fleeting moment he wondered if Pinky had had something to do with this. He looked up at the sky, but it was perfectly clear. He saw that the big white bird that had been sailing toward them had now reached the shore. It clambered up onto dry ground and began to waddle imperiously in their direction.

Billy took out of his pocket a bag of peanuts. He shelled a few and threw them in the direction of the bird, which waddled forward, ate them rapidly, then came right up to where Billy sat on the bench and eyed the bag of peanuts.

"Ulysses, this is Arthur," Billy introduced them.

"Ulysses?"

Billy did not give an explanation. "Did you know that trap?" he asked, indicating the chessboard.

"Of course. I don't know why I didn't see it coming."

"The past can only travel in one direction, but the future comes from several directions at once. It's hard to know where to be looking." Billy threw a handful of peanuts on the ground. The swan advanced upon them.

Whatever lift the run had brought was rapidly leaving Arthur. He was taken with the desire to go home and look upon his house and family, to check upon the dryness of the basement floor and the ordinariness of whatever activities Pinky and Teddy were engaged upon.

He stood up. "Next week?"

"It would be a pleasure," Billy said.

Arthur reached over and brushed some of the hairy green seedpods that had fallen onto Billy 's shoulders. "Okay, then," he said and trotted off slowly.

The swan raised its head and watched him for a moment, then returned to the peanuts.

In the far corner of the yard there was a birch tree whose branches hung down to the ground and made a small and perfect cave. Teddy, carrying his petri dish and magnifying glass and tweezers, parted the branches and crawled in. He gazed around for something he might add to his formula that would do the trick. He considered the small caterpillarlike seedpods that hung from the birch tree. He considered the velvety petals of the violets that grew in little clumps just outside the shade of the hanging branches. But neither of these seemed quite right to him.

He lay down on his back.

He peered up through the arrowhead leaves and thought about how, when he had succeeded with this particular invention, he would invent a formula for flying and he would be a famous person. The sun, though still high in the sky, was now beginning its downward journey. By closing one eye and moving his thumb fairly close to his face, he was able to block out the entire thing, which was an extremely puzzling phenomenon, since he knew it was supposed to be about a million miles wide and his thumb, he knew, was much smaller than that. He wondered if the explanation to the problem had something to do with relative weight. Possibly the sun, being made of fire, was very light, and his thumb, being made of blood and bone, was much heavier. He made a mental note to weigh his thumb on the bathroom scale when he went inside. He sighed and, shutting his other eye, was enclosed in the sharply fragrant noise of someone mowing a lawn in one of the adjacent yards. A large black and gold bumblebee, mistaking him for a rose, buzzed in under the tree and circled hopefully around his head. Teddy started in alarm, then decided the wisest thing to do would be to lie back and pretend he was dead. He felt the bee, for just the briefest of moments, touch down on the inside curl of his ear, as if imagining it a petal. It took all his willpower not to move, but he did not, and a second later he heard the bee lift off grumbling into the air.

He opened his eyes and, finding himself alive and unstung, sat bolt upright.

At just this moment, Oedipus, who had been enjoying a brief nap under the peony bush, awoke, stretched, and leaped lightly onto the top of the chain-link fence that divided their yard from Susan Edelman's. He stood there balancing regally in the long gold afternoon light, gazing down the stretch of small backyards with proprietary interest.

Teddy looked up just in time to see the cat flick his white-tipped tail and jump down lightly into the extravagantly flowering yellow tea roses in the adjacent yard.

Meaning no profanity or disrespect, but simply as a form of warding off, Teddy said, "Shit," to himself silently.

The cat, once again, approached the bush with the pink buds. Two or three of the flowers were just beginning to open and, even in his anxiousness over the cat, Teddy noticed a deep crimson color peering out of their insides. The cat turned and lifted his tail and watered the base of the bush thoroughly.

Teddy glanced anxiously at Susan Edelman's back door. At first he saw nothing there, but when he looked closer, he thought he could just make out a shape, squat and sinister behind the door screen.

"Ed!" he whispered. "Ed!"

The cat sauntered down to the next rosebush and settled in a shady spot beneath the leaves and began to wash his ears.

"Ed!" he hissed and tried to imitate the *chiccch, chiccch* sound his mother made when she called him. The cat looked up at him indifferently, then went back to his ears.

Teddy studied the fence between the two yards and measured his chances of climbing over it. He could probably manage it, he thought, but then he looked at the roses and shuddered. He had a horror of those thorns.

Susan Edelman opened her screen door and stepped out, preceded by a long thin shadow. Teddy saw that she was holding something out, a little tidbit of something between her fingers. Teddy shuddered. Could she possibly have known that the cat's great weakness was chicken skin?

Teddy had the feeling that, although Susan was not looking at him, she somehow was looking at him, and he was stricken with the sensation that he could not move, or, at any rate, could not move fast enough to outwit whatever fate awaited them.

Oedipus lifted his head and sniffed. Then he stood up and, with false casualness, started to saunter in Susan Edelman's direction.

Susan smiled. It was a terrible smile.

The cat came up to her feet and stopped. From out of nowhere, Susan produced a large red-and-white-checked tablecloth and dropped it over the cat. Before Teddy had a chance to give a word of warning, she had gathered the ends together like a sack and had the cat dangling off the ground, hissing and writhing.

Now she looked straight at Teddy. "I thought I told you to keep this cat out of my garden."

Teddy stared at her, unable to say a word. She shook the tablecloth a little, experimentally.

The cat yowled. "I think you should go get your mother," she said.

Of course. His mother. He should have thought of this right away. He turned and ran for the back door, shouting, "Mom!"

When his mother appeared in the doorway, he was appalled for a moment by how small she was. Why, she was even smaller than Susan Edelman. He stared at her in bewilderment.

"Mrs. Edelman has Oedipus in her tablecloth," he whispered.

Pinky took the scene in at a glance. Teddy was reassured to see that, almost immediately, several little curls of his mother's red hair escaped the confines of her rubber band and sprang out around her head.

"Put the cat down," she said.

"I asked you politely to keep him out of my garden."

"Well, I talked to him, but he doesn't get it, you know, about how that is your backyard and this is ours. Cats don't think in little rectangles like that. Surely you can see that."

"I see a cat urinating on my roses, which is not acceptable to me. This rose right here," she said, indicating the bush with pink buds and the deep red insides, "will soon be one of the most valuable roses in the United States."

Teddy saw that, as his mother came forward, she was holding on to her distress very carefully, as if it were an overly full glass of milk. She lifted her palms up slowly, in a way at once queenly and supplicating. "It's a beautiful flower, but he can't possibly hurt it and don't you see it's impossible to keep him in the house? He's been waiting for this backyard all his life."

"Well, he may have been waiting for your backyard, but I'll teach him now to stay out of mine. Let's see if he can land on his feet." Susan Edelman hefted the wriggling tablecloth and disappeared into her house.

Teddy, fascinated, looked at his mother. She was, he could see, thinking furiously. He had the feeling he was watching some massive movement of troops or storm clouds. She gazed first at Susan Edelman's back door and then up at her roof. Teddy knew that whatever his mother came up with, it was not going to be scientific.

"Quick," she ordered Teddy. "Call the fire department. Dial 911."

Of course. Teddy's hopes soared. It had been a long time since she had called the fire department.

"Tell them it's an emergency. Give them our address. Do you know it?"

Teddy nodded solemnly. He liked numbers.

"Tell them to come around to the back of the house next door because an old lady at that address is threatening to throw herself off the roof."

"But—"

"No buts! Just call. Now!"

When he got back to the yard, he found that his mother was now somehow standing in Susan's backyard, shading her eyes and looking upward, and there was Susan herself, way up high, dangling the checkered tablecloth out over the edge of her roof.

"Stop right there, Susan!" his mother yelled. "There are powers you can't see, right there with you, and they're going to remember this. The cat is an innocent bystander. It's not a good thing to murder an innocent bystander."

At this moment, the man halfway down the street with the pigeon coop must have opened the door, for a large cloud of pink and gray pigeons appeared over Susan Edelman's head. They made one circuit and then another in perfect synchronization. The way they all did everything at exactly the same time, as if they were all listening to one single commanding voice that nobody else could hear, reminded Teddy of when they had gone to see the Rockettes at Radio City Music Hall last Christmas, and he watched them hopefully.

Susan Edelman looked up at the pigeons and then down at Teddy's mother. "Vermin!" she shouted. "They're all vermin!" She gave the tablecloth an angry shake.

Teddy knew that during his own lifetime Ed had already used up three of his nine lives—one when he slipped out into the hallway of their apartment building and got into an argument with a German shepherd and lost the tip of his ear, one when he was playing with a piece of green thread from his mother's sewing box and swallowed the needle at the end of it, and one when he fell from their fire escape onto the fire escape two stories below. However, Teddy had no accurate count of how many lives the cat might have used up in the days before he, Teddy, had been born, and for all he knew, Ed might be at the end of his allotment.

Teddy decided to try praying. He had no idea of the procedure, since his father had always discouraged discussion of such matters. But he folded his hands and closed his eyes. He had some notion that praying was supposed to be done in the dark.

"Oh, dear gods in heaven, please strike Mrs. Edelman dead with a bolt of lightning and bring my cat safely to the ground. Amen." He made a brief mental pause, then added a polite, "Hallelujah!"

When he opened his eyes, six large, handsome men wearing heavy black waterproof coats with luminescent yellow stripes were standing among the roses in Susan Edelman's garden. The one standing at the front, who was not the largest or the handsomest but was somehow the most significant and prepossessing, and whom Teddy presumed to be the chief, looked up at the roof. Then he looked down at the ground. He seemed to be measuring the distance. He took in the back door and the fences on either side of the yard. Then he beckoned to one of his men and whispered something in his ear. The fireman quickly disappeared around the side of the house. The chief whispered to another of his men and that one went in through the back door. Teddy could see from the way the other men watched him that they were ready to do his bidding at the drop of a hat.

"Her name is Susan Edelman," Teddy's mother said.

The fire chief looked at Pinky for the first time. It was a look Teddy recognized but did not understand or like.

"She's distraught. She's beside herself," Pinky said in a low voice.

"What is it that she has in that cloth?" the fire chief inquired, also in a low voice.

Teddy's mother colored and then shrugged. "Who knows? Maybe it's something valuable she wants to take with her."

The fire chief looked at her with serious attention, but at last he tore his gaze away. He turned toward Susan Edelman and took a step closer.

"What seems to be the problem, Susan?" he called up in a loud clear voice.

The woman on the roof looked down at him angrily. "This is really none of your business. Don't you people have fires to put out? It's outrageous that taxpayers' money should go to such meddling."

The fireman's gaze did not waver. Teddy saw how he was trying to hold her right where she was with his eyes. "What better cause is there than this, that we should be on call help each other? We're here to lend you a hand. Come down and think things over one more time. You're feeling hopeless, but hopelessness passes. Don't let a little bad luck, or whatever it was that happened here today, make your destiny for you. You're not a coward. Anybody can see that. Choose for yourself."

Now she looked amused. "This is the kind of thing you guys think about, is it, while you wait around for the bell to ring—about courage and destiny?"

He looked up at her seriously. "Of course. But we think about other things, too. We remember things and we worry about things. We think about our families. We think about food."

She shook her head and gave the tablecloth another little swing out into the air. "You're interfering in something you don't understand, Mr. Fireman. Something that is really a very private matter. But let me tell you something: I've had a lot of time on my hands, too, and I don't know much about courage and destiny, but I have given the question of bad luck a lot of thought. Far more than it deserves. I have pondered it from right side up and wrong side down. I know exactly where a little bad luck ends and the end of the world begins. You have nothing you can teach me. Now I suggest you step back a little."

"Don't do it, Susan!" the chief commanded, but she ignored him and took a small step closer to the edge.

Teddy gave a sob.

Susan looked down and nodded at Teddy's mother.

At this moment, one of the firemen appeared on the roof. He lunged forward and grabbed Susan Edelman around the waist. And, at the very same moment, just before she and the fireman tumbled backward together, she tossed the tablecloth lightly out into the air.

Arthur walked slowly back from the park. He gazed, without really seeing it, at all the casual greenery of the Brooklyn neighborhood, the trees and little front yards, the flowerpots and window boxes. His head ached with a distant ominous thudding.

He had just turned the corner to his own block when he saw the fire engines.

He stopped and groaned inwardly. Then he forced himself to pick up speed and jogged his way down to his new house.

As he approached, he saw that the crowd standing around on the sidewalk was a motley crew of old ladies, children, and dog walkers, and they all turned and looked at him with interest as if they knew just who he was.

"What's going on?" he asked.

A boy a couple of years older than Teddy, holding a skateboard, said, "They showed up about ten minutes ago and they all went running around to the back of Mrs. Edelman's house."

He felt a most unexpected release of pressure from around his temples. It had not been Pinky, after all. At this moment, however, there was the sound of a window screen being pushed up and everyone looked to see a woman's stiffly coiffed head emerge from the third-floor window of the house on the other side of Arthur's. The man with uncombed blond hair, who was sitting on the house's front steps, looked up at her, too.

"Hey—you, there, young fella!"

Arthur realized after a moment that she was addressing *him*.

"Yes?" he said, stepping forward reluctantly.

"You better get your hiney around to the back and straighten things out before your wife starts a riot."

"My wife?" he said with a sinking heart.

"Yeah, you know the one I mean—the little redheaded one. She's the person called the fire department. I heard her send your son inside the house to do it."

"I see," said Arthur gloomily and headed like a condemned man down the alley to Susan Edelman's backyard.

When he got there he found a small circle of firemen huddled around a red-checked tablecloth that lay on the patio. Pinky stood in the middle of them, her hands over her eyes, but peering through a crack between her fingers.

Arthur marched right up to her. "Did *you* call the fire department?" he demanded.

She ignored him, but, with her hands still over her eyes, nudged the stern-looking fireman standing next to her with her elbow. "Tell them to open up the tablecloth, for crying out loud!"

The chief looked down at her uncertainly, then he looked over at his men. "Open it up," he said quietly. One of the firemen knelt down and gently unfolded the tablecloth. Sitting in the center of the cloth with its outer leaves curling slightly away from its middle was a large yellow cabbage.

"Where is my cat?" screamed Pinky.

Dully, Arthur felt the sorrow of it again, that he had taken a wrong turn somewhere, and he thought how if only he could retrace his steps and go back to that particular juncture where he had taken that turn, surely, it would be but the work of a moment to find his way into that universe where order and logic reigned, and the paths he chose would go straight where he expected them to, and firemen would put out fires and not spend their summer afternoons rescuing cabbages.

"I saw the cat out on the front steps eating something that looked like a piece of chicken skin," Arthur said.

The fire chief, Arthur noted, was staring at his wife. Pinky smiled back at him radiantly. "I'm so sorry. I'm sure this must be very confusing, but I had no idea what she was going to do and it seemed like the kind of emergency the fire department would know how to handle. You guys were incredible."

The firemen, Arthur observed, folded the tablecloth before laying it on the patio table. One of them paused to examine the cabbage critically and, after a brief moment of hesitation, stuck it in a voluminous pocket and followed the others out.

7. The Art of Matchmaking

*K*en had little doubt that his plans would succeed. He decided to give Katya a week or so to think things over and to feel the full impact of what it would be like to be left the sole caretaker of such a young child. Meanwhile, he called Mitchell Newman and told him that he would need a baby nurse capable of total discretion and a check made out to Katya's name.

"You have the baby?" Newman asked.

"I will in a few days."

" 'O happiness! Our being's end and aim!' I can't wait to meet the little fellow."

Ken said nothing, feeling unsure of his ground, as he always seemed to be when talking to Newman.

"I was quoting Alexander Pope, by the way." Newman laughed that peculiar hoarse laugh of his, as if he were trying to clear popcorn out of his throat. "Anyway, I'll have the check sent down to you, and your baby nurse will be waiting for you this evening in the observation area so you can get to know each other a little."

It was hot as hell. As the week had gone on, it had gotten hotter and hotter. At breakfast, Teddy's mother said it was so hot it was a wonder that everyone's underwear didn't just spontaneously combust. His father didn't seem to hear a word she said, but after Teddy questioned her about what she meant, he went upstairs and took off his underpants and wore his shorts without them, which was cooler anyway.

Then he went out into the backyard with his tweezers and petri dish and crawled into the little cave under the birch tree.

There wasn't a breath of air and noise traveled so quickly and easily through the unresisting stillness that the sound of a dog gnawing on a bone, several houses down, was as loud as if it were right here under the birch tree with Teddy.

Seeing a black ant lugging a huge crumb of something purposefully past his foot, Teddy lifted it up with the tweezers. The ant, startled, dropped its crumb and Teddy dipped it into the petri dish, which today contained a viscous, sweet-smelling liquid, including three drops of tincture of iodine, a pinch of Dr. Scholl's foot powder, a dab of Perry Ellis aftershave cologne, a tablespoon of strawberry jelly, and a crushed spiderweb.

He lifted the ant out of the mixture and dropped it into the palm of his hand and observed it closely. The ant, bewildered and shocked as we all are when the hand of fortune lifts us up and changes the program without a word of warning, just sat there gazing around.

Nothing happened.

After a few minutes, Teddy, with a sigh, gently put the ant back down on the ground. Then he stuck his head out from between the branches of the little birch tree and felt the sun hit him full in the face. It occurred to him that this might be a good day to see if he could fry an egg on the sidewalk. He crawled out from the cave and went into the house.

In the kitchen, he put two eggs in a plastic bowl, but as he turned to leave, he happened to notice, sitting up on top of the refrigerator, the watergun still in its big cardboard box. He put the eggs down carefully and pulled over a chair. He lifted the box down and carried it over to the kitchen table as gently as if it were a newborn baby and then stood there gazing raptly through the clear plastic window at the intricately fashioned barrel and trigger. His father was at work. He decided to take the gun outside with him. He just wanted to feel it nearby for a while. He would not open the box.

He stepped out the front door and carried the bowl and the box out to the sidewalk. He put them on the ground. Then he got down on his hands and knees and felt around for the hottest spot.

He had not been patting for more than a minute when he felt a strange vibration beneath his fingertips. What could it be? He was pretty sure that his father had told him that earthquakes were very rare in this part of the world. He sat up anxiously and looked around. There, down the block, was a boy coming rapidly toward him on a skateboard.

He watched with some alarm as the boy skidded to a stop right in front of the watergun box. His hair stuck up in spikes and he sported a copper and silver antenna implant over his left eyebrow in the shape of a hammer, and a small, snap-open infolinker on his left wrist. His irises were bright red.

"Hey, that's prime," the boy said, one foot on the skateboard, one foot on the ground. He was looking at the gun.

Teddy said nothing. The boy looked older than him, perhaps nine or ten and indifferent to scientific procedure.

"It works better, though, if you take it out of the box."

"We're sending it back to my grandmother. My father and I don't believe in toy guns." The boy raised his eyebrow, which made the silver and copper antenna implant catch the sunlight. There was no one else on the street.

Teddy waited for the boy to go away, but instead he sat down on the curb and looked around with a bored and proprietary gaze. The boy softly patted the top of his head, reassuring himself that the spikes were still there.

Teddy decided the wisest course would probably be to ignore him. So he continued to feel around till he found what he thought was a particularly hot spot and drew a careful circle around it with a piece of chalk.

He reached his hand into the bowl and lifted out one of the cool white eggs. With a gentle tap, he cracked the egg against the curb and then opened it over the circle. Into the stillness the yellow yolk in its clear slippery sac slid out onto the sidewalk.

The boy cleaned his ear with his pinky and watched with interest. Teddy held his breath.

The egg sat there like a small jelly bull's-eye, a little yellow sun fallen flat upon the sidewalk. It didn't cook.

"Try putting it out on the street."

Teddy looked over at the boy, surprised. "What?"

"Try putting the egg out there in the street."

"Why?"

"Why? Because the street is darker than the sidewalk."

"So?"

"So? So dark gets hot faster than light."

"How do you know?"

"I saw it on a holoscreen program."

"You can't believe everything you see on holoscreen."

"Mr. Wizard, Millennium Two."

Teddy did not actually have a holoscreen of his own, since his father, although an expert in computer and communication technology, was very careful about the devices he brought into the house. They did have an old flat compuscreen and Teddy had seen some of the old Mr. Wizard programs on there. "I'm not allowed in the street."

The boy rose quickly and plucked the remaining egg from the bowl. He walked out into the middle of the road without bothering to look right or left.

"Watch out!" Teddy warned, although there wasn't a car in sight.

The boy broke the egg open by squeezing it around its middle and, messily, the slimy inside plopped out onto the blacktop. Instantly it began to steam and turn white around the edges.

"Yes!" Teddy cried.

The boy stared at the egg with pleasure also.

Neither of the boys noticed a small dog with a pink bow between its ears trotting double-time toward the egg. The dog had been shaved down very close to its nub, so it looked, if you didn't take the bow into account, more like a rat than a dog.

Before the boys could stop it or even realize what was happening, the dog approached the egg, gave it a quick appreciative sniff, and then, in several greedy bites, gobbled it down.

As quickly and mysteriously as it had come, it trotted off and disappeared down an alley. Teddy gazed mournfully at the spot where the egg had been.

"What's your grandmother want with a gun like that?"

Teddy wasn't going to get into this. He gathered up his stuff.

"Yeah, I gotta go, too," the kid said and put one foot on his skateboard. "What's your name?"

Teddy considered giving a false name, but could not think of one. "Teddy."

"Orlando," the kid said. He pushed off and skimmed away. In a moment the sidewalk was empty again.

In the evening Ken went down to the quarters that had been set up for the baby and opened the door with his identikey. A small older man of strangely shrunken-looking aspect rose from a chair and approached him deferentially. He handed Ken an envelope. Inside was a note that said: "This is Maurice, who will be your nanny. Although fundamentally quite hard-hearted, he is very good with children. Not only does he owe me a favor which will ensure his silence, he is a deaf-mute."

Maurice was neatly dressed in gray slacks and a clean white hospital jacket. He looked at Ken. Ken was, somehow, not thrilled with this arrangement, but he nodded to the little man, who nodded back without smiling.

"Do you read lips?" Ken asked him.

The man nodded.

"Good. It will probably be a day or two before I bring the baby in here, but please be ready. The child will, of course, need to be tranquilized for the trip, so expect him to be asleep or very sluggish at first."

Maurice nodded again.

Ken looked around the rooms to see that all was in order and then returned to his office.

That night the cat got up onto Teddy's bed and with his usual air of condescension surveyed the situation. Try as they might, they had not been able to keep him in the house and he had just returned from a satisfying evening of trespass and hunting. Now he cleaned his perfectly clean face fastidiously, as if the scene before him did not meet his own tight standards of tidiness. Then, casually, he made his way up to Teddy and, turning himself around once, twice, three times, he made himself comfortable in the crook of Teddy's arm.

Teddy, on the other hand, seemed worried and distracted.

"What is it, Dewdrop?" Pinky asked him. She'd been telling him the story about the time she had convinced her little sister, Audrey, that she had seen the end of the rainbow up on the roof of the tool-shed and that if Audrey climbed up there she'd find a pot of gold. Audrey climbed up on the roof, but when she got up there, there was no sign of the rainbow and she was too scared to get down. Usually Teddy liked these stories about all the things she had tricked Audrey into do-ing but tonight she had the feeling he hadn't heard a word she'd said.

"Why do you call me those funny names?" Teddy asked.

"Isn't your name Dewdrop? I could have sworn that was your name. Am I confusing you with someone else?"

"Cut it out, Mom."

"So what's wrong?"

He gazed up at her worriedly. "If you figured out how to disappear, would you give your secret to the government so that they could use it as a weapon, or would you just keep it for yourself and be a secret agent and go around stopping wars and attacks from happening?"

Pinky pursed her lips and frowned. "My grandmother, Maggie, used to be able to make herself disappear. Into thin air. It was one of her little accomplishments."

In spite of his exasperation with her, he felt the hair on his arms prickle in anticipation. This was going to be one of those stories he knew his father would disapprove of. Luckily, his mother had sent his father down to the basement to look for the air pump for the wading pool, which seemed to be losing air. His father always had trouble find-ing things he was sent to look for.

"She didn't do it often," his mother said. "I don't think she had really mastered the business. But every once in a while she'd be there and then she'd be gone. My grandfather told me that the first time he went to kiss her, it was December and snowing just a little, and they were standing at the gate by the cemetery. You remember I showed it to you when we went to visit? It's across the creek and about halfway up the little mountain there? Yes, well, he put his arms around her and he said she was warm as a little cookstove there in the snow and she smelled like a peony and he closed his eyes and he bent over her and the next thing he knew, he was holding cold air. He said he never felt like such a fool in his whole life, standing there with his lips all puck-ered up and the wind whistling through his arms. He didn't see her after that for several days, and when he saw her again at last, it was at the skating pond and she smiled at him sweet as treacle pudding and sailed right on by."

Except for the twitching of the very tip of his orange tail, you might have thought the cat had fallen asleep.

"What's treacle pudding?" Teddy asked.

His mother rubbed her nose. "I don't know. Treacle was something they used to sweeten things in the olden days, I think, but I don't know what it was made of. Ask your father. He always knows things like that."

They both looked nervously toward the doorway, but there wasn't a sign of Arthur.

Teddy lowered his voice. "Did *you* ever see her disappear?"

Pinky put her hand on the cat, as if to quiet any doubts he might be having about these proceedings. "When I was eight, my parents went to Europe and left me with my grandmother and grandfather for a week. One night they had an argument about whether or not lobsters suffer when you boil them. She said one time she had been in somebody's kitchen where they were boiling one. My grandmother said that she could hear the lobster weeping and praying to its gods very clearly. My grandfather laughed so hard when he heard this that he could hardly catch his breath. After that he made himself a cup of tea and left it on the kitchen table for a minute while he went into the other room to look for something. As soon as he left the room, she picked up the little can of chili powder, which happened to be on the table in front of her, and shook it into his cup. A little later he took the tea and went into the living room.

"She was sitting there directly across from me, smiling, when I heard my grandfather let out a loud bellow and come running into the kitchen, yelling her name. I looked up at him as he came racing through the kitchen over to the sink, where he turned on the water and stuck his whole face as far under the water as he could get it, and then I looked back at my grandmother and I saw she was gone. Just purely vanished without a trace. When my grandfather had calmed down, he looked without a word at the place where she had been sitting. He made me dinner that night and didn't even bother to look for her because I think he knew it would be useless."

"Did she come back?"

"When I got up in the morning, she was there in the kitchen making blueberry waffles."

His mother was staring out into space, perhaps remembering those waffles.

"But what I don't understand," he said, "is why people get married if they're going to argue all the time."

She sighed. "When you grow up and you're a great scientist, then maybe you'll go out into the world and find the answer to that question." She scratched the cat between his tea-colored ears and without opening his eyes he rubbed his head against her hand and began to purr loudly.

"Would it make me famous?"

"Sure. Everyone would invite you to dinner and the newspapers would write articles about you and the holoscreen talk show hosts would cut off their right arms to have you on their programs."

Teddy stared up at the ceiling and furrowed his brow. "Did you ever wish for something so much you forgot to breathe?"

She smiled at him tenderly. "I've had several heart's desires that I would have jumped into a burning building for. Is that what you mean?"

"I guess so. Do you have one now?"

"Of course I do."

"What is it?"

"It's private. What about yours?"

"It would be dangerous for you to know."

When he was asleep, she went back down to the kitchen to finish cleaning up, and while she was standing at the sink, Arthur came up the stairs from the basement.

"There *is* no air pump down there," he said.

She laughed and turned around. "Oh, Arthur, you're so predictable." Then she stopped because she saw how weary and preoccupied he looked. She touched his cheek lightly, but he shrugged her off.

"Of course there's an air pump. I put it down in the basement myself, the day after we moved in. Do you think I would have sent you down there to get it if it wasn't there?"

"Well, it's not there now. Somebody must have taken it."

"Who would have taken our air pump?"

He didn't bother to answer. "Have you been using the emergency bottled water? It looks to me like there's a couple of jugs missing. You know I've told you not to touch those. If you run out, use the tap or go down to the store, but keep your mitts off that stuff in the basement."

She laughed. "I borrowed one yesterday. I needed some for the fridge. I'll get you a replacement tomorrow. It's amazing, given that you can never find anything you're sent to look for, that you'd notice that one bottle of your precious catastrophe water is missing. Listen, I'm going down to the basement and look for the pump myself. Everything is in front of your eyes, my love, you just don't know how to see it. Fran is coming over on Sunday for a barbecue and I want us to be able to put our feet in the pool."

He lifted one eyebrow. "That's an interesting coincidence, since I invited Maury over for supper on the same day."

She stared at him. "You're kidding."

"You don't look pleased. I thought you'd be pleased. What about the web of friendship and all of that jazz?"

"But Fran will think we're trying to match her up. She'll never talk to me again."

"And then who will you turn to when you need a kidney?"

"You think this is funny? What is funny about this? She'll rip him to shreds and she'll never trust me again. You have to call Maury and disinvite him."

"Maybe they'll like each other."

She stared at him in surprise. She frowned. "Do you think? Her mother will never approve."

There was a long pause. "You can't wait for your mother's approval on something like this. Do you think I waited for *my* mother's approval of you?"

"You mother adored me. You mother knew I was just what you needed."

He laughed. "Maybe if you disinvite one of them, then the entire course of human history will be changed in a single afternoon."

She felt an unreasonable small sputter and burst of hope, like a match being lit. It was as if he had reached over without a word and taken her hand. But when she looked up shyly to meet his eyes, he had turned away and opened the refrigerator and she saw that he was gazing into it with deep concentration. He was, no doubt, looking for the milk or something else that was right in front of his nose, but he did not ask her for help and she stared at his back for a moment, then, deciding she would find the pump in the morning, she went up the stairs.

She went into her little studio and flicked on the lamp and examined her painting. She had not had much time to work on it since they had moved in. It was waiting for her, she saw. But she drifted restlessly over to the back window and her gaze was immediately arrested by the oddest sight. Down below, Mrs. Edelman was dancing in her rose garden in her nightgown. There was no music that Pinky could hear, but she was waltzing—holding the skirt of her cotton nightgown out, dipping and bowing and pirouetting.

Pinky stared and then, unable to help herself, she pushed the screen up quietly and poked her head out for a closer look.

Susan Edelman continued to dance and twirl. Pinky could see this was a celebratory dance, no everyday occurrence, and indeed, at this moment Susan stopped and said quite clearly, although her voice was hoarse with excitement, "We did it!" and blew a kiss up to the sky, up into the great spread trellis prickled with the faint dots of the Brooklyn stars.

When she was done blowing girlish kisses, she turned to the rosebush that she had pointed out to Pinky the other day. Near its top, a pale pink rose with a dark center appeared to have just opened. It floated there in the darkness luminescently. It was the only open rose on this bush, but Pinky could see that there were others also just about to break into flower. Susan Edelman leaned over and inhaled this single flower as if it were a baby she had just put to sleep and did not wish to wake. Then, quietly, almost tiptoeing, she returned to her house.

8. Dinner Guests

While Pinky was laying out the plates and forks and knives, she realized she had forgotten to bring the napkins. She went into the house to get them, and as she was pulling them down from the shelf, she happened to glance out the window at the north corner of the garden where the ivy was thick and caught sight of what she could have sworn was the flash of a blue hem and a white calf. She hurried to the door and stared out at the back corner, but saw nothing.

She stepped outside, the pink napkins in her hand, and gazed as far as she could gaze, down the long row of little backyards. There wasn't a soul out hanging laundry or pruning roses. She looked up and around at all the windows that overlooked her garden. No one looked down.

Then she noticed a purple and black cloud shaped like a woman shelling peas into a pot, trying to park itself over the one tall building in the neighborhood, which was a senior citizens' residence a couple of blocks down.

"Oh, my God," she exclaimed. "Oh, my God. Teddy, Arthur, come here!"

Teddy appeared in the doorway a moment later, and right behind him was Arthur carrying a large watermelon.

"What is it?" Teddy asked.

"Look! Look at that cloud! That's the same cloud that I saw on the night I met you, Arthur!"

Arthur followed Teddy into the yard and put the watermelon down heavily on the table and turned and frowned at the sky.

"If it wasn't for that cloud, my life would be completely different."

"This is the same cloud, Mom? Are you sure?"

She nodded, staring at the sky.

"The same cloud that startled you so much you practically chopped your finger off?"

"Yes."

"Tell me again what happened. I don't remember the whole thing."

She smiled at her son. "Well, I was standing at my kitchen window chopping a carrot and I looked up and saw that cloud right outside, practically sitting on the fire escape, and I was so surprised, because it hadn't been there a minute before, that I sliced the tip of my thumb right off. I put the knife down and ran my finger under the cold water and tried pressing on it with a washcloth and an ice cube, but nothing worked. I went looking for some gauze and adhesive, but the only things I had in the house were regular little Band-Aids and the blood just kept oozing out from under them."

Arthur sighed and rubbed the spot over the bridge of his nose, and then he went over to the grill and started pouring charcoal into it.

"So I wrapped it up as best I could in a big hunk of paper towel and went down to the drugstore on the corner to get some gauze and adhesive, and there was your father looking for unwaxed dental floss. When he happened to turn and look at me and saw the paper towel around my hand all red and wet, he passed out right there. After the pharmacist and I woke him up, I took him back upstairs for a cup of tea, and that was that."

"That was that?" Arthur repeated ominously.

"Oh, my hand stopped bleeding the second I set eyes on your father. I often think how if it hadn't been for that weird cloud my whole life would have been different and you wouldn't be here right now."

"Oh, come on, Pinky. Clouds are not permanent things that just float around and travel from Manhattan to Brooklyn and back again."

"That's the same cloud," she said stubbornly. "I'd recognize it anywhere."

Teddy squinted at it uncertainly, then looked at his parents. "But even if you and Mommy hadn't met, wouldn't one of you have made me with somebody else?"

Arthur looked up from what he was doing and frowned. "What do you mean, Teddy? That isn't the way it works. I've explained this to you. Each parent contributes half the chromosomal material."

Pinky laughed, but Arthur only glanced at her and went on. "The chromosomal material is what gives the orders for how a person is meant to grow. Half of it is in the egg and half of it is in the sperm. The part of Mom's meshugeneh story that is true, is that if she and I hadn't met, the two halves of you would never have come together. It's perfectly possible that if I had married someone else and made a baby, and Mom had married someone else and made a baby, then half of you might be walking around one side of town and the other half of you might be walking around the other side of town."

Teddy stared up at him in utter astonishment. "Have you ever met anybody like that?"

There was the creak of the side gate and Fran now stepped forward into the light of the backyard. "I meet people like that all the time," she said as she came across the lawn. She held two little white paper bags in her hand and she pushed her dark, thickly waving hair off her face and looked small and slender and perfectly capable of slaying and eating an entire dragon, scales and all.

"You know, what I never understood was—given Arthur's deep reservations about the human race and the fate of the world—how you ever got around to having Teddy in the first place."

Pinky said nothing, struck dumb, as always, by the ancient, unlikely, not entirely joyous fact that Fran had chosen her as a friend.

Fran, in any case, did not wait for Pinky's answer, but went over to the picnic table and reached out and rapped smartly on the watermelon. "How wonderful—watermelon!"

Arthur shrugged. "Actually, I hate the stuff, but my friend Maury says it's the perfect food. He says that if the whole world would eat only watermelon for a week, then everything would just fall into place."

Pinky glared at Arthur, then looked nervously back at Fran. "Listen, Fran, I gotta tell you something. . . ."

But now Fran was squatting down, looking Teddy in the eye.

"Don't tell me I've gotten bigger," he said sternly. "You only saw me last week."

"I wasn't going to say that, I wasn't going to say that at all. What do you take me for? Someone's grandmother?" She kissed him on the forehead, right where the little furrowed lines of worry were deepest. "I was simply going to suggest that you might want to lighten up a little, that you've got plenty of time before you get reduced back to dust and nothingness. And don't you dare wipe that kiss off."

She got up in one swift movement. "So are we going to get to go swimming?" She took off her sandals and stepped eagerly into the little pool. "You're going to have to lend me a suit." Fran was wearing one of those short serapelike silk dresses that were all the rage. The wide open sides showed her expensive pink lace no-bra. She had entered wearing a little pillbox hat made out of straw and twigs, but she took it off now and laid it on the table.

Surreptitiously, Teddy wiped his forehead with the back of his hand.

"Listen, Fran, I need to apologize. It wasn't intentional. I mean, everybody meant well. Arthur was just showing off to me, I think, when he did it. But he didn't ask me first and I hadn't told him that I'd invited you."

Fran, who was wiggling her toes with great pleasure in the water, looked up at her with amusement and said, "What is it? Spit it out."

At this moment the gate creaked again, and there was Maury, also holding a little white paper bag.

Pinky made a small sound of dismay at how quickly her life was speeding forward and what little chance she was getting to make right, but then she straightened herself and, studiously avoiding Fran's gaze, came toward him, smiling.

He was a tall man, who, through perpetual fasting, had reduced himself to a luminous thinness out of which his bones stuck like various doorknobs and coat hooks. She knew that he did not fast, as many people did these days, in the expectation of making himself live longer, but as part of his spiritual regime. He, too, was wearing a serape-like thing, but his was rough-woven and had sleeves and you couldn't tell whether or not he was wearing underwear. A strong, beaklike nose dominated his face and, since she had last seen him, his head had been shaved completely clean. He was gazing at them, or perhaps not at them, but at the scene in general, in a curious but detached manner.

He smiled and handed her a paper bag. "My contribution to the feast."

"Oh, that was nice of you. Thank you so much."

Arthur introduced the two guests. "Maury, this is Pinky's oldest friend, Fran. She's very shy."

Pinky watched with a mixture of jealousy and pride as Fran stepped out of the pool and came over to where they were standing. She looked disdainful and ready to be offended.

Maury did not extend his hand or anything, but stared at her, frowning, as she approached.

"And Fran, this is my friend and running partner, Maury. Pinky thought you should meet him."

"I didn't!" Pinky squealed.

"She didn't," Arthur confessed. Arthur took a pack of Juicy Fruit out of his shorts pocket and unwrapped himself a piece of gum. He offered the pack around, but nobody wanted a piece. He returned the gum to his pocket and took out a book of matches. He lit one and threw it onto the charcoal, and with a little hiss and *whoomph*ing sound the charcoal ignited.

"This is what I was trying to explain to you," Pinky said. "It's just one of those terrible crashes of fate. You know, like when you're driving your shopping cart down the aisle trying to read some word on your shopping list and somebody comes around the corner in a big hurry looking for the ketchup and you ram right into each other. It's nobody's fault, really. I mean, I had no idea Arthur had invited Maury to dinner."

Maury paid no attention to this, but continued to stare at Fran.

Arthur shook his head slowly. "And this is my wife, Pinky, professional gadabout and internationally renowned hostess."

"Really," Pinky insisted, "it's all a big accident."

Fran, who, Pinky knew, was going to make her pay, stared at her coldly. "As the Big Man pointed out, Pinky, there *are* no accidents."

"Well, but what I mean is, you shouldn't feel obligated to regard each other as people of the opposite sex or anything. Just pretend it's one of those situations where nobody's sex matters."

"Which kind of situations are those?" Fran inquired.

Pinky considered it. "Well, I don't know, like we're on a plane to-gether and we've all been taken hostage."

Even Teddy stopped what he was doing and looked at her. There was an intrigued silence that fell over the group.

Pinky looked over at the fence and saw that her cloud had grown, or risen, rather, like a loaf of bread. She looked around the yard again uncertainly.

Fran sighed and shook her little paper bags at Teddy. "Come over here," she said. Teddy got up and approached her slowly.

"Choose," she said. "But be forewarned—whichever you choose is the one you must eat. A man must learn to live with his choices."

"Can I feel them?"

"Certainly not. Life is a crapshoot, darling. Take your chances."

Fran held the two bags out in front of her and Teddy eyed them with a narrow, scientific concentration. Then he dropped to his knees in front of the bags and squinted, perhaps in an attempt to give himself X-ray vision.

Quite suddenly he pointed at the bag on the right.

Fran raised her eyebrows and stared at him curiously. "How did you know?" she asked and handed him the bag.

"I smelled sugar," he said.

He opened the bag and lifted out a cupcake with pink icing and rainbow-colored sprinkles.

"Are you actually going to allow your child to eat that?" Maury asked aghast.

Pinky shrugged. "After dinner."

"It's pure sugar and carcinogens. Why don't you just open his mouth and pour a little cyanide in? It would be quicker."

Gently, Teddy tugged the other paper bag out of Fran's hand and looked inside it. He made a face and put the bag down on the table.

Arthur looked at Fran inquiringly. "What is it?"

"Something for *you*, my prickly friend."

Arthur opened the bag and took out two artichokes. He smiled. "Well, he mighta choked Artie, but he can't choke me. What'd *you* bring, Maury?"

"Tempeh burgers. I thought maybe we could marinate them and stick them on the grill."

Arthur opened up the bag and removed several disks of a pale curd-like substance. He put them down gingerly on a plate next to the artichokes.

"I wouldn't eat those if you stuck an arrow through my eyeball," Teddy said in a low voice.

"Me neither," Fran said.

Pinky went in to trim the artichokes and put them on to boil. When she came back out, Maury was saying to Fran, "You're not really shy, are you? I didn't believe that for a minute."

"Certainly I am. I just disguise it very well. It's a very inheritable trait, but with a little personality modification training you can make yourself perfectly functional."

"Your parents were very shy?"

"Oh, extremely."

Pinky glared at Fran, but Fran ignored her. "So you avoid sugar and food coloring for health or spiritual reasons?"

"I'm just hoping for that lighted window like everybody else." He smiled at her searchingly.

"Who *is* this guy?" She stared at his face, frowning.

He smiled. "You look like you think you recognize me."

"Is there some reason I *should* recognize you?" She peered at him.

Arthur came over and put his hands on Maury's shoulders. "You probably met him in a previous life or something. Maury already met a lot of people there."

"What happened to your hair?" Teddy asked Maury.

Maury turned and looked at him and patted the top of his head. "I shaved it off. I shaved it off so there would be less between me and heaven."

"Heaven?" Teddy asked alertly. "Do you believe in heaven?"

Maury smiled at him. "Heaven, paradise, we've all been there already and we can never forget it. It's imprinted in every one of us and we all want to return."

Teddy looked uncomfortable. "My dad doesn't believe in it."

Maury sat down at the table, still patting his head. He looked over slyly at Arthur. "Your father is preparing, right now, to come back in his next life as a very holy man."

Arthur sighed and shook his head and poked at the coals in the barbecue grill. "Pay no attention, Teddy. This is it. My one and only life. It will be more than plenty for me."

"He has a short memory, your father."

Fran came and sat down at the opposite end of the redwood table looking unamused. Pinky brought over a large brown grocery bag and seated herself in a strategic position between her two guests. She pulled out an ear of corn and began shucking it. Maury took the little pile of pink paper napkins and began folding one with great concentration.

The fuzzballs hung over their heads without moving. There was a nearby sound of a baby clucking sleepily to itself and Pinky saw, with a start, that another dark cloud, this one shaped like a bowler hat, had joined the first one over the senior citizens' residence.

"Whaddaya got in your pockets?" Fran asked Teddy.

Everyone turned and looked and noticed that the pockets of Teddy's baggy blue shorts were bulging knobbily.

"Meteorites," he said and took a couple of pebbly gray rocks out to display them.

"How fabulous," Fran said. "Where'd you find them?"

"Here. In the garden. You gotta watch out for them."

"Really?" Fran asked. "Why's that?"

"Well, you wouldn't want to get hit by one."

Fran took one of the rocks from Teddy and weighed it in her hand. She glanced over at Pinky and then at Arthur.

"How ya feeling, Arthur?"

"Fine," he said gruffly.

"So how *did* you guys ever get around to having Teddy?"

Pinky saw that Maury, on her left, had taken another paper napkin and was folding it, not into a fan as with the first one, but into some new and delicate shape yet to be guessed at. He looked as if he were paying no attention to them, but then again, if you looked a little closer you saw that he was giving off a sort of proprietary air, as if he imagined he was the rower of a rowboat and they were all his passengers and even though he never looked at them, he was keeping his eye firmly fixed on a receding landmark in order to guide himself and his passengers safely to the opposite shore. It was sort of silly of him, she thought, but kind.

Fran, on her right, was weighing a meteorite in her hand and staring with determined eyes at Arthur, who was now meticulously beginning to prepare the shish kabobs.

Teddy stood at the head of the table, and she saw that he was waiting with burning curiosity for somebody's answer.

Pinky sighed. "Well, as I've mentioned to Teddy before, I won him in a bet."

Arthur stared at her in wounded silence.

"A bet?" Fran asked with interest.

"But what kind of bet?" Teddy demanded.

Maury said nothing, but looked innocently pleased.

"I wouldn't really call it a bet," Arthur said gruffly. "That's hardly accurate."

"I beat him at a game of chess."

"But you don't play chess, Mom."

"Actually, I do. I mean, I used to play chess. My grandfather had taught me how and he used to play with me a lot when I was young. After I met your father, I started to play with him now and then, but he was always much better than I, so it wasn't much fun. But what happened was that after we'd been living together for a year or so, I started to get the idea in my head that I wanted a baby. But every time I suggested this to your father, he always told me what a lousy world this was to bring a baby into, and anyway, half the problem with it was that it was overpopulated. This didn't stop me, of course, because I know some things about the world your father doesn't know and I guess I just kept pestering him and maybe I was driving him crazy, because eventually he said, 'Okay, I'll make you a deal. I'll give you six months to beat me at a game of chess and if you can beat me at just one game, I'll agree to try to conceive a child. But if you can't beat me after six months, then you have to drop the subject forever.'

"So, for six months I played chess like the entire fate of the world depended on it."

"Yes?" Fran leaned back attentively. Pinky knew it had taken her years of practice to perfect that look of There's Absolutely Nothing I Would Rather Do Than Sit Here and Listen to You with Completely Uncritical and Undivided Attention for Fifty Minutes.

Maury reached forward and set a perfect pink paper swan next to another plate. Nothing stirred.

"He didn't think I had a chance, of course." She looked at Arthur. "You were pretty sure of yourself, weren't you, buddy?"

Arthur neatly continued skewering the vegetables and chunks of chicken.

"But I went and got books from the library and every day, when I was finished teaching my classes, I would go home and practice. And every evening I would challenge him to a game."

Arthur didn't look up from his task.

"And he won every time."

Arthur poked his skewer through the heart of a little cherry tomato so that a little squirt of tiny seeds and pulp came out the other side.

"For five months he won every game and I was beginning to despair and then, in absolute desperation, I went down to Washington Square Park where the old men sit around and play chess at the stone tables and I sat there utterly embarrassed, not knowing what you were supposed to do, and I waited until suddenly I looked up and I realized that there was this very sad little senior-citizen-type guy sitting across from me. He had a funny, gravelly voice, I remember, and he challenged me to a game."

Arthur now stopped what he was doing and stared at her.

"So I agreed, and after he beat me, he asked me what I was doing there, since I was really a terrible player. He said I had an almost remarkable inability to look ahead. So I explained to him my situation and that I was desperate and I needed someone to help me practice and he said he would be glad to help me."

Arthur put the shish kabob he was working on down on the plate. "You never told me this before," he said accusingly. "Did he want something in return? He must have."

Pinky flushed. "Well, no, actually, he didn't. I mean, I said I would give him whatever he wanted, if he could help me. I offered to bring the child to him to visit every weekend. He could be like an honorary grandfather. But he only said, 'God forbid.'

"He asked me what kind of player you were and I told him that I thought you were probably very good for an amateur, but very predictable and unimaginative, and that it drove you nuts when I made wild moves that nobody who knew anything about chess would ever make."

Arthur sighed heavily at the memory of those moves and went back to skewering. Pinky looked at her audience.

"The guy thought about it for a while and then told me he would teach me a trap that Arthur would assume I didn't know and that Arthur would not be on the lookout for, because he would think it was just me, playing crazy. When I had got it down by heart, he suggested that for the next few days I should play as if I had given up and didn't care anymore and then I should sock it to him.

"And that's what I did. I played really lousily all week, and then on the last night I made a beautiful pesto with fresh basil and garlic and butter and I brought out a big bottle of wine. After dinner I said that it was obviously hopeless and maybe we should forget the last game, but his testosterone was not going to let him be cheated of his final little ounce of triumph and he insisted we play. So I shrugged and made the moves the guy had taught me as if I no longer cared about winning, and Arthur made all the predictable responses and fell right into the trap. Never ever will I forget the look on his face when he saw what had happened. Remember those old Road Runner cartoons, where Wile E. Coyote keeps chasing Road Runner around and Road Runner keeps running off the edge of cliffs and when he's dashed out into the air he always looks down and suddenly realizes that he's not standing on anything solid, and it isn't until he looks down that he crashes to the ground?"

"It was the wine," Arthur said.

Fran laughed. "It wasn't the wine. It was what you wanted. You let her set you up because it was the only way you were going to get permission from yourself to have a baby."

Maury cleared his throat humbly. "Oh, I really don't think so."

Fran turned her head impatiently and gazed at him with interest the way a snake looks at a little toad that it's about to swallow. "No? Why not?"

"Because babies happen neither by accident nor human choice. Parents are no more responsible for the creation of a child than a child is for its parents' creation. Parents are simply the bridge over which the child has to cross to arrive here. Or perhaps, more aptly, we should call them the designated drivers."

"Who *is* this guy?"

"Hard to say," Maury said with a laugh.

"Teddy, don't you worry for a moment," Fran ordered him. "Your father wanted you more than he ever wanted anything else in his life. He just didn't know it at the time."

Teddy, however, appeared to have lost interest in the conversation. He was taking the rocks out of his pockets and laying them on the table one by one in a straight row. From somewhere, through a hole in the fence or maybe from the grass at his feet, blew a small breeze that played tenderly with Teddy's hair.

"Well, since I didn't know it, I can hardly speak to the question, but I'm certainly glad that you're here now, Ted," Arthur said.

Teddy did not meet his eye or smile back, and Maury set a little pink sailboat next to another plate.

"Maury, you going to be offended or revolted or anything if we eat this chicken?" Arthur was rinsing his hands with the garden hose.

"You gonna eat it like that or you gonna cook it?"

"Cook it."

"Will you remember to stop and give a brief prayer to thank the spirit of the creature who gave up its mortal breath to feed your mortal breath?"

"Arthur won't pray," Pinky said. "He'd feel like he was pawning his soul to the devil."

Arthur said nothing to defend himself. He went over to the table and put the corkscrew into a bottle of red wine. He twisted it and gave it a good yank and, with the release of the vacuum, out came a low and distant rumble of thunder. No one seemed to notice but Pinky.

She lifted the tempeh worriedly in her hands. "Can we shish kabob this?"

"If you can shish poor Bobby, then I guess you can shish my tempeh. You got any tamari?"

"Would you mind getting it yourself? It's in the cupboard over the stove."

While Maury was gone, Teddy picked up his rocks very carefully, and put them into his pockets one by one, in size order, starting with the largest.

"I'm going out front for a while," he said, and with that, he crossed the lawn and disappeared down the alley.

Pinky shucked corn and kept her eye on the ladder that climbed straight up into the sky. At the top sat a plain gray bird looking sharply down at the earth. At the bottom sat Oedipus staring up at the bird.

"That's the funniest ladder, don't you think?" Pinky said to no one in particular.

"What's funny about it?" Arthur asked. He had returned to the grill and was drinking his wine and turning the chicken.

"Well, the way it just stands there and goes straight up into the air."

"Pinky, you know what it's for, don't you?"

She looked at him uncertainly, but at that moment Maury came through the back door, holding in his hand, not the bottle of tamari, but the poisonous green watergun. From the way that he hefted it, Pinky could see that he must have filled it with water.

"Wow," said Maury, grinning with delight. "This is unbelievable." He lifted the gun and sighted along the barrel toward Pinky's cloud on the back fence. Then he abruptly pointed the gun upward and shot at the bird sitting on top of the ladder.

"Ratatatatattat!" he yelled. A great plume of water shot into the air and, catching the sunlight in the upper regions, came back down toward them in a mist of falling gold. The bird, untouched, stared down at them curiously.

"Let me try!" Pinky said.

"Don't, Pinky," Arthur said in a low warning voice. He chomped unhappily on his gum.

"Don't what?" she said defiantly.

"We have an agreement about this."

"What we most certainly do not have is an agreement about this."

"We have discussed this issue several times and we've agreed to send the gun back to your mother. Could I have the gun, please, Maury?" Arthur held out his hand, but Maury stepped back gleefully.

"Pinky's mother?" he asked. "This wonderful device belongs to Pinky's mother?"

"My mother-in-law sent it to Teddy as a gift, but Pinky and Teddy and I have decided to send it back."

"*I* didn't decide any such thing!"

"Pinky, we've talked about this. We're Teddy's parents. We need him to understand our beliefs about how we use reason to solve conflicts, and how we never glorify violence or playact at it. If we let him have that gun, we're betraying all our principles."

"It's a toy, Arthur. It's a piece of plastic."

Arthur stared at her, chewing wearily on his Juicy Fruit. "It's discouraging, you know, to spend all those hours talking to you and then discover that all the words are just water through a sieve."

"Don't talk to me like that, Arthur Sorenson, like I was just another idiot sent to ruin your day. I *heard* you. I've heard every word you said about guns and violence, and some of it works for me and some of it doesn't."

Maury smiled and lifted the gun and said, "Raatattattatt!" And gave each of them a little squirt in the chest.

Arthur blinked. One of his eyes had drifted noticeably higher than the other. He appeared not to notice that he'd been shot.

"If I understand you correctly," he said, "you're saying you agree with me in principle, but it is not convenient, at this time, to hold to these principles."

"But Arthur, I'm talking about our child! Our son, who always acts like he's about one hundred and ten years old, and who thinks if he steps on the wrong crack in the sidewalk, he's going to trigger two earthquakes and a tornado, and who thinks that when he grows up, he alone is going to be held responsible for finding a cure for all the known earthly diseases. Our son, who needs to be encouraged to play."

"He has a questioning mind. He has a serious temperament. He's not interested in that gun because he knows it's a piece of corrupt and evil junk, spawn of a society that is so addicted to consumerism that it is forced to prey on its own young without thought for the future."

"But Arthur, he's a wimp! He's seven years old and he's a little old man already. What good will all his conscience and his questions do him if doesn't know how to play and nobody wants to play with him?"

"When there's somebody worth playing with, he'll play."

"This is what I mean, Arthur! This is what I mean. You're always walking in the wrong direction because every morning you get up and put your pants on backwards! If you want peace, everybody has to play with everybody else. You can't be such a snob."

"A snob? You think I'm a snob?"

Fran cleared her throat delicately. "Would you mind if I interjected something here?"

"Oh, Christ," Arthur muttered. "Now we're in for it."

Pinky had to smile to herself. Fran's eyes glittered as she nodded first to Pinky, then to Arthur, and seemed to gaze, not at them, but at a distant garden where the first pair of opposite-sexed gladiators prepared to fight to the death for the entertainment of the gods.

"You both seem to agree that you want to pass on to your child the message that violence is a poor solution to conflict. Right?"

They nodded at her.

"I think at least you are succeeding in presenting a unified front on a moral problem you both consider important. Around the specific meaning of the watergun, however, you seem to have different ideas. Maybe, at bottom, you're both afraid of something."

There was a silence. Pinky gave her attention to the large black bowler hat slowly growing and engulfing the senior citizens' residence. Was she afraid of something?

"What is it you fear will happen, Arthur, if Teddy gets hold of this gun?" Fran kept her gaze steadily fixed on Maury as she asked this question.

"I'm not *afraid* of anything, Fran, but I want him to know that guns are not playthings."

"Are you afraid that if you let him play with it he will become mean and nasty, that when he gets older he will be more likely to play with real guns? Or," she said, smiling cunningly, "are you afraid that if you give him the gun you are somehow handing him the goods to turn and shoot you?"

"Baloney."

Fran pushed her thick dark hair back from her forehead and said, "What you might think about, Arthur, is that when children play at violence they are testing the limits of what is allowable and what is not. They are tapping into and examining their own feelings of aggression and hostility and discovering how to come to terms with these feelings without being overwhelmed by them. It is very important for a child to discover that he can pretend to shoot his father and his father will not die. Even more important, a child needs to discover that it takes more than an angry wish to knock someone dead."

"Why's she talking like that?" Maury asked, staring intently at Fran.

"She's a shrink," Arthur said.

"A shrink! Of course! I should have known!" He rapped himself lightly on his shiny head with the watergun. "I detest shrinks, you know," he said to Fran.

"This is the kind of news that can completely wreck a person's day."

Pinky got up from the table nervously and took the corn into the house. When she came back she had the tamari in her hand. Arthur took it and carefully sprinkled it over the chunks of tempeh and vegetables that he had meticulously skewered. Then he began laying all the shish kabobs on the grill.

Maury started shooting at the fuzzballs. Every time he hit one with the stream of water, it quivered and danced.

Arthur did not look up from what he was doing. Pinky thought that anyone who didn't know him well would assume that his mind was mostly on the job of methodically arranging the shish kabobs so that they were lined up in two perfect rows, instead of thinking furiously how to get the gun out of Maury's hands and hidden away in the house before Teddy returned.

The cloud shaped like a bowler hat now tottered forward slowly and blotted out the sun. Pinky had been waiting for this, but everyone else looked around in puzzlement. The birds, the insects, the radio playing next door fell silent. And then again, from somewhere nearby, there was the happy chuckle of a baby. The stillness in the garden and the rumbling of the slate-gray sky that seemed to have come down to touch the tree drew everything in the garden close. The table with its pink paper shapes and glasses of wine looked beautiful, ready for whatever ceremony was to come in the heavy still light.

Teddy reappeared silently at the table. His pockets were fuller than ever with knobs and bulges, and the breeze, a little wind, blew through the garden and lifted the edges of the paper plates. He stopped where he was and stared at the gun, which Maury now had pointed at a squirrel lying stretched out on a branch overhead as if it were dead.

Maury pulled the trigger and hit the squirrel, which opened one small beadlike and unreadable eye and looked around, then puffed up its tail over its back like an umbrella and closed its eye again.

Pinky glanced at Teddy and reached for a taco chip. "Didn't you have toy guns when you were growing up, Arthur? Didn't most of your friends? And isn't everybody you grew up with a wimpy systems analyst or lawyer or English professor? My Uncle Lowell told me that when he was a kid he made himself a slingshot and stole my grandmother's button box and used up all her buttons in one afternoon shooting at birds and squirrels, and did he turn out to be a gun freak or a war mongerer? No. He drove a Greyhound bus between Scranton and Buffalo for forty-five years and never once did he shoot any of his passengers or family members, either."

"Anybody else?" Maury asked, and offered the gun to the group.

Pinky saw that Teddy was tensely trying to find something else to look at besides the gun or the grown-ups or the air quivering around the grown-ups.

Arthur reached forward and firmly grabbed hold of the nozzle of the great green watergun. He looked at Maury and dared him with his eyes to shoot him again. Maury turned back at him a gaze as limpid and obscure as the gaze of a flower.

"You see," Arthur began, "you see what I'm afraid of is that these stories of Pinky's—these chess games and these reappearing clouds, her grandmother's buttons and her hats that turn into birds—I'm afraid . . . that they give a false impression of happy endings lurking everywhere, of the kindness of the human heart. What about all the other stories— the wars and the genocides and the ethnic cleansings, the Stalins and the Pinochets and the Bin Ladens? What about what happened to my grandfather in 1944 and how his little brother was lost and never heard from again?"

Teddy was staring at his father with a frown of deep concentration. "What happened to your grandfather in 1944 and how did his brother get lost?" he asked.

"Oh, Arthur, not now," Pinky said.

Arthur looked at her and then at Teddy. "I'll tell you some other time. The point is, despite all of your mother's stories, most of human history is driven along by violence and cruelty."

"I don't believe that at all," said Pinky. "There is as much kindness and cooperation as there is the other stuff, and besides that, people learn from history. You and me and Fran and Maury will never get within two hundred miles of shooting anybody. And neither will Teddy. And his having a watergun will not make the smallest fart of a difference here."

"I think you're wrong, Pinky. For most people, murder is a capability that's just on the other side of the fence. All it takes is for somebody to cut you off in traffic or come over and pee on your roses. It's part of the human condition, part of our chromosomal inheritance. We have to understand it and be on the watch for it all the time." Arthur pulled the gun from Maury's grasp.

Maury laughed as he watched Arthur put the gun on the table. "The way I look at it, all our enemies are gifts—the ones outside of us and the ones inside, too. Each time you learn to live with one and rise beyond it, you have moved yourself another step along in the direction we are all intended to move—up and out.

"This is like a law of physics or something that I missed?" Fran asked, chewing on a celery stick.

Maury laughed. "Could be. You were absent from a lot of those classes, as I remember."

Fran stopped chewing. She frowned and leaned forward and looked at Maury more closely. "Oh, my God, it's Maury Weintrob!"

"Well, that certainly took you long enough."

"What are you doing here?"

Maury laughed. He was as radiant, Pinky thought, as a daffodil. "Me? What am *I* doing here? What are *you* doing here?"

"Who's Maury Weintrob?" Pinky asked.

"I went to junior high school with him. He had uncombable hair that he tried to part on the side. He was not skinny."

Maury waited.

"He used to sell the answers to the math homework for other people's desserts and he used to quack whenever Mr. Duckman, the physics teacher, turned his back to write on the board. He was a bra strap snapper."

"Is this true?" Arthur asked.

Maury beamed. Fran continued to examine him in suspicious astonishment.

There was a loud crack of thunder and the afternoon poised itself into a perfect stillness, like a button that has rolled to the edge of a table and stopped for a moment, uncertain whether to continue forward and over the edge or to roll back.

"Oh, my God," Pinky exclaimed, "Ed has a bird."

At this moment Oedipus, wiggling through a shallow hole under the fence, slid into the backyard. He had in his mouth the plain gray bird that had been sitting on top of the ladder a few moments ago. The bird, Pinky could see, was alive, but trying to keep a very low profile.

"Drop that!" Pinky commanded.

The bird looked up at her hopefully.

She started toward the cat and there was a brilliant fork of lightning and a great rush of wind.

"Put that bird down," she screamed.

Oedipus, divining that there were those here who would deprive him of what was naturally and inexorably his, started slinking rapidly away toward the alley.

"Stop him!" Pinky yelled.

"Head him off at the pass!" Fran suggested and tried to circle in front of him. The cat slunk lower and doubled his speed and slipped right between Fran's legs like a snake.

"The gun, Dad!" Teddy yelled. "Use the gun!"

Arthur looked at him and then the gun in puzzlement. He touched it with his fingertips and then, as if he had received a shock, withdrew them quickly.

Fran, seeing what was needed, snatched the gun up and aimed.

The wind blew around and around the small garden with rising excitement, then lifted one of the lawn chairs up and flung it against the fence.

"Shoot him! Shoot him!" Teddy yelled. "Shoot him between the eyes."

Fran aimed at the cat and frowned with concentration. Then she pulled the trigger and a long plume of water shot forth and hit the cat square in the face, drenching the bird as well.

The cat stopped in his tracks and turned on her a look of pure astonishment.

Fran took this opportunity to blast him again, giving a little grunt as she pulled at the trigger.

The cat quivered and opened his mouth for moment and the bird fell out onto the grass.

Teddy ran forward, and as he did, the bird gave a little flutter. The cat crouched.

"Oedipus!" Pinky screamed. "Don't you dare!"

Oedipus, however, possessed by his dark and lovely intentions, apparently didn't hear a word she said.

Fran leaped forward and grasped the cat by the tail.

Definitely not a cat person, Pinky thought, as the cat turned, hissing furiously, and raked Fran's forearm with his claws. Fran let go of the cat.

This, however, was enough time for the gray bird to gather half its wits. It tottered forward, flapping awkwardly, toward the ivy in the back. Every time it lifted its wings, a brilliant stripe of white appeared like a signal hidden in its underfeathers.

"Mockingbird," Maury commented, but he didn't move, just sat looking on with interest at the unfolding scene.

"Oh, it's hurt," Pinky cried. "Catch it gently, Ted, and I'll take care of Oedipus."

Pinky ran across the grass and threw herself on the wet, spitting cat. "Hold still, darling," she whispered to him.

Teddy followed anxiously behind the bird, his hands out, trying to figure out how to grab hold of it. The wind blew harder now, with a loud keening noise, and whipped the branches of the trees back and forth. The sky was dark.

The bird flitted in front of Teddy just out of reach.

"Help him, Arthur," Pinky shouted, but Arthur, trying to protect the shish kabobs, was struggling with the large black domelike cover that went over the grill.

"Cup your hands, Teddy! Cup your hands and catch him gently around the middle," Pinky advised.

Just as the bird reached the foot of the ladder, Teddy lunged forward and missed him, falling into the ivy. The bird, recognizing a last chance when it saw one, stretched open its long, elegant gray wings, and flaunted its white stripe at them. Then it shot itself up into the air and landed neatly on top of the high, back fence. It sat there on its perch, gazing down at them.

The garden, which only a short time ago had been so hidden and becalmed, had been cast adrift into the storm. The wind leaped and howled. There was a flash of lightning and then a great kettledrum of thunder. Fran was running around the yard trying to collect all the flying cups and plates and sailboats and swans. Arthur, who had finally managed to get the cover onto the grill, now turned and looked around and, spotting the three stripes of blood that trickled down Fran's wounded arm, recognized that he was going to pass out. He sat down on the bench next to Maury and put his head between his knees.

Teddy saw none of this, but was distracted by a sound like a little voice laughing inside the wind. He looked up at the sky, but then realized that the sound was not coming from above, but from down below, inside the tangle of ivy. He leaned forward and parted the leaves and gazed in bewilderment at what he had found.

"Mom," he called.

Pinky released the cat and ran to the back corner and crouched next to Teddy at the base of the ladder, and just as the first drops of rain came down, hard as bullets, she saw the baby. He was strapped into his little reclining baby seat. Next to him on the ground was a tightly packed diaper bag. He had been studying Teddy with sleepy interest, but now he turned and looked at Pinky and gave a low, pleased chortle, as if to say, *What luck, running into you here, of all places*. She, too, thought he looked vaguely familiar.

Part Two

9. Pinky's Theory

*O*n that first day the baby had been rather sleepy and slow in his responses, but by the next morning he was as wide awake as a firecracker. It occurred to Pinky that he had been drugged. The bag that had been sitting next to him in the ivy was thoughtfully packed, with several changes of clothing and enough diapers, baby food, and formula to last a few days. It seemed to Pinky that whoever had left him in the garden had carefully planned the whole operation.

So she told Arthur that he could say whatever he wanted, but she had no doubt that this baby had been intended for them and that clearly here was a case of finders keepers. Imagine how many other doorsteps or Dumpsters or city agencies he could have landed in, and yet he landed right here. Under the circumstances, Arthur could not possibly consider throwing him back out into that whirling terrible cesspool he was always raving about.

Arthur didn't say much in answer to this. She wasn't sure he was even listening. He took the baby from her and gazed down into the brown eyes with the little flashes of light and gold like minnows darting through dark water. The baby managed to keep a straight face for about thirty seconds, as if he recognized the seriousness of the situation and was trying to show that he could behave as responsibly as any other baby, but then he cracked up. His little body stiffened with delight and he let out a long string of *mmmmmmm*s and vowel sounds and then he made a little spit bubble. For a second Arthur looked alarmed and his arms tightened up, and the baby, perhaps perceiving that he had frightened him, switched his vocalization to a soft crooning sound.

Pinky stood very still. She had a sensation that she'd had once or twice in dreams, of having walked through a door and found herself in a green and lovely place that she'd forgotten all about.

"Of course," Arthur said, not looking at her but at the baby, "if someone legitimate claims him, we'll have to give him back."

"Of course," Pinky murmured soothingly, knowing this would not happen.

"I'd like to name him Bernard."

Teddy had just come in to wash his hands, which were purple from something he had been mixing up. He looked at his father with curiosity. "How come?"

Pinky came back from her green place with a start. She watched Arthur sharply.

"It's a funny name. Why would you name him that?" Teddy said.

Arthur didn't answer for a while. Pinky waited, holding her breath.

"After my Great-Uncle Bernard, who I never got to know. It would be a nice way to honor him and remember him. What do you think, Pinky?" He held her gaze.

She sighed. "Sure. It's a good name."

Arthur lifted the baby up in the air in front of him and, frowning, hefted him as if taking his measure, as if he were a small heavy object the purpose of which he had not yet a clue. The baby, delighted to find himself so high up and perhaps assuming that someone was now about to teach him to fly, flapped his arms and legs helpfully.

Sometime in the next week, Arthur called an attorney, a friend of a friend, and posed the situation in a theoretical way. The attorney advised that the best thing to do in a case like this was simply to take the stand that one had adopted the baby and make no report to an official agency for at least two years. After that time, assuming that no one had come forth to claim him, it would be a simple matter to petition the court and make things legally correct.

When they took him to the pediatrician, the doctor said that Bernard was in excellent health except for a moderate heart murmur that should be monitored, although chances were the baby would outgrow it without any outside intervention.

Pinky wasn't worried about either the medical or legal questions raised here. She had several reasons for believing that it was a deliberate intervention of a watchful and divine influence that had dropped the baby off in her garden, and, that being so, she had no doubt the baby traveled under the protection of a wide umbrella.

Within a week or two, it was clear to her that he was the baby she had been yearning for, a cheerful, busy, heedless child. He was constantly on the move and into everything.

She was deeply relieved for Teddy, who now would not only have someone to lecture to about meteors and invisibility and chemistry experiments, but also someone to demonstrate to him that all the really good unifying theories of the universe must begin with playing around and not worrying so much about will happen next—by feeling around with your hands and yanking things you cannot see off the table and down onto your head, or by trying to leap out of your father's arms and into the branches of the fuzzball tree, or by trying to eat the bars of light coming in through the venetian blinds. All this kind of experimentation or risk-taking Teddy had nervously managed to avoid, which had somewhat limited, she thought, the scope of his imagination.

Pinky feared that Arthur would now find a whole new set of anxieties to cultivate, but that wasn't exactly the way it went. In fact, she was delighted to find that the arrival of the baby seemed to lift a weight from Arthur's shoulders. His headaches were farther and fewer between, and when the baby was in his arms he was often nearly light-hearted. It was true that she often caught him looking out the windows or standing in the doorway scanning the horizon as if he were looking for trouble, and it was true that he was constantly trying to discourage her from taking the baby outside the house, but he was concerned, no doubt, because the baby wasn't legally theirs yet.

She wondered and worried a great deal about who had brought the baby to them and why. An infant would have been one thing, but what misfortune or turn of events could cause a mother to give up her ten-month-old baby? She felt sure, somehow, that whoever had chosen them, had chosen them quite deliberately. She wished she could meet this woman and find a way to at least reassure her that all was

well now, but Pinky saw no way to track her down without perhaps at-
tracting unwanted legal attention to the situation.

It was curious to her that Arthur made no effort, either, to find out
where Bernard had come from. It was as if he knew, as she did, that
this baby had been meant for them all along. And this might have
been the reason, she thought, that soon after the baby arrived he began to wake her in the middle of the night almost laughably hard-up,
his hands on her thighs or her shoulders, pulling and kneading at
whatever limb he had happened upon, until she somewhat confusedly
slid herself up against him and nestled her face against his furry chest
or rough cheek and half slept, half swam to meet his own desire.
Toward the end he would be even fiercer and sadder-sounding than
ever, as if he were looking for the place in the darkness where, after all,
it was the two of them who had created Bernard.

From Teddy's point of view, of course, the baby was a serious
mistake.

He tried explaining germ theory to him and Bernard listened carefully and then went right back to picking up pennies and sticking
them in his mouth—also silver gum wrappers, other people's dirty
spoons, anybody's key chains that he could get hold of.

The baby also played this very irritating game of constantly dropping things overboard from his high chair and then squawking loudly
until someone picked up whatever it was and gave it to him so he
could drop it once more.

"Gravity," Teddy explained to him. "It's a force of nature. You
can't see it. It's invisible. If it wasn't there we'd all just float off into
space." It was obvious from the way he whacked his little spoon gleefully against the high chair and then flung it onto the floor that he was
missing the point, that he was lacking the necessary soberness to be a
good scientist.

But the worst thing was the moonwalker. Teddy's grandmother,
the same one who sent the watergun, sent it in the mail soon after
Bernard arrived. It was the very latest thing in baby equipment, a large
inflatable yellow doughnut on wheels. It had a little seat suspended
through the middle. You dropped the baby in, tightened the seat belt,
and set the baby free. The walker could go forward, backward, and
could rotate dizzily like a merry-go-round. If the walker came to the

edge of a step, an automatic braking device was activated and the walker locked in place and emitted a loud beeping. But as long as there was solid ground for it to run on, it was silent and swift. After it arrived, nothing Teddy was working on was safe anymore.

If Teddy took out his meteorites and lined them up carefully on the coffee table, within minutes the baby would come careening over and, ignoring whatever organizational principle Teddy was working on, would quickly rearrange things. He'd then pick up one or two rocks and begin babbling to them in a lively and interrogative voice, pausing now and then, for all the world, as if he were waiting for a reply.

He seemed unable to grasp the rules of physical encounter, and he had an astounding number of accidents. Whether he was in the moonwalker or out of it, he was always pulling things down on his head and bumping into things and, of course, putting the wrong things in his mouth. Teddy was frightened of what the consequences might be if Bernard got his hands on the wrong test tube.

It baffled him how unworried his mother was. She seemed not to comprehend the danger at all. In fact, she had never been more carefree. Teddy felt the full weight of the position he was in settle down inexorably on his shoulders.

As for the cat, the cat avoided the baby pretty much like wildfire.

When Ken Fishhammer came to Katya's door again, he was surprised to find her wearing a small white dress and looking as cool and unhurried as some flower that blooms only by moonlight. He stared at her uneasily, since this was not, in his experience, the way women with young children usually dressed or looked.

He had, downstairs in his car, a car seat, a diaper bag, and enough chloral hydrate to keep a smallish child sedated for several days while he adjusted to his surroundings.

"May I come in?"

She stood aside and allowed him to pass into the interior of the apartment.

Before he sat down on the sofa, he handed her an envelope.

She looked at it without expression, then sat down across from him and opened it. She gazed at the large check, then returned it to the envelope and handed it back to him.

"The baby is gone."

He stared at her.

"Gone? Gone where?"

"He is gone to relatives."

The number of obstacles that had been thrown in his way was simply astounding. But he had long ago come to believe that it was nature's driving imperative that her mysteries be made known. That that was what we were here for, what evolution had spit us out onto the sand for, to discover, to find out how and why. He did not think there was much else worth doing than to make oneself one with this cause, and so he held in his fury.

"Where are these relatives?" he asked.

She hesitated. "You know where my sister and I have come from."

"You sent the baby back there?"

She shrugged.

"How can you imagine that, after all your sister went through to bring you out of that black hole, she would have wanted her child to go back there?"

"My sister did not like you."

He ran his tongue over his front teeth. "Supposing I find out where the baby is, and offer *them* this money. What will you have gained then?"

She flinched and looked behind herself nervously.

His eyes narrowed in suspicion and he followed her gaze, but saw nothing.

"You're quite sure the baby has gone to relatives? It is not too late to change your mind about this course of action." He tapped the envelope against his knee.

"Money will be of no use to this baby."

"But what about you?"

She said nothing.

He folded up the envelope and put it in his pocket. "You'll have a few days to think this matter over. Then it will be too late. You have my number."

10. The Accident

$\mathcal{A}$ rthur knew, as soon as he saw the baby smiling up at him through the slashing rain, where he had come from. But it took a week of observing his laughing and babbling good spirits, his reckless curiosity, his remarkable tolerance of frustration, his placid acceptance of every bump and scrape, before Arthur reluctantly came to the conclusion that Marina had somehow managed to steal one of Fishhammer's genes and bestow it upon the baby.

Arthur was pretty sure that one way or another Bernard would be dead by the time he was twenty-five.

Perhaps Marina had believed that Fishhammer had succeeded in separating the happiness gene from the HDR disorder and its early death program.

Arthur didn't.

Life was a package deal. And from all of the studies that he had carefully read, he had concluded that genes that were linked in this way were too interdependent to be successfully teased apart. Fishhammer was blinded by his own obsessions and a culture that yearned to be excused from struggle and discomfort.

Arthur was sure that if the baby's own reckless cheerfulness did not kill him, the misfirings caused by his DNA certainly would.

What was odd was that he didn't find himself dwelling upon these eventualities much. When it happened he would probably be thrown into a black pit of despair from which there would be no hope of climbing out. But now he rose every morning as soon as the baby began to hoot and make proclamations from his crib, and went and stood in the boys' bedroom doorway. Teddy slept on, but when the baby spotted Arthur, his babbling riff would change to a delighted crow of recognition. Arthur would lift him out and carry him down to the kitchen, and to-gether they would eat some Cheerios and sliced bananas and read the news. Then, if it was a laser truck day, Arthur would carry Bernard out to the front stoop.

The baby, who loved dogs, the moon, gum wrappers, the cat, keys on key chains, rubber balls, bananas, applesauce, mashed carrots, birds, mirrors, open windows, Teddy's chemistry equipment, bath time, bugs, his new father throwing him in the air, the clanging of pots and pans, swinging on swings, his new mother singing, but who loved— more than all of these put together—laser trucks, would bicycle his lit-tle legs and flap his arms with great excitement.

Arthur admonished him to be more serious, to consider the truck's cargo, the burned up ashes of all the neighborhood's unrecyclable waste and pollution, but the baby's enthusiasm was unshakable. He babbled and cheeped, and when the sanitation guys jumped down, he watched them, enchanted, as they zapped the garbage in the cans with their zappers and then dumped the ashes into the back of the old truck. When they were done, he called out to them imperiously and they would pause to greet him, their voices deep and hoarse with the long years of inhaling the rich fumes of garbage.

"Hey, Shorty, when you gonna come down here, already, and help us with these here big cans?"

The baby, never shy, would yell out to them and flap his arms, in-dicating that he was perfectly willing to go off with these greasy guys and their truck full of ashes, but Arthur would hold on to him tightly until the truck had rumbled off down the street

Then they would go back inside and proceed with the day. By now Pinky and Teddy would usually be up, Teddy out in the backyard with one thing or another, Pinky in the kitchen puttering about.

Arthur knew that he was going to have to tell her. He saw that clearly. He had made a mistake in not telling her about the jelly jar in the first place. And now, of course, she would need to know about Fishhammer's chromosome so that she could cope with the inevitable when it happened. In those first weeks, each morning as he put the baby down on the kitchen floor, he considered it. But he was feeling so oddly at peace with himself, it was hard to know how to begin.

~~~

Not much more than a week or two after Bernard arrived, Maury appeared at the door one evening with some organic strawberries and a container of alfalfa sprouts.

Teddy ate several of the strawberries and then took an extremely, almost microscopically small nibble of the alfalfa sprouts and then spit it into the garbage and got a Devil Dog and some potato chips from the cupboard to wash down the taste.

Maury took the strawberries and the sprouts over to Bernard, who was rampaging through the house in his walker. Bernard stopped right where he was and, ignoring the strawberries, stared at the tiny green seedlings, transfixed. He leaned over them and touched them softly with his nose and his tongue, and then he did something that seriously unnerved Arthur, who was watching from the other side of the room. He began to croon. He crooned a low, reverential sort of tune without a melody. It was exactly the sort of tune the mice used to sing every evening at sunset. When he was done singing, he lifted a large tuft of the sprouts from the carton and stuffed them happily in his mouth.

Teddy came over and handed him a potato chip and a piece of Devil Dog, but Bernard ignored these and took another tuft of sprouts.

"That's a great sign," Maury pointed out, "that he prefers the perfectly balanced to the sweet or salty. Could I hold him for a while?"

"Sure," Arthur said. He lifted him out of the walker and handed him over to Maury. Bernard smiled and reached up and patted Maury's shiny head.

"Uuumloov," he said.

"How's it going here?" Maury asked looking toward the kitchen, where Pinky was getting them some lemonade.

"Uhh . . . okay . . . actually pretty good," Arthur said, the words coming uneasily to his tongue.

Maury eyed him with amusement. He held on to the baby gently and permitted himself to be fed squashed strawberries. Then the baby wiggled out of his grasp and went on about his havoc-wreaking business. Maury sat for half an hour or so watching him tear the place up and then he took off, saying he had forks in the road that awaited him.

About a half an hour after he left, Fran showed up bearing an audio recording of North American songbirds and a music box with a lid inlaid with turquoise. When the lid was opened, it revealed a hologram of a little boy ice-skating on a silvery pond. His red scarf was flying out behind him and the snow was coming down. He was skating to the tune of "The Blue Danube." Teddy had had very little experience with holograms and he was completely enchanted by the little box.

Bernard looked at it cursorily and then forgot about it, but he was riveted by the songbirds and, as the recording played, wheeled himself all about the living room, peering under and behind things trying to figure out where the birds were.

The grown-ups sat contentedly watching the children, until Bernard managed to shut his finger in the door of the cabinet where Pinky kept her old collection of favorite TV episode video recordings (*Buffy the Vampire Slayer*, *Friends*, and *Frazier*). He let out a small yelp, but could not get himself free. By the time they realized what had happened, the knuckle of his tiny finger was blue and bleeding. He looked at it curiously and put it in his mouth.

"Does he always do that?" Fran asked.

"Do what?" Pinky asked, carrying him over to the sink in the kitchen where she could wash the finger off.

"React like that when he gets hurt."

"Like what?"

"Like not crying or yelling his head off."

Pinky laughed. "Yeah. He's a tough little boyo."

Fran looked at Arthur, who was standing in the doorway of the kitchen, but Arthur had nothing to say.

Teddy got into bed that night and put the music box next to him on the pillow. Every once in a while he would open the box and the music would come tinkling forth into the room and the little boy with the red scarf would skate around and around in a circle.

"How do they do that?" Teddy asked his mother, who sat beside him.

"What?"

"Make him look so real like that." Teddy put his finger on the boy and his finger, of course, went right through him.

She laughed. "I have no idea."

"Is he a picture of a real boy?" he asked.

"Probably. He's made of light and computerized photos, I imagine." Pinky leaned over and stuck her nose right into the little whorl of hair at the back of her son's head. She breathed him in as if he were a wild sweet rose she had just met by surprise at the side of the road. The warmth of his scalp made a complicated perfume of dirt and sun and peanut butter and jelly and salty little-boy sweat. She thought about how, when she was done, she would go over and smell the other one, who was asleep in his crib, and he would smell like a completely different kind of flower, much simpler, a little milky and a little shampooey. And then she would go downstairs to Arthur, who when last heard from was whistling a Chopin prelude and dragging the laser bins out to the curb for the garbage pickup tomorrow morning, and she would sniff him and he would smell of aftershave and Juicy Fruit and some essence of Arthur that she could not name, and together these three flowers would complete a bouquet, enough to make her dizzy.

"Who was the Bernard who got lost in the war?" Teddy asked her.

Pinky stopped sniffing his head.

Teddy snapped the music box shut.

"That's not my story," she said at last. "You'll have to ask your dad."

"Did anyone in *your* family ever get lost in a war?"

"Actually, my Great-Great-Great-Grandfather Cornelius did. That was the Civil War, when the North was fighting the South."

"What happened to him?"

"He went off to be a soldier for the North and for a while my Great-Great-Great-Grandmother Helen and her son, John, who was *your* Great-Great-Great-Grandfather, got letters from him. But then the letters stopped coming and after about a year Helen decided he must have been killed in battle and she went and got herself remarried."

"And then what happened?"

"And then what happened was that Cornelius came home because he'd only been wounded and had spent a long time recovering in some nice family's farmhouse, and he wasn't really dead at all. And when he got there he found his wife in the kitchen with another man. When Cornelius realized what was going on, he rushed back to the war."

"And?"

Pinky considered it. "And he fought with a terrible rage and sadness and no care for himself, but he managed to stay alive until the horrible bloody thing was over and then he went back to the farmhouse where the people had taken him in and he discovered that the old farmer who helped care for him had died while he was gone, but his wife, who was quite young, was still there, and he married her and they had many children."

Although, actually, the way family legend had it, Cornelius had rushed back into battle and then really did get himself killed, but Pinky was in far too good a mood to pass that news on to her son.

Although it was a very warm night, Teddy pulled his fish quilt all the way up to his chin, just as he always did. He held his thumb up in front of his face, watching anxiously how it seemed to move as he opened and closed alternate eyes. Pinky saw that she hadn't fooled him for a second and that he understood perfectly well how hard it was to get definite information that stayed in one place and did not keep shifting shiftily around the room.

After Teddy was asleep and she had taken a deep sniff of the baby, she went downstairs and curled up on the sofa next to Arthur and inhaled him deeply, too.

Arthur was, first of all, used to the inexplicable things she did and, second of all, was nearly happy. He put his arm around her and kissed her head. She smiled up at him in delight.

"That was a close one, wasn't it?"

"What was a close one?"

"The way Maury showed up and then Fran. They almost ran right into each other. I think it's going to be soon," she said. "I can feel it coming."

"What do you mean?"

"They will both happen to come visit at the same time and then destiny will fulfill itself, just as you predicted."

"Just as I predicted? What are you talking about?"

"You said maybe they would meet and the course of history would change in a single afternoon."

He frowned, puzzled. "I must have been kidding or I said something you misunderstood."

"That was exactly what you said. I didn't misunderstand a thing. You know more than you know you know, Arthur. Next Saturday I bet they show up at the same time, and then, kaboom!"

"Kaboom?"

"Just like it was with you and me."

He looked into her face more closely. "You're kidding me, right?"

Ken had had an academic acquaintance with Marina's father. It was, in fact, through this connection that Marina had found her way here. Ken now used what he knew of her family to try to track down the baby. But although he tried every avenue, he came up with nothing.

When he considered it, he saw that it was not that obstacles were constantly being thrown in his path. This was just the appearance of the thing. It was simply that most of a human life, like most of the human genome, like most of evolution, consisted of wasted space, useless data, wrong turns, and false starts. The bits that contained real information, the moments of forward movement, were rare and easy to miss. It was up to fellows like himself to keep their eyes open, to keep watching and looking.

So he continued to search tirelessly for some clue as to where the baby had gone. He checked all the immigration records between her country and this one. He tried to determine if she had made any friends who might know what had happened. He followed Katya about for several days and got hold of her e-mail records.

Nothing.

Then one morning there was a memo in the corner of his computer screen.

> Did you ever meet Arthur Sorenson's wife, Pinky?
> She's also very fond of babies.
>   Mitchell

Ken, who would have much preferred to completely ignore the existence of Mitchell Newman, understood that to do so would be a fatal error.

He made a request for directory service and in a very few seconds the printer had silently spat out the Sorensons' address on a small pocket-sized piece of paper.

One afternoon, Pinky, noticing that Bernard had actually tired himself out enough to fall asleep in his moonwalker, checked on Teddy, who was working with an intently furrowed brow on his research project, then tiptoed upstairs to look at her painting.

There, suggested by just a few small dabs of black and warm brown, rose and white, sitting in one of the red-leather booths of the Chinese restaurant, resting her cheek upon her hand was a small young woman. She looked out through the plate-glass window into Pinky's eyes. Pinky did not recognize her, but was very pleased with the success of this figure, particularly the use of white to suggest the light in her eyes or, perhaps, the drying up of some tears.

Pinky quickly gave her a pot of tea and a tiny white teacup and then added to the painting the suggestion of a middle-sized, rascally-looking black dog tied up to the lamppost outside of the restaurant.

While she was doing this, Teddy was gazing into his vial of formula with a terrible frown. There must be an answer. He had a feeling the problem lay in the coating action of the formula, that he needed some way to make the stuff stick. He had tried several different coating agents, including honey, toothpaste, and shampoo, but none of them had been successful. The formula had turned a thick pond-slime green and its smell was none too inviting. He stirred it now with a popsicle stick and sighed.

At this moment there was a shattering and then a tinkling sound from the dining room, and then an imperious cry of dissatisfaction from Bernard. Teddy, of course, completely ignored this, but Pinky jumped up and raced in to investigate.

Bernard, who had awoken refreshed from his little nap, had looked around and found himself alone and still in his walker. Spotting a wooden train engine on the coffee table, he zoomed over and picked it up and decided it would be fun to watch it disappear. He rolled over to the window and discovered, to his surprise, that the window was closed, for Arthur had shut it in the middle of the night when he had awakened to what he thought was a distant roll of thunder. Having very little experience with closed windows, Bernard, with the toy train in his hand, whacked the glass. He whacked it several times and, on the third whack, found to his astonishment that his hand, clutching the engine, went right through it.

This was all very interesting, but after dropping the engine and seeing it completely and mysteriously vanish out of the world, he tried to withdraw his hand and bring it back in the house, and his wrist immediately became impaled on a long sharp Christmas-starlike ray of glass.

When Pinky arrived, she found him poised there, his arm outstretched, babbling and trying to pull himself backward. She did not immediately grasp what was going on, for he looked merely stuck and impatient to go with his adventures. Then, however, he gave a harder pull, and he must have torn into a vein, for now blood began to ooze out and drip down onto the floor in large red velvety drops.

Pinky could not breathe. "Don't move, baby, don't move!"

But the baby, who at this time of day was in a hurry, having a lot to take care of—moving the pots and pans around in the cabinet, taking out all the packets of seeds and old coasters and bits of string from the kitchen drawers and dumping them on the floor, interviewing the cat, attempting, again, to get hold of the green pattern in the living room rug—he pulled once more and there was a small ripping sound and more blood.

She grabbed at the baby's wrist and tried to pull it off the glass, but the piece was jagged and snagged on some inside tissue of flesh. The blood spilled out faster.

"Teddy!" she screamed. "Teddy!"

Teddy was slow to appear. Perhaps he couldn't hear her.

For a mother, this kind of time lies outside of the usual continuum. Her child has suddenly vanished in a department store, or she sees, from her greater perspective at the top of the stoop, that the car that is coming too fast down the street will intersect in just a few moments with the path of the child hurtling after the ball. Time jogs out of its usual orbit and the moment, which is generally tiny, no bigger than a marble, contains within it so much—a heightening of the senses and a straining of every ounce of willpower to return the child safely to the moment before and an odd assault of disembodied memories: a whiff of the baby's head, maybe, the weight of him on her hip, herself struggling to jam his little foot into a blue sock—it threatens to collapse in upon itself and explode.

Most of the time the moment is over in a few seconds and the child is found hiding behind a rack of winter coats or he stops at the curb as he has been taught to do while the ball rolls into the street and the car goes speeding by, and the mother takes a breath again and wonders, just briefly, how near we stand to the edge and how closely we are guarded.

But, of course, in this case—since Bernard was stuck—the truth of our terrible and precarious position announced itself plainly in front of her.

The blood oozed out steadily and the pain, Pinky thought, must be terrible. She tried again, gently, to remove his wrist from where the glass went through it, but when she did this, the blood seemed to come more quickly. Pinky squeezed the baby's arm tightly. "Don't move," she begged.

Teddy appeared in the door. He stopped when he saw all the blood.

"Call 911. Tell them the baby put his fist through the window and is stuck on the glass and I can't get him off and the bleeding won't stop. Give them our address very carefully. Tell them your mother said to get here as fast as possible."

Teddy would probably have been tempted to stop for a moment and take a closer look at the blood and question Pinky curiously about the situation, but he was somewhat taken aback by the appearance at Bernard's side of a small and semitransparent woman he thought he might have seen somewhere else recently, but certainly never before in his own dining room. She put her fingers to her lips and made it clear from a single and eloquent gesture of her lovely hand, through which he could clearly see the window curtain behind it and a painting of his mother's on the wall, that she, too, wished him to call 911.

Pinky was filled with gratitude toward him when Teddy did not stop to ask whatever was on his scientific little mind, but wheeled around and disappeared toward the phone.

The baby lifted his hand weakly to try to wave bye-bye, but could not complete the gesture.

Pinky swept the little curly dark locks from his forehead with her free hand. "That's right. That's Teddy. Don't worry, everything will be all right. Just hold still." Purplish, bruised-looking circles had appeared under his eyes. His breathing was quick and labored.

Bernard tried to smile at her and then lowered his head to the tray in front of the walker.

There was blood all over the place—all over him, all over the floor, and all over Pinky.

He whimpered. The little roses that usually glowed in his cheeks were gone.

"Just hold on, baby. Everything's going to be fine."

At this moment, Oedipus padded into the dining room alertly, his nose lifted, following the scent of the blood. When he saw Pinky crouched there, holding the baby's arm, he stopped.

Bernard looked in the cat's direction and rallied a little. "Dardee! Dardee!" he whispered. He didn't lift his head, but tried to move his feet forward in the cat's direction. In doing this, he wrenched his arm, but it still remained stuck. He gave a small groan, whether of pain or frustration or desire to get hold of the cat it was impossible to tell. Then he turned his head toward Pinky and his eyes rolled up into his head.

The fire truck and an emergency medical vehicle arrived at almost the same moment.

Several firemen came in first, dressed like giant bees in their black and yellow jackets. Behind them were the medics in white. They carried a stretcher.

The fire chief took in the situation immediately and produced from his voluminous pockets a small delicate hammer. He gave the glass a smart tap and the long sharp jagged piece on which the baby's wrist was impaled broke free from the pane. He lifted the baby out of the walker with the glass still in his arm and the blood oozing down and laid him on the stretcher. Delicately, the fireman pulled out the piece of glass and handed it to someone. Then he put two fingers on the baby's wrist and listened for his breathing.

"He's lost a lot of blood and his pulse is not good," he said in a low, coaxing voice, "but he's breathing." Pinky knew that he was trying to deliver information and, at the same time, encourage the baby's spirit to stay on board.

"Let's get this wound closed up and then get him out to the ambulance." He continued to speak in a low, encouraging voice as if he were concentrating all the huge strength that his years of breaking down doors and hoisting aloft great gushing hoses of water and hauling unconscious people out of burning buildings had caused to grow in him, and putting it into his hands and voice for the express purpose of convincing the baby to hold on.

To everyone's surprise, Bernard's eyes fluttered open and he stared into the fire chief's face with interest.

"This is a tough little boyo," the chief said.

Bernard struggled, perhaps wishing to be lifted up, but the chief put a firm hand on his forehead and shoulders. "Keep your diapers on, there, cowboy."

"Pfllllf." The baby smiled at him.

"Pfllf, yourself. Stop squirming around. You're messing up your mother's floor."

But in a couple of minutes the emergency medical guys had finished cleaning and bandaging the wound. "Let's go, Orson! We gotta get this kid outta there."

The chief nodded and looked steadily at the baby. "Okay, amigo. You heard the man. It's emergency room time for you. We're going to pick you up and take you outside and we're going to go for a fast ride. You like fire trucks? You like ambulances? We got the whole package out there for you."

"Mamboo," Bernard murmured hopefully.

"That's the spirit. This is gonna hurt a little, but don't worry, it's for a good cause."

The chief looked over at Pinky worriedly and suggested she might like to ride over in the police car with her older son.

Pinky said no. She would ride in the ambulance. She instructed Teddy to get in the police car and she would meet him at the hospital.

The chief and the medic carried Bernard out on the stretcher and when he got outside and saw the police cars and the fire trucks and the ambulance, he tried to wave at everyone with his good arm.

They lifted Bernard up and placed the stretcher gently inside the waiting ambulance.

Pinky followed him.

She crouched down on the bench near the medic, who immediately placed an oxygen mask over Bernard's face and then proceeded to open a drawer full of shiny steel hooks and probes and needles and to extract one of these needles and fit it to a long thin tube that was attached to a plastic bag of clear fluid.

Across from where she sat were several large green and silver machines with dials and accordion-folded rubber hoses and lots of other unkind steel instruments, hanging from hooks.

"Any history of anemia or easy bruising?" the medic asked her as he continued to fiddle with his needle and plastic tube.

She shook her head dumbly.

"Any allergies?"

Again she shook her head.

"Okay. We'll get a blood type and they should be all ready for us when we get there."

The medic lifted Bernard's free wrist up and prepared to insert the long thin needle.

Bernard looked up at him over the oxygen mask. Then he gazed around the interior of the ambulance with interest and apparent pleasure, as if the inside of an ambulance had long been on his list of hot spots he'd like to visit.

The medic tried inserting the needle and, meeting some resistance, swore softly. He withdrew the needle and hovered over the baby anxiously. "Sorry, fella. These little veins can be hard to find, but we'll get there, don't worry."

"Tarboo," Bernard said in a muffled voice from behind the mask.

"Right." The medic smiled. "You're an awful sweet little guy." This time the needle slipped in and found its mark. The baby shivered slightly, reached up, and tried to touch the medic's eyelashes, but, finding his reach was not long enough, sighed and passed out again.

11. Bernard Goes over the Fence

*O*ne evening a couple of days after Bernard came home from the hospital, Arthur had a date to play chess with Billy, but as it turned out, it was raining.

Arthur took an umbrella and, without allowing Pinky to pin him down to exactly where he was going, walked slowly down the block over the smell of wet summer sidewalks, in the wrong direction. It was early August. Johnny Pitsacado sat in his usual spot on the front stoop, his hair lank and uncombed, a brown paper bag by his side. He nodded as Arthur went by.

Arthur circled around the block and then stopped in front of Billy Edelman's house. Seeing no sign of Pinky watching from the windows, he opened the gate and went up Billy's front steps.

He stood nervously between the two gray stone geranium pots until Susan let him in.

She took his umbrella without a word and whacked it, hard, against the doorframe and stowed it away in an iron umbrella stand. Then she led him silently down the dark hallway.

He followed her into a room lined with books and furnished with several large dark-colored armchairs. In the middle of the room was a table made out of some heavily polished red-colored wood. Billy was at this table contemplating the chessboard.

When Arthur sat down, Billy looked up with a little grunt of surprise and then looked over at his wife, who stood watching them in the doorway. He smiled at her, but she did not, Arthur noted, smile back. After a brief pause, she turned and left them.

"So, you told your wife you were coming here?" Billy's face was the color of the sea on a cloudy morning. Next to him on the polished table stood a small crystal vase with one very large wet rose. Even Arthur, who knew nothing about flowers or roses, was startled by its fleshy-looking pink petals and strong fragrance, and when he leaned over to inspect it more closely, he saw what looked almost like a dark crimson face staring up from the flower's interior.

"Not exactly. That's an unusual-looking flower."

"How's your little son?"

Arthur smiled. "Well, he's home."

Billy raised his eyebrows. "He's back on his feet?"

"He never was on his feet yet, exactly, but he's okay. He lost a lot of blood and they had to sedate him to keep him on the IV, and he has twenty stitches or so in his arm, but he's okay now. He's over there ripping the pages out of an old voicelink directory and eating them." Arthur was a little surprised at himself, at how quickly he had recovered from this near-catastrophe, at how unworried he found himself to be about what would happen next.

"You know, I have to admit, I'm a little confused about him. Was he with you when you moved in?"

"No, he was with his aunt for the first few weeks."

"Well, sounds like you were lucky."

"Yup."

They played the first few moves of the game without speaking. After around twenty minutes, Susan appeared holding a ceramic snack dish such as his own mother used to entertain with. It had three different little hollows for snacks. Susan had filled the dish with black olives, peanuts, and, lastly, with neatly trimmed celery-heart sticks.

The older man shook his head somberly, gazing at the dish, then he raised his eyes at last and looked at his wife, who stood watching him also. "Thank you, Susie. You're a genius. I was just thinking of olives and peanuts." He reached for her hand as if he would squeeze or kiss it, but she backed away, no expression on her face, and turned and exited.

Arthur pretended he hadn't seen this and took Billy's knight. "Check."

Billy gazed ruefully at the spot where his knight had, just a moment ago, stood on its little green felt bottom, full of possibilities.

"I'm actually better outside, for some reason," he said. He contemplated his position and moved his bishop forward three spaces.

The game developed slowly and unevenly—the pawns standing around in little clumps chatting. Billy played as he had before, without much apparent knowledge of the game, but imaginatively and erratically. Arthur felt confident and in fine form. He was beginning to get a picture of Billy's style and he waited impatiently for the board to open out. He knew that he had a strength, not reliable, in the endgame, where with a sudden flash of clear sight he could sometimes see all the possibilities opening up ahead.

At one point there was a brief skirmish and hostages were taken—a rook and a pawn from Arthur's side, the queen's bishop from Billy's. Arthur thought about this little advantage that Billy had gained and finished off the olives. He studied the board carefully and, with a sudden burst of light, he saw a path that would almost inevitably resolve itself into his own victory if only he could draw Billy's attention over to the corner and tempt him into exchanging bishops. He moved his queen's knight over the heads of the crowd and put it down. He waited with an expressionless face to see if Billy would do what was needed.

At around seven, when Arthur had already been gone for about an hour, the rain stopped suddenly and the sun came out. The day had already seemed gone and the addition of this extra hour filled Teddy with inspiration and energy. He pulled a chair up to the pantry shelf and was poking around, looking for something he might try on his formula, when, way in the back, he came upon a very interesting-looking old brown bottle with a cork in the top. It had a round fat bottom and a high narrow neck with a dusty crimson ribbon tied around it.

"What's this?" he said to his mother, who was at the sink washing dishes.

She turned to look, then came over and took the bottle from his hands and stared at it curiously.

"Well, my goodness, this is my grandmother's cherry cordial. Where did you find this?"

Teddy told her.

"Your father must have been the one who packed it up and then put it away up there." She smiled. "She used it as a medicine, and people said it had all sorts of strange and wonderful properties. She gave me this bottle right before she died. She said I should only use it very sparingly, so I put it away and I forgot all about it."

Teddy got down off the chair. "Could I smell it?"

She lifted the bottle up and considered it. Then she set it on the counter and pulled on the cork, which came out with a soft whooshing sound. The air immediately filled with a strangely sweet and spicy fragrance.

Teddy bent over and sniffed at it. "Could I put some in my formula? Just a little bit?"

Pinky thought about it again. "Well, I don't know. I'm not sure how she'd feel about that."

"Who?"

She frowned at him. "My grandmother, of course. Anyway, there's quite a bit of alcohol in this stuff, as I remember, and it would probably make your ants quite drunk. Let me give you something else you could try, something she loved to use."

Pinky went over to the pantry and rooted around and brought out an old bottle of molasses. "Nobody uses this much anymore. It's a nice old-fashioned ingredient and it's good and sticky. You're not drinking that formula you're making, are you? Just trying it out on ants?"

"Ants and bugs."

She handed him the bottle and he took it solemnly and announced he was going out into the backyard. Bernard, hearing this, flung down the voicelink directory he had been pulling the pages out of and crawled rapidly over to where his brother stood and, using Teddy for support, pulled himself into an upright position and said, "Wamba," in a commanding tone.

So Pinky took out the portable talking playpen with its many buttons and levers and flashing lights that Bernard pretty much ignored, and put it in the back and stuck Bernard in it. She told Teddy and Oedipus to watch him like hawks and she went back inside to finish vacuuming the living room.

The cat immediately leaped the fence and went directly to Susan

Edelman's prize rosebush and lifted his tail and peed on it. The look on his white and orange face as he did this deed was one of sober and far-away intentness. It was a workingman's look, a washing machine re-pairman's kind of look. He had an important job to do, one of those jobs that keeps the world going around as it should. When he was done, he gave his tail a final flick and then he leaped up, light as an ap-ple blossom, to the top of the fence and jumped back down on his own side. He walked across the lawn, shaking his paws as he went, since everything was wet and glistening. The sun lowered itself slowly and carefully, palish and pink, like an egg lit from within, down into the gauzy clouds that were still breaking up along the horizon, as the crick-ets and the cicadas, one by one, picked up their instruments and began to sing the song in praise of this particular day which had opened itself up at the last minute. Soon they were singing with reckless abandon, since the flipping pages of their tiny wired-in calendars told them they'd all be dead within a matter of weeks. The air smelled of wet roses, basil, cut grass, sunflowers, and petunias.

Pinky whizzed through the living room, humming and banging the vacuum cleaner into chair legs as she went. Then she straightened and picked up sofa pillows and threw baby toys and paraphernalia into the old covered toy chest they kept in the hallway. When she was done, she slammed the toy chest closed and scanned the living room with satisfaction. Then she went to the back door to check on her children.

Teddy was bent over in the grass poking at something and Bernard was holding on to the padded railing of his playpen, crooning softly to himself, his face raised to the fuzzball tree. The cat was nowhere to be seen, but standing at the fence, gazing at Bernard, was Mrs. Edelman. Pinky watched her uneasily, but Susan did not even seem to see her. She looked frozen, caught by surprise, like one of those old photos you find in a shoebox of a stiff, ornately attired woman, trying to see out past the frame where she perceives, dimly, a crowd of grandchildren and great-grandchildren staring in at her.

At this moment, Pinky heard the doorbell ring far away inside the house.

Pinky did not like the idea of leaving her children alone in the yard with Susan Edelman staring over at them in that weird way, but what was she going to do? She imagined that no harm would come to anybody if she left them on their own for a few minutes. She went into the house to answer the door.

At the door stood a man whose handsome nose and shiny-looking pocket pencil looked vaguely familiar.

"Mrs. Sorenson? I don't know if you'll remember me, we met once at a university party. My name is Ken Fishhammer."

She smiled at him, remembering instantly. He had been famous before his fall and now he was notorious, though she wasn't exactly sure for what.

"Yes, of course."

"I was wondering if Arthur was at home. I was passing through the neighborhood and thought I might catch him in."

"Well, no," Pinky said. "He's not here right now."

"Oh, that's too bad. Do you know when he'll be back? I was looking for some information I thought he might have."

"I'm sorry, I don't think he'll be back for a couple of hours. Would you like me to leave him a message to call you?"

"Sure. That would be fine, but I'm wondering if you'd mind if I used your voicelink. The battery on my cell seems to have gone out and I need to make a call."

She led him inside and handed him the voicelink. She was glad that she had had a chance to straighten the room. "I'll be right back," she said and left him alone. When she came back into the room a few minutes later, she found him sitting on her sofa, staring glumly about.

"Everything okay?" she asked politely.

He looked up at her and shrugged. "Oh, it's my wife," he said. "She's been having rather a hard time. Depression, I guess."

Pinky was not the sort to be surprised by confessions like this. Her heart immediately went out to this woman she had never met. "I'm sorry. I know how hard depression is on everyone in a family. Is this a regular problem or did something particular happen?"

Ken paused for a moment and looked at Pinky, as if deciding how much to tell. "She's depressed because she can't have any more children. She had to have some surgery a couple of years ago."

"How many children do you have?"

"Well, we have two, two girls, and I know it might seem crazy, but she always had her heart set on a third."

Now Pinky felt, suddenly, an electrical overload in the atmosphere. She smoothed her hair back from her temples and discovered that several strands had escaped from the elastic rubber band, so she reached back and pulled it off, gathered her hair together, and slipped the elastic back around it. She gave it an extra twist this time and felt her scalp being pulled tight. "It's hard to have your heart set on something like that, I know. But couldn't you adopt?"

"Well, to tell you the truth, that's why I came to talk to Arthur. Last month, I accidentally found out that Marina Kulagin, who was the lab assistant on one of my projects, had given birth to a baby just a little while before she died in a car accident. Her younger sister, Katya, had the baby for a little while, but apparently this baby has been sent back to relatives in Marina's native country. I'm trying to track him down. I'd like to bring him back and adopt him. I feel sure that this is something that Marina would like, since I could offer this child so much, and I believe that a baby might be my wife's salvation. As it happened, Arthur was working on that same project and I wondered if Marina might have told him anything about her family or if he knew anything else that might help me."

She found she could not take her eyes away from his. He was looking at her very calmly, but intently, gauging, she thought, the blush that had risen to her cheeks. She saw that he was lying about something, but exactly what, she couldn't tell. "Would you excuse me for a minute? I need to check on my son. He's awfully quiet."

She walked across the room, unhurriedly, and saw there was—thank the forces that be—not a baby toy in sight. When she entered the kitchen she took a deep breath of panic and ran through it and out the back door into the little yard.

She raced over to the baby in his playpen, where he still stood singing to a large apple-pie-shaped cloud. She scooped him up and held him to her breast and gazed around the yard urgently, trying to figure out where she could hide him.

At that moment her gaze met Susan Edelman's, who was still standing at the fence watching them. Pinky knew better than to think about what she was about to do. She simply took another deep breath and then strode over to her, carrying Bernard.

"Susan, please. I need your help. Take the baby into your house and keep him there until I come to get him." She did not wait for Susan to answer but lifted the baby over the fence and held him out. Susan blinked once and took the baby in her arms. She gazed at Pinky for a moment and then turned toward her back door.

Pinky watched her disappear inside and then she lifted the awkward playpen, which sang "Hush, Little Baby" mockingly at her as she dragged it out of sight into the alleyway.

She ran back into the house, breathed several deep breaths to calm herself, then entered the living room.

"Sorry," she said. "He's seven and he's working on some top-secret experiment. I'm always worried he's going to blow us all up." She smiled and lifted her hands. "Anyway, I doubt that Arthur is going to have any information for you about this baby. My husband talked about Marina once in a while, but never in a personal way. Personal information is not really Arthur's line of business. He heard about her death, but I don't think he realized she'd had a baby. He never mentioned it to me."

Ken gazed at her impassively for a moment, then made a small face of disappointment. A little too casually, he looked around the living room. She looked around with him, but what was there to see? "Well, look, if Arthur happens to remember anything, would you have him call me?"

"Sure."

To her immense relief, he stood and turned toward the front door. Then he stopped, as if a thought had struck him, and asked her if he could take a look at her backyard. He and his wife were thinking about a move, and he was wondering what kind of gardening space he might get around here. He was a big gardener.

She led him to the backyard and he stood on her back patio gazing around carefully, although she didn't get the feeling that he took in a single flower or fuzzball. The sun was nearly down and the air was soft and warm and smelled of the wet grass. Teddy was crouched, transfixed, over his petri dish in the back of the yard next to the birch tree.

"That's your son?"

"Yes. He gets a little obsessive."

"Necessary for progress. Nice garden. I could live with this."

The thought of this terrible cold guy and his wife, who Pinky imagined had stiff sculpted hair and wore a fur coat, messing around in her garden or holding her baby made her want to scream.

Almost rudely, she hurried Ken back through the kitchen, through the dining room, and into the living room toward the front hall. They had almost made it home free when she spotted them, right there at the foot of the stairs on the bookcase, the box of recyclable Cloud-Soft disposable diapers. On the top of the box was a plastic teething ring of colored keys. She had meant to bring them upstairs later. She inserted herself quickly between Ken and the box, and when she looked up at him, her face burning, she could not read from his expression whether he had seen them or not. He smiled at her mildly. She ushered him through the hall and out the front door.

"Don't worry," she promised. "If anything turns up, I'll call you! Goodbye, goodbye!"

Arthur shifted in his seat a little restlessly, as if he were bored with what was going on in the center of the action. He took out a piece of gum, unwrapped it, and popped it in his mouth. He watched with indifference as Billy moved his bishop forward and lifted his hand. He seemed to think about what Billy had done without great interest, then nudged his own fellow in the black pointed hat three spaces sideways.

Billy studied this with suspicion. Then brightened as he appeared to realize the possibilities. He lifted his bishop and—Arthur could have sworn—at this critical moment, there was a strong extra gust of scent from the rose. The older man paused and frowned. He stared at Arthur's trap. He wrinkled his nose. Holding the white bishop up by the point of his little cap, he waggled it thoughtfully in the air. He put the bishop back down where it was and returned his attention to the center of the board. He pushed a pawn forward.

Then he leaned forward to sniff at the rose. "My wife bred this rose. It's taken her years. She's done it completely naturally. She's an extraordinary woman."

Arthur made no comment.

"I met her in the late seventies in a club, a small place. They had a lot of live bands. Where'd you meet yours?"

"Pinky, you mean?" Arthur, who didn't remember that particular afternoon very well, shrugged. "Oh, in a drugstore."

"I used to go to this place with my pal Arnie. We'd go to hear the music, but one night in August—it was around this time of year—I turned around and there she was. There was a big crush and it was dark—it was always like that in those places—but she was wearing this little white dress. She looked so cool, like it was only the beginning of April where she was standing, and, on top of it, she was so beautiful. She was definitely one of the most beautiful women I'd ever seen." Billy leaned back and seemed to be remembering Susan as she was on that particular evening. Then he looked at Arthur. "It's your move," he reminded him.

Arthur, who found himself only mildly interested by the story, idled his queen a step forward. Billy glanced casually at the board, moved *his* queen a step sideways, and then continued. "On one hand, I didn't think she was likely to even give me a second glance. I was pretty fond of myself, but she looked out of my class. On the other hand, I knew that I was seeing what I wanted, which wasn't too usual with me. I was a sort of a noncommittal kind of guy. I could easily have dropped the matter, not gotten myself worked up, and forgotten about it. Often I think back to it. How easily things could have gone another way." He sighed. Arthur wondered if he was thinking about his son. "It's your move," Billy reminded him.

Arthur moved a pawn.

"But anyway, I went over to her, where she was standing, and I said, 'Excuse me, but I wonder if I could ask a favor of you.'

"She was there with another girl and I remember the other girl looked pretty entertained by my appearance, but Susan . . . Susan looked at me the way a true queen looks at her subjects, with a certain distance, of course, but also kindness and attention. I was very grateful and I determined to make the best of my opportunity. So I said to her, 'My wife is sitting at the back of the bar and she bet me five bucks that you wouldn't dance with me.' I pretended to wave to somebody at the bar and then I looked at Susan and I said, 'Please, won't you help me win five bucks and help my wife see what a true treasure of a guy she's got on her hands?'

" 'Well, of course,' she said, and she took me out on the dance floor. She was a really fantastic dancer. And I wasn't bad myself. And by the time the set was over, I was pretty sure I had run into my destiny. But, naturally, I knew better than to crowd it."

Arthur couldn't help smiling. He thought how Pinky would have loved this, this story of first encounter, deception, and true romance. He watched Billy move his knight.

"So, after the dance, I thanked her and went back to the bar and didn't bother her for the rest of the evening, but after that first night, I came again and again looking for her. Whenever she was there, I would ask her for one dance only. I treated her with the greatest respect and formality, letting her know that even though it was the seventies and a lot of people were treating their marriage vows with the same seriousness as a car lease, I, personally, was an old-fashioned guy and would never cheat on my wife, but that I *was* feeling some regret about not being a free man. We began to meet sometimes for lunch or dinner. We spoke of poetry and traveling, our dreams and our disappointments. She was a very high-strung, sensitive, shy type of girl, but she felt safe with me, since she knew I was already taken, and after a while, I saw that she was beginning to return my feelings for her. I made a great tender tragic thing of our friendship and then, eventually, I invited her home to meet my wife."

Arthur frowned and looked up from the chessboard. "But you had no wife."

"That's correct. I borrowed some nice dishes and set out candles and when she arrived and looked around the room, I got down on my knees and said, 'Forgive me,' and I explained the true facts of the case and I asked her to marry me. It's your move."

Arthur laughed. Then he castled, which was not, at all, what he had been planning.

Billy tilted his head first to one side, then to the other, like a bird eyeing a caterpillar crawling slowly along the branch beneath it. He dove forward suddenly with his queen and snatched up Arthur's knight. "Check."

Arthur stared at the board in astonishment. He had been had. He moved his king back.

Billy moved his queen forward. "Checkmate."

Arthur laughed again. He saw that he had gotten what he deserved for allowing himself to be distracted.

"It was a pretty good marriage as those things go, but after we lost our son—and there were some other things that happened, too—she was never the same. She's very . . . fragile."

Occasionally, in the last couple of weeks, the thought had occurred to Arthur that he might ask his neighbor for some advice on how it was you went on after losing a child, but sitting here now, he did not find himself really in the mood for such instruction. When he looked toward the window, he was, furthermore, caught by surprise to find that the day was not yet over. In fact, a last-minute sunset was elbowing its way through the clouds.

"What worries me is what will happen to her if I go first. I've got a bad thumper." He patted his chest.

"But listen," Arthur said, "they're doing a lot of great work with artificial hearts now. I could hook you up with a very cutting-edge person over at the university."

Billy smiled. "Already got one. Completely cow and plasmic tissue." He patted his chest again. "It worked really nicely for a few years, but now the rest of my general organ committee seems to have gotten ticked off—ha, ha—about the situation. My body is producing some sort of acid or something that's begun to eat away at the thing. The doctors tell me there's nothing much they can do and if they put another one in, it'll happen again."

"There must be medication to slow the process down?"

"Nothing seems to be having much effect. But don't look so upset. It isn't your bad luck, it's mine. And I'm used to it. In fact, I'm working on a plan."

Now, Arthur had not had a real live headache for several weeks. But he knew immediately, from the pressure in his head and the loud ringing in his ears, that he definitely did not want to know what this plan was. He put his hand over his eyes.

"I'm sorry," he said. "You must forgive me, but I think I'd better go."

In his confusion and discomfort, he did not hear the bustle and footsteps in the hallway. When he looked up and saw Susan standing in the doorway holding a rosy-cheeked and curly-haired baby who was patting her face delicately with the palms of his hands, he imagined that this was one of those absurd hallucinations he sometimes got with his headaches. The baby, however, turned as they entered the room and took one look at Arthur and screamed, "Dardoo!" in delight. He held his arms out in excitement, but when Arthur only stared at him baffled, as if he were a mere phantom passing through a dream, the baby turned his attention back to Susan's face, which he touched delicately with one finger and then two. Then, carried away, he pinched her cheek hard between his thumb and forefinger and pulled. Susan did nothing to stop him, but stood there with an odd look on her face, as if what was going on was not what was going on, but as if she were listening to the wind soughing in the trees, or to a voice she recognized but couldn't quite make out. Finally she said, "Your wife handed him to me over the fence. She said he was in some kind of danger."

Pinky watched Ken Fishhammer get into his car, and she stood there on the top step until he drove away down the street. When his car had turned the corner, she ran down her front steps and over to the Edelmans' house. She put her finger on the doorbell and held it until the door opened.

Arthur stood there holding Bernard in his arms.

"Arthur?" she exclaimed.

"What happened? Why did you give the baby to Susan?"

"What were you doing in there? Is this where you went?"

"I was playing chess with Billy. Let's go home."

When they were back inside the house, they stood there in the hallway and looked at each other. The baby patted Arthur's cheeks.

"So what happened? Why did you give Susan the baby?" he asked her again.

"Ken Fishhammer was here."

Arthur closed his eyes and thought about it. He realized that the moment had arrived and he was going to have to tell Pinky. The baby, seeing Arthur chewing on his gum, tried to pry his jaw open with sticky little fingers.

"He was looking for Marina's baby," Pinky said. "He wants to adopt him. He said that Marina's sister told him she'd sent the baby back to Eastern Europe, but wouldn't tell him any more than that. He was trying to track the baby down. He thought we might know something."

Arthur tried to say something, but it was difficult with the baby's fingers in his mouth.

"You knew, didn't you? You knew that he was Marina's baby?"

Night was nearly here, but no one had yet turned on a light. A firefly blinked on and then off in the tree outside the window and then the street lamp came on. "Well? Did you?"

"I wasn't sure, but I thought it was pretty likely."

"Why didn't you tell me?"

"I didn't know if that would have been the right thing to do," he said, half truthfully. "I didn't know if Marina would have wanted anybody to know where the baby came from. I didn't really know what had happened, only that Marina had died."

The baby was like a little firecracker spluttering and sparking here in the dusky evening. Arthur walked into the living room and sat down on the sofa and threw Bernard up in the air and then caught him. Pinky stood over them, watching.

"Well, what is going on? Why would Marina's sister bring him *here?*"

He took a deep breath. "I think Marina must have left her some instructions in the event of her death. She may have thought it would be too big a job for her sister. She knew very few people here in this country, but she and I had worked together for a couple of years and she may have thought I was reliable and trustworthy. She may have suggested that her sister bring the baby to me in the event something happened."

Pinky waited for more, but Arthur paused to throw the baby up in the air again. Bernard was caught in the light of the street lamp. Anyone looking in would have been astounded to see this baby who appeared to be flying all by himself.

Pinky thought about what Arthur had said and she knew it was true. In a way, there was no one more reliable and trustworthy than Arthur. You could hurl at him plagues and locusts, genocide and orphaned babies, and he would throw up his arms to catch them with a perfectly straight face, these being exactly the sort of things he expected the world to toss around. Yes, this was surely the reason she had instructed Katya to bring the baby here.

Arthur held the baby still in his arms and took another deep breath. "Pinky—" he began, and at this moment Teddy came racing into the room, his hand held out in front of him.

"I did it! I did it!"

"What?" Pinky asked. "What did you do?"

"I created an invisible ant. Turn on the light!"

Pinky reached over and turned on the little table lamp. She and Arthur and the baby leaned over Teddy's hand. There was absolutely nothing there.

"This is what I've been working on! A formula for invisibility. And I finally got it! It was the molasses. I dipped the ant in and he disappeared. But you can feel him on my hand. Here, Dad, I'm going to put him on you. You have to concentrate hard, because he's tiny."

Dutifully, Arthur held out his hand and Teddy gently pushed something no one could see onto his palm. "Do you feel it?"

Arthur sat very still and then, after a minute, since he really had no capacity for untruth, he said, reluctantly, no, he couldn't feel anything.

"But Dad!" Teddy protested.

"Here, let me," Pinky said. "Your dad wouldn't feel an invisible ant if it came up and peed on his foot."

Teddy frowned, but then very gently lifted whatever it was from Arthur's palm and pushed it onto Pinky's.

Pinky concentrated very hard. She closed her eyes. She widened her nostrils. "Oh, yes! I think I feel it. It tickles. It's a big one!"

Teddy glared at her in disgust. "You're making it up. I told you, it's very tiny."

At this moment, Bernard leaned out of Arthur's arms and dipped his head toward Pinky's hand.

"Watch out!" Teddy yelled desperately. "He's going to eat it!" And, indeed, Bernard, as if he had spotted something there that absolutely must be tasted, stuck his little pink busy tongue out and licked Pinky's hand.

"No!" Teddy shrieked, and he grabbed Pinky's hand and began desperately feeling around. "It's gone!" he sobbed. "It's gone. I hate this baby! I hate him! I've been working on this since I got my chemistry set and now it's completely messed up."

"Calm down," Arthur commanded him. "It's all right. If your formula really works, all you have to do is go outside and get another ant."

Teddy shuddered and slowly stopped crying. Pinky put her arms around him. "It's okay, Peachblossom," she said. "Everything's going to be okay."

"No, it's not," he said, and pushed her off. He left without looking back at any of them. They heard the screen door to the backyard open and shut.

"He'll never find an ant now. It's too dark," Pinky said.

The baby wiggled out of Arthur's arms and slid down to the floor, where he quickly pulled himself up on the coffee table and started trying to climb on top of it. Arthur grabbed hold of him and put him on the sofa beside himself and gave him his keys.

"Fishhammer will be back," Arthur said worriedly. "He's a very persistent son of a bitch."

"But what do we have to worry about, really?" Pinky said. "Marina sent the baby to us and now he's ours. Look how happy he is living here in our little house."

Arthur did not say what he thought, which was that this baby would be happy living in a cardboard box with Lizzie Borden and Bluebeard the pirate, to whom Ken Fishhammer was almost certainly directly related.

12. Katya

*T*he next morning arrived clear and bright and cooler. Pinky was excited about what she had decided to do. While she waited for Arthur to come back from his run, she went into the sunroom and attempted to bring some order out of chaos. She tidied up and dusted, and the baby followed her about in his walker, trying to catch the dust motes and knocking things over. When he knocked over a stinky, viscous-looking substance in a plastic container, she sponged it up quickly and took the container back to the kitchen and rinsed it out and threw it away. The baby followed her into the kitchen and hung around trying to sing to the birds, who were arguing a difficult point in the hedge outside the window. When she was finished washing the dishes, she lifted Bernard up and carried him outside.

Arthur found Pinky and the baby on the front steps waiting for him. She was holding Bernard by his two upraised hands and giving him little lift-boosts as he stretched his legs to climb laboriously up to the top. When he got to the top, he crowed, then instantly spun around and headed back downward.

At the bottom she scooped him up and went over to Arthur and kissed his sweaty mouth. Bernard yelled loudly, his arms out toward the steps, complaining that he wanted to go up again, but she ignored him.

"Listen," she said, "I need to get some stuff for the baby. He's been living in practically the same three outfits since he arrived. I need to get a couple of things for myself, too."

Susan Edelman came out her front gate and walked past them. She carried a pocketbook and a large shopping bag. She did not glance at them or say a word.

"What *is* her problem, one wonders?" Pinky said.

"She's unhappy."

Pinky looked up at him sharply. "What do you know about it?"

Arthur shrugged.

"Ordinary garden-variety unhappiness or ravening wolves from the north unhappiness?"

Arthur looked mildly annoyed. "It's hard to rate that kind of thing, since it seems to be the ratio between the inside state of the person and the outside events that determines the final total. However, in my estimation, it's more than the ordinary garden variety."

Arthur, she saw, was not going to tell her what he knew. This was just like him. She was never sure if it was a strong code of ethics about keeping other people's business confidential or if it was that he simply didn't find other people's business that interesting. She would have to circle around from behind when he wasn't prepared and see if she could noodge it out of him. Meanwhile, she had other important matters to attend to. "Well, anyway, I'm going shopping."

"You've got enough stuff in your closets to clothe several Mongolian hordes."

"Everything has green-bean stains on it."

"And the baby doesn't even wear clothes."

"Now is a very good time to look for winter things."

"Winter things? It's August and you're going to go out and look for a sale on mittens?"

"I'm just being practical. You're always criticizing me for not being practical."

"Well, fine, you wanna take a shot at being practical, be my guest. But you don't really need to take the baby along. Just bring one of his current outfits and measure the sizes against that one."

"I don't want you to worry. You have nothing to worry about. He's ours, I'm telling you. Nothing is going to happen. I will either keep him locked up in the stroller or glued to my own personal body. I'm going to find him a perfect blue shirt. And if you're really that nervous, why don't you come along?" Although she knew he wouldn't, she knew there was no sound he hated more than the sound of women rattling hangers in a department store.

Arthur sighed. He unhooked the baby's fingers from Pinky's and helped him struggle up, and then down, the steps. Then, reluctantly, he handed the baby over to Pinky and said, "Don't use public transportation. Take the car and don't talk to strangers."

She laughed. "You're so predictable. Teddy is in the backyard. Keep an eye on him. I'll be back in a few hours."

Pinky drove down the block and around the corner. Then she pulled over to the curb and took out her street map and studied it very carefully for several minutes.

Bernard squawked, eager to be on with things, to find out what was coming next.

"Hold on," she said. "I gotta figure something out. We got an important stop to make before we do the shopping thing. Your destiny is involved. How are you at reading maps?"

"Gaah!" he yelled and struggled valiantly to free himself from the restraints of the car seat. But, finding himself unequal to the task, he settled back philosophically and looked out the window for diversions.

Katya answered the door. Pinky watched her carefully. Katya looked inquiringly at Pinky, then down at the baby.

She let out a small gasp and then, for a curious moment, her face warmed and opened and across it passed, in succession, several little sailboats of emotion.

Pinky watched this intently and noted, too, how by the time Katya looked up at her again, her face was empty.

It was too late, of course, for by now the baby was yodeling wildly with his arms out to his aunt.

Someone down at the end of the hallway opened a door and peeked out. Both Pinky and Katya looked at each other sharply.

"Don't worry," Pinky said in a low voice. "I'm not bringing trouble, but I have to ask you a few questions. Please let us in."

Without a word, Katya stood aside and Pinky entered the apartment with the baby still on her hip, yelling gorgeous nonsense commands to Katya.

They all stood there in the small shabby living room.

"We call him Bernard," Pinky said. "What did you call him?"

"Andre," Katya replied reluctantly. "How did you find me? I cannot take him back."

"I know the secretary at the university. She told me where to find you and, of course, I don't expect you to take him back. He is my heart's desire."

They looked at each other over Bernard. "Sit down," Katya invited at last.

Pinky sat down on the sofa and stood Bernard between her knees. For a moment he was silent and he stared at her smiling, waiting. She took a deep breath. "I had been praying for him steadily and nonstop for the last five years. Not in a religious way—I don't believe in God, really—but there are forces out there—and I know sometimes you can get them to move in a certain direction on your behalf. I prayed to all the dead people I know, too. Sometimes they'll lend a hand. I'm not offending you, am I? Do you believe in God?"

"No."

"No, I didn't think so from your face. Did your sister? What I'm thinking is that Arthur must have mentioned to her how much I wanted another child."

Katya shrugged. "That I do not know."

"But somehow she must have told you that she wanted you to bring the baby to us."

Katya was quiet for several moments. "Yes, she let me know that."

Now Bernard interrupted loudly, "Pakadooo!" He wiggled out from between Pinky's knees.

Katya watched him curiously. "He is so big now," she said with a sigh.

"Have you ever seen a baby who looked so much like the sun coming up in the morning?"

"I have not known many babies."

Bernard caught hold of the coffee table and picked up a spoon that was lying there. First he tasted it carefully, then he pushed it down his shorts inside his diaper and turned and looked toward the window.

"You know what he is thinking?" Pinky asked Katya.

"Yes." She smiled again, more broadly this time.

Bernard measured the distance from where he was to the window.

He let go of the coffee table. He took a step and stopped and gazed around himself in surprise.

"He is walking!" Katya exclaimed.

"It's his first time," Pinky whispered.

They held their breaths and watched him. Now he took several very fast jerky little steps, apparently hoping that if he moved fast enough, he would keep himself upright, but by the fourth or fifth step he was walking at such a tipped-forward angle, he soon lost his balance and toppled into the compulink screen, banging his chin and biting into his own upper lip with his bottom teeth.

Katya started forward, but Pinky put out her arm and held her back. Katya looked at her and sat down. The two women did not move. Each felt the other sitting there not moving, watching Bernard to see what he would do.

He should have been howling, but he was not. He gave one small whimper, then snuffled and snorted and shook his head clumsily, like a bear cub. He looked around himself, clearly only interested in trying to figure out how he'd gotten so quickly from up there to down here. A trickle of blood was running down his chin, but he did not appear to realize this. He thought the situation over and then pulled himself up on the stand that held the screen and started tottering again toward the windowsill.

Katya went into the kitchen and brought back a wet cloth. She looked at Pinky, who nodded. Katya carefully cleaned off the baby's lip and chin. Then she sat back down next to Pinky.

"When was he born, exactly?" Pinky asked.

"His birthday, October three."

"Yes, that's about what the doctor guessed. He's a little young to be walking."

They both watched him proudly for a while.

"Last week," Pinky said, "he got a very big piece of glass stuck all the way through his wrist. He almost died." She pointed at the gauze bandage still taped around his wrist.

Katya gazed at her without comment.

"He hardly cried at all. At the hospital the doctor said he had never seen a baby with such a high pain tolerance. He asked me a lot of questions I didn't know the answer to."

Katya was watching Bernard, who after several tumbles had landed himself, at last, at the windowsill. He fished around in his diaper and brought out the spoon.

"Did your sister have any trouble with her pregnancy or the birth?"

"No."

"What can you tell me about it?"

"We are in the Chinese restaurant when she has her first pain. We are waiting for such short time and the pains begin to come very sharp, very quick. I call for the taxi. This taxi driver is a coward and afraid he will have to stop his car and help me catch the baby. So he goes across every red light. In hospital they put her in the room and leave us. They do not believe he is coming so fast, but my sister holds my hand and calls upon my mother. When Andre's head is coming, I yell for the doctor, but no one comes. My sister pushes. There are his shoulders. I put out my hands to hold his head and there is big wave of water rushing at me. My dress is all wet in blood and water and there is very strange smell, like wet mud. In my hands is lying Andre very quiet. His eyes are looking at me. Then come many doctors and nurses and someone takes him away, but he is still looking at me, very happy. He makes a noise like a small horse passing wind. The doctor he hits Andre on his feet to make him cry. But Andre does not cry. He was even happy on the first day."

Pinky was so pleased to hear this story. She closed her eyes and inserted herself there in the room with Katya and Marina and the blood and that weird muddy earthy smell that she remembered very well.

When she opened her eyes, Bernard was sliding the stolen spoon over the windowsill and out into the air. It immediately dropped from sight and vanished. "Brookafal!"

"Listen, was it possible your sister took drugs or anything? Something that might have affected his brain or his pain tolerance?"

Katya looked at her indignantly.

"The doctor asked me this," Pinky explained sheepishly.

"No. Never."

"Did she drink alcohol? Wine, beer?"

Katya shook her head angrily. "No, no. My sister was very strict in her ways."

Bernard, having accomplished the task of making the spoon disappear from sight, turned and crowed at them with his wide rosy smile.

"He is so contented and pleased with everything. It is . . . almost unnatural."

Katya shrugged. "I said this same thing to my sister. But she said our grandfather was just like this."

"Oh, yes? Was he? Was he? That is so good to know. What about your sister? Was she a lighthearted sort of person? Please tell me a little about what she was like."

Katya thought about it and then answered carefully, "It is hard to know how Marina would be if our life was different. But she is too shy and serious and full of feeling about what is happening in our country. Always she is worrying about everyone and their children and their old people. This is why she thinks she is going to be a doctor. She is the first one born and too full of conscience. Maybe this is the fault of our parents. But after they are murdered she is more full of these things even than before. She is very hard with herself and she is very hard with me and makes me study and study and so I will get myself ready to take the chances that come in the world. I know this is right, but it does not fill me with love for her. Our time here in this country is filled from every morning till night with working.

"But then, one day, I see that something is different. My sister is more dreamy and not looking at me so much. She is looking at something invisible in the air. In a few weeks I see she is pregnant. I cannot ask her, of course, where does this baby come from, or she will be very angry with me, but now things are better here because she is laughing sometimes and she is always telling me, how happy this baby will be. 'Too late for you and me,' she says, 'but this one will remember his true secret heart that everyone else has forgotten.'

"When I question her how she knows how the baby will be, she laughs and says it is because of our grandfather and because of the mice. I think she is mad, but I am trying not to worry. In our family I have seen sometimes how to be pregnant makes a woman grow strange and then she is all right again when the baby comes." Katya fell silent and seemed to be thinking of her crazy sister.

"So, was she all right again when the baby came?"

Katya frowned and then she looked at Bernard. "I don't know. Everything was so different when Andre came. She was so busy watching over him. And somehow, he was just as she said."

"What about the father? Do you know anything about his father?"

Katya looked at her oddly and then shrugged. "I never meet Andre's father."

"Do you have a picture? Of your sister?"

When Katya took one down from the wall and brought it over, Pinky was not particularly startled to see how the woman in the photo rested her cheek in her hand and stared straight into the eye of the beholder in just the same way the tea-drinking woman in her painting did.

When Pinky arrived home with Bernard, Arthur was waiting for them on the front steps. What was remarkable was that he was not only delighted to have the baby back in his arms, he seemed to be looking at her, too, in an unusual way, as if she had been gone for weeks instead of just a few hours. She showed him the blue shirt she had bought and Arthur actually praised it. Pinky was filled with gratitude for her good fortune. Then Arthur said she'd better go out to the back because Teddy was all worked up about something.

She found him under the birch tree. He had been crying.

"What is it, my little Creamsicle? Why are you sad?"

"It's gone."

"What's gone?"

"My invisibility formula. It disappeared."

"Oh, no, Teddy, you probably just misplaced it. Where did you have it last?"

"I had it where I always had it," he said to her angrily. "On my laboratory table."

She drew in a breath. "In the sunroom where that big mess was?" she asked.

"Yes." He gazed up at her and must have seen how flushed and stricken her face looked.

"It's okay, Mom. There's nothing you could have done. I just didn't think about it, how if I finally got it right, of course the formula and the dish would disappear, too. I patted everywhere with my hands, but it's completely gone." He looked out at the clear bright afternoon grimly, as if the sky were dark and full of rain and hail and off in the distance there was a tornado planning to make its way right through this backyard, and as if he knew he was the one who was going to have to lead everyone to safety.

13. Red Wine

A week later, on Sunday morning, Pinky looked out the front window and saw Celia Pitsacado walking by carrying a salmon-colored silk parasol. Celia was their neighbor on the left and she had already leaned over the fence several times with a cigarette dangling out of her mouth to tell Pinky and Teddy a series of stories about the days of her high-heeled youth, how she had met the love of her life who she could never marry because he was married to someone else, how they had had a child anyway and her lover had kept two households, how she lived with this because she wasn't the jealous sort (live and let live was her motto), how their son, Johnny, however, was a hopeless bum (he was the one out on the front stoop with the paper bag) and she had done everything for him, but it was no use. It must be some kind of tainted blood in the genes. But things could always be worse, she said. If you wanted to cultivate a positive attitude you needed to keep this right up there in the front row of your mind.

As she went by this morning, Pinky tapped on the window and waved to her. Celia waved back and continued down the street.

Teddy changed into shorts and a white T-shirt and went out front and fixed himself there as solid and leafless as an old tree stump. The sky was hot and thin, the back of his ears itched, and there was somewhere nearby a faint, persistent ringing of bells. The slow Sunday morning river of baby strollers and people going to the corner for the paper, meandered past him without a second glance.

His life, he saw, was pretty much over.

He sat on the steps for what amounted to several years, until he had perfectly memorized the dull solid, rhythm of the old ladies and the autoprams and the dog walkers, and until he knew that he was doomed to loneliness and failure.

Then, from the end of the block, he felt rather than saw a disturbance in the molecules, a windchill, a reshuffling of the cards.

In a moment, Orlando stood in front of him, blocking the view, one foot on the ground, one foot on the skateboard. He didn't say anything.

Teddy noted that he wasn't wearing his bright red contact lenses today, so his eyes were a regular brown. He was carrying a watergun. It was a small watergun, certainly not the same deluxe model as the one Teddy had that was still sitting on top of the refrigerator, but he carried it with unquestionable authority.

Orlando scratched at a mosquito bite on his arm, then, with a practiced gesture, removed the gun from his shoulder and shot it up into the top of the crabapple tree. In a moment a cool splatter of water fell back down upon their heads and faces.

"So where's yours?"

There was an odd color around this boy, Teddy saw, golden and yet dark on the underside, like a storm traveling off.

"It's on top of the refrigerator."

"Well, why don't you go get it?"

Why? Teddy considered it and then, when he looked down, lo and behold, there was a Y-shaped crack in the sidewalk. It wasn't a perfect Y, but a Y with a diamond shape on the end of one of its arms. He considered it slowly. Why? Y? A bee floated down out of the crabapple tree and he lifted his head sharply. The bee zigzagged off. Another bee went by. He wondered if bees stung other bees. Then he wondered if bees kissed other bees.

He looked at Orlando. Then he rose and went into the house as quietly as moonlight coming in the window at midnight. There wasn't a sound. The baby must be napping.

He lifted a kitchen chair up and carried it over to the refrigerator so that it wouldn't scrape across the floor. Then he climbed up and brought the watergun down. He put the box on the table and cautiously opened the end flap and slipped the poison green instrument of destruction out and laid it on the table. Then he carefully replaced the flap on the box, carried it over to the chair, and put the box back on top of the refrigerator.

He looked around cautiously, hugged the big gun to his chest, and slipped back through the living room and out the front door.

Orlando was sitting on the front steps waiting for him. "Did you fill it?"

Teddy shook his head.

"Here, let me show you."

But Teddy did not want his assistance.

He unscrewed the detachable tank and filled it up at the spigot by the side of the house.

When it was filled and back on the gun, the gun was very heavy, but he lifted it awkwardly and pumped it three times and shot it into the air. The arc of water went high, high, high, then came pattering down around them in a golden shower.

"Flip on the audio switch."

Teddy fumbled around and then pressed it—a small red button on the side. The gun emitted a loud high-pitched beeping sound like a fire engine backing up. When he pressed it again, it squealed like a pig being slaughtered.

"That's really prime," Orlando said.

Teddy switched the audio off. He flipped another switch and pulled the trigger and the gun shot out a great cloud of bubbles.

"Shoot 'em! Shoot 'em!" Orlando blasted away at them with his gun and when Teddy was able to figure out how to reset his, he shot at the bubbles, too. It was very satisfying.

When the bubbles were gone, there was a silence. "Now what we do," Orlando said in a soft voice, "is we wait for toxomutants."

"What?"

"Toxomutants. We watch for them here, behind this hedge."

And the two of them crawled in behind the hedge and hunkered down.

The light in here was many shades of green and tasted of dust and the rankly sweet little blossoms that grew along the outward side of the hedge.

"What's a toxomutant? What's it look like?" Teddy whispered.

"Hard to tell. There's all kinds of mutations in this world and some are good and some are bad. The toxomutants are bad. They have evil powers that hurt other people. Sometimes they look strange and different. But sometimes they look just like other people. The difference is on the inside, in the blood. You have to stay alert. Keep your eyes open. See? There's one now!"

Teddy looked and saw Susan Edelman come around the side of her house with a large watering can.

"That's Mrs. Edelman."

Orlando nodded. "That's right. A toxomutant."

"She has evil powers?"

"She has poison toad skin. It secretes acid. If she touches you, your own skin just falls right off."

They both contemplated her for a few moments as she bent over the urn of geraniums. "Let's give it to her," Orlando said. "Just once. In the butt. But lie very still. She won't be able to see us from where she is. When I count to three."

Orlando counted very softly to three and then they both shot their guns in her direction. The two streams of water had to make their way through the hedge and then through the tops of a patch of bright red salvia plants before they could reach Susan. By the time the water reached her, the power of the stream was somewhat dissipated and instead of hitting her butt, it hit her ankles. Susan looked down at her legs in puzzlement. She touched them and felt the wetness there and then looked up at the sky. She checked the bottom of the watering can for leaks, then went back to the geraniums.

The boys shot at her again, choking back their laughter.

She looked at the sky, then turned slowly around in their direction. Teddy closed his eyes, but he felt her in the itchy hairs at the back of his neck.

She seemed to look right through the hedge, right at them, he was sure of it, but she didn't say or do anything, only stared in their direction for a moment, then finished watering her geraniums. When she was done, she turned and went back where she had come from.

They breathed a sigh, both together, at the same moment.

"Look! Here comes another one," Orlando whispered.

Teddy looked and there was the small dog that had eaten the egg they had fried in the street. Its hair was growing back in little gray spikes. You could see that eventually the hair would probably cover most of the dog's eyes and legs and it would look like a walking frying pan scrubber, the kind Teddy's mother kept by her sink. It was headed right toward them.

"Shoot him! Shoot him, quick!"

Teddy lifted the gun again and together they soaked the little dog, which skittered sideways on the sidewalk, then stopped and shook itself vigorously and matter-of-factly, as if this kind of thing happened to it all the time. It looked around with interest, but as if it weren't really expecting an explanation, and then took off in a different direction.

"That was close," Orlando said.

"Why? What would have happened? What's his power?"

"Radioactive eyes. He's got radioactive eyes. He can bore holes through steel with them. You don't want him looking at you."

Suddenly there was a cry from the window behind them.

"Eee! Eeee!"

They turned and there was Bernard, fresh from his nap, standing on the sofa banging at the screen.

"What's he wearing?" Orlando asked with some disapproval.

"Nothing," Teddy said. "As soon as my mother puts a diaper on him, he rips it right off."

"He's your brother?"

Teddy shrugged.

"How ya doin', Nerfball?" Orlando called out to him.

Bernard, delighted at being addressed, bounced up and down on the sofa.

"That don't look right. Your mother oughta put some clothes on him."

"He's one of those bad mutants," Teddy said slowly.

"Yeah?"

"I don't think he's human."

"Yeah?"

"He wrecks stuff. He wrecks stuff all the time. And he sings. I don't know what his power is yet, but I know he's got one."

"Looks like a mutant to me," Orlando said. He looked at Teddy and they lifted their guns and shot a long hard stream of water right in through the window and hit the baby square in the face.

The baby, water running down his dark hair in little rivulets, stared out at them in shock and surprise.

"You gotta know how to keep these little shitballs in line," Orlando said.

But now Bernard let out a scream of impatient delight.

Teddy turned and saw his father jogging toward them from the park.

"Get down," he whispered fiercely and pushed Orlando flat on the ground, with his hand conveying the message that they must not move, which he wanted desperately to do. He wanted desperately to leap up and go fleeing down the block with the gun in his hands, but he knew that staying right here where he was, was really the safest thing to do. For his father would never notice them lying here in the shadows because his father listened carefully to people and he saw many things, but what he saw were inside things, things he was thinking about or trying to figure out. He didn't see what was on the outside. He often walked right by people he knew on the street, or was unable to find the butter right on the top shelf in the middle of the refrigerator, and he could easily fail to notice two boys with large waterguns hiding behind the hedge in front of his house.

And this would have been exactly what would have happened had Orlando not found it necessary to reach over and scratch at his mosquito bite, and in so doing, accidentally jammed his elbow into Teddy's side, causing Teddy's grip to loosen on the watergun. The gun fell with a little clunk to the ground just as Arthur reached the top of the front steps, and even then, he probably would not have done more than look quizzically behind him. However, Teddy, in his rush to pick up the fallen gun before it could be seen, accidentally activated the pig-squealing button.

Arthur stopped where he was and then walked down the steps, peering into the hedge. In later years, when Teddy recalled this moment, it was always difficult to explain to himself how his father could possibly have grown so large, not, in this case, in an outside-peering-down-at-them sort of way, but in way where he seemed to fill Teddy from the inside, darkening the vision in one eye.

By the time his sight had cleared, his father had gently removed the gun from his grasp and was now nodding in a not-unfriendly way at Orlando. Orlando, without expression, nodded back at him, and then shouldered his gun and continued on down the sidewalk on his skateboard.

Oedipus slept most of the morning away in the shadows next to Susan Edelman's back patio. He was a master of disguise and he curled himself up to look just like one of the empty clay pots she had stacked up there. She did not notice him at all as she went in and out with her watering can and her pruning shears.

At around noon, smelling something lovely and unfamiliar—Susan's Sunday pot roast—he stretched and noted that she had left her back screen door ajar. He padded inside and looked around curiously. The kitchen was too tidy and clean for his taste, everything Formica and polished, no pots with little bits of food left in them standing about, but he lifted his nose and followed the path of the meat smell so clearly laid out in front of him. In a few moments he was disappointed to find himself coming right up against one of those hot walls he was always hitting in Pinky's kitchen.

However, being both philosophical and unquenchably curious in the manner of all his forefathers, who had managed to survive long enough to reproduce and pass their genes along to him, he drew in one last breath of pot roast and then turned and headed into the dark, carpeted interior of the house, all his senses alert.

In the next room was a man sitting in a chair. The man, very still in the dim light, did not notice Oedipus, did not look up as Oedipus passed over the thick carpet and came to a stop under the heavy mahogany table and gazed up at its underside as if he were gazing up at the ceiling of a cathedral. The cat rubbed the side of his face and body against the heavy carved table leg, leaving a scent the man could not smell, and then, pausing only briefly to stare again at the man, passed forward into the next room.

In the next room there was an even bigger table and coming from the center of the table a familiar fragrance. Oedipus jumped onto a chair and then stood with his paws on the edge of the great shiny swimming surface and gazed into its middle distance at the glass bowl holding the bunch of pink-and-crimson-faced roses. He stared at them for a moment, but then jumped down and passed into the next room.

In the next room, which was the one that faced the street, there was a yellow stream of sunlight that had managed, triumphantly, to find its way through an unnoticed crack in the bottle-green drapes, and hanging in this sunlight was a white wire box, and sitting on an unnaturally round and smooth branch suspended through the middle of the box was a sight that stopped Oedipus right in his tracks.

It was one of those two-footed flappers that drove him so wild with desire. He loved the delicious way their little bones cracked. Unlike the man and the roses, this creature stared at him attentively, first through its right eye, then through its left. Then it sidled over to one side of its cage where it hoped less of itself could be seen. Oedipus sat down. He measured the various angles and distances. His tail twitched with the effort of composing his natural energies in the direction he needed to go. Then slowly he flattened himself against the floor and crept forward. The bird, missing none of this, looked around and began sidling rapidly from side to side along its perch, perhaps on the theory that a moving target would be harder to take down.

Oedipus slid forward more quickly. He looked neither to the right nor to the left and heard nothing of the sounds of the street outside nor anything that might have been happening in the house behind him. There was a crackling in the air, an electrical charge, perhaps generated by a gathering in close of all the spirits of all the cats who had preceded him. He paid them no heed, however, and if they tried to warn him to look behind him, he failed to hear their voices. So when a strange and circular darkness came rushing down over his head a moment later, he was taken completely by surprise.

Early in the evening, Pinky looked out the front window and saw Celia Pitsacado returning home. She looked pleased with herself, although her footing was a little unsure, the back straps of her shoes having been pushed down in the manner of one who has worked up a blister or two. Pinky also saw, to her astonishment, that her parasol was now green. Pinky knew this transformation must be a sign of some sort and she was trying to figure out what it might mean when Arthur came up behind her and asked her what she was looking at. Startled, she turned around and faced him.

"N-nothing," she stammered.

He looked at her curiously. "Where's the baby?" he asked her at last.

She nodded toward the upstairs. "He fell asleep."

"And Teddy?"

"He slunk by me about half an hour ago. He had one of those little black clouds following right behind him. I guess he's still upset about his formula."

"Sit down here for a minute, Pinky," he said hoarsely. "Let's talk a little."

She gave him a radiant smile and sat down on the sofa and drew him next to her. "Arthur," she said, and touched his face. "You seem to be feeling so much better lately." She waited for him to speak, but he couldn't seem to figure out where to begin. For a brief moment she imagined that he was going to say he loved her.

"Listen, I want to talk to you about the baby."

She smiled again, not really disappointed, knowing that most of the time between people was spent in separateness, and that you had to wait around in the darkness with great patience and faith for those brief moments on which everything else depends, when the match strikes the box and there is a little sputter of light.

"Yes, the baby. He's really helping you lighten up, I think."

"I think so, too," he said simply. "But what I wanted to talk to you about was Marina."

"I know all about Marina."

"You do?" he said, looking at her uncertainly.

The doorbell rang and, startled, they looked out the front window and saw Fran standing on the front stoop. "Let me in." She waved to them. "Once you let me in, you can ignore me, if you want. I've really only come to see your children."

Pinky got up and let her in and was examining her beautiful blue silk sundress when the doorbell rang again. It was Maury. He was damp and shiny with sweat, and wearing nylon running shorts and a white singlet.

"I ran down. Across the bridge. I thought I'd just drop in and see the children."

Pinky looked at them and then at Arthur triumphantly. "You'll both stay for dinner," she commanded. And I will be the lightning rod of your destiny, she thought.

Fran had brought with her, as a gift for the children, a lava lamp. Maury had in his backpack another container of sprouts and a wooden whistle that made a sound just like a train going by in the distance.

They plugged in the lamp and watched as the purple puddle of lava heated up and began slowly and eerily to stretch and curve itself into snakes and question marks, to eject from its main body little blobs that shaped themselves into new balls and little planets that floated off in slow motion to the far corner of the lamp and then came back and rejoined up with the parent blob.

Pinky watched them. It appeared to her that Fran and Maury stood carefully apart, possibly not really aware of how electrically riveted they were in their consciousness of each other.

Pinky suddenly remembered one of the supposed properties of her grandmother's cordial. This would be the perfect occasion, she thought happily.

"My God," Arthur sighed, staring into the lava, "where did you dig up this antique?"

Pinky was a little surprised to see that Bernard, who had been awakened from his nap by all the noise, did not seem much interested in the lamp. He examined its antics briefly with his head tipped to the side, then went back to hunting through the house for something that he had apparently lost. He toddled and crawled around in an unself-consciously pantless condition, peering under the sofa and table, lifting up the sofa cushions, and chattering busily to himself.

Teddy, on the other hand, who had come in from the backyard and stared at all of them without a word, turned his total attention onto the lava lamp as soon as he spotted it. He walked around and around the table and examined the lamp from every angle, trying to see into it from the top, tapping at the glass nervously with his fingers.

"What *is* that stuff?" he asked at last in a hushed voice.

In here the blinds had been drawn against the heat and only a few fine zebra stripes of light managed to slip in. The rest of the room was in dusky languorous shadow. The lava lamp did a slow purple turn. The baby's bottom flashed white as he squatted down and peered under the table.

"This is a little blob that has gotten separated from the Big Mother Blob," Maury said. "It is working on the same project that all the rest of us are working on. It's trying to find its way home again."

"I'm not working on that project," Fran said. "I'm working on the separation-individuation thing. It's the Let Me Grow Up Already and Let My Mother Drive Somebody Else Nuts Project."

"That's part of the same project." Maury laughed.

"You know what this is?" Pinky said, lightly caressing the lava lamp. "This is what a genie looks like when he's inside the bottle waiting, waiting, waiting for years and centuries for someone to take the stopper out."

Arthur put his hand on Teddy's shoulder. "Actually, what's inside there are two colloidal liquids with two very different specific gravities. When you heat them up, one separates out and lifts up more quickly than the other. It moves away from the source of the heat and when it gets far enough away it begins to cool off and then it falls slowly back down towards the source of the heat, where the cycle will begin all over again."

Pinky looked fondly at Arthur. He had on his best stone face and there was his handsomeness that was the same intent and comical handsomeness he had had when she first spotted him. It was an illusion, she knew now, the same illusion that all lovers are deluded by, the sum of several disparate parts that didn't really hold together after you had been staring at someone for several years, but now here it was again for a moment, and she leaned forward and kissed him lightly between the eyes. He did not appear at first to notice what she had done, but then he reached up and brushed abstractedly at the spot where the kiss had landed as if he were brushing away a shadow.

He was so predictable, she thought happily.

With a little grimace, Teddy took one last look at the lamp and slipped out silently from under his father's hand and headed for the back door.

Bernard had been busy pulling all of the newspapers out of the newspaper basket and was now crumpling them up and arranging them into a nestlike structure around himself as if he were a large mouse or hamster. As his brother exited to the outside, he looked up alertly and pulled himself to a standing position and toddled over to the back door and demanded to be let out also.

"Come on," Pinky said. "Everyone outside. I'm making grilled tuna. We need to set the table. Bring the tamari. Help me carry stuff. You eat fish, don't you, Maury?"

"Well, it depends," Maury replied tranquilly as they stepped out into the still evening. "Everything must be eaten in the right time and place. Nature intends for certain foods to be eaten in winter, others in summer. Some are meant to be eaten when we're ill and some when we're getting ready to run a race. You have to pay attention to your insides and your outside. You can't just shove anything and everything into your mouth."

"I *knew* I must be doing something wrong," Fran said.

"Come on," Pinky urged them. "You guys move the picnic table under the tree. I have something very special I want Fran and Maury to try."

When the table was moved and the cups and plates were set down, Pinky held up the old brown bottle. "My grandmother's cherry cordial. This stuff was famous all over Scranton. Strangers used to come knocking at the door offering her money, but she would never sell it. Teddy found this in the back of the pantry. I believe it's the last remaining bottle. Arthur, I'm not giving you any, because it's got a spice in it I know you don't like. You can have some of the Merlot instead." She poured him a glass of wine and then, very carefully, she poured out three glasses of her grandmother's cordial. She gave one to Maury, one to Fran, and one to herself. She didn't plan to drink any. This was a special occasion and from the little she remembered of her grandmother's stories, she thought it might be wiser for only the two friends to enjoy the honor.

Maury sniffed at it curiously. "Interesting," he pronounced. Then he lifted his glass. "L'chayim."

Pinky was about to lift her glass as well when she saw, to her horror, Teddy in the back of the yard, brandishing a long scratchy-looking stick and poking Bernard in the chest with it.

"Wait!" she yelled to everybody. "Don't drink yet." She made sure they put their glasses down, then she hurried to the back of the little yard, where Bernard was gazing mildly into Teddy's ferocious face.

"Chickpea!" she said in horror, divesting Teddy of the stick. "What are you doing?"

"He's bothering me. He's bothering me on purpose. I'm working here."

She crouched down and took his hand and kissed it. "He just wants to see what you're doing, sweetie. That's the way little people learn things."

Teddy wiped the kissed hand on the back of his shorts. "Let him learn things from somebody else."

Pinky said, "Hey, no wiping off of kisses. They're full of vitamins. It stunts your growth when you wipe off kisses. Look at your father."

Teddy eyed her disdainfully. "Can I have my stick back?"

"If you promise not to poke anybody with it."

"Fine."

Pinky gave him back the stick and scooped up Bernard and went back to the table.

"I have sprouts for you, Bernard," Maury said to Bernard.

Maury lifted the green cardboard container of stringy seedlings and Bernard, realizing what it was, wriggled from Pinky's arms and rushed forward across the grass to him.

Maury laughed. "He always looks as if he just finished mainlining something. As if he knew that any second now the big rush was going to hit. He's a gifted child. I wonder if it comes from the father's or the mother's side," he mused slyly. "Or maybe it's just a spontaneous generation thing?"

"He takes after me," Pinky said excitedly. "After me and his grandfather!"

Fran turned toward her and blinked. "But you're not related, Pinky. You know that."

"Of course we're related. Or we're going to be related very soon. You think it's just genes that make people into relations? That's crazy. What about breathing the same oxygen for a few years? I mean, you breathe the air into your body and then you breathe it out and then whoever you're living with breathes that same oxygen in. You don't think you're constantly passing lots of little microscopic bits of yourselves back and forth that way? And what about food? Some lady who says she's your mother feeds everybody in the family the same meat loaf every Friday. Of course you all start to look alike and fart alike. It's only natural. And what about germs? Everybody knows that germs pass a lot of information into people's bodies. I get a cold and I give it to Arthur and Arthur gives it to Teddy. Well, of course this brings us closer together, how could it not? There're a million different things that happen inside a family that make people related."

Maury said to Pinky, "I know what you mean, I think. But I see it differently. It's not that people become related after the fact, it's that they have simply been related all along—bound together by a past connection or obligation or unfinished business—something that occurred way before their parents got into the chromosomal act. I think it's possible that the two people can miss knowing this, but often, after they have been hanging around together for a while, the smoke clears and some aspect of the truth reveals itself and the people have a chance at working things through—taking care of business, as it were."

Fran laughed impatiently. "No matter where it comes from, this little guy is very unusual. Almost nothing seems to frighten him and he hardly ever cries when he gets hurt. He must have a higher natural endorphin level than most people. I've been doing a little research and I think he's just one of those lucky ones on the high end of the scale. I wonder if it will affect his learning."

"Yow!" Bernard yelled as he reached Maury's knobby knees and tried to grab the sprouts.

"You think his endorphin level might affect his intelligence?" Arthur asked anxiously.

The baby grabbed the container of sprouts and held them very close to his face. He inhaled deeply and waited.

Fran said, "I don't know if anybody knows much about this stuff yet. It seems to me common sense that fear and pain must teach us a lot in the early years. But maybe they also stop us from developing other parts of ourselves as well. Maybe a person with very little of those things might develop into someone with completely unique gifts."

"But I'm sure you've got to have them to get started on moral development," Arthur said morosely. He leaned over and ran a finger down the line of the baby's cheek. "He'll become an arsonist or an ax murderer."

The baby smiled, but did not take his eyes off the sprouts. His face was almost, but not quite, touching them.

"A serial rapist," Maury said, considering.

It seemed to Pinky that all distances between all points in this yard had gotten unaccountably smaller. The distance between Fran and Maury was almost nothing.

"A sociopath," Fran said. "Like those guys I work with at the hospital."

"And are they a happy-go-lucky bunch?" Arthur asked.

But nobody answered.

Bernard pulled a bunch of sprouts out of the carton and rubbed them against his cheek. Then he took off toward the back corner, where Teddy was examining the undersides of some old discarded bricks.

Pinky saw that the moment had arrived. "A toast to them all!" she said and lifted her glass. She waited for everyone else to follow. She pretended to sip her cordial, but only wet her lips. There was, and she remembered it now, a strong fragrance of radishes mixed in with the cherries. What she was hoping was that Fran and Maury would look at each other as they drank.

"To us all," Maury said cheerfully and took a sip. He blinked as if a little surprised by the flavor. Pinky watched him closely. His eyes were on Fran.

Fran raised her glass to her mouth, but at this moment her pocket-link chimed in.

Fran stopped her glass in midair and sighed. "It's my mother," she said.

"Don't answer it," Pinky suggested anxiously.

But Fran put her glass down, reached into her bag, and pulled the little phone out. "I'm going to take this inside," she said. She rose and went into the house.

Pinky saw Maury follow Fran with his eyes as he took another sip of the cordial. "This has quite a little zip to it," he said.

In the silence that followed while they all waited for Fran to re-emerge, Pinky set Maury to chopping onions. She snapped the beans. After a few snaps, she looked up and happened to see the plain gray bird sitting on top of the ladder again.

"Why *is* that ladder there?" Pinky asked.

"It's to make it easier for the angels to come down and drop off the babies," Maury said.

"It's a ladder for hanging laundry lines," Arthur corrected him. "I can't believe you didn't realize that, Pinky. You hang a rope on a pulley from one end, and hang the other end at your window, so you can put your laundry out to dry. Look next door. The Edelmans have it all set up."

Pinky looked and saw that he was right. "How wonderful!" she exclaimed. "Why didn't you tell me before? We need to get that set up right away. I love laundry that's dried in the sun the best, don't you, Maury?"

Maury nodded. "Absolutely."

"You can bring your laundry down here once it's working, and I'll dry it for you."

Before he could reply to this offer, Fran returned. She threw herself into the white plastic lawn chair with a groan.

Pinky put her glass back in her hand. "Drink. I'm sure you need it."

Fran just stared at the drink.

Maury looked up from the onions. Large tears ran down his cheeks. "What did she want?"

"She wanted to tell me what Elsie had to say about the cemetery plot."

"What cemetery plot?" Arthur asked.

"And who's Elsie?" Maury asked.

Fran sniffed at her cordial, but still didn't drink. "Elsie used to be my father's accountant. But last year my father came to my mother and said he wanted a divorce so that he could marry her. My mother isn't well known for her generosity or self-control, but she responded very uncharacteristically. She said she understood, that people changed. The concept of 'forever,' particularly in marriage, should certainly be discarded. People needed to shed their old skins from time to time or they would suffocate. This was going to be a growth opportunity for everybody. When she spoke about Elsie, she spoke of her as if she were a sister.

"She pretty much let him have whatever he wanted in the settlement. But I knew that whatever it was that my mother was up to, conscious or unconscious, it didn't bode well for my father. My mother has spent her entire adult life focused on wearing my father and me down to little stumps. People need their little projects. I couldn't see my mother giving hers up, and on the one occasion when the four of us were together in one room I saw my mother lift her foot and sniff like she smelled dog shit. I don't think Elsie saw this, but I know my father did.

"It's also been interesting to observe that, although my mother has given the appearance of being perfectly at ease with all that's happening, somehow the divorce has still not gone through. One little detail or another gets in the way and seems to hold things up. But last week my father called me and said he thought everything would be resolved by the end of the month. My mother called me the next day and asked me if I'd like to go for a little drive in the country with her. We could take a picnic. It's rarely worth the labor to try to worm my way out of one of her invitations, so I went to Zabar's and got some nice fruit and cheese and stuff and we got in her car and drove out towards Long Island. After about an hour, she pulled into this cemetery, looked at me from the corner of her eye, and began to drive slowly up this hill through these great big trees that looked about a hundred years old. When she got to the top of the hill and stopped the car, I said to her that this was not exactly my idea of a drive in the country. She gave me the same withering look she always gives me, like she can't believe I'm the one who's her kid instead of some other undeformed person, and dragged the picnic basket out of the car and started down the other side of the hill through the gravestones."

Fran paused and put her untasted cordial down on the table. "I don't like cemeteries. This was a beautiful cemetery, but I don't like the things."

"Don't you?" asked Maury. "You should just think of them as being sort of recycling centers. As a place where you stop on the big journey, where you get to rest for a moment before you get re-formed into an oak tree or a dog or a basketball, or whatever you're going to be next. I always enjoy my little vacations there."

"Cemeteries are where the worms eat their way through your eyeballs, take a rest, and then eat your brains," Fran said.

"Well, yes, of course, that, too," he agreed.

Pinky stared fixedly at Fran's glass, trying to draw her attention to it.

"So did you get out of the car?" Arthur asked.

Fran sighed again. "Well, of course. Just like I was this great hulking pimply twelve-year-old, and then I tromped down the hill after her."

"And?" Maury asked.

"She stopped under a tree at a little grassy rectangle. She opened up the picnic basket and spread out the checked cloth and sat down and started to eat.

"I wasn't all that hungry, but I could see she had something on her mind, so I sat down and I nibbled at some bread and waited. I admit it was a beautiful spot. There was actually a little stream burbling somewhere nearby and way down at the bottom of the hill you could get a glimpse of the Sound. After she finished eating, my mother announced that she had bought this plot as a gift for Elsie's birthday, which was coming up soon. She asked me if I thought Elsie would like it.

"It was hard to know what to say. She told me that she thought it was a unique gift, but practical, too.

"I asked her if she had gotten my dad one also, but she just shrugged. She said it wasn't *his* birthday. I decided I'd be much better off not making any further comments, so we ate a little more and then I took her home. When she got out of the car, she told me she was going to have the deed hand-delivered on Elsie's birthday."

"And?" Arthur asked.

Fran picked up her glass again, then seemed to think better of it and put it back down. "And yesterday was Elsie's birthday. Elsie called her today and my mother wanted to report what had happened."

Everybody waited.

Fran looked around at them. "Elsie was outraged. She called my mother a fat, devious cow. She said she knew perfectly well what was going on here and that she had manipulated and tormented my father for thirty-three years with this sort of demented warfare, but she wasn't having any part of it. She said that she planned to live to a very old age like her mother and her grandmother and that when she died she was going to have her ashes scattered in the Botanic Gardens and that she was going to give the deed to the plot to her Uncle Claremont who was ninety-seven and on his last legs."

"And what did your mother say to that?" Pinky asked.

"My mother told her that it was never a good idea to bury someone in a spot that wasn't meant for them and she recommended to Elsie that she go and take a look at how beautiful the place was before she made any rash decisions."

"And?" Pinky asked.

"Elsie hung up on her. My mother sounded very pleased."

Teddy, who had been drawing slowly closer and closer to this conversation, now came over and put his petri dish down on the table and looked curiously at his godmother. "What I don't understand," Teddy said, "is why, when you're dead, everything doesn't just look black."

Everyone stared at him. His knees, Pinky noted with affection, were covered with dirt.

"I mean, if you're dead and you can't see anything, then why doesn't everything just look black?"

Arthur smiled. "It's hard to imagine, isn't it? But if you can't see anything, then you're not seeing black or white or anything at all."

Pinky was puzzled by the anger with which he looked at his father. "But blind people can't see and they see black."

"That's different, though. Blind people are alive and conscious and they can sometimes see or describe various amounts of light and dark. Though, if they've been blind since birth, I don't know what, if anything, they understand they're seeing."

"No, listen, Peachblossom, when you're dead you go back to where you were before you were born and you're part of everything—the wind and the trees and the ants and the stars—and you don't hear things or see things anymore. You just are."

Now he turned toward her and stared at her irritably, and after a minute he said, "Stop calling me those stupid names."

She had, of course, always known in a dim sort of way that this moment was bound to arrive, but that it should arrive here, now, so soon, did not seem possible. She went over to Teddy and hunkered down in front of him, half laughing, half crying, and grabbed him around the waist. Unable to stop herself, she exclaimed, "But Teapot, but Periwinkle, my own true Blueberry Child, I just call you those names so you don't get lost in the woods, so you know it's really me and you don't get mixed up and go wandering off with somebody else's mother."

"Cut it out, Mom." And he wiggled out of her grasp as easily as if he had turned himself from a boy into a speckled trout right there in her arms.

She watched him swim away and almost, but not quite, missed the fact that at this moment Maury reached over and lightly touched the back of Fran's hand. Fran, she thought, did not even look up. "Try that cordial," Pinky urged her. "It's really delicious."

"PINKY!" Arthur said sharply. What was it? She looked around. The air was going into that long half-light of a summer evening. The light-hued flowers—the impatiens, the white roses and petunias—began to stand forth, while the others receded into shadow. Arthur rose and hurried over to Bernard, who was in that back corner again, by the laundry ladder. He was squawking and shaking his hand. Arthur hunkered down and caught hold of him.

"Come here, Pinky. Come here and see this." He had that peremptory worrywart tone in his voice that he had when he was afraid, when he was sure that the world had at last come to an end and he wanted her to stand next to him and somehow convince him he was wrong.

It was awful and lovely, the way he needed her but couldn't see it. She felt a rush of gratitude for his dependableness, for his essential decency, which made it possible to predict him from a mile away. At least with him one always knew where one stood.

As she drew close to them she saw that there was, indeed, something funny with the baby's hand. He held it tightly shut and she could see that the wrist was puffy and swollen-looking.

"Let me look."

She took the baby's fist gently in her hand and slowly uncurled it.

"Deedeedeeagwoo," the baby explained.

In middle of his palm was a large, lifeless black and gold wasp.

"Oh, he's been stung!" Pinky cried and brushed the insect off his hand with a cry of horror. It fluttered to the ground like an old leaf. Bernard cried out at the loss of his treasure and bent down to retrieve it, but Teddy was there before him, lifting the thing up by one of its wings.

"You can hold it while I look for the stinger. Then you have to give it back to Bernard."

Bernard complained loudly, but she shushed him and said he would have it back in a minute.

Carefully, she examined Bernard's palm, which also was swollen. "Look, there's the stinger. Hold his arm steady," she instructed Arthur. "I'll pull it out." Gently and steadily she pulled the little black barb from the base of Bernard's thumb. "Give me the wasp, Ted, and get me some mud. It'll help draw out the poison."

Reluctantly, Teddy gave the wasp over to her and went off. In a minute he came back carrying a nice dollop of mud inside one of his petri dishes. Pinky smeared this around Bernard's thumb and almost immediately the hand began to look better.

Bernard looked relieved. "Da dee dee ablue," he tried to explain.

"He's so dumb, I'll bet he just picked that old wasp up right in his bare hand," Teddy conjectured.

"Any other kid would have been screaming his head off," Fran pointed out.

"Oh, baby, baby, what are we going to do with you?" Pinky lamented.

Bernard tugged at her hand and she realized he wanted the insect back. She handed it over and he put his face up very close to it, very reverently, just as he did with the sprouts. He began to half croon and half hum.

"You are so weird," Pinky said, and laughed.

As if this were the signal, Bernard flipped his hand over so that the wasp hung upside down. It should have, by rights, dropped to the ground, but it hung or stuck there. Gravity seemed to have no influence in this case and then, in a second, the wasp gave a little flutter of its wings, straightened them out, and flew out from under Bernard's hand.

Pinky screamed.

"Hey, that wasp was dead," Teddy exclaimed.

"Just stunned," Arthur said with a frown.

The wasp lifted up, hovered near the top of the wooden fence, then dipped and disappeared over the other side.

"I'll have to look and see if there's a nest around here somewhere," Arthur sighed.

Pinky pulled her small adopted son close to her body and kissed his forehead.

Now, here everything became completely silent. Not a cicada cleared its throat. Not a snake rustled in the grass. Later Pinky wondered whether it was that she had lost her ability to hear, or whether it was that time simply froze so there was nothing to hear. Or maybe it was that everybody breathed in at once so there was a sudden drop in air pressure so no sound could carry. But whatever it was, the silence passed and Pinky leaned back from her kiss nervously and looked at Bernard.

Bernard—as if he were brushing away a shadow—swatted lightly at the kiss with his free hand.

With a shock, it came to her why it was that he had always looked so naggingly familiar.

She gazed at Arthur and then back at the baby and then she stood up. Arthur was looking straight at her as if he wanted to say something, but she excused herself and went inside and put her head down on the kitchen counter and wept.

When she was done, she combed her hair and damped down her freckles with a wet paper towel. Then she went back outside and served the tuna fish gallantly and courteously, never once meeting her husband's eyes.

Halfway through dinner, she noticed that Fran's blue silk dress was no longer blue, but a deep purple.

"My God," Pinky said. "What happened to your dress?"

Fran looked down at it and smiled. "It's light-sensitive. You haven't seen this before? This stuff is all the rage. They do something to the fabric."

It wasn't until much later, after Fran and Maury were gone and the children were in bed, that she told Arthur that she didn't know how she could have been so stupid, but she had just realized who Bernard's real father was, and why hadn't he told her? But before he could answer, she was so overcome with fury that she told him she didn't want to hear it, whatever it was, and would he please just pack his bag and go. He tried several times to get her to listen, but she went into the bathroom and locked the door and didn't come out until after she heard him leave.

After he was gone, she walked through the house weeping silently, not wanting to wake the children. It wasn't until she looked into all the rooms of the house, searching for she didn't know what, that she realized the cat was missing, that he must have been missing since morning.

Part Three

14. Maury's Dream

$\mathcal{S}$ usan left the cat under her laundry basket all that afternoon.

She told Billy that she was allowing Cleopatra, the canary, out of the cage for exercise and he was not to go into the front room. She herself went in periodically to make sure that all was well. Toward early evening she came in and found the cat trying to lift the basket by jamming his nose and paws under its rim. She carried her portable compulink station from the kitchen and placed it on top of the basket.

On her subsequent visits to the room, she could hear the cat scratching anxiously away from the inside and mewing occasionally, but he was no longer able to get his paws under the rim.

She covered the birdcage at nine and went to bed.

At around three in the morning she rose quietly and dressed herself.

Billy did not wake up but lay on his back, breathing harshly through his open mouth.

When she entered the study, she had with her everything she needed, including her thickest gardening gloves and a large piece of chicken skin, which was what, she had noticed, Teddy usually used to entice the cat back into the house. By now the animal would be hungry and if he knew she had food perhaps he would cooperate with her.

She held the chicken skin outside the laundry basket for a minute so that he could get a good whiff of it. Then she lifted the compulink station off the top of the laundry basket and set it on the floor.

Crouching down, she raised the rim of the basket slowly and reached in. "You can make this easy or you can make it hard," she told him. She lifted the basket a little higher.

Out of the dark hole, sliding right under her mittened hand, sprang Oedipus. He went right for her eye, as if he'd been planning it, and he probably would have gotten it, slashed into the blue iris, if she had not butted her head down and straight into his nose. His claws caught her ear and the side of her neck.

She pulled him off furiously and grabbed the thick loose ruff of skin behind his neck with one hand. He clawed and jabbed futilely at the air. Blood dripped into her hair and mouth, but she wiped it away with her sleeve. She opened the thick canvas duffel bag she'd brought down from the attic and dropped him in. He clawed at her valiantly, but in a few moments she had managed to zipper it shut.

She went into the bathroom and washed herself up as best she could, then carried the hissing and writhing duffel bag out the front door and down the steps. To her immense irritation, there was Johnny Pitsacado, leaning up against his fence and staring down the empty street. She had no choice but to walk past him, since the car was parked a little ways down the block. He stared with bleary curiosity at the mewing, shape-shifting object that she clutched in her mittened hand, but she ignored him entirely.

When she got into the car she put the bag on the seat next to her and drove down to the warehouse section below Third Avenue. She pulled over in front of the sanitation department building, then got out and went around to the passenger side. She opened the door and lifted the duffel bag out and put it down on the sidewalk. Gingerly, she unzipped the bag part way and stepped back.

Nothing happened. There was no sound or movement.

"Well, good luck," she said.

She walked back around the car and got in and drove home and went to bed.

When she got up in the morning, she could hear them, calling and whistling. Later in the day, when she looked out the window, there they were again—the woman, the little boy, and the baby in an old-fashioned stroller—going up and down the street posting notices and stopping passersby.

The rose, considering the attentions it had received from the cat, was doing extremely well. With the cat now out of the way, Susan was sure it would surpass all those that had come before it. An examiner from the All-America Rose Selections would be arriving in mid-September.

Meanwhile, Arthur went to stay with Maury. He had no way of knowing if Maury's behavior was unusual or just his regular thing. Maury lived on the fifth floor of a five-floor walk-up. The air-conditioning was not working, or possibly Maury had disabled it. This wasn't clear. The furniture was old and beanbaggy, the place dusty and crowded with musical instruments and CDs.

Arthur wasn't sure how he felt, although he knew it wasn't good. It was difficult, given his own leaden sense of himself, to figure out if Maury's preoccupied look of dour concentration was his usual after-work look. Maury came home almost every evening from his job at the Transit Authority and changed into a loose serape-type shirt and a pair of shorts and pulled out his favorite drum and drummed away. The drum was short and wide, with a single face carved on it. The face seemed to be growing out of the side of the drum. It was tilted upward and its mouth was open either in a wide O of surprise or pain. Or maybe the guy was yodeling. Maury would take this drum on his lap and he would slap it alternately with the palms of his hands and then his fingertips. Sometimes he would chant along with his drumming, a wordless guttural-sounding chant, and when he stopped he would pass his gaze slowly over different objects in the room, attentively, sadly, watchfully, as if he were expecting some answering response.

Now that Arthur was staying in the man's house, he noticed that Maury carried with him an unusual scent—flowery but spicy, with a hint of radish. Arthur had never smelled an aftershave cologne like it. He was on the verge several times of questioning Maury about it, but something always made him hold his tongue. After a while, being preoccupied with his own affairs, he stopped noticing it anyway.

Maury had an extra futon mattress that he had put in a corner of the living room for Arthur. When the evening seemed to have reached its conclusion, Arthur would go and lie down on this. It was like lying on packed dirt.

In the first week while Arthur was staying with Maury, he tried several times to call Pinky, but she screened all her calls, refusing to pick up the voicelink. She also put a block on all his e-mail communications.

He was sorry that he had not tried harder to tell her about Marina's request and what he had done. Although, when he thought it over, he decided that if he *had* managed to tell her, he might well have ended up here at Maury's anyway. On the other hand, he could not help feeling angry that after all this time, after living with him for practically nine years and knowing very well the sort of person he was, she could jump to the conclusion that she was undoubtedly jumping to, and that she would not at least give him the courtesy of listening to the explanation he wished to offer.

But then again, maybe his explanations didn't amount to a hill of beans anyway; maybe, for all his belief in his own modest magnanimousness, what he had done simply boiled down to the same sort of vanity and foolishness that drove the rest of his fellow humans.

The more he went around and around with these thoughts, the more they slowed him down, as if he had, in the last few days since he had come here, gained ten pounds. He went up and down Maury's stairs hearing the harshness in his breath.

He didn't sleep well, either. He lay in the stifling heat of Maury's small junk heap of an apartment and stared out at the pale light of the windows and when he did fall asleep he would wake a half hour later, as if he had heard, right down below on the street, the roar of the world, like a motorcycle on fire, driving itself straight to its doom.

He had been staying at Maury's for several nights when he woke up into the darkness with a start and saw that someone was sitting across the room on the sofa. The air was hot and still.

"Maury, is that you?"

"Sorry," Maury said softly. "Did I wake you?"

"What are you doing out here?"

"I had a dream."

Arthur sat up slowly and leaned against the wall. "A nightmare?"

"Not exactly."

"You want to talk about it?"

"I'm trying to remember, but it's not all clear."

Maury sat in silence for a while trying to remember, then he said, "I was standing, I think, in the corner of a crowded room holding a tray with some wineglasses on it. Three, I think. There was a party going on, or some sort of big convention. But I knew I couldn't be part of it until I had given away these last three drinks. I felt good, though. I was pretty sure it wasn't going to be a problem to find people to take what was on the tray. Across the room, I saw this little knot of people talking and laughing. Their backs were to me, so I couldn't see any of their faces, but I thought I recognized voices. Then someone stepped aside and I saw a woman . . ."—Maury hesitated for a moment—"a woman who I knew. She looked up at me and put her finger to her lips, signaling me not to talk. Then she started to come my way, but she did it very slowly, stopping to chat with this person and that person. She also seemed to be taking off her clothes, one piece at a time. Somebody lifted one of the glasses off my tray and then somebody took the second one. I knew that when this woman finally finished all this chitting and chatting she was going to be right in front of me and she was going to be naked. Nobody else seemed to notice what was happening except her and me. Every once in a while she would look at me from the corner of her eye. I was very aroused, but I couldn't move. My hands were sweating and it was all I could do to keep the tray from falling. And then, just as she was almost in front of me, something happened. A dog jumped through the window and came running across the room in my direction. A black dog. I was so scared it was going to knock the glass of wine over that I grabbed the glass by its stem, and when I did, the stem snapped and the wine spilled all over me. Then I woke up."

Arthur, who rarely remembered any of his dreams, and when he did remember one would never have divulged any of the details to another adult, wasn't sure what he ought to say. "Wow. A dog, huh?"

"Yeah. A dog. A warning, I suppose."

"What kind of warning?"

"Well, I suppose a warning about the feelings I'm developing for this woman."

Arthur was surprised and didn't say anything for a moment. "Have you ever had feelings like these before?"

"On many occasions."

"But you resist them? Is that it?"

"Oh, no. Almost never."

Arthur sighed. "It's a hard temptation, I guess."

Maury didn't say anything. Next to him on the floor under the window was a big potted cactus. It was flat on the top like a little table or a footstool. It had long ago died of neglect, but its dried shape and thorns remained intact. Now Arthur saw Maury reach over in the dark and lightly run his hand over the top of the thing as if it were a little cat or dog.

"Nature is very keen on keeping us reproducing," Arthur said. "She makes the bait almost impossible to see through for many people. At least until it's too late."

Arthur could see the outline of Maury's arms as he lifted them over his head in the dark and stretched. "I don't look at it like that, exactly. I look at falling in love as an occasion to get things right. To work old mistakes through again."

"You're talking about your past lives?"

Maury laughed. "You tend to oversimplify me. Which is easy to do, I guess, since I tend to oversimplify myself. But the way I see it, it's more that when we fall in love we tend to be drawn back to the scene of old crimes in the hopes of freeing ourselves from them. And sometimes I believe that's karmic stuff we're working on, mistakes from past lives, and sometimes I suppose we are reenacting scenes from our childhood just like the psychologists say. But maybe it's not so simple to separate these things, because who knows who your mother or father was in your past life anyway? Maybe your mother was your wife last time around."

"You're kidding."

"Sort of. But in any case, the problem is that it's easy to fall in love, but very difficult to actually use the opportunity in a successful way. Most of the time we simply repeat ourselves."

The men sat silently for a moment, then Maury smiled. "Why are you here, by the way? You never really told me. I assume it has something to do with your strawberrry jelly jar."

Arthur rubbed his eyes and made a face. "Pinky guessed that I was the father of Bernard, but I never really had a chance to explain what happened and I suppose she jumped to some incorrect conclusion about my relationship with Marina."

"Ahh. I wonder why you delayed so long telling her."

Arthur didn't answer this right away. "Well, at first I wasn't so sure that telling her was the right thing to do. I wasn't sure that it would have been fair to Marina. And then, when I decided that it was more important that Pinky know than to protect Marina, there were always interruptions. It's hard to picture what it's like in our house, but you can't drink a cup of coffee without being shot in the face with a water-gun or somebody falling out the window."

"Well, but why don't you tell her now? That is, assuming you really understand what happened."

"I can't get in touch with her. She won't read my mail or answer the voicelink. In any case, I'm not sure how much my explanation will improve the situation."

In the hot still darkness, the two men sat for a while without moving. Arthur was just beginning to drift off when he was startled back into the room by Maury's voice.

"I know what you should do."

"What?" Arthur asked, a little confused.

"You should invite her friend Fran over for dinner here. If you explain the situation, I'm sure she'll help you."

"What on earth makes you think *that?*"

"She's a kind person."

"No, she's not."

"Well, she'll help because she wants what's best for Bernard and Teddy." Maury patted his cactus with a little nervous pat.

"Why do you keep that thing around?" Arthur asked at last.

"What thing?"

"That dead cactus."

Arthur could just make out Maury's smile in the darkness. "To remind me not to sit on it."

Pinky entered the bedroom cautiously that evening. Teddy had been coldly furious with her all week and had permitted not a single bedtime story.

The baby was deeply asleep in the crib. His limbs sprawled. His mouth was slightly open. He had that deceptively mild and exhausted look a hurricane has when it's done for the day.

She lay down next to Teddy and he didn't say anything. The missingness of the cat was so strong, it was almost as if you could reach over and touch it—a dark empty spot on the bed between them. Teddy just stared away from her out the window. It was hot and still, so she decided to sing him "Good King Wenceslas," one of his favorites.

"Good King Wenceslas looked out, on the Feast of Stephen.
As the snow lay 'round about, deep and crisp and even.
Brightly shone the moon that night, though the frost was cruel.
When a poor man came in sight, gathering winter fuel."

She sang it all the way through, all the verses. When she was done, he remained lying with his back to her. "Why don't you love Daddy anymore?"

"Who says I don't love Daddy?"

Teddy turned over and looked at her. "Why isn't he here with us? Why did you make him go?"

She was silent for a very long time. Then she said, "Did I ever tell you about the time I took your father to meet my Uncle Forest?"

"No."

"Well, it was a few months after I'd met him in the drugstore."

"When you saw the cloud and cut your finger and he fainted?"

"Right. I took him to my Great-Uncle Forest's house for dinner. I took him there because I was pretty sure your father would like him. Uncle Forest liked to play chess and he was a very interesting man who had fought in the Second World War and he had traveled all around the world and he had a very bad opinion of human beings in general and he thought we were all going to hell in a handbasket, but he was still very kind and funny. He also had only one arm. He had had the other one blown off when he was fighting overseas somewhere in the war. I took your father to my uncle's for the evening and my uncle, who had learned very well how to do things with one arm and who still loved to cook even though he was an old man, made us a dinner of scallops and mussels and rice with wine, which was wonderful, and your dad and Uncle Forest talked a lot about politics and history and after dinner they played chess. Your father won one game and my uncle won the other, so the evening was very harmonious and lively.

"I knew your dad had had a good time, but on the way home I said to him, wasn't it too bad about Uncle Forest's arm? Your father looked at me like I was crazy and he asked me what I was talking about. I said I was talking about the arm that Uncle Forest didn't have, the one that had been blown off in the war. I said, 'Didn't you notice at all that he had one sleeve of his shirt pinned up so that it didn't just go flapping around?' He said no, he hadn't noticed, and he actually asked me if I was sure that he was missing an arm.

"And I loved it that your father didn't notice something like that, that it wasn't important to him, a thing that would make other people stare and maybe be horrified. I knew it was the mark of a very good man."

"So why did you make him go?"

"Because he doesn't see things," she said sadly. "Because he doesn't see what's right in front of his nose."

Teddy was tired. "But you said that's why you loved him," he protested.

"Yes, yes. But the reason why you love people is sometimes the reason why you can't stay in the same house together. One of the things your dad has never been able to see is me and what I mean to him, and this has made him do something very, very stupid that has hurt me."

"What?"

"He's going to tell you that himself one day, when he figures it out."

Teddy was beginning to feel sleepy and his mother's answers floated around in his head like muffled woolly sheep. Then he felt an odd sensation pass through his hand—a touch, not solid, a warmth that sliced right through and then left. His eyes snapped open. He thought he saw someone pass through the door, but whoever it was, was gone. He looked at his hand a little nervously, but there was nothing to be seen. He closed his eyes again.

When Teddy was asleep, Pinky got up and went downstairs and checked the lock she had put on the gate in the alley. Then she locked the back door and the front door and went to bed.

15. Japanese Beetles

$\mathcal{T}$he cat had been gone for over a week. Susan passed among her roses, holding on to her tender feelings in an upright, soldierly way. She pinched off a yellowed leaf now and then and felt how the petals had gathered the drops of moisture from the wet night air. She grew none of those genetically engineered monsters here, those great puffy cabbages with no fragrance, but only pure lineage flowers—China teas, species roses, and damasks. She had some newer roses, too, but they were all cultivated through cuttings and graftings. These she grew mostly along the fence that stood between her own and Pinky's yard. The "Tropicana," with its blushing orange, was brilliant in the early morning sun, and she could have found it by its scent with her eyes closed. She leaned over one of the flowers and drank in its fragrance.

The aching in her shoulder grew less. She turned to her "Sombreuil," which grew well over her own head, nearly six feet, and, careful not to prick herself, pulled down one of the creamy white-petticoated flowers. Its scent was not so strong, something like the distant smell of an apple you've been carrying around in your pocket all afternoon. She held it to her face for some time, then she let go of it carefully and turned.

Sometimes as she did this, in that last moment she would imagine that the rose would be gone, but there it always was.

It was a grandiflora, tall with long spraying stems, spilling over now with flowers. And she knew that soon it would be recognized for the startling feat that it was.

She had been working on this rose for years so that it would breed true, would show, within its thickly petaled pink bowl shape, this deep crimson little face. And because here in this little fenced-in rectangle of earth there was actually an almost fair field, an opportunity to keep good luck and bad luck within her own hands, she appeared to have succeeded. The shrub itself had grown two feet this spring with deeply glossy green leaves and soon it had begun to produce beautiful large arrow-shaped buds. She had been filled with excitement and anticipation, sure that this would be the year she would succeed. Then, at the last minute, the bush seemed to hesitate. She had thought perhaps the buds were blighted, for she had never seen flowers wait so long to open. She had been terrified that all her work was going to be for nothing, but then one morning she came out and found two of the buds had burst open and revealed the dark red facelike stain of color at its center. By afternoon there were a half dozen more flowers, and two days later the bush was covered with the rich dark flowers. There was nothing else even remotely like it, she knew.

Her only remaining worry had been the cat.

If, perhaps, she could have done it another way she would have, but cats, she knew, could take care of themselves. Unlike roses.

She lightly ran her hands up the side of the bush and felt, with a growing calm, the thickness of its stems, the rich fullness of leaves and even of thorns. Then, as she reached under the base of a flower to check its tightness and width, she felt, with a shock, a familiar little shape.

She pried it off with a firm careful tug—it clung tightly with pronged feet for a moment, then surrendered. She dropped it onto the slate path and crushed it with her foot. She rubbed the bottom of her shoe in the grass.

It was nothing. It was a misfortune no greater than a single Japanese beetle that had now met its final destiny. She pushed the old shadow of dread away. She had only to be vigilant, she had no doubt, and all would be well.

A drop of rain hit the back of her hand and then a moment later another pinged against her cheek. She gathered her tools and carried them into the house.

It was one of those late summer rainstorms that catches everyone by surprise. One minute the sun was shining, and the next minute, like a curtain drawn across a stage, the sky was dark and the rain was coming down in fat splattering bullets, and then in great gray streamers and slashes. In the busy parts of the city people huddled together beneath awnings and in doorways, grumbling and exclaiming in wonder. The streets were no longer streets, but creeks and rivers, rushing and plunging toward the sewers that could not contain the torrents pouring into them. On Teddy's block the dry midsummer maple and sycamore leaves torn off by the force of the rain plugged up the two sewers in front of his house and, in no time at all, the street was no longer a street but a lake rapidly backing up onto the sidewalks.

"I'm going out there," Teddy announced. "I'm going to sail the remote-control boat Grandma sent for my birthday."

"Good idea," his mother said wearily. Teddy had been underfoot all day, refusing to go back to work on his vanished experiment and plaguing her with questions about what happens when people travel at the speed of light, if you can see them, and what it would feel like if they touched you as they went by.

She put his blue rain poncho on him and a pair of rubber boots and opened the front door and let him out.

He stood there for a long moment, staring at the lake in front of him. Twenty minutes ago it had been a regular Brooklyn street, now here it was dark and dangerous-looking, with little whirlpools and no bottom that could be seen. He looked for any cars that might dare to come down the street, but there were none in sight. He lowered his boat into it carefully and stepped back and pushed the button on the remote control. The boat spun around wildly for a moment, then righted itself and headed for the middle of the lake as if of its own accord. It took Teddy several minutes to figure out how to guide the thing with any accuracy. But after a bit he started to get the hang of it.

Completely absorbed, he was startled when a man's voice addressed him from behind.

"Excuse me, are you by any chance Arthur Sorenson's son?"

Teddy looked around and saw a tall, very wet-looking man in a white shirt and a green baseball cap. The rain was stopping now, but the man's hat had not caught up with this turn of events and drops of rain dripped plentifully from its brim. The man had a long straight nose and in his pocket one of those shiny mechanical pencils that

Teddy admired so much. Teddy wondered where the man had come from so suddenly. There had been no one out on the street a moment before.

"Yes."

"How do you do? I'm Ken Fishhammer. A friend of your father's from the lab at the university. You look just like him. I was just passing through the neighborhood. I thought he lived around here someplace. Is he at home?"

"No."

The man waited for more information from Teddy, but none was forthcoming.

"Ah. Too bad. I would have liked to say hello. Is anyone else at home?"

"Just my mother."

"No brothers or sisters?"

Teddy considered it. "The baby is asleep in the kitchen. My mother brought him in because of the rain. Usually she lets him sleep in the backyard for his nap."

Ken considered this information with interest. "What a good idea. Fresh air and all that."

"That's what she says. She says the fresh air is what makes his hair so curly."

"Interesting theory."

"I don't think she knows what she's talking about."

"I guess you'd have to test it out. Take a bunch of babies with straight hair and put half of them in the backyard for their naps and keep the other half inside. Then you'd watch what happened to their hair."

Teddy looked to see if he was teasing, but he appeared perfectly serious.

"So what are you working on these days?" Ken asked. "I remember your father told me you were a budding scientist."

"Nothing. I was working on a formula for something. But I've given it up."

"Given it up?

"It was an experiment. But I'm done with it. It's not any good."

"Oh, that's a shame. Are you sure? Most successful science just comes from being stubborn, I think. You gotta hang in there. What kind of formula was it?"

Teddy, who usually gave nothing away, was moved by the gravity of this man's attention. "I was making a formula for invisibility and I worked on it for months and I finally got it to work on an ant, but then the formula disappeared."

Fishhammer continued to stare at him, puzzled. Then he began to laugh. "So, actually, your formula was a complete success."

Teddy, taken aback, frowned at the wet lake at his feet.

"Oh, I'm sorry," Ken said. He put his hand kindly on Teddy's blue-ponchoed head. "I'm not laughing at you. I'm really not. It's that I know just how you feel. Nature is such a slippery devil, isn't she? No sooner do you think you've got the answer in your hand than it dissolves. It vaporizes. But you shouldn't give up. You really shouldn't. There are very few scientists with true imagination like yours, and imagination is what's needed. Imagination and stubbornness. Everything may depend on us in the end. Just keep on trying different ideas out. Perhaps this experiment was a dead end, but if you keep your mind open, another direction will come to you."

Teddy was knocked into silence by this. He had no idea what to say. He would have to think it over in private.

Ken looked at him and then at the house for another moment. "Well, give my regards to your dad for me." He turned away.

At the last minute, Teddy, unable to restrain himself, said, "Excuse me . . . I mean, I have a science question. Maybe you would know the answer."

Ken stopped and turned back to look at Teddy. "Science is a big place, but what's your question?"

"If someone ran by you at the speed of light and just reached out and touched your hand as they passed, what do you think would happen? Would it go right through you?"

Ken stood there thinking about it, looking intrigued. "This is far from my field, but yes, I would suppose you're probably right. Either that or it would kill you. It would depend probably on the amount and angle of impact. Has someone run past you at the speed of light recently?"

"I think so."

"Lucky you. I have a hunch that you have a promising career in front of you. Let's keep in touch." He turned away again.

Teddy, suddenly remembering his boat, looked out at the lake. There it was, sailing serenely away. It had almost reached the distant shore on the other side.

Maury's outside buzzer rang just as the storm was beginning to subside.

"Let her up, will you?" Maury was gliding around, putting the little finishing touches on his dining table, an ancient piece of furniture with metal legs and a gray linoleum surface. He had covered it this evening with a brightly covered cloth with an orange and red African sort of print. He had laid down silverware and differently patterned china plates, and at each place, a paper napkin folded in the shape of a lily.

Arthur pressed the button and a few minutes later the doorbell rang. He opened the door and Fran stood there, soaked through to the skin, the rainwater dripping from the tips of her flattened hair onto her gray linen dress. Maury came and stood behind him. Arthur felt him give a little sigh. Nobody moved.

"So should I come in or do you want to come out here in the hall-way and talk?"

"Come in, come in," Maury said.

She followed him into the middle of the little cluttered living room and, again, everyone stood there.

Fran shook her head and little drops of water flew through the air. She sneezed.

"We need to get you dry," Maury said. "Follow me."

Fran followed him into his bedroom. When she emerged again, she was wearing a pair of his gym shorts and a T-shirt and was toweling her hair dry. Her nose was red and her eyes were watery. "I've got a si-nus infection. This was just what I needed, getting stuck in a fucking monsoon. What did you call me over here for, Arthur?"

Arthur looked at her uneasily. "Well, actually this wasn't my idea."

"Oh, what a coward you are, Arthur." Maury laughed. "Fran, would you join us for supper? Something very simple."

Now Fran noted the festive table. "Well," she said doubtfully, "that's nice of you, and I guess, since I can't taste anything, I'm not in danger of making any offensive faces in case you made something really weird, which I suppose you did." She pulled a wet tissue out of her wet purse and blew her nose.

Maury looked at her thoughtfully. "I have an excellent cure for si-nus infections."

"Such as?"

"A neti pot. It's a little teapotlike device that you fill up with warm salty water and then you put the spout in your nose and you gently pour a little water in. It will help clear your sinuses."

"What I need to clear my sinuses are some major antibiotics. I don't suppose you got any of those around?"

Maury looked at her in horror.

She sighed. "Keep your yarmulke on. I was just kidding. Nobody who's anybody takes antibiotics anymore, do they, Arthur? Not unless it's for something really big, of course."

"Well . . ."

But Fran ignored him and started rummaging around in her purse again. "Here we go."

She lifted out a little white squirt bottle, uncapped it, and stuck it in her left nostril and squeezed. Then she did the same to her right nostril.

When she was done, Maury took the bottle out of her hand and examined it with a look of disapproval. "You get a lot of sinus infections?"

"Constantly. You know how they held Achilles by the heel when they dipped him in the River Styx so it turned out that his heel was his only weakness? That's what they did with me, except with me, they held me by the sinuses."

"So the rest of you is invulnerable?"

"Precisely."

"You know these sprays are toxic and addictive?"

"You want quick and easy solutions, you gotta be willing to swal-low a little poison. Where's the food?"

Maury looked at her—longer than necessary or customary, Arthur noted—and went into the tiny kitchen and brought out a platter with several nice-looking zucchinis, halved and grilled and stuffed with something colorful and spicy-looking. "Brown rice, garbanzo, tomato, onion, garlic."

"Wow! Those are gorgeous," Fran said.

Arthur thought he actually saw Maury blush.

Maury served each person half a zucchini, then offered around a bottle of sparkling melon water.

"This is delicious," Fran exclaimed. "You'll have to give me the recipe."

Maury looked at her again.

"Not for me, of course. I don't cook. But my mom loves to try new things."

"So how's your mom doing?" Maury asked.

Fran lifted her fork and pretended to stab herself in the heart with it. "My mom continues to be all that she has ever been."

"Meaning?"

"Meaning that I called her the other night and, somewhat to my surprise, she wasn't home. When I asked her the next day where she'd been, she said she had been having dinner with my father."

"With your father?" Maury asked.

"Yes. I, too, was somewhat taken aback, but she merely said, 'Why not? We're old friends. For thirty-two years I cooked dinner for the guy. Now let him take me out once in a while.' She was smug.

" 'Excuse me, but what about Elsie?' I naturally asked her.

"My mother merely said, 'Let her eat with somebody else now and then. I'm sure she's got other friends.'

"I wondered, of course, if Elsie knew, but the very next day there was an interesting new development."

Maury and Arthur looked at her expectantly.

Fran blew her nose again with relish, and then took another bite of zucchini. "My mother called me to tell me that apparently Uncle Claremont had passed on and she wanted me to call Elsie and remind her not to bury Uncle Claremont in the cemetery plot. She was sure that it would bring Elsie very bad luck if she did so."

"Did you call Elsie?"

"Of course not. I'm not getting anywhere near this one."

Arthur, who had barely touched his food, leaned back in his chair. "What kind of bad luck do you think she's talking about?"

Fran shrugged. "Who knows? My mother entertains a lot of very interesting notions about the nature of life and death and the forces which work invisibly around us. And she's probably not beyond attempting to practice a little voodoo on a rival like Elsie. In any case, I had it from my father that Elsie remains uncowed and went ahead and had Claremont buried in the plot. Lucky fellow. It's really a beautiful spot."

"What's your father think about all this?" Maury asked.

"My father is a man who keeps his own counsel. This, I think, he learned to do over the years while living with my mother. You gotta play your cards very close to the vest when dealing with a person like her."

Fran and Maury ate silently for a while. Arthur stared out the window.

"So how ya doing, Arthur?" Fran asked. "Pinky asked me to find out."

"She knows you're here?" Arthur asked sharply.

"Nope. But she's worried about you."

"I'm a little worried about him, too, actually," Maury said, looking at Arthur thoughtfully. "He's a man with a lot of things to say and not enough tongues to say them."

Fran picked up her lily-shaped napkin and blew her nose into it. "And who would he say these things to if he could find the tongues to say them?"

"To Pinky, of course. I just need to get her to listen to me for a minute," Arthur said.

"And that's why you've called me here? To intercede on your behalf?"

"Yes."

"But why should I do this? You've broken her heart. What could you possibly say to her now that she's discovered that the baby who she thought had fallen straight out of some little hole in the floor of heaven is actually your baby by another woman?"

"She's laboring under a big misapprehension."

"What kind of misapprehension?"

"I can't tell *you* that. I've got to tell *her*."

Fran looked at Maury, but Maury merely offered her another piece of zucchini.

"She doesn't want to hear a lot of lame excuses about how you got carried away right there on the laboratory floor in front of the mice."

Arthur looked at her angrily. "She should know me better than that. That's not what happened. If you want to find out the true facts of the story, then you've got to get Pinky to listen to me. Once she hears my explanation, I'm sure only a very short time will elapse before she blabs it all to you."

Fran looked at Maury. "Do you know what he's talking about? Is it going to be worth my while?"

"I suspect you'll find yourself pretty entertained," Maury said.

"But you're not going to tell me?"

"It's not my story to tell."

Fran sighed. "Well, I'll give it some thought."

When they were all done eating the zucchini, Maury cleared the table and brought out a rice pudding sweetened with honey. They talked about other matters, the rapid spread of the new strain of influenza in Japan, Fran's new patient who had killed his wife because he believed she was the leader of a vast ninja conspiracy. When they were finished and Fran had gone off into the evening, still wearing the gym shorts and carrying her wet dress, Arthur sat for a long time just staring out the window.

Maury cleaned up and did the dishes and then sat down next to Arthur.

After a while Arthur turned and looked at him. "Was she the one in your dream?"

Maury looked at him, but didn't answer.

"Do you think she'll call Pinky?" Arthur asked him.

Maury smiled. "Before the night is out. I'd bet my neti pot on it."

16. Paradise

Oedipus, who took things as they came, wandered for a couple of days, nervous but exhilarated, through the deserted streets and alleyways, sniffing alertly at the sharp mélange of greasy water and wooden pilings and the rank fermentations from the garbage bins. Sometimes he caught the gleam of other eyes watching him and once, when he slipped through a hole in a fence, he nearly stepped on a large, hairy stinkbarker sleeping on top of a rubber tire. Oedipus froze in his tracks staring at it. It was similar in aspect to the stinkbarker that had chewed off his ear three years ago. He backed up slowly and then turned and slipped through the hole again.

After a night or two, he was drawn to a green smell, not the same as the green smell that came from his own backyard, but a rough and recognizable cousin to it. He followed his nose and found himself at the edge of a large and overgrown vacant lot.

In the back of the lot was an old dresser that had fallen on its side and its drawers had come slightly open. Oedipus sniffed it carefully for any current residents, but finding none, he crept into one of the drawers and was content.

He woke up hungry, however.

It was the dark cool time before the sun rose and there was a hush that was more like a breath held than a silence, when the shapes of things were still not quite separated from each other, but about to be separated.

Oedipus stretched cautiously and then crouched in the grass and waited. He waited a long time and then an invisible creature sent, like an arrow upward into the grayness, a short questioning whistle. There was quiet for a moment and in the quiet he felt, more than saw, the condition of light change, a gathering of form in the upper reaches along the roofs and the antennae. Then another creature answered and then another, and soon the cat saw that the darkness was being dispelled.

On this particular morning, when the singing had finally lifted the sun up into the air, there was, because of the refraction through the mist, a sudden burst of light like glass shattering.

The cat's ears went back and his eyes went wide. He watched alertly, and when nothing more happened except that the light gradually settled itself down into the drops of dew that hung like diamonds from the grasses and weeds, he looked up into the tree where the two-legged flappers, now that they had accomplished their task, were making an incredible racket, arguing and whistling and congratulating each other.

It came to him, with an undeniable quiver of pleasure and anticipation, that up there perched his breakfast. He felt quite glad that he was hungry and that things had been arranged so.

The trick, he knew, was not to try to sneak up on the one you wished for, but to have the one you had chosen come to you. You must lie hidden behind something. You must wish for the thing sideways, not straight on, your mind suspended, focused on something else, and all the while you must slowly, carefully reel it in, what you wanted, as if it were on the end of a string. When it came down into the grass, you had to wait until it had drawn near enough to you, scenting its own dark appointment. It was no use leaping for what you were after unless you could get it by the neck in one leap.

It took him three tries.

The first time he warned the skyflapper off with the twitching of his tail. The second time the creature took off at the last possible minute and Oedipus, who knew he had made a perfect approach, assumed it must have been tipped off by one of those whisperers who, invisible and unfathomable, give out occasional lifesaving advisories.

The third time, however, luck moved over to *his* side. What happened was that suddenly, from high up in the tree, he became aware of two creatures screeching and fluttering and chasing each other down through the branches. They tumbled lower and lower through the tree as they screeched and pecked at each other's feathers. The cat was filled with a frenzy of thirst. He swallowed at the dryness in his throat, realizing that he hadn't eaten for a very long time.

The two flappers dove for each other's eyes and underbellies. It was a puzzle what they argued about or if it was really an argument at all.

Oedipus kept his eyes on them steadily, never faltering, and gradually he pulled them down closer and closer to himself.

When they landed, at last, in the scrubby grass, they struggled and pulled at each other's feathers. The cat knew that the moment was his. Neither would even see him coming. He positioned himself taut and wound tight as a slingshot and then he let himself go and flew through the air.

He landed on the back of one of the creatures. They both stopped for moment and stared at each other in horror, only now realizing the triviality of what it was they quarreled about. The one who remained free stared in mute sympathy and apology into the eyes of the other, whose tiny neck was delicately but irretrievably gripped in the cat's teeth. Then he flew off.

Oedipus tossed his captive into the air and then, with his paw, neatly pinned it down and snapped its wing. He let go of it and crouched, watching it. After a few minutes of sitting frozen, the creature picked itself up and attempted, wing dragging, to flutter into the underbrush. The cat, aroused, let the little bird go a little ways, then he leaped and grabbed the broken fellow by his neck and flipped him, again, playfully into the air.

When the bird landed, twitching in the grass, the cat stood over him and waited for him to look up and meet his gaze. When he did, and they appeared to understand one another, the cat picked his capture up in his jaws once again and snapped its neck.

Oedipus's patience fled and he was filled with the certainty of hunger. He pulled the wings from the flapper, ripped open his breast and tugged out the entrails. He made a quick and bloody meal. When he was done, he buried the tiny bones and feathers under some loose underbrush and then climbed atop an old cement pipe and washed himself. It occurred to him that he had somehow, by some stroke of destiny or luck, found his way into Paradise. With a certain self-consciousness he did not look up at the top of the tree, where he knew there were others watching him.

A day or so after Fran's dinner with Maury and Arthur, Arthur received an e-mail from Pinky saying that if he would like to come see the children, tomorrow evening would be a good time.

Arthur found Teddy sitting on the top of the stoop.

"Are you back to stay?" Teddy asked accusingly.

Arthur shook his head sadly. Arthur sat down next to his son. "No. Just to visit and see everybody. I've missed you very, very much. How are you?"

"Okay, I guess."

"How's Bernard?"

Teddy shrugged. "He's still in trouble all the time."

"Does he worry you?"

"No. He pesters me. When are you coming back to stay?"

"I don't know the answer to that question yet."

Teddy didn't say anything for a while. It was a hot, muggy evening. Every once in a while someone would walk past the stoop, people returning from work, dog walkers, a couple of teenagers entwined in each other's arms. No one looked up at them.

"Well, if you're not going to answer that question, tell me about the baby who got lost in the war," Teddy demanded.

Arthur looked at him. "You sound angry."

"I'm not angry. But nobody answers my questions. I don't like it."

"Well, all right, then, I'll tell you about that, but you probably won't like it."

Arthur then sat for a while staring at something down the street. Teddy thought maybe he was looking at the pigeon coop, but then he decided that he wasn't.

"My grandfather's baby brother was named Bernard. You know something about Hitler and the Holocaust, don't you?"

"Yes, you told me. They wanted to get rid of all the Jewish people."

"Right. That was a big part of it. Well, one day they came to the town in Poland where my great-grandparents lived with my grandfather and his little brother, Bernard. Bernard was just a baby at the time. They rounded up all the men, including my great-grandfather, and put them up against a wall and shot them. My great-grandmother took the children and went and hid in the cellar. She put my grandfather in a secret hiding place under the cellar steps and she hid Bernard, who was sleeping, in the potato bin. She climbed into an empty barrel. The soldiers found my great-grandmother and my grandfather, but they didn't find the baby. The Germans took the two of them to a concentration camp, where my great-grandmother died. My grandfather was young and strong, however, and he survived. After the war was over and he got out of the camp, he went to live with a family in France, and it wasn't until he was much older that he was able to go back and look for his little brother. But he was never able to find him. My father looked for him, too, when he grew up. But whether the baby had died or they just couldn't find him, they never knew. Somehow, it was something my father could never get out of his mind."

"And he was always sad, wasn't he?"

Arthur tentatively put his arm around his son. Teddy sat there stiffly in his embrace. "What makes you say that?"

"I remember Grandpa. I remember how he was. He was always in another room reading the newspaper."

"Do you remember your grandmother? The one who was my mother?"

"She used to sing to me."

"Oh, yes," Arthur said. "I'm glad you remember that. She was a little bird. She loved to sing. She sang in many languages—in English and Yiddish and German. She was always trying to cheer my father up, I think, but that wasn't really possible. What had happened to his family had hurt him too much."

"You miss your mom and dad because they're dead now?"

"I think I always missed my dad because he was never really there. So after he died, it didn't seem all that different. But my mother, well, you know . . . that was very hard. I keep thinking one day I'm going to open some door and there she'll be."

Teddy put his hand in his father's hand. "A ghost?"

"Oh, no, not really. Just my mother there, folding laundry and singing."

For a while, they sat there silently, watching the late August street, holding hands, then Arthur said, "I need to go inside now and see your mother and the baby. Do you want to come with me? No? Okay. Well, I'll come back out here in a little while."

Pinky searched his face. Besides looking a little thinner, it was the same old face, worried, too sober, and a little baffled, as if he'd been accidentally misplaced in a parallel dimension that was slightly, but critically, different from the one he had been meant for.

She patted her hair down and then the minute she took her hand away the curls shot right out again.

"Bernard is in the kitchen. He and I were just finishing dinner."

He followed her wordlessly. Teddy's chair was pushed back and his hot dog abandoned halfway. Bernard was leaning out of his Gerber Skylift Baby Seat and trying to get hold of the hot dog. The seat was hydraulic and had been sent last week by Pinky's mother. Babies were not supposed to be able to operate the seat themselves, but Bernard had discovered that by twisting himself 180 degrees around inside the harness and reaching down with Pinky's long wooden serving spoon that she had left on the high chair so he could whack things and make noise, he could reach the control buttons. As the seat went down, it gave out a very eerily unpleasant electronic rendition of "Eensie Weensie Spider." Bernard had managed to get it almost on level with the kitchen dining table. But when he saw his father come through the door, he stopped what he was doing and lifted his arms up with a loud whoop.

The baby's hair, though dark, curled and stuck out damply around his head like Pinky's. He wore a pair of royal blue overall shorts—no shirt. Pinky saw that he looked exceptionally handsome. His cheeks were rosy and his dark eyes with the flecks of gold in them lit up ecstatically. He waved the wooden spoon at his approaching father.

"Eh, eh, eh!"

"How do you undo this harness?" Arthur asked, trying to free the baby.

"It's incredibly complicated. Why don't you leave him in there until he's finished eating?"

Arthur crouched down to get a closer look at Bernard and Bernard tried to feed him a pea. Arthur ate it gratefully and stared at the baby's face with the intentness of a man lost in the frozen tundra trying to light a fire. Pinky wondered what it would be like if he looked at *her* like that.

"I saw Teddy out front," Arthur said.

Outside they could hear it beginning to rain again. The rain made a sound like handfuls of rice being thrown against the windows and out of the sound rose the strong, pleasing smell of warm outdoor things becoming wet—the grass, the leaves, the dusty cement patio.

"How is he doing?" Arthur asked.

"He's angry."

"At what?"

She shrugged. "You name it, he's pissed off at it. It hasn't been a great couple of weeks for him. But I guess since he always expects the worst anyway, he isn't as bad off as he might be. I just wish he'd go back to his experiments."

"Listen, Pinky, I need to talk to you."

"I know. Fran called." She faced him and waited for it, whatever it was, knowing that it needed to be gotten through so it might as well be now, even though it wouldn't make any difference, because, after all, what could he say that would clear his name? Nothing. Sorry wasn't going to do it. She had loved him, she supposed, for this spotless little piece of him, his predictable true North Star self. It was a paradox because it was the piece you couldn't get hold of. It was that if he said something or promised something you could rely on it, *always*, as far as it went. And now it was gone. And whoever it was who was standing here in front of her, it was the same face, but it wasn't the same Arthur Sorenson who had passed out in the drugstore when he saw her bleeding finger. It was some imposter, though he was getting a headache, she could see. And suddenly she realized this made her nervous because something always seemed to happen whenever he got a headache.

He still couldn't seem to find the place to begin, or the crux of the matter, or to get around the fact that words were never going to pin it down exactly. They were just going to be approximations and they were going to have to do.

"Listen . . . Pinky . . . how much did you know about Marina?"

She looked at Bernard, who, seeing that his father's attention was diverted, had returned to the problem of the hot dog. "Enough," she said.

"You know that her parents were murdered? They were intellectuals who wrote letters and signed petitions. They weren't a threat to anyone. No one claimed responsibility, but a group of armed men showed up one night and barred the doors to the house and then burned it down. Her sister was at a friend's that night and Marina returned late and when she found the house on fire, she tried to get in and save her parents, but it was too late. She was very badly burned, particularly on one side of her face. Marina, of course, could never forgive herself for not being there when they needed her, but she knew she had to get herself and her sister out, so she used some of her parents' university connections, and it was Fishhammer who sponsored their visas. He had no interest in her politics, which I believe may have become rather radicalized after what happened to her parents. He needed somebody who would keep her mouth shut about the project he was working on."

Pinky stared at him, thinking of the photo Katya had shown her, of Marina looking right into the camera, her cheek resting on her hand so that side of her face could not be seen. "Are you telling me that you made love to her because you felt sorry for her?"

"No," he said, frustrated. "You have it all wrong. Well . . . of course she'd had a very hard time. But it wasn't that. . . . I'm trying to explain to you the background of what happened. She came to me and she asked me—"

At this moment, Teddy came slamming through the back screen door. He stopped in his tracks and he looked at the assembled company. He looked at his father for a long moment and then his mother, and then his eye was arrested by Bernard. "Why is that baby turning blue?" he demanded.

Pinky was aware that Arthur turned with her.

Bernard met her eyes with his. They were wide open and protruding slightly. What threw her off for a moment was that he did not look at all distressed, but instead taken by surprise, as if he had spotted, coming through the doorway of the kitchen, some unexpected and rather fascinating sight.

She looked where he was looking, but couldn't see anything, and when she turned back to him again, it came to her that something had gotten caught in his throat and that he was suffocating.

This time, seeing death hovering over the child that she had waited for with such longing and impatience, she was furious. She stood up, knocking the chair over, and yelled, "Bernard! Bernard!" as if she could bully him out of his state of asphyxiation.

"Damn it!" Arthur yelled. "He must have gotten that hot dog."

Bernard waved his hands and gazed at them fondly, but as if they were very far away and receding fast.

His eyes went up inside his head.

Perhaps things went very quickly. In retrospect, it was hard to say. "Teddy, call 911. The address is 566 Charleston Street," Arthur ordered.

"I know," Teddy said and ran out of the room.

"Pinky, help me with these straps." They struggled unsuccessfully together with the extremely complicated buckles and harness and then Pinky grabbed the scissors off the shelf and cut him loose. Arthur grabbed him up.

Teddy came in and said the satellite must be down because he couldn't get a voice line or an e-mail.

"Christ," Arthur said.

He pulled the baby up against himself and, with his balled fists at the bottom of Bernard's rib cage, punched in again and again. Nothing happened.

Pinky felt as if she had been picked up by a big wave and was being tumbled around and around while being dragged out to sea.

"Let's take him outside! We'll flag down some help," he said.

The rain had stopped, but there was no one there. Where was everyone? Only Johnny Pitsacado, of no use to anybody, was leaning nearly unconscious up against the NO PARKING sign in front of his house. "Help us!" Pinky yelled. "Someone go get the fire department!"

Arthur laid Bernard down on the sidewalk and tilted his head back.

He opened Bernard's mouth and stuck his finger inside. "I can't feel anything. It must be way down there."

Pinky ran up Celia Pitsacado's steps and banged on the door.

When Celia answered, Pinky breathlessly explained what was going on. Celia came tripping down the steps and knelt next to Arthur on the sidewalk. "Get Billy Edelman to drive 'round to the firehouse," she ordered Pinky.

Pinky turned and ran up Susan and Billy's steps. They answered the door together and Billy did not hesitate. "I'll get my car keys." He reappeared a moment later wearing only one shoe and stumbled down his steps and into his car and took off. From the corner of her eye she saw Susan Edelman standing at the top of her stoop. She seemed to gaze at the crowd as if she were a sailor's wife staring at an empty horizon.

"A! B! C!" Celia Pitsacado said loudly. "Airway, Breathing, Circulation. Did you feel anything in there?"

Arthur shook his head no.

"Let me try, please. I was a nurse." Arthur stared at her and moved back reluctantly.

"Do you know what's in there?"

"We think it's a piece of hot dog."

"Shit." She tilted back Bernard's slack little blue face and opened his mouth and breathed into him and watched his chest. "There's a little something going in there, but not much. Did you Heimlich him?"

"Yes, but nothing came out."

"I'm going to try again." She picked the baby up and with one foot on the curb held him face down against her knee. She whacked his back five times, then laid him down and blew into his mouth again. Pinky thought she saw his chest rise slightly. Celia looked inside his mouth, listened for breathing, and checked his pulse. "If there's a pulse, it's so faint I can't catch it, but there's a little air going in. Let's do CPR. You!" she ordered Arthur. "Five chest compressions after each time I breathe. Put your hands here."

Arthur knelt beside Bernard and pressed the heels of his hands one on top of the other against the baby's sternum.

"Five times now! One, two, three, four, five! Now I breathe." She leaned over Bernard and breathed steadily into his mouth, then looked up at Arthur. "Your turn again. One, two, three, four, five! Keep at it!" She breathed into the baby again.

When they had done this three or four times, she ordered Pinky to check for the pulse.

Pinky put her fingertips against Bernard's neck. She felt for the pulse angrily. She saw how sad she was going to be. This came to her like a flash of lightning lighting a room up briefly in the middle of the night in the middle of a dark storm. She'd never seen such sadness before.

"I don't feel anything."

"Shit!" Celia said again. She looked into Bernard's mouth. "I can see! But I can't pull it out. Go back to the chest compressions. We've got to get that air going in there."

Johnny Pitsacado was watching his mother. It wasn't clear to him what was happening, but he had a dim sense that it was something out of the ordinary. He leaned up against the NO PARKING sign and squinted at the little scene before him. He looked around slowly and then, just as he saw the little boy on the front stoop watching him curiously, he felt something very odd. He held his breath. It was as if someone had laid a hand against his chest, a warm light little hand, and then that hand went right through him to the other side. As it went through, it burned like a hot poker. He breathed deeply, trying to catch his breath, and when he looked down he expected to see a black hole with the charred remains of his heart sticking out. But instead he saw nothing out of the ordinary at all. His T-shirt, the same dirty white one he had been wearing for three days, was still intact. His heart was nowhere in sight. He shook his ear as if he had water in it, and as he did, another peculiar thing happened. The cars, the trees, the summer twilight all came into focus. He looked at them as if he had not seen them for years. Something, he realized, must be wrong with that little baby who always smiled at him with such good fellowship when he went by in his stroller.

Johnny tilted his head and shook the water out of his ear again, and made his way over to the little crowd gathered around Bernard.

"Here. You're not doing that right," he said.

Celia Pitsacado lifted her face from Bernard, looked around, and, seeing who it was, stared in astonishment. This gave Johnny the opportunity he needed and, without hesitation, he bent over and picked up Bernard by the heels, gave him a good shake like he was a ketchup bottle that needed some encouragement.

The little piece of hot dog came flying out.

By the time the first Modular Emergency Unit arrived, Bernard was sitting up and laughing. When Modular Emergency Unit Two arrived a few minutes later, they snapped themselves together, took an event history from Pinky and Arthur, and then said that they needed to take Bernard over to the emergency room so they could get a better look at him.

"Not a chance," Pinky said.

"Maybe it's a good idea," Arthur said.

"You would be taking a serious and unnecessary risk if you did not allow us to take him for an examination."

A fire truck came wailing down the crowded street and pulled up behind the emergency units. The chief jumped out and came over to where the medic was listening to the baby's heart. The chief asked him what was going on. Pinky could tell from the sober and careful tone of the medic's voice that he held the chief in high regard. He finished up his report by turning to Pinky and saying accusingly, "This person, the mother, will not permit us to take the standard precautionary measures."

The chief turned and gazed into her eyes. He did it rather gingerly, as if he expected some small electrical or explosive device to go off.

"Why don't you humor them?" he said in a low voice.

"Forget it," she whispered back.

"There's good reason for these procedures. They have lots of experience."

"Look at him," she said.

Everybody looked at Bernard except for Arthur, who watched the fire chief suspiciously.

The firemen had started passing the baby around, laughing and tickling him and sticking their faces in his face and letting him pull on their noses.

"Could I have my child back now, please?" Pinky asked.

"Of course," the chief said. "But if you're not going to agree to let us take him over to the emergency room, you'll have to sign a release."

"Fine," Pinky replied.

The firemen turned the baby back over to her. Pinky received him with a great sigh of relief and held him tightly against her breast, while Arthur signed the papers. The baby murmured into her ear, softly and reassuringly.

When Arthur was done signing the forms, Pinky looked around at them all. "We appreciate everything that everyone did. Thank you, Johnny. Thank you, Celia. I need to take the baby inside now."

She turned around and walked, trembling, up the front steps. Arthur and Teddy followed her, but when she got up to the top, she turned to Arthur and told him that she needed some time to herself now. He could come back in a few days.

Arthur kissed the boys. "Please call me if the baby has any problems," he said to Pinky.

She nodded and watched him walk down the steps. He stopped for a moment to say a word to the firemen and the medics, who were still standing on the sidewalk talking softly to each other. Then he headed down the block. When he was gone from sight, she readjusted the baby on her hip and followed Teddy inside.

After Pinky had gotten the children to sleep, she went into her studio and turned on the little light and sat down in front of her painting. She stared at the little tea-drinking woman, who, her chin and cheek resting in her hand, gazed straight out at her.

The doorbell rang.

She looked through the peephole before she opened it. It was the fire chief.

She opened the door. He had gray eyes, she realized, with a darker ring, blue, around the iris. She'd never quite seen eyes like them before. He stared at her seriously, inquiringly, but the way he stood there— no longer in his coat and rubber pants, but wearing sneakers and jeans and a black T-shirt—it was clear that he had no doubts about his own presence.

"You want to see the baby?" Pinky asked.

"No, that's all right. I just wanted to make sure he was okay."

"He's okay."

"You want to keep a very close eye on him. He is a remarkable child. The gods are always a jealous crowd. The fire department will not always be nearby."

"Okay," she said. Now she looked at him more closely and she saw that his dark hair was threaded here and there with gray and that he was not as young as she had first guessed. She had been fooled by the odd mixture of lightness and gravity with which he carried himself. He was watching her with just a note of amusement. Patiently, she thought, waiting for her to catch up. It came to her with a little shock that he wasn't here only to check on the baby.

As soon as he saw this jolt go though her, not wishing to give her any more time to think it over, he drew her in and kissed her.

It was, she recognized, a wonderful kiss. It smelled of smoke, and it tasted strongly of luck and danger, despair and devotion, and faintly of tarragon. It galloped through her like a horse without a rider, over streams and up hills, crashing through the trees, and jumping fences. She had never had such a kiss before. When it was done, she put her hand between them on his chest and looked around. They were standing on the front stoop and the sky was dark and the street was empty. She wondered if anyone had seen them.

She pushed him back gently. "Go back to the firehouse. I'll call you if I need you."

17. The Experiment

$\mathcal{B}$ ernard was asleep in the backyard in his playpen. One hand was wide open, the other was fisted under his cheek. There was a moist spot where he had drooled a little on the playpen sheet. In his dream the cat came through the yard and, seeing Bernard asleep, stopped and called him by his old name, Andre.

Teddy sat on the front stoop and peered into the plastic container that held a yellowish brown mixture composed of mayonnaise, dill weed, iron pyrite, and a dab of sienna yellow from his mother's oil paints. He sat back and sighed and looked around for inspiration, but all that came was a prickling sensation as if an ant were walking quickly down the back of his neck.

He closed his eyes. Probably he was imagining this. He waited for the sensation to go away. But it didn't. If anything, it increased in intensity.

When the skateboard stopped in front of him and there was silence, Teddy thought the matter over.

"Hey, what's going around?"

Teddy turned himself so that the container was half hidden behind his back. "My cat disappeared."

"Crappachino. I used to have a parakeet, but it got caught in the ceiling fan. You should of seen the feathers all over the place."

Teddy chewed this one over in mute horror for a few moments. Then he said, "Something else happened."

"Yeah?"

"My mother won't let my father live in the house anymore."

"Was he beating her up?"

Teddy looked at him sharply. "No."

"Well, my dad was beating my mom up. That's why she threw him out. It was a couple of years ago. Sometimes we go see him."

"Mine came to see me the day before yesterday."

"Did he give you the gun back?"

"We didn't talk about the gun. My brother choked on a hot dog and the fire truck came. He's all right now. He's taking his nap in the backyard right now. My mother won't let me play back there till he wakes up."

Orlando grinned. "Too bad, huh? What a little mutant. What are you hiding behind your back?"

"Nothing." He shifted himself and hoped that the container could not be seen, but Orlando reached around him, monkeylike, and grabbed it.

"Phew!" he exclaimed. "What's in here?"

"It's a scientific formula," Teddy said breathlessly, trying to grab the container back.

Orlando took a sniff at it again. "What's it for?"

"I'm not sure. I only started with it today. I'm just experimenting."

"What's in it?"

Teddy listed the ingredients.

"I used to do stuff like this. Once I put some baking powder and some vinegar and some flour and some red food coloring into an old perfume bottle and I made a great exploding nail polish for my sister for Christmas."

"I'm not making exploding nail polish. This is a serious experiment."

"Well, then," Orlando said, gazing into the formula, "you need serious ingredients."

"Like what?"

Orlando stared up into the sky for inspiration. He snapped his fingers. "I know! Your brother's sleeping in the back?"

"Yes."

"Can we get in there?"

"My mother's been keeping the gate locked ever since my father left. But I know where she keeps the key."

"Can you get it?"

"Yes."

"Well, it'll just take a couple of minutes and then we'll lock it right up again."

Teddy looked at his spiked, glittering hair and at his neon-red eyes. "What are we going to get?"

Orlando grinned. He took out of his pocket a gleaming little instrument, something between a Swiss army knife and a laser ratchet set. "A little blood. He won't feel a thing."

Once Teddy had opened the gate with the stolen key, the boys slipped down the alley and into the backyard. They had not gone more than a few steps when they heard a sound that stopped them both in their tracks. It was the sound of weeping—a soft, heartbroken, womanly weeping. They looked at each other and tried to turn around, but before they could, the weeping stopped and a voice, although choked and breathless, called out sharply, "You boys, come here. I need you."

They approached her with reluctance and regret, but it was too late to run away, and when she told them they could climb the fence into her yard, they did so obediently.

When the boys got up close to Susan, they saw tears glistening on her little wrinkled iron face. She held up to them in the palm of her hand a gorgeous and gleaming thing, a gold and emerald eye, a jewel for a rajah's finger.

"What is it?" Orlando asked.

"They're all over her," she sobbed.

Teddy looked closely and saw it was a bug they were looking at, the most beautiful bug he had ever seen. He put out his hand eagerly, then stopped and asked if it would sting.

"No, no, no. They eat the leaves." She gestured at her rosebush. "I want you to pull them off for me. I want you to pull them off—carefully—so you don't hurt her. Pull them off and drop them in this bucket." Teddy recognized the smell of the colorless liquid inside.

"What are they?"

"Japanese beetles," she sobbed. "I've never seen such an infestation. You have to tug them off like this, very gently. They have something like claws on their legs. They can tear the leaves." And she demonstrated how to pull a beetle off, tugging on it slowly and insistently until it finally let go of its own accord. She dropped it into the bucket with a hiss of distaste.

"Bloodsuckers! Parasites! Vermin!" She stared down at the gleaming jewel struggling in the alcohol. "I'll give you a dime for every one you pull off."

Orlando lifted the leaves and a calculating look came into his eye as he saw the number of beetles glistening beneath them. He grabbed hold of one gamely and gave it a little tug. It let go of its lunch with obvious reluctance, then hung there caught in Orlando's fingers, paddling its wiry legs uselessly as it tried to find something to grab hold of. Orlando dropped it in the bucket and they all watched it slowly cease motion as it drowned.

"Get to work!" she said. "There isn't much time." She stood there for a while, until she had satisfied herself that they knew what to do, then she said she would be back in twenty minutes to check on them. She went into the house.

Orlando picked quickly and efficiently, but Teddy kept turning to stare into the bucket, to watch how, very suddenly, the bright, jewel-like color of a beetle would go out as if a light had been switched off, then he would pause and look at the roses.

It wasn't an unpleasant task for a summer afternoon. It was sort of like berry picking. It would have been nicer to see the beetles piling up in the bucket if they weren't going to their deaths, if there wasn't something quiet about this garden that Teddy didn't like. In Teddy's yard there were always bees buzzing and birds calling and crickets playing the violins. In this yard there was a strained silence. As if everyone were holding their breaths.

"You better hurry up," Orlando said. "I've already picked thirty-two. I hope you're counting."

Teddy wondered how fast the bugs could multiply. If they just left them there, would they take over the whole garden? Then the block? Then the world? He didn't share these thoughts with Orlando.

When Susan came back out, they had almost picked the bush clean. She gave an exclamation of satisfaction. Then she handed them each five dollars. Orlando looked at the money in his hand and the money in Teddy's hand angrily and then said, "I picked way more than him. I picked sixty-three. You said a dime apiece."

She looked into the bucket. "You think I have the time to stand here all day counting beetles? Work it out between the two of you. And go down the alley when you leave. I don't want you climbing my fence anymore like a couple of chicken thieves."

"You told us to climb over," Teddy pointed out, but she merely glared at him.

When they arrived out front, back into the hot sunlight, Orlando demanded that Teddy give him two dollars.

"I worked just as long as you," Teddy said calmly.

"But I picked more."

"So what? Most people get paid by the hour, and if you hadn't been in my backyard, I would have done the whole job by myself."

Orlando reached forward swiftly into Teddy's pocket, but instead of coming up with money, he came up with a handful of glittering beetles.

"You were stealing her beetles!"

"That's stupid," Teddy said. "They weren't her beetles and she didn't want them."

"She was right about you. You *are* a thief! Give me my money." Orlando grabbed Teddy by the shoulder and squeezed it pretty hard. Teddy let out a yell of surprise. He stared at Orlando and then, without thinking about it at all, he stepped on Orlando's foot. Once he had done it, he experienced a solid gush of something so satisfying and surprising, he immediately stuck his elbow out and stabbed it into Orlando's chest. This gesture, too, felt so ripely correct, he hardly noticed the punch that Orlando landed on his ear. He stepped forward and, with both hands wide open, pushed Orlando so hard that he fell backward, landing on the bottom step of the stoop. Orlando grabbed Teddy's ankle and pulled him down on top of him.

At this moment, Johnny Pitsacado, looking wide awake and neatly combed and washed, came strolling by. He stopped in front of the boys and watched them wrestling for a minute. Then he pointed over them and yelled, "Holy shit! Will you look at that? The house is on fire!"

Orlando and Teddy stopped what they were doing and looked

first at Johnny, and then at the house, which stood tranquilly and without a trace of smoke or flame right behind them.

Both boys simultaneously realized that they had been had. It was too late, however, to return to what they were doing. The momentum was gone.

"Your knee is bleeding," Johnny pointed out to Teddy.

Teddy saw how clean and fresh Johnny looked, and that he was wearing strawberry-pink sneakers with silver toecaps. "I'm going in," Teddy said. He picked up his container and went in the house.

Inside he listened for his mother, but there was no sound. He slipped into his laboratory and there he squeezed some blood from his knee onto his finger. He shook the blood into the formula and then stirred it with a spoon. Instantly it turned a deep rusty red. It shone out at him like rubies or a fire truck coming down the street. He had no idea what the power of the thing was meant to be, but he was sure he was going in the right direction.

At six-thirty Maury was standing in line at Zabar's, waiting to buy some smoked salmon.

Someone spoke his name.

He turned and there was Fran, holding a large plastic take-out container of Greek salad. He found himself able to look at her face for only a moment, so he focused, instead, on her bare right shoulder, which had three silver concentric circles tattooed on it.

"What's that cologne?" she asked, leaning in closer to sniff at him.

"I'm not wearing cologne."

She turned and sniffed at the man in line behind her. Maury saw, to his intense dismay, that the man grinned at her invitingly.

"No, it's not you," she said to the man. She turned back to Maury.

"It is the natural incense of my fresh and innocent soul."

She stepped even closer, so close that if he had put his arms around her and pulled her in, just a little bit, her breasts would have just lightly tipped up against him. He didn't, however, move, although little beads of sweat gathered at his temples.

"I like it," she said, "but it's not a soulful smell. There's something peppery in it. You eating a lot of peppers?" Suddenly she frowned. "I just remembered something."

"What?" Now that she was frowning, he was able to look at her, as if a little cloud had gone across the sun. It was an exquisite frown, a lacquered Chinese box of a frown, filled with other little boxes inside of boxes.

"I had a dream. You were in it. I'd forgotten all about it."

He had to breathe deeply and calmly, down low in the depths of his abdomen. Of course she'd had a dream about him. A dream such as his own did not stand all alone without an answer. He waited for her to tell him.

She looked around without seeing anything, frowning, trying to remember. "That smell was in my dream. What was it? Now I remember. There were a lot of things going on, but in this part of the dream, I was sitting in a café in Italy for some reason, drinking lemonade, and the waiter was putting a plate down on the table in front of me. The plate was loaded up with all kinds of elaborate foods. I didn't recognize any of them, but there was that same peppery smell. When I looked up to tell the waiter I hadn't ordered any of this, I saw it was you."

"And?"

"And that's all I remember about that part."

He took five deep even breaths, straight from the center of his desire, trying to tame it. "That's a good dream," he said. They were almost at the front of the line. "How's your mother doing?" he asked hoarsely.

She frowned. "Funny you should ask. Something rather weird happened yesterday."

"What was that?" He kept his eyes upon her as if he feared that if he looked away even for a moment, she would disappear.

"My mother called me to say that Elsie was very upset because when she came home from work the other night she found a pair of muddy boots sitting on the mat outside her apartment door. She said they looked just like Uncle Claremont's—the boots he was buried in."

"How did your mother know this?"

"Good question. Apparently she had dinner with my father again the other night."

"Ahh."

"I asked my mother if she might possibly have had anything to do with this footwear at Elsie's door. My mother laughed and said she had warned Elsie that Uncle Claremont would never rest easy in that grave."

Maury had now reached the front of the line. He paid his money and waited for Fran to pay hers. Then they walked out of the store together and stood on the sidewalk.

"I wonder what size they were," Maury said.

Fran looked at him.

"The boots. Imagine walking around in those for an hour or two. Now, there might be an opportunity for enlightenment. Could you find out if Elsie would like to get rid of them?"

"You're kidding, right?"

Maury smiled. "Sort of. How are your sinuses?"

"Not great. Still clogged."

"How about I take you to a good Japanese place and we'll get some sushi with an excellent wasabi dipping sauce?" He saw that she was staring at him in amusement. He blushed, but went on. "Furthermore, I will quietly admire your beauty. There is no vitamin or tonic so good for the overall general immune system as having one's beauty quietly admired. I guarantee that this, along with the wasabi, will clear your sinuses by the end of the evening."

It was that time at the end of a summer day when the temperature drops enough to lighten the collective footstep. The busy river of people parted with only a few curious glances and went around them. Soft lights began to come on in the store windows like fireflies.

"I'm having dinner with my father," she said at last and waved her paper bag at him. "I'm bringing the salad. Perhaps another night."

He was half relieved and half crushed to death. He considered her offer. He could suggest another night. But since, as a general rule of thumb, he did not make plans more than twenty-four hours in advance, knowing that such overplanning could delay or frighten off one's destiny, he merely nodded his head and wished her a pleasant dinner.

〜

When Pinky went into the backyard to check on the baby, she found that the gate was unlocked and that there was no sign of Bernard anywhere. For several minutes, she raced around the garden and then down the alleyway, peering in the shrubbery, calling his name. But he was nowhere to be found. When she frantically questioned Teddy, she noted the look on his face when she mentioned the gate and kept at him unrelentingly until he admitted that he had left it unlocked, but closed. Bernard was there when he had last left the yard a while ago. He did not mention the Japanese beetles to his mother.

Pinky picked up the voicelink and dialed Arthur's pocket number.

But as it fell out, Arthur had gone straight to the park from work and accidentally left his pocketlink on his desk. He had a date to play chess with Billy. He sat under the tree with the leaves like little green fans and ate a hot dog with sauerkraut and mustard. He watched Billy playing a very neat-looking elderly gentleman in suspenders and a pressed white shirt.

Arthur saw that although they both played politely, there was an air of murderous determination to the game. The elderly gentleman had the advantage.

The air was still and heavy. Ulysses the swan sailed up, accompanied by another swan. The two birds stopped in the shallow water and waited there rather menacingly for someone to throw them something to eat. Arthur threw them each a piece of his hot dog roll. They stood where they were, but snapped their long strong whiplike necks forward and swallowed these pieces down in single gulps.

"Watch your fingers," Billy warned him.

The birds waited for more, but when nothing came, they turned to preening their back feathers haughtily.

Arthur saw that Billy was uneasy. He stared at the board and then he looked around at the trees, the lake, the two swans preening themselves. He looked at his opponent, who was studying the board in a bloodthirsty, self-assured way. It was the other fellow's move.

Billy cleared his throat and in an offhand manner addressed Arthur. "He got caught in a fishing line last week," he said, indicating Ulysses the swan. "Can you imagine the asshole who would leave a hook and line around a place like this? It was a mess. The hook was stuck in his neck, under his beak, and the line had gotten twisted around his leg, so he couldn't move his head."

"So what happened?" Arthur asked.

Billy's opponent, trying to concentrate, frowned.

"Well, I knew it wouldn't do me any good to call the Parks Department. It would take them days to do what needed to be done. So I went home and got a pair of Susan's heavy gardening gloves and a little pliers and a scissors and I came back. I found somebody willing to help me, and we got hold of the bird and I cut him loose. The hook was the hardest part, but it was caught in the feathers, not the flesh, and the bird actually stood still while we were doing it, like he knew what we were up to. We ended up just pulling the feathers out. You can see where he's still missing a couple."

Arthur peered at the bird.

"And that's the end of the story, right?" the elderly man asked irritably.

"Well, actually, no. When we were done, he wouldn't get back in the water. He just kind of stood there, hissing a little. When I got up to head home, he started following me."

"The swan?"

"Yeah. I had gotten across the road and I heard all of this honking behind me and when I turned around, there he was, right in the middle of the street and all these cars swerving around him. He was watching me and trying to scare the cars off by flapping his wings at them."

The elderly man pursed his mouth and stared at Billy and then at the swan.

"Susan would have shat kittens if I brought a swan home with me. So I turned around and stopped the traffic and then I led him back into the park and down to the lake. But he still wouldn't get in the water. So finally I took off my shoes and waded in there and he followed me. Once he was in, he started heading right out to the deep part, like he thought I was going to just dive in there and swim along with him. When he saw I wasn't following, he started back toward me, but I kept shooing at him with my arms. It was getting dark and finally, I guess, he gave up because he swam away and disappeared in the reeds over on the other side.

"Your move," Billy reminded the other guy.

The elderly man shook his head. "What a lot of baloney." He made, Arthur noted, an amazingly injudicious move.

Billy smiled. He moved his knight's pawn two spaces forward.

Everybody studied the board. It was immediately clear that the other fellow was now going to lose his queen and, shortly thereafter, the game. He made a clicking noise in the back of his throat, bowed his head angrily, then rose and stalked off.

Ulysses lifted his head and watched him depart.

"He always hangs around when I'm here, now. He's keeping an eye on me. Sort of a bodyguard thing, I think," Billy said.

A little ways down the edge of the lake, two boys pulled something out of the water on the end of a fishing line. From here it looked like a turtle with two heads, but it could have been any kind of discarded debris covered with weeds. Whatever it was, the boys were arguing over it.

"Play?" Billy asked.

Arthur sat down across from him. He played white. He did not allow Billy to talk. Every time Billy cleared his throat or opened his mouth, Arthur put his finger severely to his lips.

He knocked all of Billy's footmen one by one off the board, until the middle was a completely open smoking meadow. Then his queen dashed out, connecting his rooks, and, in a few swift moves, he had Billy by the throat.

When he announced the checkmate, he leaned back and waited for Billy to speak, but Billy was silent.

Arthur, when he looked out at the lake, found himself able to ask the question he had been wanting to ask.

"When your son died, did you regret that you'd had only one child?"

It took Billy what seemed a very long time to pull his gaze away from the board. "We didn't have one child. We had two."

Arthur was taken by surprise. The headache, which had been so mild up to this minute he hadn't even noticed it, now expanded rapidly like a balloon or a small, head-sized air bag. It pressed up against his eyeballs and the inside of his skull.

"A girl."

"Where is she? She's grown now?"

"She's thirty-two. She's been in an institution since she was four." Billy was still staring disappointedly at the chessboard. "A little spot where something wasn't right with her genes. Three chromosomes instead of two. If they'd known then what they know now, they might have been able to do something about it. But you have to catch the problem while the baby is still in the womb. It was a long time ago. She never learned to walk or talk."

Arthur managed to say that he was sorry.

The older man nodded. "She's in a place not far from here. It's not a bad place, as these places go. But, of course, there isn't anybody there who remembers when her birthday comes around, or who can imagine how beautiful she would have been if she had been able to keep her tongue in her mouth and hold her head up straight. And, of course, you have to keep watch—things have a way of disappearing: clothes, blankets. You have to keep an eye on these kind of things. We go a couple of times a week."

"Does she know you?" Arthur asked.

"Sure. Sure. She lights up when we come in. She's ours. She isn't anybody else's. Last month she got pneumonia. It wasn't the first time. Her lungs are weak. She was very sick. But this time they thought she might die. I went every day, but what was so hard was not knowing what to do, what I could do for her that would make any difference, and then one of the nurses pointed out how dry her mouth was and suggested I could moisten it with these little wet cloths, and once I could do that, it helped me. Although it also quenched my excitement at the prospect that she might die, at what it might mean to me. Does that sound awful?"

"I wouldn't presume to judge such a feeling."

"The chances are that she will outlive us. It's hard to bear, thinking about how it will be for her when we are gone, when the world is emptied out of anybody who might love her even a little."

"But you have some sort of plan, don't you? You mentioned it to me last time."

Billy looked, again, at the lost game. "That's right. I do."

"So, what is it?"

"I got a gun a few months ago. It was surprisingly easy."

The swans were gone. "What on earth do you mean?" Arthur demanded. The ducks were beginning to come up on shore and to settle in the long grasses for the night. There was a loud chorus of crickets and other violin-playing insects.

Billy shook his head."I was thinking that when the time was right, I'd just take us all out for a drive to Coney Island or something."

"If this is a joke, it's a poor one."

"Who's joking? I'm not joking."

"You actually have a gun?"

"In the back of my study closet inside an empty chess box."

"You just tell these stories as a way of distracting your chess opponents," Arthur said angrily.

"We're not playing chess," Billy pointed out.

"You were going to tell me this story while we played, but I wouldn't let you talk. Now you're telling me this as a way of exacting revenge."

Billy shook his head heavily. "Revenge?"

Arthur felt ashamed of himself and very tired. His head was throbbing and to think his way through this in a straight line wasn't easy, but he managed to say, "Forgive me. My mind is not clear. Pinky and I have separated. I guess you know that. I've been staying with a friend up on the Upper West Side, but I wonder if you'd mind putting me up tonight. The trip seems like too much right now."

Billy lifted his eyebrows and looked at Arthur searchingly, but Arthur volunteered no more information.

"Of course. You're welcome to stay."

"What about Susan?"

"What about her?"

"Will she mind?"

"Almost certainly. The trick is to act as if you notice nothing."

Pinky tried calling Arthur every few minutes. She tried his office, his pocketlink number, and she tried calling him at Maury's. She got Maury's service message that said: "Whoever you are, you are just the one I have been waiting to speak to. I'm not sure where I am right now, but I will call you as soon as I get back from wherever it is. Leave your name and number, if you're so inclined. Otherwise leave it to destiny, which knows its business."

Pinky slammed the receiver down.

She thought of calling the police, but she wasn't sure what the baby's legal status was now. Would they demand a birth certificate? Arthur would know, but where was he?

She tried to calm herself. It seemed to her most likely that Fishhammer had taken the baby, and that, certainly, he had every reason to care well for him. She and Arthur would bring him back eventually, but meanwhile, no possible harm could come to him.

She fed Teddy dinner, though she could eat none herself. She did not notice his dreamy preoccupation. When she finally got him to bed, unable to restrain herself, she called the fire department and asked to speak to Orson. Someone told her that he was off duty for the night. Was it an emergency? She said that it wasn't and hung up.

Back at Billy's house, they played one more game of chess. Arthur would not have stopped Billy from speaking if he had wanted to. He did not particularly care if he won or lost at this point. What he mostly wanted was for the evening to be over so that Billy would go to sleep and Arthur could do what it was he knew he was obligated to do. Then he could go back to Maury's apartment with a clean conscience in this matter and lie down on his futon that was like packed dirt and stare at the ceiling and prepare for the weight of all his guilt and sorrow to gather enough mass and tonnage to crack the earth open and allow him to sink down out of sight.

Billy stayed silent and Arthur won again. There was no sign or sound from Susan. Billy said he was tired and asked Arthur if he would mind if they turned in.

He brought Arthur to a room that was clean and neatly swept, almost bare. There were no toys or banners, books or baseballs. But in one corner of the room sat, neatly, a pair of basketball sneakers, and Arthur knew that this had been the boy's room.

This didn't frighten him, since he knew there was no such thing as ghosts, but a cricket had found its way into the room and it was doing that ventriloquist act crickets did, throwing its voice around so that it sounded like it was somewhere where it wasn't at all.

When the cricket at last fell quiet and there were no other sounds in the house, he tiptoed out of the room and down the stairs toward the study. At the bottom, though, in the dark, he was disoriented and he heard an unnerving sound, like a distant woman weeping. He dared not turn on the light for fear of drawing attention to himself. He touched the wall and felt a bookcase and then bumped into something protuberant and sharp like the antlers of a moose, but in a moment, brushing up against coats, he realized he had found the coat tree in the front hall.

He turned around and went the other way, patting the wall carefully until he found an open doorway. He stepped in and shut the door behind him and felt on the wall for a palm sensor or a light switch. There was none, but at last he found a little table lamp and was able to turn it on. He was in the study. It was almost, he felt, too easy. He went to the closet in the back and there, on the top shelf, was the empty chess box with the old black revolver inside. Nauseated and terrified of the thing, he lifted it up between two fingers as if it were a wasp and slid it into his pants pocket.

Leaving the house, he closed the front door behind him and paused to make sure he heard the lock click. Then he stopped again, sure he heard a woman weeping. Was it the same woman he had heard a few minutes ago, or was this was a different woman? Perhaps there were always women weeping all up and down the city at this time of night.

He looked around, a little reluctantly, to see if he could see where the sound was coming from. He did not have to search far before he spotted Pinky sitting on his own front steps, crying her eyes out.

18. Arthur Explains

$\mathcal{H}$e was telling her about the jelly jar and the happiness gene. He explained to her that his motives were not at all what she imagined, that although he would never be sure that what he had done was right, he had *wanted* to do what was right. They were sitting there in the dark in the living room, Pinky at one end of the sofa, Arthur at the other. He had expected, when the moment came, to feel relieved, but there was no relief in sight. The baby was gone and he knew that if Ken had taken him where Arthur thought he had taken him, then there was no hope of bringing him back.

All the while he was talking, he managed not to look at her face, but after he was finished, she was silent for such a very long time, he wondered if she had taken in what he had said. He glanced at her and saw that the light that came in through the curtains was blue and diamondlike, and it struck her head so that her hair glinted and sparkled. For some reason she smelled of smoke.

"So you're telling me this was all some kind of science experiment?" she said at last.

Perhaps it was the loss of the baby, or that he had had to wait so long to tell her this story, but his voice, when it came back into the silence, had an exasperated note of despair in it, like the voice of a man who has broken down on the side of a dark road and then discovered that he has left his pocketlink at home on the dresser.

"No! It wasn't just a science experiment. I'm trying to tell you! Marina didn't care about that part at all. She just wanted a baby—a happy baby."

"Which was exactly what I wanted."

"Pinky, we have Teddy. We didn't need another baby."

"We didn't need Bernard?" She sat up and the shadowy leaves in her hair rippled and fluttered. "How can you tell me we didn't need Bernard?"

He stared at her. "But Bernard isn't the issue. If we had had another baby together, it wouldn't have been Bernard."

"Of course it would have been Bernard. Maybe there would have been some minor changes, if it had been you and I, but how can you believe that the essential Bernard would not have found his way to us?"

"Pinky," he groaned. What he wanted, he recognized, was a small thing. He did not expect to find his way back to where peace and rationality prevailed, to where no guns existed and people didn't fly planes into buildings full of people, to where no one bioengineered virulent influenza germs and let them go in reservoirs in Japan, to where swans didn't follow people home, and to where babies could sleep in their backyards without fear of being snatched away. What he merely hoped for was that he be forgiven. Somewhere, however, he had, once again, taken a wrong turn. "Pinky, even if our germ cells had combined to create a baby something like Bernard, he still would not have had Fishhammer's gene. Marina stole that from him, I think."

"Fishhammer's gene is what makes him happy, is that what you're telling me?"

"Yes. I think so."

"So you're saying that Bernard is not really Bernard, that he would be somebody else without this gene, and that Fishhammer didn't take him for his wife, but for his science experiment?"

"That first part is hard, Pinky. But I believe that Bernard is as much Bernard as you are you. We're all shaped by things or influences that have come to us from other people and I suppose you could look at the happiness gene that way. As for the reason that Fishhammer took him, yes, I suppose it's for his research. But that's assuming that Fishhammer was the one who took him. We can't be sure of that."

"What good would Bernard do him? What would he want with him?"

Into his mind came some of the tests that Fishhammer carried out on the mice. "He wants to observe him. Then he wants to write a paper about it and get it published in some big scientific journal."

"That's it? That's *it?* He would steal a child so he could write a paper for a science journal?"

"Well, I think he also hopes to reroute evolution and the path of human destiny."

"What do you mean? Say what you mean!" She was impatient and angry. He had imagined when he finally told her about the jelly jar she would be interested only in understanding what had gone on between him and Marina, but, of course, now that the baby was gone, her interests were elsewhere.

"I think he thought that if he could get his gene to work, he might begin a whole new race of happy and reasonable and well-behaved human beings."

"Bernard isn't well behaved!" she yelled, as if this were the worst thing of all, that Bernard should be so misunderstood. Several more strands of her hair came undone and twisted upward into the pool of light that illuminated her head.

"That's true," Arthur sighed. He remembered his few weeks of being happy. They already had a distant dreamlike quality. How much more reliable and familiar misery seemed.

He tried again. "Look, what I wanted you to understand was that I agreed to Marina's request because I knew what she had gone through, what she had suffered."

She put her hands down in her lap and made herself still. "So you are telling me it was a political thing, that there was nothing personal in it?"

"I don't think I was thinking politically, exactly. It was more that I knew she'd been through a hard time and I could see that she was a good person and I imagined that she'd have a difficult time finding a partner."

"Why? Because of her face?"

"Well, partly."

"Would you have loved her if it hadn't been for her face?"

Arthur bent his head and tried to breathe through his exasperation. "I didn't love her because I didn't love her. It had nothing to do with her face."

"But it's a terrible thing, to make a baby with someone you don't love," she informed him.

"Pinky, I don't know what to say to you. I don't know what it is you want, but I need you to know that there was nothing sexual or romantic in my decision to agree to her request. It was, I thought, a kindness. Now I realize my mistake. I'm sorry for it."

"You're sorry you made Bernard?"

"Pinky," he admonished.

"Why should I believe any of what you say?"

"Because you know me."

"No, I don't."

He leaned forward and reached into her little pool of moonlight and took her hand. "Please forgive me."

She tipped her chin upward proudly, but kept her gaze upon his.

He waited. He thought he might have felt just the slightest answering pressure of her fingers, but then she pulled her hand away. "You have to go find him," she said.

"You mean Bernard?"

"Of course."

"Well, if he's where I think he is, that's going to be next to impossible. He's inside the jaws of a machinery that you can't comprehend."

"Where do you think he is?"

"If Ken took him, he took him to Venturetech. That's where Ken went after he got booted out of the university. It's a huge multinational bioresearch company. It's Mitchell Newman's company."

"Oh, I've heard of him. Nobody's seen him for years, right? His wife and son died in a car accident. He has enough money to rule the world if he wants to."

"I have no idea how much money the guy has, but the point is, that place has a security system God Himself couldn't get into."

"You don't believe in God. I'm sure there's a little back door somewhere."

"You don't know what you're talking about. You have no experience with this. I worked for one of these companies, remember, back before I took the job at the university."

For a couple of minutes, he thought she was actually giving due consideration to what he was saying. She chewed on her bottom lip and stared up at something on the ceiling. The fine curls of her hair that had escaped stood around her head in a red mist. Her freckles stood out in the lamplight. Then her gaze snapped toward him, as if she had suddenly made up her mind. She rapped the wooden arm of the sofa with her knuckles.

"Pay attention, Arthur," she said. She opened her bare arms up as if she were holding something large in them. "Here's the earth. What are the chances of its being here? You told me that according to the theories, its chances of getting made and of becoming the right sort of place for life to show up were not good, right? Maybe about a trillion to one, but here it is. And here *we* are. According to *your* story, we made it through out of a jillion sperm. Now, you may think this doesn't *mean* anything, but I do. Bernard came to us from out of the blue. There's only one thing we can do. I'd be out that door in a second, but I think it better be you. You're the one who can get in there and if you don't give it a try you will never forgive yourself."

Soon after Fishhammer got Bernard in the van, he gave him an attractive chloral hydrate–laced lollipop. Bernard had eaten only half of it before he was asleep.

When he woke up the next morning, he was in a crib in the strange bright grassily carpeted room with its three fruit trees. One wall of the room was composed of a dark open doorway and a great silvery one-way mirror. The room was pleasantly temperature-controlled. Bernard called out questioningly and, in a moment, the deaf-mute—the man who called himself Maurice—came in and stopped and stared at him.

This was what he saw. He saw a baby with perhaps no one extraordinary feature, but who shone out into a room in a way that was hard to account for. He stood there holding on to the bars of the crib, no bigger or smaller than a baby should be, in a pair of royal blue shorts sagging soggily in the seat. His legs were plump and creased. He wore no shirt and he had a little jutting Buddha belly. He had a lot of curly dark hair that obviously the mother had had no heart to cut, so that it fell into his eyes. His face was plump and round. One might be tempted to take little pretend bites of it and then revert to kisses. His eyes were dark as coffee beans, but clear and bright and full of movement. Even so, he stared into Maurice's eyes quite steadily.

Maurice lifted him up. Bernard looked at this fellow human with pleasure and the man gazed back at him curiously.

Their faces were close. Bernard touched the man's mouth and then worked a couple of fingers inside and pried it open. Maurice breathed gently upon the baby's hand and face as Bernard leaned in closer and peered inside his mouth.

When Bernard pulled his head back, they stared into each other's eyes and appeared fully satisfied with what they had found.

Maurice brought the baby over to the changing table and clumsily stripped him down. Bernard was delighted with the novelty of the man and the strange room. He peed straight up into the air and wet Maurice and the front of his white jacket.

"Aaabba!" he declared.

Maurice grabbed a towel and patted himself dry, keeping one hand on the baby. He then rediapered him and, in spite of very little cooperation from the baby, managed to pull onto him a clean pair of shorts and a T-shirt. He lifted Bernard up and set him on the floor.

Bernard surveyed the room with a crafty eye, then zoomed across it tipsily as a humming top. He babbled and sang his commentary as he went from corner to corner, climbing and touching and knocking things down. Maurice stayed close beside him.

Bernard stopped for his first long pause at the table piled high with bright toys. The alphabet cubes, the colored plastic rings that sat in graduated size on their little pole, were flung through the air. The cloth books were roughly examined and dropped on the floor. The fat peg people in the yellow school bus were summarily turned upside down and tumbled onto the table. Some were stowed down Bernard's diaper and some he carried in his hands across the room.

"Eh, eh, eh!" he demanded, and climbed up onto the sofa. Bernard peered curiously behind the sofa into the darkness and then dropped the peg people down there, one by one. He stood there for a while gazing into where he had thrown them, but when the peg people did not return, he climbed off the sofa and headed at a speedy waddle toward the fruit tree with the bright red disk fruits. He stood under it, gazing up at its heavily loaded branches, and appeared to consider the distance. It wasn't a tall tree and its lowest fruit hung nearly within his reach.

"Oodoo," he said and grabbed the slender trunk and tried to pull himself up on the edge of the large wooden planter from which the tree grew. He got one foot up and lost his balance and fell backward, banging his head on the side of a chair.

Maurice hurried over to him and helped him up and examined the little head. The baby, of course, was not in the least perturbed and smiled at Maurice, babbling wildly. "Ooodoo, doo, ad. Oodoo, doo." He wiggled energetically, until Maurice tired of trying to hold on to him and set him again on the floor.

Now Bernard paused and, after a lot of hard work, managed to pull his T-shirt off one arm. Then, tired of this effort, Bernard stopped and took his bearings again. He looked around the bright room, but this time his eye was caught by the dark doorway at the other end. He seemed to give a little sigh. He stared at it. He said, "Poompah." Then, as if under a reluctant obligation, he headed in its direction, the T-shirt hanging crookedly across half his bare chest.

He toddled into the second room, the one that stood behind the one-way mirror. This space had no windows. Maurice followed him and put on the lights and flipped the video switch, which turned on all the video cameras mounted strategically around the walls.

A camera recorded the baby's expression as he stood looking at the steel examining table, the tiled floor, the grid on the wall hung with the many sharp and electrical instruments, and the small chair with the leather straps and buckles.

The baby's face had gone quite still. He looked neither happy nor sad nor frightened. And, after all, why should he, the older man thought? He was far too young to have any associations with such things. Nevertheless, he could not help thinking that the child was gazing calmly, with acceptance, as if he understood perfectly well what it was he was looking at.

A moment later, Bernard turned with a small sigh and headed back toward the sunny room. One of the peg people slid down from his diaper and out of his shorts onto the tile floor, and Bernard, not noticing it, put his foot down on top of it and slipped and pitched forward into a metal cabinet, scraping his arm.

Maurice picked him up and carried him over to the sink and washed the cut, then brought him into the other room to the high chair and strapped him in. From the cabinets behind the chair, Maurice pulled out some cereal and a banana, a spoon and a bowl.

Maurice parked himself in front of the high chair, his back to the camera, and watched the baby feed himself a merry, highly action-packed breakfast. Part of the banana was consumed, the rest was ungently squeezed between Bernard's fingers and then smeared artistically about his person and the high chair. The cereal met a similar fate. Somewhere in here, Bernard managed to work his other arm out of the T-shirt, so now the shirt hung like a lobster bib about his neck. Bernard talked loudly to his food during the whole meal.

Maurice, tired out, watched him sleepily. His eyes were half closed when Ken Fishhammer came into the room silently.

Ken looked at the baby and then stood over Maurice, frowning.

Maurice sat up.

"Take the baby out of the high chair. Why is his shirt like that? Take it off, please, and clean him up. We have a lot of work to do."

Maurice removed the shirt and cleaned up the baby and then unstrapped him and put him down on the carpet.

Bernard did not hesitate, but came over directly and greeted Ken with much fanfare. After a while, when Ken did not respond, he worked his way over to the little rug area where some blocks were arranged on a low shelf. Ken wrote some instructions on a piece of paper and handed it over to Maurice. He then went and hid himself behind the one-way mirror and took copious notes.

Bernard seemed completely enthralled by Maurice's attempts to frustrate him. First, they played with the blocks. Every time the baby built a tower, Maurice would pull one of the blocks out so that the tower would come tumbling down. The baby laughed hysterically. Then Maurice took a small box from the shelf, marked "A" and extracted from it a little card and a gorgeous toy fire engine tied to the end of a thin, nearly invisible nylon string. Maurice read the card and then put the fire engine on the floor just within the baby's reach, but every time his chubby fingers got near enough to touch it, Maurice jerked it forward. Again, Bernard thought this hilarious, but he did not give up trying to grab hold of the engine, finally attempting to pin the toy down by throwing his whole body on top of it instead of using just his hands. When Maurice finally untied the string and put the fire engine in his arms, Bernard lifted it with the greatest tenderness to his face as if it were a little bird fallen from a nest. Maurice let him hold it for a minute, then pried it from his grasp and put it away. He took out another box, this one marked "B." Looking inside, he first extracted the card and read it. Then he removed a large black hatlike object. He turned it so the open side was up and laid it on the floor. He waited for Bernard to come over and look inside. As soon as Bernard was almost close enough to touch it, Maurice pressed a little remote-control button and out of the hat shot a big rubber head with a disfigured, Halloweenish face. Its tongue stuck out and its eyeballs protruded redly and there was a big, gaping bloody wound on its cheek. Even the mother of this face would have reeled back in horror and dismay. Bernard, however, being made of some stuff for which no name yet had been thrown out of the air, toddled forward and hunkered down and reached out to stroke the wounded cheek. The face let out a terrible scream. Bernard tipped his head to the side and considered it. Then, again, he laughed. Maurice shot the head up and down a few times and made it howl, but Bernard remained obdurately tickled by the performance.

Ken, taking rapid notes and watching from behind the one-way mirror, was filled with a careful and tempered glee. After a while, he came out and looked at the deaf-mute. Then he picked up the dark-haired child and carried him into the other room and strapped him into the little chair. The baby still had no shirt on. He tried to avoid the baby's eyes, but somehow he couldn't. He was startled and very unnerved to see that Bernard immediately knew all there was to know about his sins and that, for some reason, in Bernard's eyes, these sins were already buried beneath the earth and the grass was growing over them.

Later in the afternoon, when Maurice went out for a dinner break, Fishhammer sat down and watched Bernard, who looked now a little wan and tired, but as cheerful as ever. Outside, it had begun to rain, but in here, the room seemed sunny and bright.

Ken's pocketlink rang.

"The baby is astounding," a hoarse voice said.

"You've seen him?" Ken asked.

Newman did not bother to answer this. "Now, what I'm interested in knowing is whether you are simply a sadist or if there is some clear scientific protocol for your little revelries."

Ken Fishhammer was extremely annoyed. "I have devised a very careful set of trials and tests for the child. I have written these out, along with their rationale, very carefully. They include observations of the child's tolerance of cold, heat, fear, hunger, frustration, and fatigue. You are welcome to examine these protocols. You are *not* welcome to tap into my video recordings for surveillance purposes. I don't want you looking over my shoulder."

Newman said, "I want to remind you that it is my hospitality which protects and enables you. Science is one thing, but I will not tolerate any indulgence of morbid appetites."

"You know my work and you know what this project promises. I have a lot of data to collect, but I believe it will all simply confirm my hypothesis."

Newman coughed, but could not clear the roughness in his voice. "Assuming that this baby proves to be what you believe him to be, it is your opinion that you could use this vaccine on any human embryo?"

"Yes. I have no way of knowing exactly how Marina introduced the chromosome vector, but she probably used some fairly simple mechanical means which could be easily done anywhere. If I'm right about this, the world will soon be banging down your door. Who will not want this for their children? Venturetech should prepare itself."

"Have no fear. I am always well girded." There was a soft click and Fishhammer found himself holding only the silent receiver.

He snapped his pocketlink shut and turned to see that in the process of trying to crawl behind the changing table in order to pick up one of the small disk-fruits that had rolled there, Bernard had gotten his head stuck between one of its metal legs and the wall.

Bernard wriggled forward and wriggled backward, but he couldn't extricate himself. He twisted his head this way and that. But the more he twisted, the tighter his head seemed to be caught.

Fishhammer sat there watching him. The cheek and the ear turned toward him were bright red, little veins protruding. The baby tried to move forward again.

Ken bent down and put his face in front of Bernard and smiled at him. Bernard stopped wriggling for a moment and smiled back at him and then he tried to reach out and grab Ken's pen from his pocket.

Ken backed off and stood up.

He lifted the table out of the way and the baby was free.

At this moment, Maurice returned from his dinner. He saw the baby sitting on the floor quietly touching his bruised and purple ear. He bent down to him to pick him up.

Ken put his hand up peremptorily, signaling him to wait. Maurice stood back.

Bernard now slowly pulled himself up, using the table to bring himself to his feet. He appeared to be listening to something at a distance. He cocked his head to the side and then turned around in a little circle two or three times like the arm on a compass, then he stopped where he was, still wavering uncertainly, sniffing the air. When at last he was settled on the direction he wished to be facing, he began to make a sound that was not exactly a croon or a hum or a warble, but any or all of these things rounded up together.

Ken turned on a little portable tape recorder sitting on a shelf. He stood there listening with a look of some disquiet on his face. Then he turned to the older man, whom he found watching him curiously.

Ken flushed. "Give him a bath," he ordered peremptorily. "We have a lot of work to do tomorrow."

Oedipus lived in the bottom drawer of the dresser for a number of days. He didn't and couldn't count them. His adjustment to the new pattern of daily rounds was easy and natural. There was the pleasure of catching his own bloody little meals, of finding his way through the alleys and the tall grass, of being loose from his former responsibilities of having to watch over the humans. But greatest was the pleasure of knowing himself surrounded by unknown danger and finding himself a warrior rising to the occasion. He was, at first, a little clumsy, a little out of tune. But each day he could hear this melody, this answer to the question that had been hidden from him, more clearly. In the day, when it was hot, he slept, but the nights were gentle and perfumed with the scent of peril and he stalked his way through them in ecstasy.

Until one night it began to rain. His mother, whose voice he had never forgotten, had not mentioned anything to him about rain in Paradise.

It rained all through the darkness and all the next day. Oedipus crouched miserably in the dresser drawer, trying to avoid the little drips dripping in through the rotten wood. But eventually there was no dry corner left and, driven additionally by hunger, he reluctantly jumped out into the wet grass.

He saw right away that there was no question of hunting. There was nothing out here to hunt. All the small furry and feathered things were no doubt crammed contentedly together in some dry nest arguing and telling foolish stories and nibbling on their stores of absurd seedy little snack foods.

He stood there, his fierce light gone out, sodden, whiskers dripping in the rain, not having a clue where to go next.

And then he suddenly had a vision of Teddy's bed, with its warm jumble of blankets. How could he have forgotten? As if he were standing right there in the room, he saw, quite vividly, an image of himself going around three times in the bedding and then settling himself into the hollow he had made. Standing here in the rain, he could smell the scent of peanut butter and tuna fish. But where was Teddy? He looked for him in his mind's eye, but could not find him.

All he could hear was that strange sound that Teddy made when things were not well for him.

Teddy was weeping for him, he realized. How could he not have known this—that Teddy would be heartbroken? How could he so easily have forgotten his true work, the charge that had been laid upon him so solemnly?

He understood that he must find Teddy and his nest of blankets, but how? There were no stars, there was no moon, and he did not know how to read those things anyway.

At this moment, he heard them—a pack of wild junkyard stink-barkers somehow loosed from their confinement. They came pelting around the corner, a middle-sized black fellow with a white ear in the lead, baying and yelping, overflowing with the thrill of finding themselves free, looking for whatever mayhem they could make, a ripe garbage can to knock over, a baby left unattended in a stroller, a wet cat lost far from home.

The fur on Oedipus's back rose straight in the air. Without pausing for breath or thought, he dashed out of the lot and into the street, only a few yards ahead of this coarse and flea-bitten, spotted and brindled horde. At the sight of the cat, they could hear their ancestors howling encouragement on the distant frozen tundra, and, gleefully, they fanned out and closed in on him.

Oedipus did not look behind him. Fear goaded him. He kept himself low and he zigzagged and he ran with the speed of an electric current. The dogs kept right at his tail. Near the top of the hill, he dashed under a car and cowered, panting, while the stinkbarkers surrounded him and tried to work themselves and their slavering snouts far enough under the automobile so they could grab him with their bear-trap junkyard teeth and rip him, still alive, into small edible portions. They were, however, too big. Only their leader, the black one with the white ear, might have been compact enough to worm his way under the chassis of the car, but he merely stood in the rain watching over the action, serenely authoritative. Every once in a while he lowered his head calmly and looked in at the cat. Oedipus shivered. He had, in general, no great respect for dogs. In his experience, they were not very intelligent, nor did they have much skill at delaying gratification. He looked around at them and thought he might be able to wait them out. The black one, he knew, he would have to find another way around.

The others barked and yipped and snorted and poked their paws as far under as they could get them, but Oedipus stayed in the safe middle space. If one got too near, he hissed and raked at the intruding paw with his sharp claws. Eventually, one by one, discouraged by this and by the rain, they took off into the gray, miserable afternoon. Only the black one with the white ear stayed about, and he made no attempt to dislodge Oedipus at all. It came to Oedipus that he was waiting for the others to disperse so that he could have him all to himself.

When the two of them were alone at last, the black dog lowered his head and peered under the car. He bared his teeth grinningly and displayed the unquestionable authority of his lower jaw. The dog moved back and paced once, slowly, about the car, then he looked in again and gave a low warning growl.

Oedipus made a dash for it and knew the dog was right at his back. Up the long long hill he flew, looking desperately for an avenue of escape, but all of the houses were attached so there was no way to cut into the backyards. He darted from laser bin to laser bin and wove in and out of the parked cars, but always he felt the dog was right behind him. Each time he reached a corner, the dog forced him out and across the street. It was a rainy, slow afternoon, and as luck would have it, each time he crossed a street, the intersection was empty—until he reached Fifth Avenue, where a big green van came barreling down from the north. Oedipus ran diagonally, with the speed of terror. He heard the screech of brakes and a thud, but without turning to look around he reached the other side of the street and, spotting the open doorway of a fruit and vegetable store, he ran into it and darted under a bin of potatoes and onions.

He waited in the dusty, strangely scented half-light for the dog. But the dog didn't show. No one showed. No one seemed to even realize he was there. Gradually, the hammer of his heart stilled itself. He watched many feet pass by his hiding place. Once in a while, someone stopped and rooted around in the bin over his head.

At last, lulled by the warmth and his own exhaustion and the peaceful comings and goings in the store around him, he fell asleep.

19. In Front of His Nose

*A*rthur took a leave of absence from the university and went to Venturetech and applied for a job. It almost seemed too easy, but in Arthur's experience the left hand often had no idea what the right hand was doing in big places like these. Within a few days after the baby had disappeared, he was working at Venturetech on a project involving the use of an anti-aging cream made from genetically altered soybeans. At first glance, the results were very promising, since the cream seemed to melt away wrinkles. The only problem was that when it was rubbed into the skin, it put its user into a mild state of euphoric torpor, leaving them staring in place for twenty minutes or so, until the cream was completely absorbed. The subjects invariably could not account for this time in any accurate way, but all seemed to have the feeling that they had been occupied in some unusually satisfying manner. None of the subjects could wait to try it again.

Several experienced biodata interpreters like Arthur had been put on the project to see if they could untangle the threads of what was going on, ostensibly because it seemed unlikely that the cream could be made to meet federal licensing regulations if the secondary effect was not removed.

The office they gave him was on the twelfth floor. The chair was good. It was an Ortho Body Molder, with automatic and manual temperature control. The computer screen was an XPG2000 with a 3D video card. There was no window, but the artificial light was full-spectrum, and there was a Spenser Microwave/Air Purifier/Coffee-maker with seven coffee selections. Next to the desk stood a small lemon tree in a pink ceramic pot. The tree was loaded with lemons.

Arthur came in each morning and fed any new data into the program. He cleaned up the original files and, as they had asked him to do, began to sort through the data. As far as Arthur could see, no one felt any particular urgency about this project, and this allowed him the freedom he needed to make his investigations. Each morning he would break for lunch early and head for the cafeteria. He took a different route each day and made careful mental notes of the offices and laboratories he passed by, later recording these observations in his notebook. He saw no sign of Fishhammer or Bernard.

In the afternoons he explored the research facility through the eyes of the computer. The security system they used was exquisite. There were roadblocks and red-alert security checkpoints everywhere. Fishhammer's name didn't turn up in a single personnel file. Not that Arthur expected it. If Fishhammer was here, he would be well hidden. If Bernard was here, probably only one or two people would even be aware of his presence. More than that would cause too high a risk.

Venturetech, as Arthur expected, not only was involved in developing and expanding upon its own current products, but had a long list of completely new projects it was investing in. There was, of course, a great deal of agriculturally related work, but in the last few years, Arthur noted, there was a preponderance of projects that focused either on aging or on the repair of damaged sensory modalities. Many of these projects, although perfectly sound in their stated goals, managed to turn up bizarre secondary effects or find their way into murky legal waters. Arthur was interested in what he found, though not particularly surprised, either by the problems that the researchers were encountering or by the risks the company was taking.

Arthur could only begin to imagine what was hidden from view in this building, if this was what was open for examination in the general compulink records.

For three days, he found nothing. Each night he went back to Maury's and called Pinky and told her what he could, which, of course, amounted to no more than a hill of beans. He did manage to get from the company archives some glossy public relations information about Mitchell Newman—about Newman's humble beginnings, his lack of formal schooling, his dogged persistence in educating himself through long hours spent in the library reading everything he could get his hands on, his photographic memory, how he built Venturetech from a couple of cosmetics lines to one of the largest multinational bio-research companies in the world, his many philanthropic contributions, his love of gardening, and the eccentric way he watched over his company, taking on menial jobs and chatting, incognito, with his employees. He was known to occasionally give away large sums of money to strangers he met whom he thought deserving. At the very end, there was a small article about the tragic car accident and the death of Newman's wife and two-year-old son. This accident had happened a number of years ago.

When he relayed this information to Pinky, she said that Mitchell's wife had been very depressed.

"What are you talking about?" he said impatiently.

"I remember hearing it on the news. She'd been having trouble with depression. She was being treated for it. What they weren't sure of was, when she went over the railing, was it because she had decided to commit suicide and take the baby with her, or was it because she was very high on some anti-depression medication that her husband was experimenting with in the company? Either that or it was just an accident."

Arthur didn't recall that the company archives had touched on any of these questions. "What's the difference?" he said.

"What do you mean, what's the difference? Don't you think it's different to accidentally ecstatically go driving over the side of the Brooklyn Queens Expressway than to kill yourself in a fit of despair?"

"I don't know. She and the baby ended up in the same place either way, right?"

"Just find Bernard," Pinky said angrily and hung up.

Teddy waited with his mother for something to happen. Each day he would check on his formula. It was always still there. When he lifted the lid on the container, its purple-red interior gazed up at him darkly. He gazed back at it with a confused mixture of emotion, triumph and exaltation, uncertainty and fear. He did not touch it; he couldn't quite bring himself to dip any ants or spiders into the ruby pudding. He wasn't quite sure why, but he knew that his creation was not yet complete. He did not yet know what was needed, but he knew that he would soon find out. He stared into it, savoring it, soothing the soreness that couldn't be put down. That his father, his cat, his brother were all gone was surely, in some manner, his own fault. He had not been paying enough attention, he had been too busy with his own business, and somehow in here, in this unfinished potion, lay the answer.

One day he came upon Susan Edelman weeping over her rosebush because the Japanese beetles had returned. She looked almost like a girl. She asked him if he would pick them off for her again. He looked her in the eye and refused and told her it wouldn't do any good. They'd just come back, he told her. There was probably some answer to her problem, but he had too much on his mind to think about it right now. Maybe she could figure it out herself.

She stared at him in surprise. Her gray hair was in disarray and he saw that it wasn't that she was really looking younger, but that inside her face was another one that she might have been carrying with her all the time and he just hadn't noticed before. She turned it away from him now as if she realized what it was he had seen, and hurried into the house.

At night he asked his mother for the stories about herself and her younger sister, Audrey. His mother told him the story about her and Audrey and the thistle cap, the one in which his mother made a terrible, prickly hat out of thistle seeds and bribed her younger sister with some caramels to put it on her head. Audrey had beautiful blond curls, which his mother was very jealous of. Audrey put the hat on and then, of course, found, when she tried to remove it, that she couldn't. All of her beautiful hair had to be cut off. His mother got in a lot of trouble.

The next night she told him the story about Audrey and the Christmas dress, the one in which Teddy's grandmother took Pinky to Macy's and told her they needed to pick out a beautiful dress for Audrey for Christmas, and his mother, who was feeling put upon and bored and not at all inclined to choose something nice for her unimportant little sister, chose an ugly plaid and pleated item. Pinky's mother kept asking her if she was sure this was the right one and Pinky kept impatiently answering yes, and then, on Christmas morning, when she opened the box with the name "Pinky" on it and the big red ribbon, there was the plaid dress she thought she had chosen for Audrey.

Teddy had always loved these particular stories, because he loved to imagine his mother being a mischievous little girl, but now, when he listened to them, he was filled with an awful sense of loss and a certain amount of shame for all of the ill will he had borne against his new little brother. He lay in the dark, thinking about them all, about himself and Bernard, about the other Bernard and his great-grandfather, about his mother and her sister growing up in Scranton.

It was strange how he felt both utterly powerless and yet guilty. There was something not fair about this. What was he supposed to do? He didn't know, yet he felt certain that the responsibility rested with him.

During the day, he carried his little container of bloody potion with him everywhere and took it out again and again, although only when no one was looking, and stared into it hopefully.

On the fourth day, through what appeared to be pure accident, Arthur managed to hack his way into the camera surveillance system. He sat there, delighted with himself, switching from channel to channel. There were many cameras. They covered all the exits and entrances. They covered the elevators and the hallways. They covered the cafeteria, the library, and the pharmaceutical stockrooms. Arthur was able to watch hundreds of people coming and going, rats being injected with toxins, monkeys "accidentally" being born with extra thumbs, dirty laundry being carted off to trucks in the back bay area, technicians picking their noses while they examined blood samples under microscopes. But, of course, nowhere did he see Fishhammer or his son Bernard.

When he called Pinky up that night and reported what he had done, she was ecstatic.

"I knew you could do it!" she exclaimed.

"I haven't done anything, Pinky. Even if Bernard is in the building, which we can't be sure of, he will probably be somewhere where the surveillance cameras don't go. Chances are, since he would be part of a completely unapproved research project, he's being kept at some underground level apart from the regular facility."

"You just keep your eyes open, Arthur Sorenson. You keep them as wide open as you are able. He's going to be right in front of your nose. I just know he is."

The next day, Arthur searched tirelessly. He switched from floor to floor and kept his eye on everything: the labs, the front desk, the laundry room, the janitors going in and out of supply closets. Nobody looked even faintly like Fishhammer and, of course, in the whole building there wasn't a baby to be found.

He switched the program to automatic so that he got a continuing sweep of the building and tried, meanwhile, to do some work on his assigned project. He kept his eye half on the compuscreen and half on the data sheets in front of him. At around noon he began to feel the faint signs of a headache and decided he'd better go get himself something to eat.

He stood up and stretched, and his eye, as he turned to go out of the room, was caught by the sight of an odd little fellow passing across the compuscreen. The fellow was coming along the hallway in the back of the cafeteria. He was an older man, shrunken and a little stiff, but he held himself very upright. He was wearing a white medical jacket and he was carrying a box of disposable diapers.

The morning after Oedipus spent the night under the onion and potato bin, he crept out very carefully and slowly into the front aisle of the little store. Almost immediately he heard a gasp of surprise. The gasp came from a woman sitting over a crate of lettuces. He stayed where he was and watched her approach. When she reached him, she bent down and very cautiously scratched him between the ears. He had several favorite massage spots. This was one of them and he immediately broke out into a loud approving purr. The woman chittered to him softly and a little excitedly, though he recognized none of the words. After a few minutes of this, she picked him up and put him down on the floor behind the counter. She spoke to him rapidly and touched him on his back. He understood her to mean that he should wait right where he was, while she went to get him something to eat. He waited until he heard her footsteps die away and then he jumped up on the counter and sat down next to the cash register, where he had a good view of his surroundings. It was still very early morning and the sun was just now rising up above the roofs of the buildings. A long sharp ray of pure yellow light fell across the peppers and zucchinis and onto the counter next to him. As it has been decreed that cats must not waste such opportunities, he stepped into this puddle of sun and began to clean himself.

He had not been at this long when a man came through the front door carrying an empty bin. Seeing the cat, he gave an exclamation of annoyance, put the bin down, and approached him with a determined step.

Oedipus was just deciding which direction to run in when the woman reappeared from wherever she had disappeared to. The cat was filled with the conviction that the bowl she was holding contained at least a couple of shrimp. Hoping for the best, he froze where he was.

The argument that the couple broke into was a long one. It went softly at first and then loudly, up and down the scale.

He listened to this patiently. The fugue of melodies was clearly one that had been played many times before. It held within it a great collection of grievances and frustrations, yearnings and misunderstandings. It went around and around in a circle and then ended up back at the beginning and started again. The performance seemed comforting and familiar, but since cats didn't do this kind of thing, he failed, as always, to grasp the point.

Anyway, he waited them out. As luck would have it, in the end the man went angrily back out the front door. The cat could see him through the windows, rearranging the pyramid of oranges. The woman, also, watched him for a while. Then she sighed and came over to Oedipus, and, speaking softly and distractedly, as if she had more or less forgotten who he was and that he was the starting point of the whole business, she put the bowl down in front of him. Oedipus took an appreciative sniff. Inside the bowl there was a lovely chicken broth, some unfamiliar vegetables, and three nice-sized shrimp.

20. The Rescue

*A*rthur didn't get his hopes up. The fact that the fellow was carrying disposable diapers, didn't necessarily mean anything at all. It was perfectly possible that they were illegally cloning babies all over the building. Or they could be using diapers on the monkeys.

Nevertheless. He followed the little man's movements carefully.

The man went down the long hallway behind the cafeteria, then stopped in front of a door marked HOUSEKEEPING and slid his identikey card into the slot. He pushed on the pneumatic bar and the door opened.

All afternoon, Arthur watched the spot where the man had disappeared, but saw nothing until around three, when the fellow emerged carrying a tray of dirty dishes and went into the kitchen entrance behind the cafeteria. He came out a little while later with another tray. This one appeared to have two bowls of macaroni and cheese on it, some Italian bread, a bottled water and what definitely appeared to be a sippie cup.

Arthur sat in front of the screen all the rest of the afternoon, watching. He did not dare to take a break for food or anything else.

At seven o'clock, the little man appeared, holding the tray with the dirty dishes left over from lunch. Arthur watched him go into the cafeteria kitchen and then watched him emerge again. This time, he did not return directly to the door marked HOUSEKEEPING, but turned left and went to the elevators. He pressed the up button and got onto the elevator alone.

Arthur switched to the elevator cameras in that wing, but although he sat pinned to the screen for half an hour, to his bafflement the man did not appear to get off anywhere. Arthur waited and waited, but there was no sign of him until around 7:40, when the basement elevator opened again and the little man appeared, as if he had been riding up and down all this time. He headed straight back to Housekeeping.

Arthur knew that he had to get through that door, although he had no particular reason to believe that he would succeed and, if he did succeed, had every reason to believe he would be putting himself and Bernard—if Bernard was actually there—in serious danger. But Bernard was his own child and, more than that, the beginning of something new and probably the end of it, as well, if someone did not watch over him very carefully. What choice did one have in such matters? You went forward and hoped that what you did was for the good, and that the good you did would outlast you for a few months or maybe a year or two. The practical question was, how was he going to get in? His own identikey card would not work down there, he was sure. It was programmed only to admit him to his own office.

Arthur switched idly from camera to camera, trying to think of some way he might gain entrance. He noted that the building was beginning to fall quiet, that most workers had already left for the day, although Jolson was still down there in the laboratory preparing a new batch of soybean cream. Jolson was a dour fellow who never seemed to go home. Perhaps he had no family, or perhaps he had more family than he wanted, or perhaps he was merely keeping busy as a means of pushing back the dark night that was falling all around them.

Arthur noted that a new rotation of security personnel had come on also. Down at the desk that stood at the entrance to his own wing, the night fellow had just settled in. He was soberly attired in his blue uniform, although the company's logo of a hand pulling fire out of a hat shone brightly from his hat brim and jacket pocket. He was opening up a cup of coffee that he must have just picked up from the cafeteria. The cup, also, carried the company logo.

Arthur took out a pack of gum and slipped a piece into his mouth. He was visited by an absurd idea, a plan of sorts. He did not spend too long examining it, knowing that if he did, it would dissolve into little wisps of nonsense. Feeling almost boyishly excited, he checked the cameras again, and then he got up, carrying a sheaf of data printouts, and went down to the end of the hallway and buzzed the buzzer on Jolson's door. In a moment the grim-looking fellow opened the door and looked at Arthur questioningly. Arthur waved the papers at him.

"I seem to be missing some numbers here," Arthur said. "I have nothing for your last control group. Could you feed them to me again? I wanted to run these percentages tonight before I left."

Jolson sighed, but said nothing. He went over to a long table piled high with papers, and while he was sifting through them Arthur moved casually about the room, examining this and that, peering in at the dwarf piglets in the cages, lifting up some discarded soybean pods, frowning into the contents of some sort of separator machine. When he saw that Jolson was paying no attention to him, he picked up one of the little vials of cream and slipped it into this pocket.

After he had written down the numbers Jolson gave him, he apologized for the disturbance and returned to his office, where he carefully brought the vial out onto his desk.

Outside he heard a loud, prolonged rumbling and drumming. Either a storm was going on or some sort of military attack was in progress.

He opened the soybean cream and stared at the oily gray contents. Teddy would have loved it, he supposed, though the stuff had an earthy musty smell that the researchers would have to find a way to mask. He took the pack of gum out of his pocket and laid the four remaining sticks of Juicy Fruit on the desk. He looked at them thoughtfully and then donned a pair of clear impermeable plastic gloves. Using a rolled-up paper napkin as a brush, he dabbed the tip into the cream and then carefully brushed the stuff around one end of each stick. Then, handling them with extreme gingerliness, he replaced them one by one in their original package and put the package in his pocket. When he was done, he walked out of his office and strolled down to where the guard sat at his desk. He looked up as Arthur approached.

"Hi," Arthur said. "I'm new here, could you direct me? I need to find my way to Personnel. They wanted me to come up and sign some papers."

"They're on the fourteenth floor, but I doubt anybody's up there now."

Arthur looked at his watch. "Oh, yeah. I guess you're right. I lost track of the time." He sighed. He pulled the pack of gum out of his pocket. "Is it raining yet? I know they were predicting rain."

"You didn't hear it? Thunder and lightning—boom! It's coming down like Niagara Falls. Forget the umbrella. You might just as well put your trunks on and swim home. There's gonna be floods."

"Seems like we've had a lot of that this summer."

"World's coming to an end."

Arthur looked him over curiously, but couldn't tell if he was joking or not. He held up the little pack and offered it to the guard, who nodded. Reaching over the desk, he slid a stick out. He unwrapped the gum and put it in his mouth and then rubbed his fingers together, no doubt wondering where the oil had come from. Arthur watched curiously as the fellow relaxed. He settled back into his seat and rested his head comfortably against the back of the chair, his face tipped upward. His hands lay loose and open in his lap. He gazed at the air right in front of his eyes, as if he saw something of great interest there.

"You okay?" Arthur asked him.

The fellow made no answer. The expression on his face was one of pleased recognition. Whatever it was the guy was seeing, it looked worth taking a time-out for. But Arthur had no time to waste.

He shook the guard's shoulder gently and then a little harder. The man did not shift his gaze, but seemed to relax a little farther into his chair.

Arthur removed the guard's hat and then, as gently as he could, he worked the man's jacket off first one arm and then the other. The fellow did not resist, but actually leaned forward a bit, as if to help.

Arthur figured his own pants were close enough in color and did not bother with those. Luckily, he did not have to search long for the identikey. Arthur was pretty sure it would be programmed for universal recognition. He pressed the fellow's hand down on it for activation, then put it carefully in his own pocket.

Not sure how long it would be before the guard woke up, Arthur strode toward the elevator and only had to wait for a few seconds before it appeared. He rode down to the cafeteria and, when he got out, took a right and then a left. He found himself in front of the door marked HOUSEKEEPING.

He slipped the activated card in and pushed the door open.

Arthur stood there, holding his breath. In front of him was a winding green tunnel lit by soft incandescent globe lights. For a moment, in his overwrought condition, he thought the door had opened upon an outside path threading through an overgrowth of trees, but then he realized it was merely the dark green of the strange carpeting and the corridor that had thrown him off.

He still held the door partly open, but now he turned and took a wad of gum from his mouth and jammed it into the lock mechanism and allowed the door to shut softly behind him.

Looking more closely, Arthur now realized that the corridor or tunnel or whatever it was did not lie flat, but descended gently and then turned a corner and disappeared, so that its end was not visible from here. He stepped forward and found that the ground beneath him was as soft and giving as a grass lawn. He passed a couple of unmarked doorways and stopped at them, listening, but heard no sound. When he turned a bend in the corridor, he saw at the far end a bright yellow doorway. The corridor stopped there.

As if a band of wire or perhaps a string on a musical instrument were being tightened, Arthur felt an unpleasant vibration start up in his head. He walked quietly down to the yellow door and stopped.

From inside he thought he could hear a soft murmur or babble.

He tried the identikey, but now that he had used it once, it had deactivated itself. He knocked firmly on the door. "Security!" he called out.

In a moment, the door opened, just a crack, and the little man stood there gazing at him. They were disquieting eyes, Arthur thought, sharp and gray and somehow younger-looking than the rest of the man's face.

"There's been a report of a security breach somewhere in the building," Arthur said. He flashed the badge from the guard's jacket pocket. "Have you seen anybody or anything unusual?"

The little man stood peculiarly still gazing up at Arthur. Then he shook his head no.

"I need to come in and take a quick look around."

The man hesitated and then stepped back and allowed Arthur to pass him.

Arthur's breath was taken away. The change in light was astounding. Although there were no windows in here either, bright late summer sunshine seemed to flood in. It was like coming, abruptly, upon a wide clearing in the middle of the woods. There were even fruit trees. The apples and peaches hung gold and deep pink. He had never seen such round and fresh and succulent-looking fruit. Then his eye was caught by the red disk fruits. For a moment he forgot all about Bernard. Normally not a man much tempted by new and exotic foods, he found himself longing to try one. He reached out cautiously, but as his hand touched the tight red skin, he felt a touch on his shoulder. The little man shook his head.

Arthur turned away from the tree and gazed about himself. There was, to his sharp disappointment, no one in here but themselves.

Then he spotted an open doorway at the other end. He knew, by the further tightening in his head, that this was what he sought.

He looked at the little man, who made no move to stop him, and went toward it.

The light in here, although bright, was completely different. It was fluorescent, harsh, and bluish. Standing in the middle of the floor appeared to be a chair of some kind, very straight-backed, with many appendages and straps and buckles. Standing next to the chair was Bernard, who turned and stared up at him. Arthur saw that his child was in some sort of harness, such as you might use on a dog. The harness was attached to a lead that was clipped to the chair.

The room spun nauseatingly for a moment, and when it cleared he wasn't sure how he held himself upright. But, to his own surprise, quite abruptly he was filled with a vast, radiating calm that seemed to spread downward in a quick heat from that central aching throb at the back of his neck. He felt his heartbeat slow immediately and he turned and smiled at the little man.

"Hey, a baby! I love babies." He turned back to Bernard and, putting himself between the baby and the little shrunken man, he crouched down and reached out.

He pulled his hand back with a shock. It was almost as if a low voltage of electrical current had passed through him.

Arthur turned back to the man. "Cute guy. You use the chair for restraint? You doing some kind of research?"

The man did not answer.

The chair had monitors and a little swing arm tray, such as one saw on a dentist chair, with an array of needles, syringes, and probes. Bernard now crowed softly and pulled against his leash with excitement.

Arthur wanted to get him out of here very badly, more badly than he had ever wanted anything else. He stood up, though, as if he had lost interest. He walked around the room slowly and examined the walls and ceilings and cabinets.

"Well, I don't see anything out of order," he sighed. He came over to the little man and took the pack of gum from his pants pocket and offered him a piece. Bernard's jailer stared at the gum with narrowed eyes, then smiled and reached forward and pulled out a stick. As soon as he popped the gum in his mouth, he noticed the oiliness on his fingers and rubbed them together. A moment later his whole body relaxed. He gave a loud sigh of contentment and stared transfixed, just as the guard had done, at what appeared to be some highly engaging sight.

Arthur touched the man, but the man made no answering response.

Losing no time, he turned back to the baby and, in order to undo him from the harness, lifted Bernard's arms. Now he saw the perfect little burn marks. Some looked like they were already healed, but one or two of them were a hot, inflamed red, oozing slightly. Arthur groaned and undid the clasps and picked up Bernard and held him tightly against his own body, rubbing the child's face against his own. The baby's skin was damp and too warm and he could feel his heart beating.

Bernard murmured at him softly, reassuringly.

"Let's go." He carried the baby through the observation room and then out into the sunny room beyond. It was but the work of a moment to pass under the fruit trees and reach the door on the far side. He opened this slowly.

He looked out into the long green winding hallway, and seeing no one about, he hoisted the baby up and sped quickly along the soft shadowy tunnel. They turned the curve and passed the silent doorways and ascended the path. At the end was the door through which Arthur had entered. He pushed on it forcefully.

But it didn't give.

He pushed on it again. It had locked shut.

He tried the guard's identikey, but, of course, the key was no longer activated. In desperation, he tried his own, but that didn't work, either. He turned around, the baby in his arms, and surveyed the hall behind them. Perhaps there was another exit somewhere.

He walked back down the hall and tried the first door. It opened without resistance, and sitting there in a desk chair similar to the one he had upstairs was Ken Fishhammer. He looked unsurprised to see Arthur.

"That was clever, what you did with the gum in the lock. It would have worked if I hadn't come along and had to spend ten minutes prying it out of there. It almost got you out of here."

"We're not staying," Arthur informed him.

"Come in and sit down. You're not leaving yet."

Arthur came and stood reluctantly in the middle of the small room, which appeared to be some sort of office. Bernard wiggled excitedly, demanding to be let down so he could start wreaking more havoc as soon as possible.

"I'm curious about my nanny. What did you do to him?"

Arthur did not bother with the question. The baby shifted in his arms and seemed to vibrate or hum softly into Arthur's distress. "Listen," Arthur said softly. "As it happens, this is my child. You have kidnapped him and you have tortured him in the name of some grotesque scientific experiment. But I am his father and now you will have to kill me before you will have the chance to go on with any more of your research."

"But Arthur, what does it matter who the father of this child is? He is not his father's child. This child is a child of a different design. Don't you see?"

"You have stolen this child in order to feed your own enormous and insatiable ego."

"I understand what you think of me, Arthur. And I guess it's not unreasonable from what you have observed. But you need to understand that I'm just a vehicle. I'm not important here. Neither are you." Ken looked into Arthur's face for some acknowledgment of what he was saying, but, seeing none, sighed. "Don't you see? This child will change everything. He is something completely new. This child is the very thing you and I have always believed cannot exist—a human who is not at war with himself, a being who hardly seems to notice pain or hunger, heat or cold, fatigue or loneliness. You wouldn't believe the things I've tried out on him, and whatever I do, he keeps smiling at me. Somehow, he manages to keep his own internal environment in constant balance with the external environment. I don't know the exact genetic mechanism yet, but I'm close to figuring it out. He is the answer to everything that ails us and everything we've ever dreamed of. I believe evolution has been working its way towards him all along."

The awful thing, Arthur knew, was that Ken believed what he was saying, and that in some unnameable way, he might even be perfectly right. Arthur looked at his son. He looked as far down into the depths of the brown eyes as he could go. Arthur loved him. It was impossible not to love such a child, but what was in there, he couldn't tell. The baby laughed and tried to launch himself into the air.

"You have no idea, yet, what he is," Arthur said. "For all we know, he may never learn to talk or reason fully. Or if he does, he may end up with no moral compass at all. He doesn't feel pain and he doesn't suffer and these are the things that tell us what is right and wrong, that drive us to live fully and justly and, yes, anxiously. Without them, what is there to stop us, all of us, from walking right off the edge of the cliff into the air? Can't you see? Look at him."

Fishhammer stood up. He was not cool, but burning with some fever. "But you know, Arthur—you of all people will understand what I am saying—if some master stroke, if some great change does not come upon us as a species soon, we will probably destroy ourselves. Our miseries and sufferings make us angry and stupid. Either by degrees or suddenly, we will terrorize and tyrannize and maim and kill each other into extinction. We have the chance here—and I don't think this opportunity has arrived by pure accident—to change the course of things."

The baby now made another attempt at getting himself released by planting his feet against Arthur's thighs and pushing himself against them vigorously and bobbing up and down.

Arthur, ineffectively, tried to still him. "There probably won't be enough room left in hell for all the tyrants and murderers you'll breed."

"Look at him," Ken gestured fiercely. "Can you imagine him turning into a tyrant?"

Arthur looked at Bernard. He laughed. "Easily."

Ken shook his head. "But what about happiness? What prize is greater than that?"

Arthur put Bernard down and Bernard stood there looking around, deciding where he should begin. "Gaaaah!" he said in a long exhalation of delight. He headed toward the open file cabinet.

"Happiness is a little thing. You make too much of it. It comes and goes. It's supposed to come and go. It's finding meaning that makes life worthwhile to people."

The baby began yanking the folders off the shelves and taste-testing the little colored tabs on their sides. Finding them, one after the other, flavorless, he threw them on the floor.

"That's a depressive speaking."

Arthur shrugged. "Well, let me ask you a question. Would you put this gene in yourself? Would you? Knowing that you might never do any science worth doing again?"

"I'm getting tired of this," Fishhammer said angrily. "The practical issue is that we are not yet sure what we have here." They both turned and looked at Bernard, who, having given up on the file folders, had now turned his attention to the power surge protector with its little red blinking light. Bernard crouched under the desk and reached forward to grab it.

"Don't let him touch that!" Ken yelled. He reached for the baby just as Arthur got to him. Each one of the men grabbed an arm.

"You're going to have to let me have him, Arthur. I'm sorry. There are so many things we need to learn from him. And I'm concerned that, although the effect on the baby appears permanent, it may be unstable. Who knows what a good jolt of electricity could do to the gene? It's important that we keep him in the kind of environment that you cannot possibly provide."

Arthur stood up and looked down at Fishhammer and the baby. "What do you mean by 'unstable'? Unstable in what way?" he demanded.

Fishhammer picked Bernard up awkwardly and stood. "Well, I

found with the first generation of mice that certain environmental forces seemed to be able to cause the organism to reject the genes and to revert to their original chromosomal codings. But when we were able to breed the first generation, the second generation seemed to increase in genetic stability. That is, the gene seemed to now have become a permanent part of the mice's genetic makeup. Unfortunately, I wasn't able to follow through on studies of that second generation because that was the point where the Committee came in and destroyed all my data and I was forced to sacrifice all the mice."

Arthur, who could not stand the sight of Bernard in Fishhammer's arms, found, to his surprise, that he had pulled out Billy's gun. He had almost forgotten it was there.

Ken stared at the gun in astonishment and then he laughed. "You've got to be kidding. You couldn't shoot that thing in a million years, Arthur. I know your sort."

Arthur frowned at him. "Of course I could. You are holding my child."

"You don't sound sure of yourself."

"Give him to me." Arthur felt his hand tremble.

"Where did you of all people get hold of a gun?"

"It's a long story." Arthur found himself feeling nauseated, but it came to him what it was that people liked about guns. It was the way they directed and magnified all your fury right through that dark little hole at the end of the muzzle. He tightened his finger on the trigger and he thought he was going to be able to do it and then he made the mistake of looking at Bernard.

Bernard, he saw, was watching him and, for once, he seemed nearly sad. He looked into Arthur's eyes and his gaze seemed to travel all the way down to the end of the world and back again.

Tears of regret and rage came to Arthur as he found that his finger would not do what he bade it do.

Fishhammer, who was no fool, grabbed the slippery thing out of his hand and turned it on him. "We're very different, Arthur. Make no mistake."

At this moment, the door behind them opened and the little man, Bernard's nanny, walked into the room and then stopped.

"Ah, Maurice. You are just in time," Ken said. Ken put the baby down and said to the man, "I want you to wait here while I go to arrange for some transportation for our visitor. I want you to make sure he stays right where he is." He held out the gun to Maurice, who looked at it for a moment, then made a small face and took it and turned it on Arthur. He pointed toward the chair and Arthur sat down in it reluctantly.

"I'll be back in a few minutes," Ken said.

The door shut behind him with a little click.

The little man kept the gun aimed at Arthur, his hand perfectly steady. Arthur—his mind a blank—watched Bernard toddling around the room, yanking things off the shelves.

After a while Bernard hunkered down on the floor. He fished around in his diaper and brought out one of the red disk fruits, slightly squashed. He sat there sniffing at and babbling to it.

"Let me try it," Arthur said. "Bring it to me."

The baby looked at him with his head cocked to the side, then he toddled over to Arthur and pressed the fruit to his lips.

Before Arthur could take even a nibble, the little man cleared his throat and said hoarsely, but distinctly, "I wouldn't, if I were you. It took me ten years to get that tree to put those out, but I have no idea if they're safe to eat or not."

Arthur turned to stare at the little man, tasting with his tongue the unearthly sweetness on his lips.

Bernard also turned and looked at the older man. Then he toddled across the room and held the fruit up to him. The man laughed. Carefully, he put the gun up, out of reach, on a shelf behind him. Then he turned and lifted the child into his arms. "You are a real charmer, but a real devil. How did you get hold of that piece of fruit? You weren't supposed to be able to reach it." The baby patted him kindly.

The little man looked over at Arthur, who was staring at him in consternation. He sighed. "I don't suppose you realize who I am?" He spoke in a cracked, uneven voice.

Arthur thought about it and decided that he probably did. "You're Mitchell Newman."

The man put Bernard down and sighed. He watched the baby head for the far corner of the room that he had not yet explored. "You know, I was thinking at first about the military possibilities of Fishhammer's gene. I've been doing a lot of thinking like that in the last few years. Weapons that might subdue without doing violence. That cream, too, the one you tried out on me today, has a lot of possibilities, don't you think?"

Arthur was staring at him in mute horror. "You would sell something like that to the government?"

The man laughed. "Or keep it for myself. The government and I do not always see eye to eye."

Arthur could not respond.

"Imagine," Newman said somewhat impatiently, "how weapons like this might change the nature of war."

"You've got to be kidding."

"Well, maybe I am. I don't know. Maybe I just wanted the baby for myself. I very much liked the idea of a completely happy human being. The thought of raising such a fellow, being near him every day, was very pleasing. My life has been too lonely in the last years. But then once I had him here, I saw I was too old for the job."

Hearing an odd metal scraping noise, both men turned and caught Bernard in the act of trying to slice his fingers off with a paper cutter. They lunged at the same time. The man grabbed the arm of the cutter in midair as it began to come down and Arthur swooped the baby up.

The two men stood up and looked at each other. "And, in any case—this is just my guess—I don't think this little fellow will last more than a year or two. I'm not at all sure Ken separated the original damaged gene from the happiness one, and even if he did, this child is on the verge of perishing every ten minutes or so. Not much of a military weapon, and I doubt I could stand my own grief."

Arthur wondered if Newman's voice was the way it was because of some damage or because of simple disuse.

"Well," the older man sighed. "I'd better get you out of here before our friend returns. Come this way."

Arthur watched him take the gun down from the shelf and put it in his pocket. He turned and pulled a manila folder off the shelf and then, instead of heading toward the door they had come in by, headed toward the rear of the office where there was another door, one Arthur would have assumed to be a closet had he even noticed it before this moment. Arthur followed, carrying the baby.

Mitchell Newman turned the simple knob—no key card or anything—swung the door open, and Arthur saw that they were looking out at a busy hallway. People came and went on various important errands and no one paid the slightest attention to them.

Newman said, "Now, you only have one more exit to get through—down there, next to the laundry pickup area. If you'd like to avoid another encounter with Ken today, you don't have a lot of time. For the future I'm going to do my best to find something else for him to do, something that will hold his interests, though I can make no promises—he's an obsessive sort. Here are the baby's DNA records. They may come in handy, I suppose, someday." His voice was becoming hoarser and scratchier, like an old Victrola record winding down. He handed Arthur the manila folder.

Arthur took the folder wordlessly and started to step through the door.

"Just a moment," Newman called him back. Arthur turned and looked at him. "My cream, please." He held out his hand.

Arthur removed the vial from his pocket slowly and handed it over. "Goodbye," Arthur said stiffly. "And thank you."

Newman made no answer.

Arthur hurried out into the busy hallway.

The baby turned to wave and Newman waved back, his face expressionless.

When Arthur reached the exit door at the end of the laundry area, he pushed it open and found himself out in the company parking lot. The rain had stopped and the sky was beginning to clear. Arthur realized suddenly that August must have ended sometime in the last few days while he was busy trying to find Bernard. He breathed in the last air of summer gratefully, and in a few minutes he had found the car, buckled Bernard into the waiting baby seat, and soon they were speeding home.

Pinky had spent the afternoon working on her painting. She had been sure that she wouldn't be able to see what it needed, that her mind's eye would be obscured by all of the horses of the Apocalypse charging through it. Yet, to her surprise, almost against her wishes, something pulled her in and she found herself remembering all kinds of things about the Golden Yen Restaurant that up until this afternoon she had forgotten: the brass wall sconces with their flickering lights, the red-flocked wallpaper, and the way the oranges they gave you at the end of the meal were cut and fanned out into the shapes of lilies. All of these things and more she added to the painting, and she saw the little tea-drinking woman watching all of these additions with approval. But when Pinky had exhausted herself and thought she could paint no more, she stood back and saw that something was still required to center the composition. Very carefully, she painted one of the dog's ears white. This was just enough to draw the whole thing into order.

She put away her paints and cleaned her brushes and went downstairs and opened the front door and, as she did, Arthur pulled up in the front.

Bernard, securely buckled into the baby seat in the rear, upright and pleased with himself, waved at her confidently through the window. She ran down the steps and threw the door open. Having her there in front of him, her perfume in his nose, he grew wild with desire and strained against his straps, crowing like a rooster on Christmas morning.

When Pinky went to change his diaper, she found the little red fruit that Bernard had stashed down there when no one was looking. She examined it curiously and then, distracted, left it on the changing table. It caught Teddy's eye when he was passing by and he carried it off to his laboratory and examined it carefully under his magnifying glass.

He could hear his parents talking in the other room. He knew that over or under the words something had changed or was about to change. Whether it was small or monumental, he could not tell. His father was telling his mother that there was a problem in the baby's heart, something that sounded to Teddy like a little "defeat." They would all need to prepare themselves for this. It was possible that the baby might not live to be very old.

There was silence then for a full two or three minutes. He wondered what they might be doing. He tried out different pictures in his mind: Perhaps they were pairing socks from the laundry basket or reading the paper or blowing bubble-gum bubbles. None of these things seemed to fit and now there was a loud crash, presumably because the baby had pulled a bookcase or other piece of furniture down on his head. He heard them shouting at each other and things being moved around and then he heard Bernard laugh.

"You see," he heard his mother say with a little gasp, as if she had been running a race or maybe crying, "You are *so* wrong. This guy is here for the duration."

It occurred to Teddy that what his new mixture was going to be was a sort of liquid vitamin that would give you the power to live forever. He removed the pit from the little red fruit, mashed it up, slid the mess into his potion, and poured half the potion into a cup. Later, when they had left the baby upstairs for his nap, Teddy tiptoed in to him. Bernard was lying on his back, sucking and blowing on the toes of his right foot as if it were a harmonica. When he saw Teddy, he stopped what he was doing right away and pulled himself to a standing position using the bars of the crib. He waited, keeping his eyes on Teddy, watching him with silent devotion. Teddy brought the little cup to Bernard's lips and the baby, his eyes wide with delight, slurped down a great deal of it and let the rest dribble down his chin.

Teddy waited for a while, watching him to see any signs of whether or not he was going to live forever, but nothing particular happened and Teddy realized he was just going to have to be patient. He wiped the baby's chin off with a tissue and went back downstairs.

21. Home

$\mathcal{P}$inky was determined not to worry about Bernard. Anybody with the eyes to see it could see that he was somehow chaperoned, that around about him rode a nimbus of light, an unbreachable force field. He was Bernard, and no catastrophe from the sky or tiny defect in his heart could outweigh the wide sum of himself.

She accepted, as well, that Arthur had returned to her still Arthur. She had been a fool to think that anything was going to really change him and, more than that, a fool to imagine that he might betray her. He was what she had bargained for, no more, no less.

If she felt an uneasiness, a sense that something was yet undone, a prick of guilt for missing something important, she decided that maybe this had to do with poor Maury.

So in celebration of Bernard's rescue, Pinky strung a laundry line from the ladder to her kitchen window and hung out a wash.

"Isn't it beautiful?" she asked Bernard.

He stood beneath the outstretched shirts and pants and pillow-cases and babbled to them ecstatically. They appeared to be flying, a motley many-colored flock of trembling garments, against the early September sky. He lifted his arms and pleaded with them to take him along, but they flew on about their business, till Pinky swooped him up and carried him off into the house, where she called Maury and got his service unit. She left him a brief message inviting him for dinner the next day. Then she called Fran.

"Oh, thank God, a distraction. You have no idea what a madhouse it is here today—an arsonist and a serial murderer and my mother has called twice."

"What for?"

"To tell me about Elsie, of course. Apparently the doorman stopped her when she was on her way out yesterday and handed her a package. Guess what was inside?"

"More boots?"

"No. A pair of glasses. Elsie claims they're the same as the ones Uncle Claremont was buried with."

"Shit," Pinky said.

"Right. Elsie called my mother and accused her of somehow being responsible for this outrage. My mother, of course, told Elsie that she was unbalanced and needed psychiatric help. Elsie hung up on her. Then my mother called *me*, purring with satisfaction."

"Do you think she had something to do with the glasses?"

"My mother is capable of wonderful things, but somehow I never pictured her as a grave robber. On the other hand, I suppose she could have easily found items similar to the ones worn by Uncle Claremont and had them sent. Though how she would have known what Uncle Claremont was wearing, God knows. I guess she could have gone to the funeral parlor and taken a look at him. That'd be up her alley. Or maybe this is all just some feverish delusion on Elsie's part, the seeds of which were planted when my mother so kindly sent her the deed to the cemetery plot."

"Or maybe it's Uncle Claremont," Pinky ventured.

There was a moment of silence on the other end. "Sending her his boots and glasses from the grave?"

"Well, you never know. You hear of things like that."

"But they're not true."

Pinky let this pass. "Listen, how about coming for dinner tomorrow? The boys would love to see you."

"Sure. Sounds nice. What do you want me to bring?"

"Just your beauteous self. We'll get drunk and celebrate Bernard's rescue."

On Friday evening Teddy was sitting in the living room working on a Lego construction. He could hear great boomings and crashings in the kitchen, but since he knew it was merely Bernard going through his after-dinner maneuvers he did not give it much thought. Occasionally he could hear his parents murmuring to each other over the din. This he listened to with half an ear. He had been relieved when he woke each morning and his father was still there, but he had noted there was a space between his parents, a dark hole inside of which something was waiting. He wondered if his parents had failed to notice it and if it was up to him to make sure that whatever catastrophe was waiting in there didn't happen.

He was startled when the doorbell rang.

He got up to answer it and found Billy Edelman on the front stoop.

"Is your father in?" Billy asked.

It was a very warm afternoon, but Teddy thought the older man looked like wherever he was it was winter and he had run out of the house without his coat on. "I'll go get him."

After he brought his father to the door, Teddy stepped back into the living room, where he hoped he would not be noticed. He had a good view of his father's back and Billy Edelman's face.

"Where is it?" Billy asked.

His father did not say anything.

"I was just looking in the box to check that it was there and the box is empty. You took it, didn't you? Where is it?"

"It's gone," Arthur said.

"What do you mean, it's gone? I need it."

"I lost it for you."

Teddy cast his imagination this way and that.

"What do you mean? What about my plan? You think it was easy to make a plan like that? Can you imagine the nights I've lain awake and the horror of planning a thing like that? The nerve it took to reach a decision like that? And then to have you come along and lift it out of my hands?"

"Yes, of course I can imagine it."

"It wasn't your business."

"Billy, you know that's not true. Once a person hears a story like that, it becomes their business. If you're a human being, it's your business. And I think you knew that when you told me your plan. I know you wanted to save them suffering, but you're not permitted to save others from suffering in that manner."

"Not permitted by who?"

"There isn't any who. It's just not permitted."

Billy groaned like someone who is trying to lift something that is too heavy to lift.

Teddy found himself wishing he could help him raise it up, whatever it was. His father, he knew with absolute certainty, was no thief, but he also knew that sometimes even just a word or a look from him could add a weight to whatever you were trying to accomplish that could make it seem impossible to move forward.

"So now what do I do?" Billy asked.

"You do the best you can," Teddy's father said.

"You gotta be kidding."

"I'm your friend. I'll help you."

"What can *you* do?"

Teddy's father lifted his palms up. "I don't know. Whatever is necessary."

Billy continued to stand there for a minute silently. Then Teddy saw him turn and go down the steps with his shoulders hunched and his head bent as if he were aimed straight into a freezing wind.

"We still have a date on Thursday?" Arthur called out to him.

If Billy made an answer, Teddy couldn't hear it. The front door closed. Teddy did not look at his father as he went by. He stared at his half-finished robot, his mind churning with questions. What dreadful treasure could have been in the box? Had his father really lost it or was it hidden somewhere? What kind of date could they have made together?

He put the robot down and reached under the table to where he had hidden the remainder of the formula. He always kept it close by him these days, and each day it became a little more red and lumpy and foul-smelling. And it also seemed to him that every morning the stuff seemed to have grown heavier. He pried the lid off and stared inside. It occurred to him that he should drink the rest of it so that Bernard would not have to live alone forever all by himself. He lifted the container toward his lips, took a deep sniff, and gagged. He put the container back down on the table.

〜〜〜

Perhaps if the cat had not stayed so long things might have turned out differently. He had not meant to stay so long. He had meant to take off that very first afternoon, but there were several matters that delayed him. For one thing, there was the possibility that there might be more shrimp for lunch. For another, he quickly discovered that the place was overrun with mice. Also, he had absolutely no idea where he was. The store was situated on a busy corner. Across the way were Top Hat Discount, Chicken King, and Stan's Pizzeria. Next door was a hardware store and next to that was a fish market. There was something about the cacophony of smells that left him clueless.

So each night he rose around midnight and hunted mice. The mice were plump and slow and insolent. He dropped the little broken carcasses one by one behind the counter, where he knew the woman would find them. He worked without shirking and then, at around six, worn out, he would lie down and sleep until she came in and gave several little shrieks of excitement and disgust. When she had finished cleaning up his handiwork, she would bring him a bowl with something wonderful swimming in a pool of broth.

After breakfast he would go out to sit in the sun in front of the pyramid of oranges. Being a handsome fellow, he attracted a fair amount of flattering attention. In fact, the quantity of scratching and stroking he could garner on a good morning was stupefying. After a while, he would simply lie down on his side, waiting for the next pair of hands to come along, purring in a kingly manner.

Each morning, after he had been thoroughly kneaded and massaged and the sun had shifted into a more glaring position, he went inside to the dusty cool of the little fruit and vegetable store and the woman brought him another bowl. He spent the hot afternoons sitting on the counter watching people come and go. In the evening he would take a little walk around the neighborhood and then he would fall asleep under the potato bin until it was time to rise and go to work.

He lost track of time after a while. Oedipus stayed out of the man's way and the man, maybe somewhat mollified by Oedipus's diligent night work, stayed out of his—although the cat never liked the look in his eye. Eventually the mice began to grow scarcer, probably because so many of them had had their necks broken and the rest had perhaps realized it was time to move on.

One morning Oedipus went outside and took up his position in front of the oranges. It was early September and the air was still and for a few improbable minutes no cars went by.

Oedipus sat there with his eyes half closed and sniffed the air. Suddenly he smelled something, a floating ribbon of fragrance, that made all his senses come alert. He opened his eyes and opened his mouth so he could get a better fix on it. There it was. It wasn't, he could tell from the thinness of its flavor, coming from somewhere very close by. It had traveled a bit of a distance to get here. But it was, nevertheless, instantly recognizable, the inedible cloying odor of that poor thornclimber with its hundred crimson faces and its feet buried in the ground. He had felt sorry for it, with its heartbroken perfume. He had tried to do for it what he could.

And now, he was sure, it had come looking for him. He had only to figure out which direction to turn and follow his nose and it would lead him home if that was what he wanted. Was that what he wanted? He hesitated for a moment and, as he did, a truck went by and then someone opened the door of the fish market. The wisp of overwrought perfume curled itself around the fumes of exhaust and the luscious stink of the fish. When Oedipus breathed in at last, the scent was so tangled into these that it was very hard to tell from where it had come. He walked a few steps up the street and few steps down. The hot dog vendor on the corner lifted one of the lids on his steam table and a pungent wash of sauerkraut filled the air. The cat sat down in confusion. He sat there for a long time, distractedly ignoring the passersby who stopped to greet him. But, although he waited until the sidewalk was hot and the sun glared at him like an angry eye, the scent did not return. When the woman came out to look for him at lunchtime, he did not, for some reason, feel hungry. He walked right past her proffered bowl and went to sleep under the potatoes.

He woke in the evening refreshed and more or less restored to himself. He was not the type to get stuck in self-recrimination. He appreciated the neatness of how things were arranged, the way, as you walked forward through the world, the world came alive and unrolled itself in front of you. What was behind dissolved quickly into a shifty half-remembered mist. He was one to learn what could be learned from his mistakes and then to forget about them. He could see through the window that the sun had gone down and the stars were beginning to salt the sky. He washed himself and stretched and found that, having skipped lunch, his appetite was back.

He noted that there was a pleasantly greasy smell of chicken coming from somewhere overhead on the counter. He jumped up to investigate and found a plate of take-out from the Chicken King across the street. There was a half a drumstick and two chicken wings left. He had helped himself to the drumstick and had just started in on one of the wings when the man reappeared. Seeing the cat finishing off his dinner, the man whipped off a slipper and, before the cat realized what was happening, pounced upon him and whacked him several good whacks of pent-up fury.

Outraged and indignant, Oedipus jumped down from the counter and took off through the front door. He ran around the corner, past the oranges, past the melons, past the pyramid of peaches, and stopped in front of a bucket of snapdragons. He waited for the man to appear flourishing his slipper, but when he did not and his own heartbeat had slowed, he turned haughtily to licking at his ruffled fur. He had just begun to get himself back in order when he saw something from the corner of his eye that made his blood run cold.

There was, he felt sure, a medium-sized black stinkbarker with a white ear, sitting right there next to the lamppost, which was just beginning to blink on. The cat turned his head slowly. The dog stood up and bared his teeth. He was not leashed.

Without giving it another thought, Oedipus began to slink swiftly up the hill. The stinkbarker did not seem to be in any hurry, but followed casually behind him, keeping his distance. Oedipus noted, however, that if he tried to change direction or move toward the safety of the houses, the dog immediately interceded, putting his uncouth-smelling body between the cat and wherever else he thought he might like to go.

When the cat tried to take refuge under a car, the dog merely crouched there grinning evilly in at him, until he moved on.

Their progress was slow and full of starts and stops, but when the last light was fully gone from the sky and the crickets were singing in full end-of-summer chorus, they finally reached the top of the hill.

Oedipus stopped and looked down beneath him with horror, for there ran the Prospect Expressway, a river of cars slamming by him at slaughterous speeds. Instantly he tried to turn about and find another way to go, but now the dog closed in on him, smiling his ugly mongrel smile.

He backed the cat slowly down the hill.

At the bottom, when Oedipus had reached the edge of the traffic, he stared into the stinkbarker's eyes fiercely and gave out a horrible caterwaul.

The dog didn't flinch. He stood there unmoving. His dark gaze did not seem to have any bottom to it, but just dropped down and down. Oedipus considered it. The dog was going to leap upon him and break his neck in one try, and then play with his body in a bloody stinkbark-ish manner. The idea of this filled him with shame and fury. On the other hand, if he leaped into the river of cars, perhaps the dog would be stupid enough to follow him and then, at least, he would have the satisfaction of taking the loathsome creature down with him.

He stared defiantly into the dog's eyes, and then he turned. For a moment he thought regretfully of the chicken wing he had not fin-ished and then the glare of lights came rushing toward him.

22. Lightning

$\mathcal{S}$aturday afternoon was sultry and overcast. Teddy was sitting on the front steps when two strange figures came up the block wearing ski pants, heavy winter jackets, gloves, and thick hats. In addition, they wore skateboarding helmets and their faces were wrapped around and around with some sort of thick cloth, leaving only their noses and mouths exposed. They were carrying waterguns and, to his surprise, they stopped at the bottom of his steps.

"Hey, what's goin' 'round?"

Teddy recognized Orlando's voice.

"You wanna come shoot a wasp nest with us? We found one down here in the bush on the corner."

"A wasp nest?" Teddy said weakly.

"Sure! You drown the wasps with the waterguns and then you whack the nest out of the bush with a stick and then you smash it."

"Oh." He had never had such a proposal before. He had little idea how to evaluate it. He turned it around and upside down and then asked, "But what about getting stung?"

"You see the way we're dressed? We got protection." Orlando sounded impatient. "That's what you gotta do. We'll help you get dressed the right way."

Teddy looked at the two of them, muffled and swathed for an expedition to the Arctic Circle. A mockingbird began to sing. The boys looked powerful and menacing. It came to him that there was nothing he would rather do than join them and then, in the same instant, he realized that he had no gun. His father had taken it away and hidden it somewhere.

He stared at them, stricken.

"Are you scared?" Orlando asked.

"No, I'm not scared."

"So what's the problem, amigo? Let's go."

"I can't," he said and blushed in shame.

"Why not?"

"My mother," he whispered. "She needs me. I promised I'd help her with something."

Somewhere was the sound of the screen being pushed up and when Teddy turned around, there was his mother, leaning out the window, smiling at them all delightedly. "Hello, fellows," she sang out. "Going ice fishing?"

"I gotta go," he said and went inside. The potion sat on the front stoop, forgotten.

While Pinky made a salad, Bernard emptied out the contents of the silverware drawer, and then wandered into the living room, where he almost electrocuted himself when he stuck a fork into the DVD player.

She caught him in the nick of time. "You gotta take it easy, baby. You're gonna wear yourself out."

Undeterred, the baby plundered onward.

He put an aluminum mixing bowl on his head. Then he got hold of Arthur's little container of mint-flavored dental floss and wound it all around himself and a kitchen chair. When he tried to move forward, the chair dragged along heavily beside him. He stopped and looked around himself, puzzled, but his headgear made it difficult to see.

"Come here, Pea Pod. Let me undo you."

She was unraveling the dental floss when Arthur walked into the kitchen. He was carrying two big bags of groceries.

"What took you so long?" she asked.

"I had to make another stop on the way." He began unpacking the groceries.

"What kind of stop?"

He took out a half gallon of milk and put it in the refrigerator. Bernard, now free of the dental floss, toddled over to Arthur and grabbed on tightly to his pants leg.

"Eh, eh, eh!"

"You want to come up and see me?" Arthur asked. Without waiting for an answer, he lifted the child up and rubbed his own face against the little soft one.

Pinky watched them. She saw how Arthur closed his eyes, trying to drink the feel of the baby in. "What kind of stop?" she asked again.

"I went with Billy to visit his daughter."

"What are you talking about?"

The doorbell rang.

"I'll get it," Arthur said. He put Bernard down on the floor and headed toward the front of the house.

"Since when do they have a daughter?" she called after him. Quick as lightning, Bernard climbed up on a chair, grabbed the salt-cellar, and began liberally shaking salt over the groceries that still lay on the counter.

"You little hoodlum," Pinky scolded and grabbed him and wrested the salt from his grasp. He smiled at her and she smiled back at him.

In a minute Fran entered the kitchen, with Arthur behind her.

Pinky stared at her admiringly. She was wearing wide black silk pants cinched tight at the waist with a fuzzy fake-tiger-skin belt and a white crepe de chine tent-style blouse that buttoned over her left breast. She wore silver sandals, and silver barrettes pulled her dark curling hair back from her temples. A gorgeous temporary tattoo of a silver dove flew from the corner of her left eye. She reached out and Pinky handed Bernard over to her.

Pinky went to the sink to wash the salt off her hands. "Arthur," she called over the water, "finish unpacking the groceries and could you lay out the chicken in this pan and pour the marinade on it? I want it to sit a little before we put it on the barbecue."

Arthur watched Fran and Bernard jealously for a moment and then turned to the counter and continued unpacking the groceries. He pulled out a bakery box. "I got a cherry pie," he announced. "You think Maury will eat pie?"

"Maury?" Fran said, looking up from the little private party she was having with the baby. "You didn't tell me he was coming."

Pinky didn't meet her gaze. "Bernard needs to see everybody. He's been through a terrible ordeal. We have to keep his spirits up." Bernard bounced vigorously in Fran's arms.

"AAAAAaahdoo, aaahdoo!" he exclaimed, and threw himself backward in a dolphinlike arch, almost loosing himself from Fran's grip.

Fran glowered at him admonishingly. "So when are you going to start talking? Hum? *Fran* is a nice word. Why don't you try that one? F-R-A-N," she mouthed. "Try it, it's easy."

Bernard grew serious for a moment. He stared at the dove coming out from her eyebrow. Then he reached up and tried to pull it off with his thumb and first finger. When nothing came away, he looked at his hand in surprise. "Darp."

"Darp? Darp? What kind of thing is that to say to me?" Fran kissed Bernard's neck noisily. When she was done she looked up and found Pinky and Arthur staring at them. "Where's Ted?" she asked.

"He's been upset about something all morning, but I haven't been able to get any explanation out of him. I think he's out in the back. Maybe you could talk to him."

"Okay," Fran said to Bernard. "Mobile Shrinks to the rescue. Let's go make a housecall." She heaved him onto her hip and headed out through the back screen door.

Fran went over to the birch tree and parted the branches and looked in. Teddy was lying on his back with his fingers in his ears. She had to say hello several times loudly before she got his attention. When he finally heard her, he sat up and looked at her and then at Bernard, who was on her hip.

"Uurdu," Bernard exclaimed.

"Hello," Fran said. She was half bent over, looking in at him. "Why did you have your fingers in your ears?"

"I was pretending I was underwater," he said.

"Oh, I see."

"Do you think sharks bleed?"

"Good question."

"That's what you always say when you don't know the answer but you don't want to admit it."

"It's not good for someone in my position to be seen not knowing things. I'm supposed to exude a certain aura of being wiser than those who are brought before me."

"Well, if sharks *do* bleed, if one of them was bleeding, do you think the other sharks would eat it?"

"Well, I suppose if they were hungry enough, they might."

"Do you think wasps sting other wasps?"

"Another good question."

"Supposing there was a terrible flood or something and you had the power to save one of your parents and not both, which one would you save?"

"Could I come in?

"Sure."

She plopped Bernard down in front of her and crawled into the dark cave on her silky knees. "Are you angry at somebody?" she asked him.

His eyes opened wide in surprise, and then quickly his face took on a stubborn, uninformative look. "No."

"Well," she said and gave him a little time, in case he had some news he wished to spill, but no further questions or explanations seemed to be forthcoming.

They watched Bernard, who was gazing around himself as if he had wandered into Ali Baba's cave of diamonds and gold.

"You know," she said carefully, "almost every decision you have to make involves letting go of one thing and taking on another. It's what's so hard about decisions. But it's very unlikely you'll have to choose between your parents—at least in that way. You can use up a lot of good energy worrying about things that will never happen."

Teddy looked at her impassively.

"It's nice that everybody's back home, though, isn't it?"

"Oedipus isn't back home."

"Oh, that's right. I forgot. The cat. But don't worry about him. I'm sure, wherever he is, he's perfectly fine."

"Owasee!" Bernard exclaimed.

"And what about this guy? Now that he's back, aren't you going to worry about whether or not to save him in case of a tidal wave or whatever? Not to guilt-trip you or anything. I'm just curious, really."

Teddy stared at Bernard, who was patting at the silver leaves of the birch tree as he babbled away. "No. He doesn't mind what happens to him. So what's the use of worrying about him?"

Pinky kept an eye on the three of them conferencing inside the tree while she arranged the coals carefully. She threw in a match and with a great whoomph and whoosh, the flames sprang up. In the stillness, they burned straight and hot. She stood back and saw that Maury had come quietly down the alley and was standing there, staring in the direction of the little commotion in the back corner. He was dressed simply in a white T-shirt and shorts and rope sandals. He stood straight and pale and looked like he was waiting to be led to his own execution.

Brushing her hands off, she sighed and crossed the lawn. She saw that he was holding in his hand a plastic container half filled with some lumpy and foul-smelling substance.

"What is that?" Pinky asked, thinking it might be something he had picked up at the health food store.

"I don't know. I found it on the front stoop."

Pinky took it from his hand and kissed him kindly. She noticed that over his shoulder, down by the park, there was a slow and heavy troop movement of clouds. She put the plastic container down on the table and then she looked up at her laundry, wondering if she ought to take it in.

"So how are you?" she asked gently.

"Who's under the tree back there?" he answered.

At that moment Bernard came bursting through the low-hanging branches. Right behind him were Teddy and Fran.

When Bernard saw Maury standing there, straight and stiff as an arrow, he stopped for just a moment and looked him over. Then he gave out a loud, "Aabwwa," and came toddling forward at breakneck speed.

Fran and Teddy ambled more slowly across the little lawn.

Not that she wasn't fully aware of how much work there was to be done, and of how much could go wrong, but Pinky looked around the garden in a rush of pleasure. The buds of the moonflower vine were tightly furled now like closed-up umbrellas. Later, though, they would unfurl and glow whitely against the darkness. The fuzzball tree was hung everywhere with fuzzballs that dangled straight and inedible as Christmas tree ornaments. She noted, too, that one of the strong middle-level branches of the tree had suddenly grown so much that it now rested up against one of the rungs of her laundry ladder.

"Did you bring me anything?" Teddy was asking Fran as they approached the picnic table.

Fran had been eyeing Maury, who was still standing in the exact same spot.

Now Fran turned and looked at Teddy. "You know what? I forgot. I don't know what I was thinking about."

"Teddy!" Pinky chided.

"I was just asking."

"Well, it's rude."

Fran laughed. "Supposing there was a tidal wave and you could save *me* or you could save this really big cupcake with pink icing, which would you choose?"

"Cupcake."

"Teddy!"

"I was only kidding," Teddy said angrily. He turned and headed down the alleyway.

Arthur passed him as he came out of the house carrying the marinated chicken. "Teddy?" he called out. But Teddy didn't answer him. "What's with him?" he asked Pinky.

"He's been in a snit all morning about something. He won't talk to me. Did he talk to you, Fran?"

Fran made a face. "You know that's confidential. Doctor-patient privilege."

Pinky stared at her. "There's a couple of things I've got to get inside. I'll be right back."

In the silence that followed, Maury finally took a step toward Fran and asked her stiffly, "How are your sinuses?"

"Better. Less snot coming out, more air going in. Thanks for asking."

"I'm glad to hear it."

Again there was a silence. Maury cleared his throat. "Isn't it a little hot for that belt?"

She looked down at her fake-tiger-skin belt, which was wide and furry. Then she looked up at him. "I have very serious principles about never letting comfort get in the way of my vanity."

"You know what I think? I think you make all these little jokes"—he touched the furry belt solemnly, then withdrew his hand and pointed at the dove flying out of her eyebrow—"in order to divert our attention from something you don't wish to be seen."

Arthur thought this was going too far. Looking around for a distraction, he spotted the plastic container on the table, lifted it up, and sniffed it. "Phew," he said. "What is this?" No one answered, although Bernard made a valiant effort to grab it out of his hands. Arthur stood up, carried the container over to the fence, and gave it a quick toss into the garden next door, then turned his back on it and returned to the table and lifted Bernard onto his lap again.

Pinky, bearing a tray with four glasses, came out just in time to see a cloud of something bejeweled and green, little winged glass beads, rise up and out of Susan's prize rosebush. Buzzing, disgruntled, lovely, it dispersed itself into the air.

"What was that?" Pinky said.

"What was what?" Arthur asked. He looked where she was looking, but now there was nothing to see.

Pinky knew an omen when she saw one. But what did it mean? She looked up at the sky and her laundry uneasily and then sighed and turned her attention to putting the wineglasses down. She set the glass with the cordial in it in front of Fran; the others she gave to herself and Arthur and Maury.

"Drink!" she said cheerfully, but no sooner was the word out of her mouth than Fran's pocketlink rang.

Fran frowned, pulled out the link, and looked at it. "I'll be right back," she said. She got up and went into the house.

Pinky saw how Maury just stood there staring unhappily at the spot where she had been. "Arthur, I think you'd better put that chicken on now."

"Where's the spatula?" Arthur asked.

"Oh, shit, it must still be inside, next to the sink."

Arthur made a silly face at Bernard and put him down into the grass. "I'll be right back."

~~~

Let loose, Bernard circled craftily around the table. Maury and Pinky kept pulling things out of his reach as he reached and patted and tried to grab whatever booty he could for himself. Finally, Maury stood up and grabbed him. He took Bernard over to the wading pool and dropped him in.

Pinky didn't say anything, but watched as her child adjusted himself with perfect goodwill to this sudden change of environment. In a moment, he was patting excitedly at the surface of the water, yelling, "Bafoo! Bafoo!"

Maury took off his sandals and put his feet in the water. Bernard stared at them with his head to the side, trying to figure out what they were and where they had come from.

"So he's going to be happy forever?" Maury asked.

Pinky turned to him sharply. "How'd you know that?"

"Grapevine."

"Arthur's been talking to you. I'm surprised at him. He doesn't want anybody to know. He says it's why Bernard was kidnapped. For some reason, he thinks this guy, Fishhammer, probably won't come back, but you never know who else might find out about him."

Bernard grabbed for one of Maury's gnarly toes and, lowering his mouth into the water where the toe was, tried to suck on it. He came up coughing.

Pinky saw that Maury was riveted. "I wonder what he did in his last life to bring him into this predicament," he mused.

"You think it was his last life did this to him? Arthur thinks it's his genes."

"Well, sure, but that's just machinery. You can take the whole machine apart and put the whole machine back together and it still won't tell you where that very first breath comes from, the one that starts the whole thing in motion."

"You think there's unseen forces that follow us around from life to life?"

"Of course."

A strange rim of yellow light was spreading around the far horizon.

"Yes. I suppose you're probably right." Pinky squinted at him.

When she looked around at the sky again, she saw that on the other side, the black cloud was slowly moving in and taking over.

Maury pursed his lips as if he were going to whistle a little tune, but instead he dipped his hand in the pool and then lifted a palmful of water to the top of his head and let it go over his shiny skull.

The back door burst open with a bang.

Pausing on the threshold, Teddy drew in several loud gulping sobs.

"Teddy, Teddy, what is it?" Pinky asked.

"It's gone," he wept. "It's gone. It was that goddamn baby! I know it was." Teddy crouched down for a second in front of the baby in the pool. "I know it was you, you little shitball!" he screamed.

The baby smiled at him.

"What?" Pinky asked. "What happened?"

"This is worst day of my life," he sobbed and ran across the dark yard and around the corner of the house and disappeared down the alleyway.

She would have gone after him, but was arrested by the sight of Fran emerging from the house, Arthur right behind her holding in one hand the spatula and in the other a fresh loaf of Italian bread. He waved them aloft like a conductor signaling to his orchestra. He put the bread down on the table and went immediately over to the grill and began to put the chicken on. Fran sat down in front of her wine-glass. Maury silently began folding paper napkins. Soon there were little sailboats sailing at each place setting. The wind ruffled and tippled at them.

Pinky thought it was odd that no one else seemed to notice that a storm was clearly on its way. Perhaps it was like a game of chicken, and no one wanted to be the first to say anything.

"Was it your mother?" Pinky asked.

Fran took a thoughtful bite of a carrot stick. "Nope." She seemed engrossed in some thought.

"Well, who was it?"

"It was my father."

"Your father?" Pinky said. "What'd he want?" Pinky asked.

"To tell me that Elsie had broken off with him."

"Oh, no!" Pinky said. "You're kidding."

"Of course I'm not kidding."

"Did he say why?"

"Isn't it obvious?"

They all gazed at her.

"Apparently she was on the verge of a breakdown, what with all this stuff being delivered to her from Uncle Claremont's grave. Then some anonymous little birdie dropped her a note about the fact that my father had been having dinner now and then with my mother.

"Elsie's going to see about having Uncle Claremont moved from the cemetery and buried somewhere else and, if she can, she'll give the plot back to my mother. She never wants to speak to my father again."

"Oh, your poor father! Is he heartbroken?" Pinky asked.

"Oh, you know, it's hard to tell with my father, but I think I detected a certain note of relief in his voice. I was never really sure what it was he felt for Elsie. Perhaps, after all, she was just a means to get himself disentangled from my mother."

Arthur, who was at the grill moving the chicken around, asked, "Do you think he'll be able to stay disentangled?"

"Well, that's the million-dollar question, isn't it? In spite of our best intentions, most of us just end up doing the same stupid things over and over again."

"Until we get it right," Maury said.

"But when does that ever happen?" Arthur asked.

"If not this lifetime, then maybe the next."

"You know what it's like?" Pinky said. "It's like you're in this room and you're trying to get out, but you can't find the door or the doorknob and you're knocking and knocking and patting the wall and finally you hit the right spot and the hidden door swings open and there it is on the other side."

"What's there on the other side?" Arthur asked.

In her mind's eye, Pinky saw a wide rolling expanse of green grass and in front of her an avenue of trees, their branches touching overhead. Picturing this, she smiled at Arthur and then at Fran.

Fran shook her head, lifted her glass to her lips, then stopped. "What is this?" she frowned, sniffing at the cordial.

At that moment, there was a great branch-shaped stab of lightning. It shot through the yellowish air, almost too quickly to be seen, and hit the ground somewhere over in the park. The crash followed only a few seconds later and a gust of wind pushed open the loose slat in the fence and went racing and whistling around the little back-yard. The zinnias, the roses, the yellow coreopsis all bent their heads respectfully.

"Shit, where'd that come from?" Arthur said, looking up. "We'd better go in or we're all going to be sleeping next to Uncle Clare-mont." He began to gather plates and napkins. "Where's Teddy? Did he come back yet?"

Pinky looked around the yard anxiously. "I don't know. Did you see where he went? He was upset about something. Teddy!" Pinky called. There was a low kettledrum roll of thunder.

"I'm up here," Teddy announced.

Everyone looked up—the grown-ups, and the baby as well.

There was Teddy, just out of reach, straddling a branch of the fuzzball tree.

"I want my watergun," he said.

"What?" Arthur called. "Come down, Ted. You're going to get your heinie fried."

"I want my gun. My grandmother sent it to me. It's mine."

Arthur was aghast. He couldn't believe it. "But we talked about this, Teddy. I thought we were in agreement." The first drops of rain shot out of the loaded clouds and splatted against the leaves of the tree and the dusty ground.

"I'm not coming down out of this tree till you give me my gun."

"Guns are not toys."

"I'm not going to hurt anybody. I'll squirt bugs."

"Listen, Teddy, I'm not worried about you. Not really. I know you know the difference between what's real and what isn't. But ideas can become real things when our backs are turned. It's important that peo-ple like you and me who are hard thinkers do the best we can and set examples for other people."

"I'm having a very bad day and I want my gun."

This time the gust of wind burst through the fence, ripping the loose slat right off. It went whooshing around the yard as if the front engine of the Phoebe Snow train had leaped the tracks. It picked up a lawn chair and threw it on its back. Then, slyly, it began to circle around the base of the fuzzball tree.

"For God's sakes, give him the gun!" Pinky yelled. "Look at how that branch is shaking. He's going to get thrown out of the tree."

Arthur looked at her unhappily and at the blackness overhead. Another zigzag of lightning shot across the sky. Ka-BOOOOM!

"Arthur, don't be a jerk," Fran yelled at him. "You're a principled guy. The best in the business. And Teddy's going to be even better than you one day, I promise you, but get him down out of that tree."

Arthur stared up at his older son miserably. A drop of rain hit him on the cheek, large and round as a pearl. Then another on his hand. He saw Maury smiling encouragingly at him, as if it were he, Arthur, who was up in the tree and not Teddy.

"All right. A compromise. I'll bring the gun out and you can have it for the rest of the evening and we'll see how you'll feel about it. Okay? Then we'll talk about it again."

"I'm gonna feel good about it."

"Maybe, maybe not. You never know. I'm going to get it. You come down, now!" He turned and headed quickly into the house. When he came back outside, he held the gun in his hand. He waved it at Teddy and Teddy climbed down low enough to grab it out of his hand. Then he jumped out of the tree and hit the ground.

Everyone went running for the house, heads bent low. Pinky was at the rear of the crowd. She saw Fran and Teddy dash through the door, and then she realized no one was carrying the baby. "Bernard!" she said and whirled around. Maury and Arthur, almost to the house, turned, too.

There was the baby, toddling away from them. He was bent forward and his hands were stretched out. "Azoo! Azoo!" he called.

Everybody looked to see what he was after.

Sitting in the grass, hungrily eating a chicken wing, was Oedipus.

"WHERE DID THAT DAMNED CAT COME FROM?" Arthur yelled over the wind.

The next moment seemed a long one and confusing, but she and Arthur, and then Maury, launched themselves in the direction of the baby. Teddy and Fran were already in the house, watching from behind the screen door.

The cat paused in what he was doing and looked up at them. The baby, almost upon him, gave a yodel of delight.

It occurred to the cat that if he wished to finish the chicken wing, he should probably take it to a less conspicuous place, and having several more lives coming to him, he turned and darted ahead and disappeared into the underbrush.

A pitchfork of lightning shot out of the clouds and struck the metal ladder squarely on its delicate top rung. The length of time it took for the deafening current to travel down the ladder and along the slender branch and down the trunk of the fuzzball tree and into the ground where the child and the cat were passing was much faster than the speed of thought or reason. Pinky said later that she could not understand nor really see what happened, but Arthur said he was sure he saw the precise white path the electricity took, just as if it were a pinball, zigzagging down an absolutely preordained pathway into the ground, where it was swallowed up.

Pinky and Arthur and Maury were flung back up against the screen door by the force of the explosion. Each felt the electricity rip through his or her body and then recede. The tree branch, with a loud noise like ice breaking, came loose from the tree and fell in slow motion onto the back of the small child, who had already been flung to the ground.

Not one of them, not Pinky, Maury, or Arthur, was ever sure how long it took them to rejoin their own senses. Fran, who was watching from inside the screen door with Teddy, said it was only a few seconds.

Arthur was the first to pull himself up and stumble over to where the branch lay covering the body of his son in a cloak of silvery green leaves and still-trembling fuzzballs.

The smell was one of the bad parts. For years to come, Pinky would wake in the night thinking that smell was with them again. It was a combination of rain and ozone and sizzled flesh. They called his name as they pulled back the branch.

"Dial 911," Arthur commanded, and Fran, from inside the house, yelled that she was on her way.

Pinky saw that he was sleeping. Right there in the rain. His eyelashes were gone and his face was bright pink and perfectly still. He still wore his diaper and the one blue sandal.

Arthur crouched and felt for his breath and pulse. Then he immediately put his own mouth over Bernard's and set to work. Pinky didn't try to stop him, although she was tired of people giving her son CPR.

Arthur pushed on Bernard's chest five times and then breathed into his mouth, then pushed on his chest five times and breathed into his mouth. Every once in a while he stopped and felt for a pulse, and then he went right back to work. Pinky noted how the rain ran down Arthur's neck and into the collar of his green T-shirt. His green T-shirt, she saw, was very wet. His hair was wet, too. He was as wet as if he had walked straight into a river with Bernard in his arms and come out the other side. She wondered if her own shirt was that wet, but she did not bother to look down and check. She did not look at the sky, either. She was aware, however, of how the thunder and lightning continued to take turns, because every little while there would be a transfixing stab of light as if someone with a huge camera and flashbulb were taking photographs of the scene before her. Then there would be a great booming crash of sound. It was not a quickly moving thunderstorm. It seemed to hang over their heads for an interminable time.

But since nothing goes on forever, there was finally a point at which she noticed that there were more and more seconds elapsing between each flash and the sound that followed, and soon the sky began to lighten. The thunder slowly rumbled off into the distance.

Arthur, however, didn't stop and Pinky called his name, but he ignored her.

When the rain also began to let up, it softened into a mist, a fine net cast out of the sky, and Pinky found herself shivering violently.

How long this went on, it was hard to say. Fran appeared from somewhere with a blanket or jacket or something, which she threw over Pinky. Then she knelt beside Arthur. She touched his wet back. "Let me have a go at it for a little while," she said. "I think I know what to do."

Arthur leaned back, breathing deeply. He wouldn't look at her, but she pushed him aside and Arthur remained there on his knees staring at the sky, breathing heavily.

"Where's Ed?" Teddy demanded.

"Where's the goddamned emergency unit?" Arthur cried.

But now one could hear the first faint approach of the wailing siren. The rain stopped altogether.

Pinky noted a streak of pink had appeared in the sky. She noted the cat on the fence and she noted the plain gray bird that flitted out

from the shrubbery and flew to the top of the ladder, where it took up
its post. Maury went out to the front to meet the ambulance and the
fire truck, and Pinky, looking around, realized that she had not taken
her laundry in.

When Orson came into the backyard with the paramedics and the
crowd of firemen, Pinky would not look at them, but kept her eyes on
Maury.

It came to her, with a shock, that he looked refreshed and restored
to himself, as if the electrocution had shaken something loose.

"How long has this been going on?" Orson asked, pointing to Fran
breathing into Bernard.

"It's hard to say," Maury answered for everyone. "I think we may
have lost track of time here."

Orson leaned down and tapped Fran on the shoulder. She turned
and looked up at him, startled. Gently, he put a hand on her shoulder
and asked her to move aside.

The ground was wet. The air was wet.

The paramedics gathered around Bernard. With various shiny instruments and gauges, they poked and prodded at him. The baby lay
unmoving beneath these attentions, his eyes closed, his limbs loose.
After a couple of minutes of this, they stopped and looked up at Orson.

This time, because she was afraid and she wanted him to reassure
her, she tried to catch the fire chief's eye, but he would not return her
gaze. Pinky didn't like this at all. She almost said something angrily to
him, but he was looking at the paramedics. He gave a small, almost
imperceptible signal with his finger.

Before, however, they could do whatever it was he wanted them to
do, the mockingbird at the top of the laundry ladder cleared its voice
and sang one long uprising note.

Maybe everyone was hoping for an excuse not to go forward to the
next moment, for no one moved. They all stayed right where they
were and looked up at the bird.

Perhaps sensing that it had an audience, that it was the bell in the
bell tower, it opened its wings and closed them. It would let them
know when they could move on and when they couldn't.

It opened its wings again, wider this time, and displayed its bars of
white. Then it flew down to the laundry line. The line swayed slightly

with the impact of its tiny weight, then grew still. It sang again. This time it was not an upward rising question but a statement of the facts. A long and ornate trill, as pure as cold water. What exactly the facts were, it was hard to say, but everybody standing or kneeling in the wet grass strained hard to hear them. They may have been something along the lines of: *The storm is over. The sky is clearing. Summer is nearly gone. From up here you can see everything.*

Then again, perhaps this wasn't the bird's message at all. Perhaps it was merely scolding its adversary the cat, who was sitting on the fence. The cat gazed at him coolly through narrowed golden eyes.

The bird puffed itself up and dropped a little yellowish green dropping down the side of one of Pinky's pillowcases hanging from the line. Then it lifted its wings and took itself off over the rooftops.

There was a faintly querulous sigh from the crowd and Pinky looked around to see who had made it.

She saw one of the paramedics staring down at something in the grass and was alarmed by the look on his face.

When she followed his gaze she found her child staring up at her. His mouth was tight and his blue-sandaled foot twitched. He was looking from face to face as if he had never seen any of them before.

"Bernard!" Arthur and Pinky said at the same moment. They knelt beside him, staring at his face, and stroked him and patted his cheeks. When Arthur leaned forward to pick him up, Orson commanded him to wait.

Arthur sat back.

"Murphy, check him over!"

Murphy was the fellow Pinky had caught staring so uneasily at Bernard. He didn't seem inclined to touch him. He looked at Orson and he looked at the baby. At last he pulled himself together and he got down on his knees beside Pinky and Arthur. Very gently and expertly he ran his hands all along the bones of Bernard's little scorched body.

When he reached Bernard's neck, Bernard turned his head sharply and bit Murphy on the thumb.

"Jesus!" Murphy exclaimed and drew his hand back, staring at the blood.

It seemed to take Orson and the other firemen a few seconds to gather their wits as well. They stared at their colleague's hand and at the baby, but then they gathered over Bernard and, keeping their distance from his little milk-white teeth, tried to hold him still.

The baby began to howl loudly. He looked around and, finding Pinky, held up his arms.

She hesitated only for a moment, really. She knew perfectly well he was hers. She lifted him up and held his wet face against her cheek. He wrapped his legs around her and clung to her fearfully and she comforted him and whispered to him until his sobbing subsided into hiccups.

While the storm had been lashing and drumming at the little backyard, the sun had gone on about its business and now it was nearly set. With the clouds dispersing quickly, great broad bands of pink and champagne and mauve ribbon appeared in the western sky. In the east, the sky darkened into a soft and holy blue.

Pinky saw that the summer was over exactly here. They had made the hot climb up to the top of the Ferris wheel and had hung there for a while. Now the ground would come quickly up to meet them. There would be roses and chrysanthemums, banks of pink impatiens and a last minute feverish flowering of the tall red and orange dahlias, but in a week or so the wading pool would be put away. She would take the children apple picking and buy Bernard a snowsuit and Teddy a new pair of boots.

Orson touched her shoulder and she was shocked from her reverie.

"It would be wise to let us take him to the hospital."

She frowned and looked into the steady blue flame of his gaze. He looked back into her own.

It took a little effort to tear herself away from this, but she did and she peered down at Bernard on her hip. "Do you need to go to the hospital?" she asked him.

He didn't answer her. He was squinting and turning his head this way and that, looking astonished and very confused, the way a blind person does when he can suddenly see for the first time after a successful operation.

"I don't think so," she told Orson.

"Well, I figured I'd give it a try," he said gently.

"Thank you," she replied even more gently. She wanted very much to give him something and looked around. "Would you guys like some bread? My husband bought way too much. I know you're always hungry."

"Yes," he said. "We always are," and he accepted the proffered loaf in its very wet wrapping. Arthur signed the release papers and then Orson gathered his men together. She followed and watched them go down the alleyway, bumping clumsily into each other like a flock of something out of their element, water or fire, who could tell? In their identical rubber coats, it would have been hard for her to tell which one was which, except that Orson was a little smaller than the rest.

In the last gold light of the evening, she saw that, in spite of how wet and bedraggled her little group was, they shone with expectation. Fran immediately put down the soaked paper plates and napkins she had been collecting and held out her arms for the baby. Reluctantly, Pinky passed Bernard over to her. Bernard looked into Fran's face. His lower lip began to tremble and he broke into a wail.

Fran examined Bernard with alarm. "Don't be a fool, baby. I'm one of your biggest fans."

The baby continued to howl.

"Give him to me," Arthur commanded and, reluctantly, Fran handed him over.

"The jig, I guess, is up," Maury said.

Pinky saw Fran turn to look at him sharply. Then she drew a breath and looked at him again. She, too, must have seen that something had changed.

The baby in Arthur's arms had just subsided into whimpers and hiccups when a breadlike shape on the top of the fence separated itself from the shadows and landed in the grass with a soft thump. Over the lawn it came, his golden eyes glowing greedily in the dusky twilight that was falling upon the yard. He came toward Teddy, who was holding out a piece of wet charred chicken skin. "Cccchhh, cccch, ccchh," Teddy called.

The baby's entire body stiffened with excitement and he tried to launch himself into the air. Arthur tightened his grip.

The baby gave out a loud many-voweled howl of protest. "Eeeyouu!"

When this did not work, when he found himself still caught tight in his father's arms, his face turned red with fury. Again he tried to throw himself out into the air, and yelled, "Eggg, eggg!"

"What is it?" Arthur asked him.

The baby looked angrily at his father and then twisted his head around again and held his hand out to the cat. He drew in a deep breath as if trying to calm himself. "Ed!" he said, perfectly clearly.

Arthur laughed happily and put Bernard on his feet in the grass. Pinky held her breath.

"Ed!" Bernard said again.

The cat, who almost never let on that he knew his own name, stopped where he was and gave Bernard a cold look. Then he dashed forward, grabbed the chicken skin out of Teddy's hand, and took off as fast as he could into the bushes. Bernard followed him and bent down and peered into the shrubbery, but after a fruitless minute, he turned around and ambled back to the table. He stopped in front of his brother and reached out and patted Teddy's knee. "Ed," he said again.

"Hey, he's talking to me," Teddy said, half pleased, half accusing.

The darkness began softly to fall upon them, so certain details were lost and other things stood forward: the moonflowers unfurling for the night from their buds, the limp wet paper plates on the table, Fran's white blouse. Pinky saw Susan Edelman's white tennis sneakers moving silently about her garden as she checked to see what damage the storm might have done to her flowers.

"You people," Maury said, "throw the most wonderful parties." He raised his arms up into the air as if he saw a football coming toward him. "I believe this is the first time I've ever been hit by lightning."

"You're not sure?" Fran asked him. She had not taken her eyes off him. In the half-light, she was practically squinting, trying to figure out what it was that was different about him.

"Well, we forget so much." He caught the football or whatever the invisible thing was that he thought he was catching and brought it slowly down and seemed to balance it on his head. He left it there and put his arms out to his sides.

"You mean from past lives and so forth?"

"And so forth," he agreed.

"Why are you waving your arms around like that?" she asked him.

"Loosening the sprockets. Trying to keep the channels open in case any spirits would like to speak with me."

"Ed," said Bernard again. He was staring worriedly at the top of Maury's head, as if he were waiting for whatever it was Maury had balanced there to fall off.

Arthur laughed again and lifted a wineglass from the table. "To the spirits!"

Pinky realized that it was the glass meant for Fran. She started forward, but it was too late.

Arthur took a sip and made a face. "Rainwater."

He looked up and found Pinky. He looked at her a long time.

It was one of those little doors swinging open, she thought nervously. It wasn't necessarily the wine. It could have been the lightning, or it could have been the fact that yesterday he had rescued his youngest child from mad scientists, or that today he had saved his older son from perishing by sacrificing one of his dearest principles.

He was still gazing at her. She couldn't bear it. Blushing and averting her eyes, she scooped up Bernard and walked away and leaned on her neighbor's fence.

Susan was standing at her prize rosebush turning the leaves over in astonishment, looking for something that apparently wasn't there.

"Are you okay?" Pinky asked.

Susan turned to her in surprise. It took her a moment. "Yes," she said. "I'm all right." She examined Bernard, his bright pink face and singed eyelashes. "Are *you*? We heard a terrible crash."

Pinky nodded. "We're okay."

Susan took a pair of gardening shears from her apron pocket and snipped one of the roses with the crimson faces and handed it over the fence.

Pinky held it carefully out of Bernard's reach as she carried it back to the table. She put it in the tall water pitcher. "Pizza!" she sang out. "Let's order a pizza."

"You know what?" Maury said. "I think I'd better be going. I've already had more excitement than is good for me. Pizza would probably put me over the edge."

"What's so exciting about pizza?" asked Teddy, who was poking around in the bushes, looking for his cat.

Maury considered this. "It's the digestion differential between the cheese and the tomatoes. The two things really go to town on each other. It's not a harmonious food. Part of it gets digested right away and the rest sits around in there all night and makes you dream about plagues and boils and locusts."

"I never dream about those things," Teddy said. "I don't even know what they are."

"Which is why it's okay for *you* to eat pizza, but not for me. I'm gonna go home and have a nice glass of wheatgrass juice and I'm going to sleep like a baby, but I could not have asked for better company on this particular evening and I want to thank all of you." Maury looked around at all of them slowly, one by one. He looked at Fran last and held her gaze for a brief moment. He seemed to be about to say something extra to her, but then he didn't. He made a little bow.

"Good night," Pinky said. "Thank you so much for coming."

There was nearly a bounce in his step, Pinky thought, he was nearly off the grass. Though he kept his head beautifully upright, as always, so that whatever it was he was trying not to spill, didn't spill over.

No sooner had he disappeared down the alley than Fran stood up as if she had made up her mind. "I'm going to go, too. I imagine you guys would like some time to yourselves and I'm amazingly tired." She slipped her feet into her shoes and picked up her purse.

Nobody said anything, so she kissed each of them in turn, the baby first, very gingerly, since his face started to crumple when she came near him. Then she kissed Arthur and then she kissed Pinky. She kissed Teddy last and looked him in the eye. "Use that gun judiciously, Ted."

The gun lay there green and gleaming on the picnic table. Teddy reached out and patted it as if to reassure himself that it was still perfectly solid. "I don't know what that means," he said, "but I'm only going to squirt bugs or use it to cool people off when they get really hot."

"Perfect," she said. Then she turned and hurried down the alley as if she had a bus to catch.

Pinky ordered a pizza anyway and after they had eaten it, she took the children upstairs and left Arthur to do the cleanup. She felt his eyes watching her go.

The children were restless and difficult to settle. She got Teddy and the cat into bed, turned on the night-light, and then she sat with the baby in the rocking chair, singing.

"I want you to lie with me," Ted called out to her. She told him that she would, as soon as the baby fell asleep. This took several tries, though, because every time he drifted off and she went to lower him into the crib, his eyes would snap open and he would lift his arms to her imperiously. At last, however, he let go of the day and she was able to put him down and cover him with his little blue cotton blanket.

"Okay," she sighed, and stretched out next to Teddy, who immediately asked her for a story.

"No, no." She yawned. "You tell *me* a story. You have to start practicing for when Bernard asks you for one."

"But what story should I tell?" he asked uncertainly.

"Tell about a boy like yourself who grows up to be a great inventor."

"But I haven't grown up yet, so I won't know what to say."

"Well, then, tell about what happened to Oedipus when he got lost."

"But I don't know what happened to Oedipus when he got lost."

"Well, then, make it up. You have a very good imagination."

"But it's probably a really scary story," he said, and lay there thinking worriedly about it. Eventually his eyes closed. In due time his breath came softly and evenly. The cat stretched in his sleep and then recurled himself up more comfortably. Pinky lay there, looking about the dimly lit room.

When Arthur appeared in the doorway, she watched him approach her and did not move. But when he was standing over her, she lifted her arms and allowed him to help her to her feet.

"Shh," she warned.

He didn't say a word, only stood there, gazing at her. The children didn't stir.

"Why are you looking at me like that?" she asked, laughing softly.

"You have something in your hair," he whispered. Although when he reached up and tremblingly pulled something out, his hand, just as she expected, appeared to have nothing in it at all.

Epilogue

$\mathcal{T}$he following week Pinky put Bernard in the back of the car and the painting in the front, and drove to Katya's apartment. Katya was studying when they arrived and Pinky saw that she had grown more remote than when they were here last. Her eye was fixed on some distant point and she let them into the apartment a little stiffly, but when she saw her gift she was drawn forward with a groan of sorrow and affection.

"It is just so that Marina would sit and look out our window. And the dog, he looks just like our Nijinsky. He is a most thieving hooligan dog. He steals food from the kitchen and makes mud on the floors. Everyone loves him too much. He is very spoiled. He runs away sometimes, a week, two weeks. Then he comes home. Maybe he has another family somewhere. But after the fire my sister and I never see him again. My sister says he escapes, but I think he perishes with my parents."

Bernard was jiggling in Pinky's arms. "Ahdow, ahdow, ahdow," he repeated relentlessly. She put him down.

Katya looked him over, but didn't reach to touch him. "He is bigger," she said, but she said it as if she meant to say something else.

Pinky watched him as he moved about the room. She wondered if he remembered where he was, but he gave no sign one way or another. He explored cautiously, approaching strange objects in this new way he had, with his palms stretched out toward things, but not quite touching them. "Ha? Ha? Ha?" he asked.

"What is he doing?" Katya asked, frowning.

"I think he is checking first to see if something is hot before he touches it."

"Something burned him?"

At this moment, Bernard, who was looking up at a little striped china cat sitting on a shelf out of his reach, tripped on the edge of the carpet and fell, banging his knee. He let out an ear-piercing howl and began to sob.

Pinky stared at him for moment, still not quite used to his doing this. Before she could move forward, Katya had lifted him off the floor. Somewhat to Pinky's surprise, Bernard allowed his aunt to comfort him.

"Shh, shh," she crooned. "You are okay, Andre. You are fine."

"Where will you hang the painting?" Pinky asked her.

Katya did not answer right away. "I appreciate this beautiful gift. Whenever I see it I will imagine that my sister and the dog are not far away here in this city. I will have to think where to put it."

Pinky saw, without resentment, that Katya probably wasn't going to hang it anywhere, but would only take it out now and then to look at when she needed to.

"I will bring Bernard again, but not too soon. I see you're working hard." Pinky nodded toward Katya's books and the compuscreen.

"That will be well," Katya said, and kissed Bernard lightly on the top of his head and returned him to Pinky.

Arthur, who was always true to his word, did whatever was necessary. He went with Billy to visit his daughter in the nursing home whenever he wished for company. He watched carefully and he saw how Billy clipped Caroline's thick nails, how Billy very gently brushed the tangles out of her thin hair, how he washed her strange face, so emptily soft and asymmetrical, so unshaped by any of those complications that usually go into making a person. He saw how Caroline looked up at her father with one big cloudy blue eye, while the other eye, the smaller one, looked off in a distant direction.

As time passed and Billy's heart grew more and more unreliable, he could not always make it to the nursing home and it became too many trips for Susan to make by herself. So Arthur went instead.

Caroline came to know him and flapped her hands and crowed when he entered the room. He did the little things that he had seen

Billy do and made sure that she had what she needed, and sometimes he sat with her awhile and read the newspaper. The room was quiet and sunny.

It came to pass one Saturday in the early summer of the following year, while Pinky was out of town visiting her sister, that Susan called at around noon and said Billy was too weak to rise from his bed. Could Arthur go to Caroline for them?

Arthur had no one to watch the boys, so he explained carefully to them what it was that they were going to see and that they must not be afraid and they must not stare rudely. Then he loaded them in the car and took them to the nursing home.

As soon as the boys walked through her door, Caroline grew as quivering and agitated as a fern caught in a gust of wind. She worked hard to lift her heavy head, to speak, to make her hands do what she wished, so that she could reach out and touch them.

At first the boys clung fearfully to their father, but then Teddy, who as always was driven by curiosity, came closer and let her tug at his T-shirt.

"She can't walk?" he asked his father.

"No."

"Or talk?"

"No."

"It's because of her genes?"

"Yes."

"Someone should figure out how to fix this. There must be a way."

"Maybe someday someone will."

"Does she have to stay here all the time? She can't go home?"

"It's too hard for Billy and Susan to care for her at home. They're not well enough. But sometimes they take her out for rides."

"Let's do that."

Arthur thought it over and asked the little redheaded nurse if they could take Caroline to Coney Island for the afternoon. The nurse, who was young and very good-hearted, kissed the boys soundly, much to Teddy's embarrassment, and gave them a wheelchair and showed them how to get Caroline in and out of it.

They drove to the boardwalk and when they got there Arthur and Teddy took turns pushing her, while Bernard trotted alongside. Caroline put her face right up into the sun and the breeze, and she drank these things in, crowing with pleasure. They brought her close to the railing that ran between the boardwalk and the beach, and when she spotted the sea, she struggled to stand up and, in her excitement, she almost tipped the chair over. So they wheeled her down the ramp and Arthur helped her out and she sat with her legs stretched out in front of her and first she patted the sand and then she tried to eat it, but it all ran out of her hands before she could get it to her mouth. Bernard, who had already ceased to see anything strange about her, who maybe imagined that she was merely a very large baby, trotted back and forth between the sea and where Caroline sat, bringing her shells and rocks, while Teddy built her a sand castle. Then Arthur took off her shoes and the boys buried her feet. She watched curiously while they did this and then she lifted her legs and crowed loudly and wiggled her toes, apparently stunned and delighted to find them still there.

When Arthur saw that everyone had had enough, he lifted Caroline into the chair and they went back up on the boardwalk and put their shoes on. Then they pushed Caroline through the noisy, milling crowd, past the hawkers in the booths, past the Wonder Wheel and the Tilt-A-Whirl and the Log Flume. They stopped to watch the Cyclone. The roller-coaster cars clattered and clanked to the top, paused to allow everyone a moment to contemplate the possibility of the doom that lay beneath them, then plummeted downward and raced off around the bend.

By the time they finally got back to the nursing home, it was early evening and dinner trays were being delivered to the rooms up and down the hallway. They had just gotten Caroline settled in her chair, and Arthur was trying to get the boys out the door, when someone began to sing. Arthur stopped where he was.

He turned around and stared at Caroline. At this moment, the little redheaded nurse came in carrying her dinner on a tray. She smiled at her patient, and then at Arthur and Teddy and Bernard standing there. "Oh, it must have been a grand day you gave her. She only does this when she's had a truly good time."

Caroline's voice was hoarse and low, almost a moan in some places, but to Arthur, the song was instantly recognizable. He listened in dismay and then he saw that Teddy, too, had recognized the tuneless tune. Bernard, who hadn't sung a note since the night of the picnic, edged toward her slowly and put his hand on her face, as if this might help him hear better.

When Caroline felt the little boy's hand, she tipped her heavy head in his direction. She looked down at him through her big cloudy blue eye, while the other eye, the smaller one, looked off at something else that only she could see, something either far behind or a little ahead of herself.

Everybody Moves

by Layne deMarin

Consultant:
Adria F. Klein, PhD
California State University, San Bernardino

CAPSTONE PRESS
a capstone imprint

Wonder Readers are published by Capstone Press,
1710 Roe Crest Drive, North Mankato, Minnesota 56003.
www.capstonepub.com

Copyright © 2013 by Capstone Press, a Capstone imprint. All rights reserved.
No part of this publication may be reproduced in whole or in part, or stored in a retrieval system, or
transmitted in any form or by any means, electronic, mechanical, photocopying, recording, or otherwise,
without written permission of the publisher. For information regarding permission, write to Capstone Press,
1710 Roe Crest Drive, North Mankato, Minnesota 56003.

Library of Congress Cataloging-in-Publication Data
deMarin, Layne.
  Everybody moves / Layne deMarin.—1st ed.
    p. cm.—(Wonder readers)
  Includes index.
  ISBN 978-1-4296-9611-1 (library binding)
  ISBN 978-1-4296-7917-6 (paperback)
  ISBN 978-1-62065-369-2 (ebook pdf)
  1. Animal locomotion—Juvenile literature. 2. Human locomotion—Juvenile literature. I. Title.
  QP301.D35 2013
  612.7′6—dc23   2011022009

Summary: Simple text and color photos present how people and animals move.

Note to Parents and Teachers

The Wonder Readers: Science series supports national science standards. These titles use text structures that support early readers, specifically with a close photo/text match and glossary. Each book is perfectly leveled to support the reader at the right reading level, and the topics are of high interest. Early readers will gain success when they are presented with a book that is of interest to them and is written at the appropriate level.

Printed in the United States of America in North Mankato, Minnesota.
042012   006682CGF12

Table of Contents

Move It

Both people and animals move all the time. They spend most of the day moving. They walk, run, jump, and climb. From the time they wake up until they go to bed, everybody moves!

People and animals both have to move to get food. They both move to stay safe. Sometimes they move just for the fun of it!

Running and Kicking

A horse has one big **hoof** at the end of each leg. It needs all four legs and all four hooves in order to run. When a horse runs very fast, sometimes all four of its hooves are off the ground at the same time.

A person only has two legs. At the end of each leg is a foot with five toes. When people run really fast, they run on their toes.

Kangaroos lean back on their tails
and kick with their **hind** legs. They
kick with both feet at the same time.
They can give very powerful kicks!

People stand on one leg and kick with the other. They need strong leg **muscles** and good **balance** to give a good kick.

Jumping and Climbing

Frogs use their legs for jumping. They jump all the time, even when they are swimming. Frogs have very long legs and strong leg muscles.

People use their legs for jumping too. Human legs are not built like frog legs, so jumping is a little harder for people to do.

Monkeys use their long arms and legs for climbing. They can grab onto things with their fingers and their toes. They can use their tails for grabbing too.

People also climb with their arms and legs. They can grab onto things with their fingers but not their toes. And they certainly don't have tails to help them hold on!

Swimming and Flying

Penguins walk when they are on land. They stand up, just like people do. When they swim, they use their wings like **flippers** to speed through the water.

People don't have flippers. When they swim, they use their hands and arms like paddles. They kick with their feet to move through the water.

Sometimes people and animals move together. People go walking with their dogs or swimming with dolphins.

People and animals move in different ways. Birds use their wings to fly through the sky. People can use a **parachute** to help them fly.

Glossary

balance   the ability to keep steady without falling over

flipper   the broad flat limb of a sea creature, such as a seal or dolphin, that helps it swim

hind   at the back or rear

hoof   the hard foot of a horse, cow, deer, moose, or goat

muscles   body tissue that connects to bones and makes the body move

parachute   a large piece of strong, lightweight fabric used to help people float safely from high places to the ground

Now Try This!

Practice moving by pretending to be an animal! Gather a group of friends. Take turns acting out the movements of a mystery animal. See if your friends can guess which animal each person is acting like.

Internet Sites

FactHound offers a safe, fun way to find Internet sites related to this book. All of the sites on FactHound have been researched by our staff.

Here's all you do:

Visit *www.facthound.com*

Type in this code: 9781429696111

Check out projects, games and lots more at
www.capstonekids.com

Index

climbing, 4, 12, 13

flying, 17

jumping, 4, 10, 11

kicking, 8, 9

muscles, 9, 10

running, 4, 6, 7

swimming, 10, 14, 15, 16

walking, 4, 14, 16

Editorial Credits

Maryellen Gregoire, project director; Mary Lindeen, consulting editor; Gene Bentdahl, designer; Sarah Schuette, editor; Wanda Winch, media researcher; Eric Manske, production specialist

Photo Credits

Alamy: Stock Connection Blue, 8; Capstone Studio: Karon Dubke, cover, 1, 4, 5, 7, 9, 11, 12, 13, 15, 16, TJ Thoraldson Digital Photography, 6; Shutterstock: Danshutter, 17, Eduard Kyslynskyy, 10, Frederic Prochasson, 14

Word Count: **385**   Guided Reading Level: J   Early Intervention Level: **17**